Pipe Dreams

by

Stanley Walker

I AM **WHO** I AM
I MUST **STRIVE** TO BE
WHAT I **WANT** TO BE . . .

Stanley Walker

Pipe Dreams

Book One

by
Stanley Earl Walker

DORRANCE PUBLISHING CO., INC.
PITTSBURGH PENNSYLVANIA, 15222

ISBN # 0-8059-4308-0
Printed in the United States of America

First Printing

For information or to order additional books, please write:
Dorrance Publishing Co., Inc.
643 Smithfield Street
Pittsburgh, Pennsylvania 15222
U.S.A.

PREFACE

I have a dream. So far I have failed to make it a reality. I refuse to give up on this dream. This particular dream is to reach out and touch someone–you.

I will try just as hard to get to you as I did in destroying my own life at one time therefore I know I will succeed. I have never lost sight of my goals. I have just taken the most difficult way around them. It is very important to me that you do not delay or destroy your dreams.

If you do not have a dream as of this moment, take time to get one. Want it, feel it, and become a part of it. It is a wonderful experience. I know, because the side I once lived on consisted of farce and misconceptions. When I had the chance to contribute to society, I took it for granted. Now I have had enough of being taunted and humiliated by the turn of events in my life caused by my own ignorance. It is my obligation to forewarn you of the obstacles that lie ahead. I write through and because of my experiences. Force yourself to understand and recognize the turn of events in this book as vital information. It is not just another story. I wish you love.

"THE BEST HIGH IN THE WORLD IS
THE FULLFILLMENT OF A DREAM"

STANLEY WALKER

ITRODUCTION

We all have dreams. Whether we choose to fulfill those dreams or not is a matter of circumstance. The quality and quantity of these dreams rest with the individual. There are those who accept whatever comes to them and those who take what they want regardless of what it costs to succeed. However, there are those of us who get caught up in the middle of these dreams. These people have difficulty in being reached. Something has obstructed our paths. In some cases that obstruction is drugs. Crack is one of those particular drugs that destroys lives.

Hence, many of our dreams go up in smoke. This crack pipe goes through the hands of millions making dreams and taking dreams. People who believe in acheiving dreams through selling this drug pursue them through ignorance, the same as those who use it. Life can be a very fulfilling experience as long as one pursues the dream that makes it so interesting. When obstacles such as crack inhibits dreams we become disoriented as well as disenchanted with life. Therefore, things and people we once considered part of us become obstacles also.

Many street dreams have very little or no substance at all. Nevertheless they are dreams. We will follow certain individuals as they pursue their dreams. Many of us live this very same way. Some make it, but some do not. Is your life affected by drugs (crack)? Regardless how one may perceive it, crack not only affects our major cities, but our smaller cities as well. This story depicts just that. My home town used to be quiet until crack was introduced into the neighborhoods. Those of us who are and have been involved with crack may relate to circumstances and situations similar in nature. Many of us would prefer to leave the skeletons where they lay. The names of people, locations and events in this book are completely fictitious and represent no persons living or dead.

Jerry is an operating room technician at a local hospital by day and a cocaine addict by night. He quickly learns the real value of friendship after becoming involved with the police. He promises to quit smoking cocaine if he is spared by the system. This he does, only to find himself caught up in another dilemma.

He loses his job. Having no success at acquiring another, he takes advantage of the instant financial security the city has to offer as a crack dealer. The friends he once cherished so dearly now had to be assets in dollars, because if they were a liability, they made no sense.

Love is a difficult commodity to find, especially within this fast paced street life. However, an exceptionally beautiful woman named Faye finds it in her heart to give herself to Jerry. She dutifully and unselfishly divides herself between being a lady, a mother, a prostitute, a drug addict and a student.

The relationship becomes a deadly trap and the world, becomes too much for her to handle. Her loyalty to everyone in her life including her friends is taken for granted. Beauty and common sense are her biggest attributes yet trust is her down fall.

CHAPTER 1

The place is Pine Bluff, Arkansas, with a population of about sixty-three thousand people. The year is 1986. The month is January. The weather is cold almost freezing, with a full moon, and partly cloudy skies, accompanied by a slight breeze.

Two men scurry down the quiet street. Jerry has on a thickly insulated coat while Duck has on a thin unlined jacket.

"Will you hurry up?" Insist Duck. "We don't have all night."

"I am coming." Complains Jerry. "I do not know about this." Sounding optimistic. "Maybe we should just go home and wait until tomorrow."

"You should have thought about that before we walked all the way over here." Argues Duck.

"Well, suppose there is someone home." Jerry suggests wanting to change his mind.

"Listen fool, I know they are not at home." Duck walks briskly with his hands in his pockets and his shoulders hunched, fighting the cold. "They take a vacation every year about this time. They always enjoy long holidays. They should be back by the end of the week. I used to work for them. Remember?"

"Yeah right, you use to steal from them. How much further?"

"About another block."

"Is that the house?" Ask Jerry

"Yeah that's it." Duck says with excitement in his voice. "Get down here comes a car." Duck forces Jerry's head down behind a row of hedges that line the front yard.

"Boy it sure is a big house! Is all of this one yard?" Duck does not bother to answer. Both men race across the front yard and around to the back of the house.

"What do you think?"

"Will you shut up and quit asking so many questions?"

Duck picks up a large rock used for landscaping, forcing it through the expensive leaded glass door. Having some difficulty. Thud! Thang! Crash! Bing-a-ling-a-ling!

"You think anybody heard that?" Ask Jerry. Looking around. His heart thumping wildly in his chest.

"I told you to shut up." Duck hisses as they enter the house. "Come on. You take one side and I will take the other. Meet back here in five minutes get jewelry, guns, money and things like that." Jerry is back at door in less than five minutes.

"What all did you get Duck?" Whispers Jerry.

"Very little money. There's a portable television, radio, and a bunch of rifles. They must collect guns. Leave what you got by the door." Jerry is still holding on to what he has. "I said leave that here. Let's go get the TV and the rifles." Orders Duck. Snatching a blanket off of a bed on the way to the trophy room, using it to wrap the guns. "We'll take the guns and television and the VCR and put them in the alley. We'll get someone with a car to come back and get them. Right now, we'll just carry a couple of the pistols, jewelry, and the money."

"How much money do we have all together?" Inquires Duck.

"Here's mine, about sixty dollars and some change."

"Is that all you got? Damn! You didn't do shit."

"You know they don't keep money around the house like that. This came out of a piggy bank of some sort."

"Fuck it. I don't know why I be bringing you along, man you are sorry when it comes to shit like this."

"I ain't no career criminal like you." Jerry responds.

"Who are you calling a career criminal?"

"Who you think? Shit!"

"Just leave this conversation alone while you are ahead."

"What are we going to then?"

"I'll just see if we can get a gram for one of the pistols and the sixty dollars."

"Okay, that's a good idea."

"I'm tired of walking. Let's see if we can get a ride."

As the two men proceed toward the west side of town Duck sees someone he recognizes. Flagging him down. In turn he offers the driver a couple of dollars for a ride as far as he will take them. It's not far from the cocaine house.

The cocaine house consists of a single trailer, which is fairly new. It sits on a small lot that contains several trees. A number of cars are parked on the lawn. A couple of them appear to be undriveable. They lack motors and tires. A street light on the corner is the only source of light that is available. It cast a shadow on the front yard. If you did not know your way around it is easy to trip over something in the yard. Beer cans are everywhere. Several youths hang around under the street light despite the cold. They serve as couriers and runners for the cocaine dealer. Not everyone is allowed to go inside. It is the runner's job to see what the customers want and fill their orders.

"You want something man?" One of them asks rudely.

"Where's Tracy?" Duck ask.

"Who are you?" Ask the young man, looking him up and down.

"What's up with you?" Another butts in.

"Tell him Duck needs to see him. It's important." Duck says, looking at him under eyed, watching him walk off.

The young man knocks on the door once and then enters the trailer. He emerges a few minutes later, and he nods his head in Duck's direction.

"He said he will be out in a few minutes."

"Okay man, Thanks." Duck nods his head in acknowledgment.

"Let me do the talking. I can get a better deal." Insists Jerry.

"Are you serious?" Mocks Duck. "You just chill out and let me handle this." The two men wait outside for fifteen minutes, before Tracy finally comes outside.

He's a black male, a big guy about one hundred and ninety to two hundred pounds, with a medium complexion and short nicely kept hair. Around Tracy's neck was a single gold necklace. On his fingers are two diamond rings, small stones, nothing fancy. He is wearing a jogging suit, and expensive Reebok tennis shoes.

"Yeah, what's up, Duck?" Tracy's voice is deliberate and heavy.

"Say, let me talk to you for a minute."

Both men walk to the darkest side of the yard, away from everyone else. One of the runners is paying more attention to what is going on than the others, watching Tracy intensely. In a voice higher than a whisper Duck tells Tracy he has fifty dollars and a pistol. He would like to trade for cocaine.

"Come inside. Let's see what you got man." Replies Tracy.

Jerry attempts to follow them but is immediately stopped by Tracy.

"Where you going bro? You need to hold down."

Once inside, Duck reveals the pistol. It is a 357 magnum, chrome plated with a large grip. Tracy likes it.

"What do you want for it?"

"I want a gram for the pistol."

"I guess that is not a bad deal." Tracy says his voice slightly higher than a mummer. Knowing the price he paid for the drugs, the trade would definitely be to his advantage. "It sure is pretty." He says, examining the weapon a little closer. "Name brand at that."

"I tell you what, I have fifty dollars to put with it." Says Duck, pausing to think. "If I can get a sixteenth."

"How hot is this toy?"

"Oh it's been a while, so don't worry about it?"

"Say baby. Get me a sixteenth all rocked up."

Tracy tells Sheila, who is standing in the entrance of the hallway leading to the bedrooms of the trailer. She holds a small caliber pistol in her grip.

Sheila is Tracy's woman. She is very pretty. Approximately twenty-one years of age, she is short about five feet three inches tall. With a medium chocolate complexion and shoulder length hair, that is very nicely styled. Her designer jeans lay very close to her body exploiting her shapely figure. The sweater is red, tightly woven, and name brand. She has on no real jewelry, just a small promise ring.

Returning from another room she gives Tracy the small, cookie-shaped piece of cocaine. He in turn gives her the pistol. Tracy counts the money Duck gives him. He passes him the cocaine rock. Duck quickly breaks a piece off the flat piece of cocaine and wraps it in a dollar bill. He hides the dollar in his sock. He thanks Tracy and starts to leave.

"I've got some jewelry that you might be interested in." Mentions Duck.

Tracy tells him to come on back if it is not past two thirty in the morning.

Outside, Duck shows Jerry the piece of cocaine Tracy gave him for the gun and fifty dollars.

"Where are we going to smoke at?" Duck asks, searching his pockets for his smoking utensils.

"I know a guy who stays about a block and half from here. We'll probably have to give him a bump to let us smoke it at his crib."

"That's cool. Let's go. It's getting late. You know we still have to go and pick up the other merchandise."

They approach the house. It is a small wooden frame house, badly in need of a paint job. Naked boards indicate the house almost has no paint at all. The yard is in bad need of grooming something the darkness fails to hide. Jerry taps on the door. A man in a pair of dingy white boxer shorts answers the door. He is thin and old looking for his age. They speak. Jerry tells him he needs a place to smoke.

"As long as I get a bump it's cool." The man replies.

They enter the house. It is desperately hot inside. The well-used gas heaters are going full blast. They enter the kitchen. Dishes occupy the rust stained sink and litter every available table and counter space. Assorted debris clutters the floor. The waste basket sits completely full by the stove. The men compete for a place to sit down, with Jerry settling for a chair barely able to hold his weight. They are the only three there. The man quickly clears the table, placing the things where ever they will lay, then virtually raking the unbreakable contents onto the floor.

Duck comments on the condition of the house to Jerry in a whisper.

"This is a nasty motherfucker. Where did you meet this fool?"

Jerry replies. "I've only dealt with him once or twice." He could not really think of his name right off. Eventually they all stand around the table. Each of them has his own individual homemade pipe 'a straight shooter'. It consists of a single piece of tubing, anything similar to a television or radio antenna, about two to six inches in length. A piece of brillo (steel wool), that is used for scrubbing pots and pans, is inserted onto the end of each apparatus to serve as a filter. This allows the cocaine to be smokeable, preventing it from being burned in an instant. A regular Bic lighter serves as a torch. Duck assumes the responsibility of cutting the cocaine into small enough hits to be smoked (called bumps or hits).

After the initial piece is smoked, Jerry and Duck ignore the man whose house they are visiting. He comments on the quality of the dope, before asking.

"Ya'll think you can spare another hit?"

Reluctantly Duck gives him another. In response to smoking another piece, the owner of the house becomes leery of his own surroundings, peeping out the windows, being extra careful not to disturb the water stained sheets covering them.

He also searches the floor for any cocaine that may have fallen by accident. Constantly picking up everything white and similar looking to a piece of cocaine, testing it before discarding it back onto the floor.

"I wish you would sit your ass down somewhere. You are making me nervous. Shit, you're fuckin' up my goddamn high. Ain't a damn thing down there. We ain't dropped shit." Gripes Duck

"This is my house." He quarrels back, his voice low and raspy. "I dropped a piece before you got here."

"You didn't drop shit." Jerry nudges Duck, indicating that he should stop harassing the man.

It is about two o'clock . . .

They finish smoking. Duck asks to use the restroom. He can't help noticing how nasty the bathroom is. The stench of urine combined with the heat comes from a small white bathroom heater placed too close to the wall, leaving scorch marks. Further evidence of the uncleanness is evident inside the commode. Around the base of the toilet is wet with dark colored water. The tub needs cleaning. Dust and dirt smear the rough surface that desperately needs refinishing. Duck closes the door. Reaching into his sock and producing the cocaine that he had hidden earlier. He breaks it into three pieces and smokes one while sitting on the toilet, fully dressed.

Ten minutes pass...

The owner of the house asks for a cigarette from Jerry. They both smoke while they wait for Duck to return.

Ten minutes pass again . . .

"It's time to go Duck." Exclaims Jerry.

"I'll be out in a minute," Duck says, having to clear his throat to get the words out loud enough for the man to hear.

"Can I have another smoke?" The owner of the house begs again.

He lights it nervously. Jerry makes a vain attempt to reach for another one himself, but decides against it. The proprietor finishes half of his cigarette, before knocking the fire off of it onto the floor by accident. Then, refusing to pick it up, stepping on it instead. Leaving his cigarette unlit he tosses it onto the table, and makes his way to the restroom. Banging on the door.

"Say man if you ain't gonna share the dope you need to get out of here."

"I'm trying to shit if you leave me the fuck alone." Protest Duck.

Duck searches the bathroom for a decent looking towel before deciding to use one of the paper towels lying on top of the toilet tank that take the place of regular bathroom tissue. Noticing the nastiness of the face bowl, he wets the napkin lightly then wraps it around his homemade cocaine pipe in an attempt to cool it off quickly. Then wrapping it in a dry paper towel and placing it in his pocket. He exits the bathroom as though he is in a hurry to leave. He is sweating profusely.

"Come on Jerry we have to go and pick up the other stuff we left before it gets any later."

The cocaine has him nervous and jittery. He fights with his body to calm himself. They walk back toward the cocaine house, stopping an individual who is just leaving, holding a brief conversation.

"I have fifteen dollars." The young man states. "I was just trying to get a piece myself."

"I have eight dollars." Offers Duck. "We will be able to get more than that if you would be willing to take us to pick up some merchandise we have stashed."

"Put your eight dollars with mine, so I can get a good hit first. I will be glad to take you."

They return to the trailer, where they buy a piece for twenty-three dollars. The young man wants to stop on the side of the street to smoke it. Jerry offers to drive. The flicker and glowing of fire from the lighters in the dark can be seen from a distance. Jerry, nervous and jittery serves as lookout until his turn comes.

Duck and the young man smoke up the piece of dope. Jerry is angry because he doesn't get any.

"Don't get mad at me that was that man's money." Duck says.

"Just forget it." Jerry mumbles.

Duck decides to ask him his name.

"My name is John." Jerry and Duck sniggles lightly.

"You ain't white boy." They ridicule, laughing louder.

They turn into the alley. Jerry turns off the headlights. John tells them to hurry because they are in a predominantly white neighborhood.

"I don't know why you are out here fucking with these white folks any way."

"I guess you want us to rob our own folks." Scolds Jerry

"Hell, niggers ain't got shit as it is boy, I mean John." Intervenes Duck. They quickly load a total of six rifles, a 21 inch color television and a VCR.

It is three o'clock when they arrive back at the trailer. Duck knocks on the door several times before there is an answer. Tracy comes to the door

"Ain't nothing going on man." He says. Talking through the door.

"Open the door man. I got something for you." Demands Duck.

Jerry and John, filled with anticipation, hoping Tracy opens the door.

"What is it man?" Opening the door slightly. "Damn I told you no later than two thirty." He growls, frustration in his voice.

"I know, I could not get back in time." Says Duck, almost begging

"Check with me tomorrow." Tracy attempts to close the door.

"Wait. I've got some jewelry, another pistol, plus some other things you might be interested in.

"Don't you motherfucker's ever go to sleep?" Protest Tracy. After hesitating, he decides to let him in, only after Duck promises to give him a bargain.

"I've got a real good deal, big shot." Says Duck trying to flatter Tracy.

Once inside he produces two men's diamond rings, a women's ring and, three gold necklaces. Tracy calls Sheila. She enters the room closing her robe. Duck catches a glimpse of her nakedness.

"Do you like this ring?" She tries it on and nods her head in agreement. "What else do you have?"

"Some rifles, a television, and a VCR."

"Do you have a shot gun?"

"Yeah, I think so. Uh, I think it's a twelve gauge or something like that."

"Go get it." Jerry and John both are standing outside the waiting car.

"What did he say?" Asks John.

"I'll be right out." Flatly states Duck. Rushing back into the house.

"What do you want for the jewelry and the shotgun?"

"I don't know. What will you give me for it?"

Tracy directs Sheila to the back room. Duck seizes the opportunity to swipe a pair of expensive shades lying on the table.

They return after a couple of minutes. Tracy picks up the shotgun and looks at it again.

"I don't know. This is not what I really had in mind." Tracy says. Knowing all the time this is what he likes. "I will give you a sixteenth."

"Naw, no way! You must think I'm strung out bad. Do you know what this stuff is worth?"

"You promised me a good deal." Tracy says acting like he is going to give it back to Duck.

"I did not say I would give it away."

"I do not know where you will get rid of it this time of the night."

"How 'bout a sixteenth and two quarters?"

"All right. I'll do it this time." Duck takes the quarter pieces and hides them in his sock.

Duck returns to the car . . .

"It's about time." Says John.

"What did you get?" Asks Jerry.

Duck shows him the piece of cocaine. "Are you crazy? Do you know what that stuff was worth?"

Jerry is upset about the transaction, and John is agreeing with him.

"I guess you could have done better?" Retaliates Duck

"We sure in the hell could have. I thought you had better sense than that, Duck! Let him sucker you like that."

"You stay out of it, John. You're just riding."

"He did the best he could Jerry" John says changing his position.

"You just stay out of it." Yells Jerry.

"Okay I will. All I want to know is where to now?" John says.

"Hell I don't know, I guess we will have to park on the side of the street."

"No way! Not with all this hot shit in my car." Shrieks John. "We can go to my place."

His apartment is located on the other side of town. They agree not to smoke any until they make it to John's place. They do not want to run the risk of being stopped.

John's apartment is located close to the street. It's a small complex average looking, nothing fancy. The parking lot is in the back of the apartments. John's place faces the street.

They enter the apartment. It is dark. John fumbles for the light switch. They proceed to the table. The inside is also average. The floors and tables are clean and so are the ashtrays. One or two dirty dishes are in the sink. The dining room as well as the living area is combined.

They gather around as Duck again cuts the sixteenth into pieces. Each again has his own smoking apparatus. John reaches into the cabinet and gets the alcohol, cotton balls, and a piece of broken hanger. Jerry and Duck do not wait to start smoking. They are using their lighters. John asks where his piece is. Duck points to it. He does not speak at the moment because he is holding his breath. He does not want to spoil the head rush he receives when he exhales. John wraps a cotton ball around the hanger, dips it in alcohol and uses Jerry lighter to light it. He does not like to use disposable lighters because of the soot produced when they are burning. He does not want to inhale the soot in his lungs.

When John asks for another piece, Duck hits him with a proposition.

"We should all stay here until daybreak. Then we can get rid of the rest of the guns and things."

"You can bet you won't be in charge of getting rid of it." Jerry says, still upset about the way Duck has handled things so far.

John agrees that it is okay for them to stay.

It is nearly five o'clock in the morning . . .

After all the cocaine is smoked, they all want a cigarette. Jerry has only one left. They take turns smoking it. John cleans everything up afterwards.

"I wish you would quit burning that pipe. You see there is nothing left."

"Lay off" Duck says calmly. "Look Jerry, this is my pipe. Let me do this my way."

"I see the reason they call you Duck your lips are burnt already."

"Lay off, Jerry."

"Anybody want a beer?" Asks John, trying quickly to keep the atmosphere pleasant. Duck and Jerry gladly accept. They sips on their beers while they wait for time to pass. They discuss whom they are going to take the other material to.

After several attempts to get rid of the stolen articles, they finally sell the television and VCR for one hundred dollars a far cry from what they were worth. They return to the cocaine house to purchase some more drugs. The only things left at this point are the five rifles and a pistol.

"Why don't you take them to the pawn shop, John?" Encourages Duck. "I would take them myself but I don't have a driver's license. We will give you part of our share, won't we, Jerry?"

At this point Jerry is exhausted.

"I don't care."

After the task is completed. They stop by the store and purchase several packs of cigarettes and a case of beer.

They again return to John's apartment, where they smoke, drink, and relax.

"What time is it?" Ask Jerry.

"Almost four o'clock." Replies Duck.

"I need to go home. My mother worries about me when I don't come home or call."

"That's your problem now. She babies you too much." Implies Duck, almost getting angry.

John decides to call it quits despite Duck's coaxing him to check on something else. Duck in turn has no choice but to put a halt to his activities, or find someone else to get around with. Jerry and John both have jobs. A little rest would certainly not hurt them.

The following Wednesday, the police knock on John's apartment door.

He answers. "Who is it?"

"It's the police."

"We have a warrant for a John Smith. Open the door."

"A warrant for what?" John asks with a bit of surprise in his voice, opening the door.

"Theft of property, and possibly burglary."

"What property are you talking about?" He asks, having some idea.

"Put your shoes on! They will fill you in on the details down at the station."

They handcuff him and put him into the police car.

The police station itself in part of a multi-structure. It sits in the basement. Its looks are very deceiving because of the design of the exterior. One would never guess it would look the way it does on the inside. In conjunction with the jail are several city offices, court rooms, and the library.

The oversized garage doors go up when the police officer calls in on his radio. They drive in.

Some information is taken from John. He is placed into a holding cell. It is no bigger than an average bathroom.

Forty-five minutes . . .

A detective comes and takes John into his office.

"Have a seat."

The rooms consist of several desks on either side of the wall. Nothing private.

"John, my name is Smith. Detective Alvin Smith. State your name."

"John Smith."

"Good, we should get along fine with the same last name. Don't you think?"

"Uh, yes sir."

"What do you know about these?"

The cop shows John a copy of the pawn slips that he used when he pawned the stolen guns.

John looks at them and shakes his head.

"What do you mean?"

"I don't know anything about them."

"Is that your handwriting?"

"No, sir it's not."

"Just a minute." Detective Smith leaves the room and returns within minutes. "You mean to tell me you don't know anything about those pawn slips? What are these?" He then shows John copies of the same receipt. "These were in your billfold." John slides down in his seat. "You want to tell me about them or do I just lock you up?" John then explains about the pawn slips as Detective Smith takes his statement. "How did you get the guns?"

"I pawned them for a friend?"

"Who is this friend?"

"The only name I know is Duck."

"You mean to tell me you pawned some guns for him and you don't really know him."

"Yes, sir, I had just met him."

"Where did you meet him?" John explains about the night, Duck, Jerry, and he met up.

"Describe this guy named Duck to me."

"He's about six feet. He's slim. I guess to be about one hundred and forty pounds. Short hair, dark complexion, clean shaven. Twenty-five, twenty-six, no older than twenty-eight."

"Describe the other guy."

"He was about five feet ten inches approximately one hundred and seventy pounds. Medium length hair. It is in a curl. He had a medium complexion, with a beard."

"About how old is he?"

"I don't know. I guess about twenty-six."

"Are you sure you don't know their last names?"

Twiddling his pencil between his fingers.

"Yes, sir."

Detective Smith calls another detective and talks to him privately for a minute.

"Do you have any idea who this Duck character might be?"

"It's kind of hard to say."

"Pull me a few photographs maybe he has a record." He says, playing a hunch.

The detective goes to the file cabinet. He returns with a hand full of photographs. "John this is Detective Simmons. He's going to show you a few pictures. I want to see if you recognize either of them in any of these."

John looks through the photographs. He stops.

"I believe this is him right here."

"Are you sure?"

"Yes, sir."

"Detective Simmons, will you check and see how long it will take to get a warrant for a James Cooper, alias Duck?"

Simmons picks up the telephone and calls the prosecuting attorney's office. He talks a few minutes before he is put on hold.

"They're checking to see if the judge is in his chambers."

"Yes, I'm here. I'll be right over. I should be back within the hour." He picks up his coat and leaves the office.

"John?"

"Yes sir?"

"I'm going to check your record. It appears that you have never been in trouble before. We are going to have to charge you with theft by receiving. Your bail won't be but fifteen hundred dollars, at the most. It won't cost but one hundred and sixty to get you out. I'll let you use my phone. That way you can make several calls. Do you have someone to get you out?"

"I think so."

"I wouldn't worry about it. You probably will get probation. That is, of course, if you have no prior record."

While, John uses the telephone, Detective Smith fills out some more paper work. John finally gets in contact with his mother. From the sounds of the conversation, she seems very upset. She will be down when she can.

"Everything okay?"

"Yes."

"John, do you work?"

"Yes, sir."

"Where?"

"At the cotton gin."

"Good."

Detective Smith picks up the telephone and calls up front and tells them to send an officer to come and get John. When the uniformed officer enters, the cop says, "Take this young man to the holding cell. Someone should be here to pick him up shortly. So don't dress him out in jail clothes."

Detective Simmons returns with the signed warrant. Smith and Simmons decide to go and serve the warrant. It is for Cooper's mother's house.

Unfortunately for James he is there asleep. He protests all the way to the jail house. He swears he does not know what he is being arrested for. They enter the police station. James passes right by the holding cell that John is in. He pauses to look. Detective Simmons grabs him by the arm and tells him to come on. He leads him to the detective's office.

"Have a seat. James. It looks like you can't stay out of trouble. Can you?"

"I don't know what you're talking about."

"Well, you will. You can tell us about the burglary or you can just sit there and look stupid. Either way, you are going back to the penitentiary. We have a statement on you already. Made by your friend Jerry. If you talk you may not get as much time." The detective tells Simmons to leave the room for a minute. "James I will try to put in a word in for you. If you cooperate." He picks up a sheet of paper and asks him, "What night did you do the burglary? It was on a Thursday, wasn't it?"

"Yeah."

"You're a damn liar. It was on a Friday. The statement says so right here. As you see, we picked up John also. If you lie to me again, you can forget about me talking to the prosecuting attorney for you. Understand?"

"Yes sir."

"What is Jerry's full name?"

"I thought you already knew that. If he made a statement you should already know."

"I just wanted to see if you were going to lie to me again."

"His name is Jerry Collins."

"Where does he live?"

"On Hurst, Sixteen-o-Two Hurst."

He finishes taking the statement from James. Then he calls the uniformed officer to come and get him. They take him to the holding tank.

John is gone. After James is taken to the tank, Detective Smith gets on his radio and calls for detective Simmons. Simmons says he will be there in about twenty minutes. Smith is finishing his paper work when Simmons arrives. He tells him about the trick he played on James. They both laugh.

"Well, we might as well get out and see what's going on. There is nothing we can do about Jerry Collins until tomorrow."

The next day . . .

The detectives go to Jerry's mother's house. Mrs. Collins answers the door. They tell her that they have a warrant for Jerry. She tells them he is not at home. When Jerry arrives home from work his mother tells him the police have been looking for him. She wants to know what it is all about. She threatens to put him out. Jerry has no choice but to tell her. She tells him that he needs to go on down to the police station to find out how much his bond is. His bond is twenty-five hundred dollars, which means he will need two hundred and sixty dollars to get out. He does not have it and does not get paid for another week and a half.

"You get ready to go and I will be back down there as soon as I can." Mentions his mother.

Jerry's mother takes him to the police station. They change him from his street clothes to jail clothes, which consist of loud orange pants and a shirt. He is on his way to his assigned cell, when he passes Duck. They lock him up in the cell next to him.

"I thought you were already in jail, man." Says Duck. "The police told me that you had given them a statement."

"You should have known they were lying, god damit!"

"I saw John the same day they brought me in. They had him in a jail, but when I came out of the detective's office, he was gone."

"Well, he's the son-of-a-bitch who snitched us off."

"How long have you been in here?"

"They picked me up last night."

"Is you mother going to get you out?"

"I doubt it. She's probably tired of my shit."

"Well, my mother is going to try to get me out, if she can. She knows I will pay her when I get paid."

Duck and Jerry talk for several hours until Jerry's mother come and gets him out. She does not want him to lose his job.

After being bonded out, Jerry decides he will stop smoking cocaine. The only thing he does for the next week and a half is go to work and return home, only because he is afraid of his mother's wrath. His mother watches him very closely. He has denied any involvement with drugs, even though he could not explain where his money was going.

Payday arrives. Jerry pays his mother as he is supposed to. Jerry makes over five dollars and fifty cents an hour, and his check is just under four hundred dollars. For two weeks, he has just over one hundred and twenty-five dollars left. Jerry goes to the liquor store and buys himself a six pack of beer and some cigarettes. He sits outside and drinks alone, thinking about Duck and what has happened. Jerry decides to go out. His mother warns him to be careful.

There is a section of town known as Third and State. This is a section of town where one might say people go who lack in class. Those people who are respected in the community would never be caught there. It consists of a series of different sleazy little clubs, or juke joints. The floors are concrete, some painted, some once painted and the paint has worn off. A couple of them have regular gas heaters placed around the room and air conditioners hanging above the doors. The water draining from the air conditioners drips at the front of the door, causing people to have to step around to keep from getting wet. Most clubs have at least two pool tables. The rest rooms have a smell that is hard to contain. The floors stay wet most of the time, either from the plumbing leaking or from someone carelessly urinating on the floor. There is no tissue paper. It must be gotten from the bar. The walls are covered with several different shades of paint. One or two have fluorescent paintings that went out of style years ago.

A liquor store sits on the opposite side of the street. Down here are winos, homosexuals, bulldaggers, drug addicts, gamblers, prostitutes, pimps and players.

There is no dress code. So Jerry decides a pair of jeans, shirt, and coat are suitable. He leaves the house just after nine thirty. The crowd is relatively small at this hour, especially during the cold time of the year.

Jerry goes into one of the taverns. He gets change for a dollar and buys a quart of beer, with two cups. Jerry asks a young man sitting at the bar if he wants to play a game of billiards. The man, appearing to be bored, quickly agrees. He also asks Jerry for a cup of beer, which Jerry obliges. Jerry is a better player than his opponent because he beats him easily. Since there is no one else in line, Jerry pitches the guy another quarter to re-rack the balls. Between the sipping on the beer and shooting pool, an hour passes. Jerry decides he will check the other joints and see if any one is around he may know.

The next crowd is considerably bigger than the one in the previous club. He orders another quart of beer and another dollar's worth of quarters. He sees a number of faces he knows but nobody he would call a friend. He places his quarter on the billiard table in line with a number of others. This places him about fifth in line. He picks an unoccupied table that has a couple of empty beer cans and bottles on it. He moves them to one side and sits down and watches for his turn on the pool table.

Half way through his beer a young lady approaches the table and sits down.

"Hey Jerry."

"What's up, uh, Faye?" Having to think a second before he is able to call her name. "What are you doing here?"

"Oh, I'm just out." She has a Champale in her hand.

Faye is a black female, attractive, five feet seven inches tall, with long off-black hair, very nicely kept. She is slightly under one hundred forty pounds, with a light bronze complexion, accented with copper colored eyes as bright as a new penny. She has a beauty mark on the right side of her face, just beside the nose, that looks artificial at a distance. Her walk is like that of a cat. Each step is deliberate and sexy. She is noticeable from either direction. Her voice is slightly high and very soft.

They talk about things that have happened since they last saw each other.

"Where is your partner?"

"Who are you talking about?"

"I can't think of his name. The tall guy you are always with?"

"Oh, you mean Duck."

Jerry's turn has come up on the pool table. So he does not answer Faye's question. He asks her to watch his beer for him. She watches as he shoots his game. By this time the number of beers Jerry has consumed has taken an effect on his game. He misses shots that he would not have missed earlier. Consequently, he loses the game. He sits back down at the table and finishes his last swallow of beer.

"Do you want another Champale?"

"That would be nice."

He gives her a five dollar bill and tells her to bring him another quart of beer in the process. When she returns, Jerry is gone to the rest room. She places his change on the table next to his beer. When he returns, they continue their conversation.

"When is the last time you smoked some cocaine." She asks curiously.

"I left that shit alone after Duck and I got busted."

"Oh."

"Why did you ask?"

"I was thinking of buying a quarter rock. I was wondering if you wanted to go with me?"

"Naw, I think I'll chill out."

The crowd has doubled in size since Jerry first came a couple of hours ago. Faye gets up from the table and mingles with the crowd for several minutes before going to the ladies' room. When she returns, she tells Jerry that she is fixing to go, and take care of some business.

"What kind of business?"

"I already told you."

"Wait a minute. I'll ride with you. It won't hurt, I'll ride for the hell of it." Jerry pours a cup full of beer and leaves the rest on the table.

As they exit, the club parking lot is quiet. All one can see is the flicking of cigarette lighters and the glow from the fire of the cigarettes. Occasionally someone lets a window down. The smoke billows out indicating activity inside.

They reach Faye's car parked on the opposite side of the street. She unlocks the door, climbs in, and reaches over to unlock the door for Jerry. She gives the car a few minutes to warm up. She lights a cigarette in the meantime, and so does Jerry.

They stop at a gas station, which is located about five blocks away. Faye pays for the gas and asks Jerry to pump it for her. He reaches in his pocket and gives Faye some money to buy a six pack of beer. While Jerry is in the process of putting his money back into his pocket, Faye notices how much money he has, secretly smiling to herself. They proceed to the west side of town.

They arrive at the cocaine house ten minutes later. The cocaine house is the same trailer where Jerry and Duck had traded the goods acquired in the burglary. As always when a car pulls up, they are immediately taken care of by one of the several couriers. Faye indicates she wants a quarter rock. Jerry seems uninterested at the moment. They drive to a secluded area. The road is dark. Trees line both sides of the street, hiding the woods that follow.

Faye reaches into her purse and pulls out her straight shooter and turns on the interior light of the car. She uses her fingernails to break the rock into several pieces. In the meantime, Jerry reaches into the sack and grabs another beer.

"This is some pretty good dope." Faye says, speaking out loud, trying to get Jerry's attention. She says it again. This time he replies unconcerned.

"Oh, yeah!"

Faye places another piece on her homemade pipe, using her lighter as a torch. She exhales the smoke in Jerry's direction. This time it works. He responds.

"Let me try a piece?" Faye quickly passes him a piece and the pipe. She knows that once he starts, she's gotten him. "Let's go." Says Jerry. After the last piece is finished.

"Go where?"

"I don't know, anywhere. Let's ride by the club and see what's going on."

"Wait I want to see if I can get another piece."

"Well suit yourself." She goes back to the cocaine house.

"Can I get a piece for twenty dollars?" She asks indignantly.

"No way, baby." The young man quickly replies.

"I don't see why not. You know I'll be back!" She yells at him.

Jerry taps her on the her thigh. He hands her a five dollar bill. She in turn hands it to the runner.

"I know you had it all the time." The runner says, taking it forcefully from her hand.

"Just give me my fuckin' dope."

He chuckles loudly.

"I don't see a damn thing funny, asshole."

"Forget it Faye, you have your dope, so lets go."

They leave and go back to the same spot as before. This time Faye chips Jerry off a piece and gives it to him. He does not dispute her action. She smokes hers and he smokes his. He feels good now.

He asks Faye, "Let's have some fun."

"What kind of fun?" She asks, knowing what he means.

"You know what I'm talking about."

"Why don't you just ask for what you want."

"I sure could go for some good sex about now."

"Are you horny or you only think you're horny?" She asks. Reaching over to unzip his pants. He fumbles to help her.

"I think you may be right. You do need some sex." She purrs. Teasing him by gently stroking his penis. Catching her hair and pulling it out of the way she places her hot mouth unto him. His body stiffens with each stroke. She gets up.

"What are you doing?" He argues. "It was just getting good."

"I know." Smiling at him. "You know you're kind of handsome."

"Fuck that, let's get our groove on."

She laughs. "Lets get another piece of dope."

"Why don't you finish? I'll buy one afterwards."

"I tell you what. You go ahead and buy one. Then we will go to my place."

"You might as well finish since you've already started." He says, almost pleading.

"Don't worry. I'll make it good to you. I promise." She then starts the car before he can respond.

Once back at the cocaine house . . .

Faye asks, for a quarter and then ask to see a half (a fifty dollar piece).

"I don't want a half." Jerry whines. "You said a quarter."

"But look at the difference. We can have a good time with this." Jerry gives her fifty dollars.

On the way back to the house, Faye teases Jerry by rubbing her fingers through his hair and play with his ear.

They arrive and enter the house, Faye tries to explain to Jerry about the condition of the house, which he hardly seems to notice.

They proceed directly to the bedroom. The bed is unmade. There are several Champale bottles on the dresser.

Faye quickly goes and removes the lamp from the table and takes the shade off before bringing it over to the bed. Jerry flops unto the bed without asking. After the first toke of the pipe, Jerry takes off all of his clothes. He lies back on the bed. Faye is trying to reheat her pipe.

"Will you come on?"

She does not answer but puts the pipe down and goes to the rest room.

When she returns she is clotheless. He really pays some attention to her body. It's perfect. There is not a blemish on her smooth tan skin. As she sits down on the bed crossing her legs, he also notices her feet. How smooth they are! He feels a woman's feet are a direct reflection of how a woman feels about herself physically. With a damp towel in her hand, she leans over and wipes off Jerry's privates. Then she teases his nature with her tongue. Jerry closes his eyes, enjoying the high and the thrill at the same time. He feels her lips as they surround his manhood and she slowly takes him inside her anxious mouth. He shivers at first, trying to keep his composure as she rhythmically massages him. She caresses his dick firmly, before sucking it hard then slowly stroking it almost making him cum. Instantly, he loses his erection.

"What's the matter? You were ready to go earlier. Now it won't stay hard."

Somewhat embarrassed. He says. "I don't know. Let's get another hit of the pipe."

This time he lets her get through smoking first. She fondles his penis while he continues to smoke the pipe. He eventually puts the pipe down and pulls Faye onto the bed. He rubs his hands over her body, confirming what his eyes have shown him. Her skin is softer than it looks. Her nipples respond as he touches her beautiful firm breast. His erection is substantial now. His sexual senses awaken with ferocity now. He pulls her to him. The temptation is too great he wants to feel the tenderness of her thighs and her pussy in his mouth. He wants to see if all of his senses agree with each other. Just as he suspected, she tastes as good as she looks and feels. She invites him to do with her as he pleases. Her womanhood throbs as she fights with her feelings, moaning and grasping for breath, pushing and pulling him to her at the same time. He finds the right spot. She tells him. "That's it, right there, don't stop."

She can't hold it back any more. She screams, her body collapsing as she reaches an orgasm. Jerry finds himself wanting to enjoy the same fate as she. He wants to release himself inside her. He pounces on her, not giving her a chance to recuperate. She doesn't mind. Reaching for his dick, she guides him to her opening. He enters her cautiously, unsure of what to expect. It feels good. He can't believe how her pussy is pulsating, gripping him and releasing him, forcing him to explode inside her sooner than he really wants to. She too reacts as she feels his warm juices. She holds him tight wanting more. They enjoy each other for a while before Faye asks Jerry if he wants to get some more cocaine.

"I really do not need to get broke. It's two more weeks until payday."

He counts his money. He turns slightly to avoid her from seeing exactly how much money he has, she again peeps his hand. He has roughly sixty-five dollars left.

"Where is the beer?"

"Did you bring it in?"

"I don't remember."

"I think you did." Faye looks for him. "No you left it in the car."

They both get dressed. Neither of them take time to put on their socks or underwear. Jerry leaves out of the door first.

When he reaches the car, he retrieves the beer. He takes one can out of the sack and tells Faye to put the rest of them in the freezer. He sits in the car and lights a cigarette. This is his last time smoking cocaine, he promises himself. It is now two forty-five in the morning.

Faye gets into the car.

"I may have to spend the night since it is so late at night."

"I did not know that you stayed with your mother. You can stay I don't mind."

When they arrive at the trailer, Jerry gets out and knocks on the door.

"What is it, man?"

"This is Jerry. I would like to get a quarter."

"Say man, come in for a minute. I want to talk to you about something. I heard you and Duck got busted."

"Yeah, man, somebody snitched us off. We know who it was."

"They don't know about yawl selling me some goods do they?"

"Oh no. We made sure they did not find out about that."

"Now what do you want my man?"

"A quarter." Tracy hands him a half. "I appreciate you being cool dog."

"No problem, I don't like snitching at all."

Faye and Jerry return to the house. He goes to the bedroom.

"Bring me a beer will you?"

"It's not cold but it's cool." She says putting the can up against her cheek.

"That's okay." When he opens it, the beer foams slightly but he catches it by guzzling it half way down.

They get naked before attempting to get high. Jerry places the rock on the table. Faye reaches and picks it up.

"This is a half, isn't it?"

"Yeah" he brags. "Tracy and I are kinda tight he gave it to me for twenty five dollars."

"I know that's right. We are going to have a good time."

Briefly arguing over who gets the residue from the pipe that can be re-smoked and produce the same high.

"Don't smoke it all." Says Faye.

"I won't."

"I really don't like anybody cleaning my pipe anyway."

"You forgot who brought it all."

"Well we're not going to fall out about it."

"What time is it?"

"Wait I'll go see. It's a little after four o'clock."

"Do you think Tracy is still selling?"

"I don't know. I'll take you if you want to go and see."

Again they make the trip. As they pull up, another car is pulling off. So Jerry goes to the door. Tracy lets Jerry in.

"It's been a long night." Tracy says.

"For me too." Says Jerry. "I have thirty five dollars. What can you do for me?" Tracy gives him a quarter and half of a quarter.

After the last of what they have is smoked, Jerry sips a beer and smokes a cigarette. Faye straightens out the room a little. She sips out of Jerry's beer, despite her dislike of it. Neither one of them has any money left. So they sit and talk.

"Damn! I spent all my money. Hell, I don't get paid for two more weeks." Angry at himself.

"Is that all you make?"

"No, I had to pay my mother back for getting me out of jail."

"I'm going to have some more money later on this evening."

Jerry lies back on the bed with his eyes closed. He thinks about what he is going to tell his mother when she asks him about his money. She wants to know where he has been, even though he is an adult. He thinks about quitting all over again. He does not blame his mother for asking questions. He knows she just cares is all. Eventually he falls asleep.

When he awakes it is almost noon. Faye is gone. She returns about two o'clock with a quart of beer and two quarter rocks. Faye takes one and gives him the other one. Jerry feels good now. Faye has come through for him. She even has a pack of cigarettes.

Faye decides to take a bath and try to get some rest. Her body is tired but her mind wants to go.

"Do you want me to take you home now, or when I wake up?" Jerry is in no hurry to go home and face his mother.

"I'll stay until you wake up."

Faye takes a bath. "I was just thinking."

"About what?"

"Get dressed. I want you to take me home for a minute."

"I thought you were going to wait."

"I was, but I just remembered something." Despite her tiredness, she agrees.

"Don't worry. It's worth it."

They approach the house. Jerry has Faye pass by the house. He wants to see if his mother is at home. Her car is not in the driveway. He is relieved. He goes into the house and leaves his mother a note to let her know he is okay.

He returns to the car. He has a man's ring, he has kept from the burglary. It is really a nice ring. A carat and three eighths total weight. When they arrive at the pawn shop, the pawnshop owner asked Jerry for some identification. Jerry shows him a social security card and his birth certificate. He allows Jerry three hundred and twenty-five dollars toward the ring.

The first thing he does is buy a case of beer, two four-packs of Champale and a carton of cigarettes. He promises himself that he is not going to spend it all. He then buys a hundred dollars worth of cocaine. Of course Tracy treats him nicely. They can't wait to get home. The afternoon won't be so bad after all. They enjoy themselves, well past midnight.

Jerry, of course, spends the night again.

"I've got to go home so I can get some rest. I have to go to work tomorrow."

"I could use some rest myself." She takes him home and starts to leave. Jerry stops her and gives her three packs of cigarettes.

"Come and check on me sometimes." She smiles and promises that she will.

Jerry sleeps until morning. His mother awakens him in time for work.

"You must have had some weekend?" Teases his mother.

"Yes, I guess you could say so." She notices the cigarettes.

"I took your beer and put it in the refrigerator. You left it in the freezer. I see you finally got smart and brought yourself a carton of cigarettes. I'll be leaving in thirty minutes. If you want a ride to work, you need to be ready."

"I'll be ready."

CHAPTER 2

It has been almost a week since Faye has seen Jerry. It is Thursday. She has to take care of her business. The weekend starts early for her. Some of the people get paid on Thursday and Friday every week. While others are compensated every two weeks. Faye has bills to pay and a growing habit to support. The moneys she receives on the first of the month and the food stamps are not enough to support her lifestyle.

The first of the month is still a week away. It's nearly three thirty in the evening. Faye puts the finishing touches on her make-up and attire, glossy lipstick, light make-up, and a pair of cheap earrings. Her hair is neatly styled in a pony tail. She is still as attractive as always, however, she is slightly underweight. The dress she wears accents her slimmer figure. It also serves its purpose, it makes easy access. Underwear and a bra are not necessary. In spite of the weather, stockings and a garter belt will surface. The purse she carriers is more like an evening bag, on a clutch purse style. The chain that once served as a handle has long been stripped away by constant use. Her coat is of imitation leather, but long in length. It also serves its purpose. She drives through town down towards third and state. It appears to be quite. She knows it won't be long before her regular customers come calling.

She leaves the area for a few minutes to get something to eat. Rich's hamburgers will do. It is conveniently close to down town and cheap. They have a special three hot dogs for a dollar. It has been the special for six months.

After she makes her purchase and attempts to start the car, it won't respond. A clicking sound can be heard each time she turns the ignition key. Before she can get out of the car, help has arrived. A young man gazing at her seizes the opportunity to make her acquaintance.

"What's wrong with it?" He asks.

"I don't know. You tell me."

"Pop the hood latch for me."

With no hesitation she pulls the lever allowing the hood to be released. A few minutes later.

"Try it now for me." He tells her.

The car attempts to crank but fails.

"Don't worry. All you need is the cable tightened up and it'll be good as new. Let me go across the street and get a wrench. You know I work over there."

"Oh do you?" She exclaims, paying attention to his name tag on his shirt. He trots across the street to the gas station and returns a minute or so afterwards.

"Try it now." The sequence is initiated and the car starts. "There you go, baby. You're ready to go. If you get a chance, bring it over some time and I'll go over it for you, and make sure everything is all right."

"Thank you, I really appreciate your help." Putting the car in reverse at the same time.

She goes back down town to her favorite club, the same one she and Jerry met in over the weekend. When she walks in, the woman attending the bar speaks.

"Hey Faye" Wilma says. "It's that time again, isn't it?"

"You know it, girl."

In the meantime Faye tears open the sack containing the three hot dogs and fries. She puts salt and ketchup on them. Wilma, reflexively reaches into the box and places a Champale and a cup on the table without being asked.

"Wilma do you have any mustard? Those damn folks forgot to put some in the sack as usual."

"Let me see. I had some around here somewhere." Wilma usually raises hell about people bringing food into the club and eating it there, when she sells hamburgers, fries, hot dogs, and other such commodities. She lets Faye do what she wants. She's a regular.

"Has anybody been through looking for me?"

"Naw, honey, not yet," and she giggles lightly to herself, snuffing out her cigarette and then emptying it into the waste can right afterwards. Wilma turns the channel on the television to one of her favorite game shows.

"Girl if had all that money I would close this place down and find me something else to do, like nothin'."

"I wouldn't have to work these streets anymore, and fool with some of these daffy ass tricks."

"I bet you run into some real fools sometimes."

Trying to chew the food in her mouth properly, Faye starts to tell her about someone she had an encounter with yesterday, but cuts it short when a gentleman walks in the door. He sits down at the bar a seat away from Faye, ordering a beer. He lights a cigarette. Wilma slides an astray his way. He responds to it by pulling it to him. Eventually it is too quiet for him. He finishes his beer in a hurry and leaves. The cigarette is still burning in the ashtray. Wilma puts it out and cleans the ashtray.

"You know him?" Ask Faye.

"No, honey. He sure left in a hurry."

"I think I may have seen him around here before I can't really say for sure." It's four o'clock and nobody has shown up of yet.

"I wonder where everybody is?"

"Don't worry child. They're liable to show up anytime now. You know they have to get their checks cashed."

Faye gets up and starts toward the door. Realizing she doesn't have her coat she turns around to get it. Wilma has started repacking the beer cooler.

"I'll be back. I'm going to see if there is anybody in the rest of the clubs."

She tightens the belt to the coat around her waist. As she exits the door, she notices that there are only four cars on the parking lot, one of which is hers, and the other is Wilma's. There's an old Cutlass that has been parked there for weeks now. One of the tires is flat. The passenger window is rolled down or broken out. If she can remember correctly at one time there was glass scattered around the car door. She dismisses the thought, finding it irrelevant. The gentleman who came in earlier is sitting in the fourth car smoking a cigarette. He blows his horn. Faye stops and looks before she makes an effort to approach the car. He beckons her with his hand. Faye smiles and goes toward the car. As she gets closer he rolls down the window. She can hear the music playing.

"Would you like to sit down a minute?" He asks.

She walks around to the passenger side. He unlocks the door. She gets in, and he turns the radio down to where it is barely audible.

want "I did not <u>what</u> to say anything in the place. I was hoping you would come out so I could talk to you. My name is Anthony." Extending his hand. She acknowledges, barely touching it.

"Hi, my name is Faye."

"I know I've seen you around. I've asked." Faye gives him an inquiring look. "I mean, you can't help but notice."

"What did you notice?"

He blushes, then chuckles.

"The things a horny man or any real man would notice."

Faye looks down toward his lap. She giggles herself.

"I was just wondering what you have in mind."

"What would it take for me to get next to you, or should I say how much?"

"You're not five o are you?"

"What's that?"

"The police."

"Oh no baby." He says reaching for his back pocket, coming up with his billfold. "See I'm not the police." She notices the pictures of kids and a woman.

"Who is that?"

"That's someone I know, a friend." He says, but his hesitation of voice and facial expression dispel the truth.

"Someone like your wife."

"What makes you say that?"

"Not too many men carry around a picture of just a friend in their wallet. Then I noticed the spot on your hand where your ring was. You can put it back on. It won't make a difference. It's not that kind of party." She says, turning her head gazing out the window for a minute.

"Excuse me, I didn't understand what you said."

"Nothing, baby, let's just get back to where we were. What do you think it's worth to you?"

She unties the belt to her coat and loosens the buttons, so he can get a better look.

"I know how fine you are, like I said I've noticed. How about fifty dollars?"

"Let's go." She says without hesitation. She places her hand on his arm as a gesture. "Uh, you'll have to take me by my friend's place first. Then we'll go to mine and take care of business."

"That'll work." He says, putting the car into drive.

When they arrive at Tracy's, she tells Anthony to give her the money. He is slow responding at first, but does it anyway. She exits the automobile, telling the runner she wants two quarters. She does not want Anthony to see what they are doing, so they go behind the trailer to transact business.

"I'm ready." She says.

Getting into the car rubbing her hands together, placing her hands up to the vents.

"Which way. Are you cold?" He asks.

Instinctively he turns the heater on high. Faye directs him toward her house. Before they reach their destination, she asks him to buy her a four pack of Champale. He does so without question.

They arrive at her house and she invites him in. Surprisingly, it is cleaner than usual. She directs him to the sofa, continuing on to the ice box, drinking a Champale when she returns. Anthony is lighting a cigarette. Faye passes him an ashtray.

"It is okay if I smoke, isn't it?"

"That's why I gave you an ashtray."

"Just being polite."

"Make yourself comfortable. I'll be right out."

Anthony in turn sheds his coat and sits back on the sofa.

Faye comes back and picks up her purse, then closes the bathroom door. She removes the straight shooter, which is wrapped in tissue paper from her purse along with her lighter. Reaching into the cabinet under the face bowl and retrieves a glass saucer and a razor blade. Ten minutes pass. She knows Anthony must be getting restless. So she hollers out the bathroom door and tells him that she will be right out. He says okay in a similar tone of voice. An additional five minutes she exits the bathroom with just a large terry cloth bathrobe and the same Champale in her hand, leaving her purse and all in the cabinet. She is very high. The drug forces her to put on a more jubilant smile. Grasping his hand, she leads him to the bedroom. She stands toe to toe with him, looking him in the eye, teasing his lips with her fingernails, which are painted bright red to match her lipstick.

"How do you want it?" She asks.

Her hands work their way down to his pants and stops at his zipper. He swallows hard.

"What ever you want to do."

"It's not how I want it, it's how you want it. You're paying." She undoes his pants and his penis is already hard. She strokes it with her fingers. He fumbles to relieve himself of the rest of his clothes.

"Where do you work at?"

"The railroad."

"How long have you been working there?"

"Close to twelve years."

"That's a long time." She lays him back on the bed and lies on top of him while they continue their conversation.

"Could we turn off the light?" He asks.

"What's the matter you ashamed or something honey?"

"No, not really."

She gets up to turn the lights off. Anthony takes a good look at what he is getting. She winks and smiles, licking out her tongue at him. The room is semi-dark, because of the time of day.

"Do you want to get under the cover too?"

He does not answer. Instead he gets up. Faye pulls the cover back. After teasing him some more she reaches onto the night stand and retrieves a condom, tearing the packet open with her teeth and slipping it onto his penis faster than he realizes. She takes him and slides him inside her.

"What would it cost to get sucked?" He asks.

She seizes the opportunity to ask him for an additional fifty dollars, and promises a good time. Faye gets up and hands him his pants. He gives her a fifty dollar bill. She neatly folds his pants across the chair. Thinking to herself. 'Motherfucker wants to get sucked. He doesn't even know how to talk to a woman stupid bastard.'

"Just a minute. I'll be right back."

She goes into the bathroom. Again she hits her pipe. This time she does it more quickly, returning with a warm wet towel. She wipes him off, the rubber still in place. He's disappointed, but dares not say anything since he does not know her. She also gives him some head quicker than he realized also, stroking him with her hand more than anything. She then takes care of business. The total charade lasts twenty-five minutes. Faye excuses herself, taking the towel with her. Returning, giving him the towel.

"Is there anything else I can do for you?" She asks without sincerity.

Kissing him on the forehead.

"I'm fine. You didn't let me down one bit."

"I'm glad." She says and goes to the bathroom, turning on the shower.

After showering, she hurriedly reapplies her make up and combs her hair back into place. On the way out she stops in the kitchen and gets another Champale. Once they are in the car, she pulls out a cigarette. Anthony reaches over and lights, it for her.

"Thank you. You're such a gentleman."

Anthony takes her back downtown. He lets her out on the corner, out of the fear of being seen. She goes back into the club.

Wilma says. "I thought you said you were going to be right back. I saw your car was still out there."

"I had some business to take care of." Before she could go on, Wilma stops her.

"Some man is looking for you. I think he may still be in the back shooting pool." Faye orders another Champale, having a habit of setting them down and letting them get hot. She walks to the back. It's Sam. He is one of her regulars. He stops shooting pool and speaks. They exchange a few words.

"Go ahead and finish your game." She says, while she smokes a cigarette and finishes her drink.

The game takes about fifteen minutes to complete. By then she is ready, realizing what time it's getting to be, knowing that it won't be long before some of the rest of her clients show up.

They leave the club. Sam already knows the routine, and instinctively takes her to the cocaine house first. There are three other cars there when they arrive, so they have to wait a few minutes before being served.

Sam stops by the liquor store without being asked, not just for her but for himself as well. He orders a pack of Champale and a pint of Canadian Mist whiskey. Having more Champale at the house than she really needs, she still never turns them down. They automatically give him two cups of ice. They know what he wants. Sam is a man of habit.

They arrive at the house. Sam goes into the bedroom. He knows his way around. Collapsing on the bed, he removes his shoes and pours himself a drink. Faye is not reluctant to smoke in front of him. She has two quarters. At this point she is not real particular about being careful not to waste the dope, because she knows there will be plenty more before the night is done. She does not bother to clean her pipe, installing a new filter, saving the old one. Sam is a regular customer all right, but he likes to bullshit more than he likes to spend money. So she takes care of business and asks him for a tip. Sam is rather tipsy at this point, so when he pulls out his billfold to hand her a twenty dollar bill. She playfully snatches another and kisses him on the jaw. It tickles him to be able to do that with his money. She then rushes him. She drives his car back to the club for him to save time and eliminate the risk of being stopped.

It's almost seven o'clock at night when she walks into the club. The juke box is playing "Crack killed Applejack." This record is very popular at the time. The crowd has thickened. The moment Faye walks into the door she is rushed back out by another one of her regulars. They go directly to her place, having no time to shower, she douches and goes back downtown.

She has one hundred and sixty dollars in her possession. She reapplies her lipstick in the car. Noticing a run in her stockings she reaches into her purse and pulls out her clear fingernail polish and puts some on the ends of the run to prevent it from going any further.

She thanks the trick, apologizing for being in such a rush.

She is really looking for Oscar, he is one of her better spenders. He's having troubles at home. So he spends more because she shows him a lot of sympathy. He's usually there about this time of the night on Thursday, but there is no sign of him as of yet. She orders a drink and sits at an empty table, using her own drink as an ash tray, refusing to drink any more.

There are quite a few female impersonators there. Faye knows them all. There is one in particular named Ted. He prefers to be called Jenny and he is rather fond of Faye. He walks over and sits at the table, having on more perfume and make-up than Faye, along with a wig, false hips, and breast.

"Hey, girl."

"Hey, Jenny."

"How's business?"

"It's not bad. Have you seen, Oscar?"

"Yeah, he went around to Ron's place. I sure wish he was spending money on me. I know he spends good. Anyway I think he saw your car was the reason he came in here looking, he only stayed a few seconds."

Faye gathers her coat, and leaves out the door without putting it on. She walks at a very fast pace, to keep from being chilled by the weather.

When she walks into Ron's place she sees Oscar at the bar sitting with his back to her. She walks over and places her cold hands on his cheeks. He turns to see who it is and smiles. He orders her a drink without looking or asking if she wanted one. She accepts it to pacify him. He tells the guy next to him to move down a stool. She thanks the gentleman for the seat. After a while she leans over and whispers in Oscar's ear, sticking her tongue in it at the same time.

"I heard that." He says.

He tells Ron he has to run. He gets up and turns his drink up, finishing it before he brings it down. He gently catches Faye by the arm and leads her out the door.

Outside he puts his arm around her as a shield from the cold. His car is parked in front of the club across the street. He unlocks the passenger side first and lets her in.

She has him take her to the cocaine house, buying herself a quarter rock, and not asking him for the money yet. Even though he knows she smokes it, she does not want him to think she wants his money for drugs, rather have him to believe the money was for a better purpose.

On the way back to her house, she has him stop by her mother's. When they pull into the driveway, her mother peeks out the glass on the front door, then opens it. Two small boys run out to the car.

Hollering "Mama! Mama!"

They attempt to open the car door, she hollers through the glass. "Just a minute!"

She asks Oscar to give her some money so her mother can go shopping for the boys and buy some food. He has been here before. Reaching in his back pocket, he pulls out his billfold, giving her one hundred and fifty dollars with no reservations.

"Thanks, baby." She unlocks the door.

The smoke from her cigarette and his cigar rolls out with the heat. "Where are you're coats?" She cries. Grabbing each one of them and kissing them on the mouth. "Hey Lil' Stevie, hey Tony." They are five and six. "How come you'll are not sleep anyway?" Her mother has kept them for her since Faye and her husband split up, over a year in a half ago. Tony is in first grade, while Stevie is in kindergarten. Faye's mother does not work. She knows what

Faye does for a living So she is rather protective of the boys. She also knows Faye drinks, she but has no idea that she smokes cocaine. She does not know what it is.

"Hi mama"

"Hi baby. The boys have been asking about you. You need to come over and spend the night like you used to."

"I will Mama. Listen, here's some money so you can take the boys shopping and buy some groceries. I have to run. I have someone waiting on me outside."

"How am I suppose to go shopping? You know I don't have a car."

"I thought you and Mrs. Annie could go. You do it all the time."

"You need to take me child. Why don't you take me when the boys get out of school?"

"Mama you know tomorrow is Friday. You have two hundred dollars pay her to take you."

"That's not what I'm talking about. You need to spend some time with the boys."

"I've got to go, Mama." She tells the boys that Grandma is going to buy them something nice. She hugs them both in one big embrace and heads toward the door. Oscar is sitting there with the car running to keep warm. "I'll call you tomorrow, Mama!" She says as she gets in the car. Her mother pulls the boys back from the doorway as they holler and wave bye to their mother.

"Hope I didn't take long."

"Take your time. You are doing the right thing to see after those boys. Do you want anything to drink? I'm going to stop at the liquor store anyway."

"I don't need anything to drink. I already have enough to drink at the house. You can buy me a pack of cigarettes and a lighter. You better hurry, they are going to be closed in a minute."

He buys his favorite gin and a bottle of tonic, along with a bag of ice. The cigars he smokes are not sold in the regular stores so he has to go one of the bigger grocery stores to buy them. Faye gladly goes in the store for him. She returns and gives him five cigars and his change.

"I bought a pack of chewing gum."

"You didn't even have to mention it."

"I know I was just being courteous."

"Are you hungry?"

"No, I'm fine."

"What about you?"

"A little bit. I think I could use some chicken nuggets." He stops by Kentucky Fried Chicken and gets a twenty-five piece orders of nuggets.

"You didn't have to order the largest one they had. The twelve piece would have been fine."

"Well, you might want to save some for later."

Oscar makes himself at home. He gets two glasses from the cabinet and rinses them out. He fixes himself a drink in one glass and Faye a drink in the other. Meanwhile, Faye goes into the rest room to slip into something more comfortable. When she comes out, Oscar has already taken off his shoes and propped his feet on the table. He knows Faye does not mind. Faye gets a chair from the kitchen and sits across from him. She shares the same table he has his feet on to fix her cocaine. She puts some in the pipe. Oscar just puffs on his cigar and watches.

"Why do you smoke that stuff?"

"Well, it makes me feel good and I can forget a lot of things. It's kind of like you drink alcohol. It makes you feel good and you forget about your wife, right?"

"Yeah it does, but you do a better job than the alcohol."

The question makes her feel a slight bit uncomfortable. So she smokes it rather hastily and puts it up.

"It's just a high. I can do without it if I wanted to. I just hate to drink hard liquor and I very seldom smoke weed."

"You didn't have to put it up baby. I just asked."

"Oh, I know I rather tease you a little bit."

She smiles, pinching him on the toes. She grabs him by the hand and pulls him up. He has his cigar in the other. She leads him into the bedroom and completely undresses him. After making him comfortable in bed she opens the gum and takes out two sticks, opening them both. She puts one in her mouth and one in his. She reaches on the dresser and gets a can of women's spray colognes and sprays herself while looking in the mirror. She then thinks of the nuggets Oscar brought. She walks into the living room and gets them along with her drink and places them on the night stand next to the bed. She turns out the light and partially closes the bathroom door, so that it only throws a small amount of light. She climbs into bed. She gives Oscar a little extra special attention and allows him a chance to get his rocks off twice. He only manages once before he is too tired.

She reaches over and turns the lamp on afterwards. She nibbles on the nuggets, really indifferent to eating. But she knows she needs to eat. He goes into depth about his problems with his wife. He tells Faye that he really loves his wife. They haven't had sex for quite a while now. He stops and asks Faye to refill his drink. She gets up and closes the box of nuggets, which is nearly finished and puts them back on the night stand. Reaching for her cigarettes, she lights one on the way to the kitchen. She washes her hands and puts fresh ice into his drink. She knows how he likes his drinks, having watched him and fixed them many times before. She gives him his drink and goes back to the living room.

She gets her pipe and pushes the brillo from end to end. a process that cleans some of the residue (which is actually unburned cocaine), out of the pipe, allowing a her to smoke what is caught in the filter. She also puts the piece she has left on the pipe. It produces a large cloud of smoke because she has smoked so much and not cleaned her pipe. There is a little bit more than she actually antici-pated. She drops the pipe and has to sit down because of the head rush she receives, followed by her heart pounding in her chest. After a minute or two she regains her composure and puts the pipe back up. She still has not gained enough of her senses to talk prop-erly, so she picks up her cigarette and goes to the bathroom. She freshens up a bit before coming out. Still naked, she sits on the side of the bed and sips on her drink.

"Are you all right?" Oscar asks.

She smiles and nods her head. Her eyes are still bulging along with being glassy. Putting her drink down she lights another ciga-rette and lays her head on Oscar's chest and just stares at the ceil-ing. She remains quiet until he starts the conversation again. He makes the comment that despite his problems at home he does not want to stay late.

"You don't have to rush off still."

"I missed the news. That's okay though; I don't regret it one bit." He kisses her on the top of the head.

"Why don't you have a television?"

"I had one, but I took it over to Mama house so the boys could watch TV."

"I'm going to get you a television. In fact, I'll do it tomorrow morning about nine o'clock?"

"You don't really have to do it. I hardly watch any TV as it is."

"Everybody should have a television baby. That way I won't miss the news when I'm over here."

They finish getting dressed and head for downtown. He drops her off at her car. She does not go to it. She goes to the club.

"Faye! Where have you been?" Asks Charlene. "I been looking all over for you."

"I was at home."

"I saw your car. I forgot that you could have been riding with someone else. I had a few sweaters but I've gotten rid of them now."

"Aw girl. Why didn't you save me at least one?"

"What are you doing tomorrow morning?"

"What time?"

"I don't know."

"It can't be at nine because I have to wait for Oscar to come by."

"Do you think you'll be through by eleven?"

"Sure."

"Why don't you come by and pick me up? I'll go get us some clothes."

"I know you have some money if you sold those sweaters."

"You know it, girl. You thinking about getting high? What we need to do is catch us a couple of tricks to get us high before we spend our money, honey."

They mingle through the crowd as if nothing is happening, looking for a new trick or a regular as long as he has dope or has some money. There are no takers at the moment. They decide to get a drink and sit down at an unoccupied table. At the back of the club. people are shooting pool. It's eleven thirty and they have not gotten a decent proposition yet, only ones that wanted to play games. They decide to go get high and then come back.

Faye drives. They go to the trailer and buy a quarter rock each. Charlene tells Faye that she knows where another cocaine house is that just opened. They supposedly sell bigger pieces for the same money. It does not matter at the moment, because they have already purchased their dope. As they are about to leave, they are stopped by two guys about to go to the same trailer. They want to know where they are going and if they can follow them. Faye asks them, "How much cocaine are you going to buy?"

One of them replies. "Probably a sixteenth for starters." Charlene lets out an audible sound.

The two guys purchase their cocaine and are following the women to the house.

They talk about what they are going to do.

"I think we just caught us a set of real freaks." They quip, laughing and giving each other some play. "Did you see the ass on them whores? Woo Hooo man!" They discuss which one gets to go to bed with whom. "You always want the best looking bitch. What about me. Shit."

"It ain't no big deal we'll probably switch anyway."

"Now you're talkin'."

Charlene is not a bad looking woman by any means. She has a dark complexion. Her hair is in a Jerri Curl. She is not as shapely as Faye and is a slight bit shorter. She has a fantastic smile, along with a gold tooth and dark piercing eyes.

The women are low on gas, so they stop at the gas station. The guys pull in behind them. Faye hands the money to the one who volunteers to pump the gas. He in turn gives it to his partner who is about to go into the store and purchase some beer. He asks the women if they drink beer. Charlene does. Faye says she has something to drink already. The women talk on the way home about how high they are going to get. They are not really concerned with who gets whom. One trick is no different from the next.

When they arrive the girls get out first and are in the house before the guys get out of the car. They bring in their beer along with a bag that once used to hold a quart of Crown Royal. It is a fancy type of bag blue with Crown Royal embossed in yellow letters with the same color draw string. Inside the house they gather at the dining table.

Three beers are taken out of the twelve pack they have purchased. One of the guys asks Faye to put the rest into the refrigerator. She does and gets a Champale for herself. The guys are well prepared. Within the crown royal bag, they have a glass pipe, brillo, pure grain alcohol, cotton balls, two pieces of cloth hanger and a couple of razor blades. As they reveal the contents of the bag, Faye and Charlene throw a smile in each other's direction. They take the cocaine that is concealed in a match box and cuts several smokeable size pieces.

The glass pipe produces a much cleaner high, so less cocaine is wasted. It is a more efficient method of smoking cocaine. A torch is used rather than a regular butane lighter. The torch consists of a stem (usually a clothes hanger) and a cotton ball dipped in pure grain alcohol or any number of other substances that will burn readily; however pure grain alcohol burns cleanly.

They are all comfortable. The guys have taken off their shirts, and after a couple of hits off the pipe, the guys are ready to fuck. The girls take one of the quarters and split it in half, putting a piece on the pipe. They then start to undress. Faye takes the bedroom.

Charlene takes the sofa. The girls have agreed to try and make them spend as much money as they can. So they make no attempt to thoroughly satisfy them. They tease them to the point where they know that they are for real but not making them mad. They go back and forth to the pipe until all of the cocaine is gone. The guys decided to buy some more dope. Charlene and the guy she is involved with want to stay while Faye and the other gentleman go and get some more cocaine.

Charlene and the man she is with smoke the quarter she bought earlier. He wants to fuck while they are gone. Charlene lets him get his rocks off, since the other dope is on the way. They do not quite get through when Faye and her date come through the door. Charlene makes him get up anyway.

They smoke the cocaine. Faye and her date get the extra piece since, Charlene and her date smoked up the other quarter. Faye lives up to her bargain as well. She takes good care of her date. But she has lost interest in them because she knows that they only have forty dollars between them. That won't be much split four ways. The guys have already spent three hundred dollars. Faye tells them she is fixing to go. So they all gather their things.

Charlene asks Faye. "Are you going to ride with us?"

Faye calls Charlene to the bedroom and asks her how much money she has left. "I have ninety three dollar."

"Can I borrow fifteen dollars until tomorrow?"

Faye has sixty five dollars. Charlene gives her thirteen dollars.

"How come you are not going to ride with us?"

"It's been a long day I'm going to chill. I'll be over to pick you up in the morning."

When they leave, Faye straightens up the dining area and her bedroom. She lights an incense to improve the smell of the house. Cursing, then talking to herself she says, "I need to clean this house up real good." Then thinking about how she felt earlier this evening when she had too much dope on her pipe. "Thank God" She whispers, lifting her eyes toward the ceiling.

It is after two thirty. Faye decides she will get herself another piece before going to bed. Reminding herself that it is Friday morning. She does just that. She returns home, runs some bath water, and soaks in the tub while she smokes her pipe. When she finishes, it's quarter to four. So she rubs down with baby oil, slips on her gown, and goes to bed. It is hard for her to get to sleep at first but she eventually does.

She is awaked n the next morning by a loud knocking at the door. She goes and answers the door. It is Oscar.

"Good morning."

"What time is it?"

"About nine thirty."

"Come on in. You have to forgive me. I'm still half asleep." Flopping back down on the sofa, she closes her eyes.

"You must have had a long night."

"It was okay."

Forcing herself to her feet, she rushes into the bathroom and washes her face and applies her make up. She's ready within fifteen minutes.

They go to Otasco. Oscar purchases a small color television on his credit card. Faye has already informed him that she has to go pick up Charlene. Therefore, Oscar doesn't linger too long. He takes the television to Faye's house and sets it up for her.

She makes it to Charlene's apartment and finally gets her to answer the door.

"I just got home at eight thirty this morning." She says, still wired up from a few hours ago. "I just nodded off, I wasn't going to answer the door until I figured out it was you. Girl, them fools last night wind up getting an eight ball from some dude. I didn't think we were ever going to finish smoking all that shit. They wanted to go back and get you, but when we drove up to the house all the lights were out. I told them you were not getting back up."

"I'm glad you didn't come and wake me up. I've been smoking too much anyway, I need to slow down."

After she is dressed and ready, she asks Faye if she is broke. Faye laughs and asks

"Why?"

"I sure could use a bump to get going this morning."

"I figured that last night when I asked you for that money. I stopped and brought one on the way. I knew you were going to spend all of your money last night with those guys. I bet you still don't know their names."

"It doesn't make any difference. I probably won't see them again anyway."

"Always let them spend the money and save yours unless you have some type of feelings for the guy."

"Girl, I don't know what I would do without you sometimes."

After getting high, Charlene is happier and ready to go steal some clothes.

They go to a small shopping center that has several ladies boutiques. Faye stays in the car. Charlene is dressed in a long dress that goes down to her ankles a girdle and regular coat. She goes into the store and returns. She has two dresses and two pair of jeans under her dress held in place by the girdle. She puts them in the car.

"I'll be back. I saw another dress I wanted."

"You're going back into the same store?"

"Yes."

"You must be crazy."

"You wait until you see the dress."

None of the clothes that Charlene gets are cheap. She gets a sweater that cost as much as one hundred and fifty dollars. The jeans are designer. Dresses cost as much or more than the sweaters. Days before, she has a sequined dress that cost six, hundred dollars.

After the first store they put all of the clothes in the trunk. They proceed to the next store. Only this time she gets some clothes she has promised to other people. They place orders and she fulfills them. After about two and a half hours, Charlene is ready to go. Since Charlene place is closer, they go over there to sort out the clothes. They tally up the clothes minus the ones they want to keep for themselves. The amount comes up to fourteen hundred and sixty dollars. They normally sell the clothes for half of what they cost in the store. Some of the people she has taken orders for do not get off from work until later that evening. Charlene goes to the women she knows are at home. She sells a part-time school teacher a dress. The dress cost one hundred and sixty dollars. The teacher pays eight dollars for it. Faye prefers to sell as many clothes as they can. Charlene wants to go and buy some cocaine right away.

"Well, since you can't seem to wait, I will put the rest with it so we can get a gram. You and me both ought to be tired of smoking."

Charlene does not want to go to Tracy's. She wants to introduce her to somebody else she knows who has just started selling. The house Charlene directs Faye to is just two blocks over from where the trailer house is located. The house is surrounded by a six foot chain link fence. The house itself is brick, with a fairly big size yard. Two pit bulldogs roam around the yard. The first thing Faye says is she is not going in there with those dogs in the yard.

"You don't have to worry about that anyway. He usually parks under the trees anyway."

The trees she is referring to line the opposite side of the street, outside the yard.

They go to the trailer anyway. Faye wants to personally get coke from Tracy. They chat for a few minutes. He wants to know when they are going to get together. He speaks freely since his girlfriend is gone.

Faye laughs and says, "Whenever you can get away from Sheila."

"We'll talk about it." He says, and pats her on the ass.

When Faye gets back to the car, she reminds Charlene that it is Friday. There is plenty of money to be made today. On the way to Charlene's house they stop to see if Mrs. Jackson has made it home yet. She has not.

"Oscar bought me a color television this morning."

"Girl, he sounds like a good trick."

"He's really a nice man. He's special in his own way."

They talk about how much money they are going to make this evening, with whom and where.

"It's three o'clock now." Says Faye.

"Don't worry, you won't miss your money, honey." Assures Charlene.

It is four thirty when they finish getting high and leave the apartment. They catch a few more of the customers who buy clothes. The only thing left now is a sweater.

Faye goes home and gets ready. In the meantime, Charlene is still fiddling with her pipe, pushing the filter back and forth, in an attempt to get another satisfactory hit. She asks Faye if she can push the filter in her pipe. She notices that Faye hardly ever pushes hers. Faye tells her no. She saves that for hard times.

"Remind me to call Mama when we get downtown" Says Faye.

It is after five o'clock when they do make it down town. Wilma's place is the first place they go. A few people have gathered already. Charlene wants some more dope. She tells Faye that she has to go.

"How are you going?"

"I can catch a ride with somebody."

Within five minutes Charlene is gone from downtown. Faye thinks to herself that Charlene sure can get around when she wants to.

Wilma complements Faye on the new dress she is wearing.

"I got it today do you really like it?"

"You sure know how to dress when you want to." Faye brags slightly on how expensive the dress is.

"I wish I could afford clothes like that."

"I have a friend that might be able to help. What size do you wear?"

"About a nine or ten."

"What about shoes?"

"Oh probably eight, eight and a half it depends on the shoe." Says Wilma.

"What size did you say again?"

This time Wilma writes the sizes down on a sheet of receipt paper.

Faye asks for a Champale and goes to the back of the club. There are some guys and girls shooting pool as a team. Several women sit at the table with a dime bag of marijuana rolling a joint. As one finishes rolling it up, the other lights it up. One of them waves at Faye. She waves back and turns to leave when she bumps face to face into a guy with a cup of liquor in one hand and a cup of beer in the other. The liquor wastes down the front of her dress. The dress consist of silk and rayon blend. The stain is very noticeable. Faye curses and calls him everything bad she can think of. He is rather intoxicated, so it really does not matter to him what she says. He mumbles a few inaudible derogatory words of his own and goes on about his business. Faye goes to the bar and asks Wilma for a wet towel. Wilma shows her the best way to do it, so that it will not leave a stain. While in the process, Robert comes up to Faye and whispers in her ear. Unexpectedly she jerks away as a reflex until she realizes who he is, and tries to put on a smile in a vain attempt. She's unsuccessful.

"Is it that bad?"

"Not really, I just got this dress today." Wilma finishes.

"Thanks Wilma."

Robert leads her back to the table and explains what he has on his mind. She agrees. While Robert is finishing his drink, the same man that wasted the drink on her dress passes by.

"You son-of-a-bitch." She says.

He approaches the table.

"Fuck you bitch."

Faye reacts and slaps him.

They start to fight. Before it gets too involved, it is stopped by Robert and a couple of other people, who are standing around. Apparently Faye feels relieved after the incident. She finishes her drink and tells Robert to come on. Robert goes to the liquor across the street and buys a pint of E & J brandy. He wants to go to his place but Faye wants to go home so she can change clothes.

When they get to Faye's place, Robert has a paper bag with his cocaine smoking fixtures. He has the type of pipe that breaks completely down and has to be put together. It is a large version. He also has a bottle of P.G.A. in his bag.

"Do you have any cotton balls?" He asks.

"No."

"Well, get me a roll of tissue if you don't mind. It does just as well."

She goes into the bathroom to get a roll of tissue. She stops and looks at herself in the mirror, then frowns at the spot on her dress. She fixes Robert a cup of ice while he is in the process of getting the pipe ready. She only wants a glass of ice water and a cigarette. They start smoking the cocaine. Faye ask Robert to unfasten her dress. She pulls it off and puts on her robe. Between the smoking and the drinking, Robert is continuously running his hand inside the robe. She tells him he might as well take it off, which he does, and he strips himself of his clothes afterwards. Before they have a chance to indulge she tells him.

"I need some money for my boys."

He says. I don't not have that much."

She does not mention it again until he attempts to perform oral sex with her. She tells him.

"I wish you would hurry up fuck. Hell, I can get the money to buy dope on my own. I don't really fuck for it anyway."

She then holds out her hand. He breaks down and gives her thirty-five dollars. She kisses him hard on the mouth and giggles.

"You know, Faye, you are a bitch."

"I thought you knew." She laughs heartily.

She reaches over and takes a sip of his brandy. She comments on the smooth taste it has compared to some other types of liquor she has tried. She drinks the rest of his drink and takes care of Robert's sexual needs, freshens up, and tells him it is time to go. He wants to know why she is acting so cold today.

"I'm not being cold toward you. I just have to make a certain amount of money this weekend. I got bills to pay, man!"

Robert's feelings are hurt, but he has no choice. Faye has her jeans on with a sweater and is standing at the door waiting, sipping on a drink she fixed.

"Where did you get the television?"

"It was brought for me."

The box it was in is still sitting by the door. Robert wraps things up and follows Faye out the door.

They go back downtown. Within the course of four hours she has made a sizable amount of money. She wants to call her mother, but she knows she goes to bed right after the news goes off. She has close to three hundred dollars. Asking Wilma to keep a hundred and fifty dollars for her until tomorrow, she thinks about Jerry and decides that she will go by and see if he is at home.

Despite the hour, she pulls up in the driveway and blows.

The light on the other side of the house where Jerry's bedroom is comes on. He slips on his shoes and pants, not taking time to put on his sock and shirt, but a jacket instead. He goes to the car to see what Faye wants.

"What are you doing?" Faye asks.

"I was just sitting in bed watching television."

"You want to ride with me?"

"Yeah, let me get my shirt."

He comes out fully dressed this time, along with his baseball cap. After he gets in the car, he tells her how glad he is to see her and that he was just thinking about her earlier that evening.

"I intended to come by yesterday but I got tied up and could not make it."

She stops by the liquor store and buys him a twelve pack of beer that is on sale at the moment, a four pack of Champale, a half pint of E and J brandy, cigarettes and two lighters. As they leave, he thanks her for the beer and reaches into the sack.

"I didn't say that was yours did I?" Jerry releases the beer and apologies. She laughs, "You know I brought it for you."

Jerry laughs himself and says, "I thought it was but when you brought that half a pint of brandy, I wondered about it. I know you don't drink liquor."

"I tasted some earlier and I kind of liked it. So I got that to keep around the house."

They head toward the dope house. Again she wants to speak directly to Tracy. She asks him for a sixteenth and a quarter. They stop by the supermarket and buy some more brillo for the pipe.

Jerry does not notice the television until Faye turns it on.

"Where did you get the television?"

"You're dipping aren't you baby?"

"Excuse me." He says as they are laughing it off together.

Jerry examines the TV and compliments her on how nice it is. Faye gets Jerry a glass as well as one for herself and pours a shot of brandy in each with ice cubes. She gives Jerry the sixteenth and puts the quarter away. He goes into the bathroom and gets a razor blade and her glass saucer and cuts it up, while she fixes her pipe. Before anything is smoked, they both undress.

Sitting side by side on the sofa they caress, fondle and tease each other. Faye makes an unsuccessful attempt to stop, but Jerry persists and downs her on the sofa. They are indulging before they know it. He complements her on the perfume she is wearing and how good she feels to him.

"I thought that you wanted to get high?"

"I do if you will allow me to do it the way I like it." Jerry says. This pleases her to know that she has some priority over the cocaine. "You in a hurry to get high?" Jerry asks.

"Oh, no baby take your time." Faye says.

Afterwards she goes and gets a warm wet towel and wipes him off as well as herself. She brings back a fresh wet cold towel to be used to cool the pipe.

After Jerry's first hit of the pipe he starts to sweat more profusely, than he was while he was having sex with her.

"Is it that hot in here to you?"

"Between this and you what do you expect? I haven't gotten high all week, to be honest."

"You poor baby." She teases. She draws letters on his chest with her fingers in the sweat that covers him like a mist on a window pane. His head is dripping sweat like the water off the roof after a rain. He goes and gets a beer and Champale and pour them into the same glass the brandy was in. "Did you get a good hit, honey?" Faye asks as she puts a piece on the pipe.

"I'm fine."

He goes and gets the television and sets it on a chair in front of them. He plugs it into the wall and almost shocks himself in the progress by touching the prongs.

"You all right?"

"Yeah, I almost got shocked was all." He puts it on the channel he wants and turns it down low to where it can barely be heard. They sit down, continuing to get high.

"You know what? I'm going to buy a glass pipe tomorrow after I make a little money. I gave Wilma one hundred and fifty dollars to keep but that is for bills. I'll come by your house tomorrow and we'll ride to Little Rock and get one. I think we're wasting a lot of dope in these homemade pipes. Besides, they get too hot and put blisters on my lips."

"You're right and I don't like to use these lighters anyway. They make me cough up that black shit."

"Jerry, can I ask you something?"

"Go ahead."

"Did you miss me?"

"You mean you can't tell?"

He puts the pipe down and moves closer to her. He kisses her on the mouth, then leads with his tongue down to her breast and wiggles his tongue around and around her nipples, as he does they arise to meet the occasion. Laying her back on the sofa and running his tongue down to her navel, he sticks his tongue in it several times before going down any further. He goes past her pussy and gently nibbles on her thighs. She is steadily trying to push him back. She slides out from under him and runs to the bathroom. He is right on her heels. She tries to stop him by backing into a corner.

"Jerry please stop! Let me take a bath first!"

She starts the water running. He is still teasing her with his hands. He gently bites her on the back. She turns around and embraces him kissing him wet and gently on the mouth.

"I'll take a bath with you. How about that?"

"You're the king, Have it your way."

He pulls her by the hand into the living room while the tub fills with water. They both put a sizable piece in the pipe and hit them the same time, then they both rush toward the bathroom. Jerry stops and turns around and lights two cigarettes, bringing his beer and her Champale and sets them on the floor beside the tub. Handing her the extra cigarette, he gets into the tub so that he sits behind her. He washes her up and down. She in turn does the same. They don't stay in the tub long. After drying off, Faye sprays cologne all over herself. He is wrapped in a towel and so is she. Jerry puts the empties into the trash and brings another. This time when he hits the pipe, instead of exhaling it out into the air, he pulls Faye close to him and places his mouth on hers, letting her suck it into her lungs. In turn she does the same for him.

He unties the towel and slides it off of her, starting his love making process all over again. He lays her on the couch and does not stop until they are both thoroughly exhausted. It is well past one o'clock. The television is hissing at them with a snowy screen. Jerry turns it off and proceeds to get high while Faye lies on the sofa. Trying to regain herself. He looks over at her.

"That will teach you about not coming to see me all week. Ha! Ha! Ha!"

He hands her a piece of cocaine. She hits it laying back, letting it take full effect. The rest of the night is uneventful, except for getting high. She tells Jerry he can push the brillo in her pipe. He looks inside it, holding it up to he light.

"You've smoked quite a bit. Haven't you? There's a lot of residue in here."

"Sure, just save me some will you?"

Faye gets comfortable on the couch and eventually falls asleep. Jerry sits up and cleans both pipes. By the time he finishes, it's after five o'clock. He picks Faye up and carries her to the bedroom, and puts her in bed. She manages a partial smile and falls back to sleep.

The next morning Faye awakens first and takes a shower. She puts the same jeans and sweater she had on late yesterday evening. She styles her hair and puts on her make up before waking up Jerry. He takes a shower and combs his hair. He goes to the ice box and gets a beer. He starts to open it when Faye snatches it away.

"You need to eat first."

She fixes some eggs, rice, bacon, and toast. She hands him a glass of orange juice. Then she sets down to eat herself.

"That's too many eggs on my plate." He says.

"You're going to need them." She promises. He smiles and gobbles them down.

After he is finished, she gives him a beer, opening it and pouring it into a glass. She also gives him a folded piece of paper. He opens it. There is a quarter rock in it.

"Where did you get this?"

"I saved it from last night. I knew you were going completely clean both pipes, before you went to bed."

"Girl, you are something else."

He gets up and pins her against the refrigerator, moving against her while he sucks her neck. She giggles and tries pushing him away. Jerry leads her to the table. Picking her up and resting her on the table, he peels away her bath robe exposing her nakedness.

"Jerry, stop I'm going to fall, this table won't hold me!" She cries. He persists, letting his underwear fall to the floor, exposing his readiness. "You just had some a few hours ago."

"That was a few hours ago." Spreading her thighs she allows him to penetrate. Jerry test the stability of the table, until he is certain it is not going to fall. He fights to keep from cumming, to no avail, he lets go.

"I know you didn't, I was just getting started." She quarrels.

"Some things just can't be helped." He laughs, putting his underwear back on.

"Go ahead and get high. It's time to get busy."

After he has hit the pipe, she gets a good bump and is through with it. He finishes the rest. He goes to the icebox and gets the rest of his beer. He grabs his coat. Faye is already warming up the car. He turns out the lights and locks the door behind him. Faye takes him home.

"Where's your cap?"

"Damn I left it!"

"I'll be back later on. You gonna be at home?"

"You know it, baby." He walks around to the driver's side and leans over and kisses her. "Be careful."

"You're home might early, considering it's a Saturday." His mother says. "Who was that you came home with?"

"Just a friend, Mom."

He goes to his room and closes the door, only to have to come back out and put the rest of his beer on ice. Sipping on a beer, he gets undressed. He falls asleep before he can finish his beer.

In the mean time . . .

Faye goes by Wilma's and picks up her money. She has made an addition one hundred and seventy five dollars. She is on her way to her mother's house. When she pulls in, nobody comes to the door as usual. She blows the horn before getting out of the car. She checks the mailbox. The mailman has run. Opening one of the letters, she puts a hundred and twenty-five dollars in it and writes a note on the outside. "Came by. I Intended to call yesterday, but worked late. Tell the boys hello. Take this money and put it up. Do not spend bill money. Love U Faye." She then takes all of the mail and slides it under the door. She goes home, takes a bath, and changes clothes.

She goes over Jerry's house and blows. By this time he has gotten up, bathed and changed clothes and is drinking a beer. He comes out the door putting on his jacket.

When he gets in the car, Faye gives him his hat.

"I don't need it now. I only put it on when my hair is not properly combed. How's it going?"

"Just great." She says. As they leave the driveway, Faye asks him if he wants to drive. They swap seats by climbing over each other. As they do Jerry grabs her in between the thighs. "Don't start what you can't finish." She warns. They stop at the gas station and fill up with gas. They also buy two four packs of Champale and a case of beer, along with some cigarettes. The next day will be Sunday and all of the liquor stores will closed. The bootleggers are twice as expensive.

They are on their way to Little Rock. They obtain a pipe from a guy there. He brings them from out of town. The law has been changed so that cocaine pipes are illegal in any head shop. Head shop themselves are on the endangered list. They have some difficulty in finding him, since Faye has only been there once, and she did not drive then. They decide to buy a sixteenth because it is about fifteen dollars cheaper in Little Rock than in Pine Bluff.

They drive, back drinking along the way.

They have brillo, so they stop at the liquor store and buy some pure grain alcohol. They enjoy the cocaine more than before and do not smoke it up as fast. They stay in for the evening and enjoy each other along with watching television. Faye takes Jerry home Sunday evening so that he can go to work Monday.

Faye decides that she will spend the night over her mother's house. It's seven o'clock when she makes it. The boys run out the door as usual. They are extremely glad to see her. She barely speaks to her mother. The boys are dragging her off to show her what they got when they went shopping yesterday.

"I see you came by yesterday."

"So you put the money up?"

"Yes, I did." The boys drag out some new toys.

"Mama I told you not to buy them any more toys."

"Now you know how those boys are. If I didn't they would have never let me rest."

"You just spoil them rotten."

"You could have went with us."

Faye just drops the subject and tells Tony to go to the bathroom and get a wet towel. He returns with one dripping all over the floor. Faye takes him by the hand leading him to the bathroom. She wipes his face and hands. Then she kisses him tickling him at the same time.

"How are they doing in school?"

"Tony, go and get Mama your school papers." Faye looks at the them, the boys try to point out whose is best. Both of the boys are smart and get excellent grades.

"Have you all eaten already?" Faye asks.

Their grandmother answers for them. "Yes, they have."

"You got anything left?"

"It may not be enough. You sure could use something honey. You look as though you are losing weight. Are you?"

"Just a little bit."

"I'm going to fix you a meal, child."

"You don't have to fix me anything."

"I don't want to hear it. If you don't have time to fix anything to eat you can always come by here and get something to eat."

Faye plays with the boys while her mother fixes her something to eat. When she finishes, the boys want to eat also.

"I thought you already ate." Faye lets them eat again. "I hope you don't have any bad dreams eating so close to bedtime." It is after nine o'clock when they get done. Faye tells the boys it is time to go to bed. They start crying and everything else.

"Don't make me whip you all."

"They just want some attention that's all." Her mother butts in.

"Come on. I'll lay down with them until they fall asleep."

Faye starts to get them ready for bed. She tells Lil' Stevie that he smells and he needs a bath. Faye runs the water for them and bathes them in a hurry. She lies down with them. It is eleven o'clock before they fall asleep. Faye's mother is just finishing up the kitchen because she sat down watched the news at ten o'clock..

Faye and her mom sit down and discuss several things. Faye tells her that she has a television. She wants to know if Faye has found anybody special yet. Faye says she likes this guy named Jerry but that is as far as it goes at the moment. She tells her mother that she is tired of the street.

"You need to start saving your money so that you will be able to settle down."

They talk until one o'clock. Faye realizes what time it is and asks her mom if she has a gown that she can sleep in. Her mother tells her that she has a couple of her own gowns in the room. As her mother goes to get the gowns for her, Faye gets up and looks at one of the several pictures of her father, who is dead. He was killed in an accident at the paper mill years ago. Faye sleeps in the same bed as her mother. As they lay in the dimly lit room, Faye's mother tells her how glad she came over to spend the night.

"Good night mama."

"Good night baby."

Faye's mother is the first to fall asleep. Faye lies awake and stares at the ceiling. Nothing is really on her mind. Her thoughts are here and there.

CHAPTER 3

A little more than two months pass. With the beginning of spring the complexion of the city has begun to change. The grass is now a mixture of beige and lime green. The budding flower and trees add an additional sign of life, as do the birds and the pesky flies that seem to be the first insects to arrive on the scene.

Everybody is eager to show off their bodies that have been hidden by the layer of clothes that illustrated the presence of winter, especially on the college campus. Walking shorts, mini-skirts, tank tops and jogging suit are all on temporary display until the weather abruptly reminds them that spring is not completely in charge yet.

Kids play outdoors after school rather than run in the house for protection from the cold. Bicycles, footballs, go carts, baseballs, basketballs, boom boxes occupied the hands of the kids. A few carry large piece of cardboard that are used for break dancing which is fading rapidly being replaced by bee bopping or rap. Kids make trips from one side of town to the other, to compare their beats with each other or to get a group started. Then they rushing home to beat the blanket of darkness trailed by the setting sun.

On the more mature side of things, teenagers as well as adult are seen at the self service car washes, particularly those who own the newer model car and trucks. Eager to bring out the shine that had been dulled by the winter, some spring cleaning begins. The night life is now completely astir, particularly downtown. Business is picking up tremendously, especially for the liquor store across the street. Beer is obtained there rather than in the club because of the cheaper price. There are more people outside than inside.

Every one is involved within their own groups. The homosexuals have their own spot, as do the winos. The prostitutes are everywhere wearing, anything they saw fit. People set up gambling tables on the parking lots. As for drugs, marijuana is about the only one that is obvious. Anybody and everybody brought or sold it. The cups, scattered glass, beer bottles, cans, and cigarette butts that litter the parking lot in the morning shows evidence of what has taken place the night before.

It's Monday afternoon. It is a pleasant, seventy-nine degrees, accompanied by light to moderate gusts of wind. It is more breezy at the beginning of April than it was all of March. Three women walk across the parking lot and enter the doors of the huge mall, which recently opened. Businesses that were once scattered all over town in various shopping centers are concentrated at The Peoples Mall, which incorporates over twenty five stores and several small booths. They have anything from shades, jewelry, clothes, toys, an arcade, along with a number of delis, a cafeteria, and a movie theater.

Faye, Charlene, and Ann are dressed comfortably. They all wear cut off designer jeans, split up the legs and tops that are cut up shirts, or blouses tied in the front, showing more of their bodies than necessary. They are out enjoying the scenery and see what the new styles for spring and summer look like. They have money but are reluctant to spend any when they have such excellent shoplifters as Charlene and Ann. They look around several hours before Faye reminds them that she has to go and pick up Jerry from work.

"Girl you sure have gotten into Jerry. He must be sticking it to you pretty good." Says Ann.

"You know how it is girl. The same way you feel about Stuart."

They all giggle. An old woman turns around and looks at them.

"I don't know why she turned around and looked like that at us. She used to get fucked pretty good herself, I'm sure." Charlene comments. They all laugh even harder now. The woman overhearing the remark is somewhat embarrassed and hurries away.

Eventually they wind up buying a pair of shades a piece before they leave. They pay for them only because they are not accessible to the public. They are handed over the counter at your request. They leave the mall and they talk about what they saw, what they liked, and what they were going back to steal.

"Where do you and Ann want me to drop you off?" Says Faye, talking to Charlene.

"You can take us downtown." She replies. "We are going to see what we can get into."

"Say Faye, why don't you take us by the trailer? So we can get us one before you drop us off." ask Ann.

"You might as well smoke one with us." Suggests Charlene.

Faye replies that she is trying to at least slow down, if not stop. Jerry said she was losing too much weight.

"Well doesn't he still smoke?"

"Sure but we try to smoke whatever we are going to smoke together." Says Faye.

"Well, hell you might as well shack up together." Complains Ann, sounding irritated.

"We've talked about it, but Jerry wants to see how he is going to come out in court. He has already talked to a lawyer. He's going to handle his case for twelve hundred dollars."

"What lawyer is he using."

"I forgot his name but we have already paid him eight hundred dollars. He said that he'll probably get probation, since he has never been in any trouble before."

"What about Duck?"

"He's already gone back to the joint." Answers Faye. "How do you know Duck?" she asks.

"Everybody should know him as much as he got around. We got high many a night. He's a real freak." Says Charlene laughing.

"He couldn't be a freak by himself." Implies Ann, searching her purse for her dope pipe.

Faye takes them by the trailer. Charlene and Ann both buy a quarter each. They ask Faye again if she wants any. She again turns them down. They want to know if they can smoke in the car on the way downtown. Faye does not mind. She just wants them to look out for the police.

They arrive downtown. Faye stops to let them out despite their pleas to make the block again so that they can finish smoking.

"Come on Ann we can finish in the bathroom at Wilma's place."

"Shit I think that girl is falling for that motherfucker, if I didn't know her better. I ain't gonna quit smoking for no son-of-a-bitch." Ann grumbles as she gets out the car.

"Aw, leave her alone. You need to find somebody besides that fucker you got. You know he ain't no good. You said that yourself!"

Charlene holds a piece of crack with two fingers, being careful not to drop it. Faye blows her horn as she speeds off.

Faye stops by the liquor store on the way. This particular store has his type of beer on sale. She buys Jerry a six pack despite the fact he is trying not to drink heavily during the week. She arrives just as he is coming out of the hospital's front doors. This saves her the trouble of trying to find a parking spot. There is no parking in the front because of the fire lane.

"Hey baby." He speaks, as he gets into the car.

He flops down and throws his head back on the head rest. Faye reaches over and rubs her fingers in his hair.

"What's the matter? You have a rough day?"

"You know how Mondays are. My supervisor doesn't make them any better." She drives off, reaching in the sack at the same time and handing him a beer.

"Thanks, baby. I need it. What did you do today?"

"Not much. I cleaned the house and went to the Mall with Ann and Charlene."

"Oh Shit! What did they steal today?" He starts to laugh.

"They took the day off." She laughs also.

"That's good. It's about time."

Their conversation continues all the way to the house. They enter the house. Jerry compliments Faye on how clean the house is. He also notices the incense that has been burned. He asks what kind it is.

"It's raspberry. I bought it the other day."

Jerry turns on the television and takes off his shoes and watches the news. Faye is in the kitchen fixing herself a glass of E and J and coke.

"Hey, Faye look!"

Hurrying to the living room, Faye spills part of her drink.

Jerry points to the television. They are showing a woman and a homosexual being arrested at the mall for shoplifting.

"That punk looks like Ted."

"Ted?"

"You know, your friend. The one they call Jenny."

"Oh, that sure is. I couldn't tell they moved the camera so quickly. I've got some spaghetti cooking on the stove. I guess I'll cook some ground beef and mix it. You very hungry?"

"I'd though you'll never ask?"

"I've pick up a pound or two this week since we haven't been smoking as much cocaine."

She pats herself on the ass and smiles at him. Jerry reaches for her but she keeps going Faye finishes cooking and brings Jerry a plate along with hers. They sit on the sofa and watch television while they are eating. After their appetites are satisfied, they work on satisfying their sexual appetites as well. Jerry falls asleep afterwards. Faye wakes him about eleven o'clock, only because he told her that he needed to go home. She tells him.

"You know you really could spend the night."

"I promised Mom that I would at least stay at home during the week days. She's kind of used to having me around the house. Especially since she and the old man got divorced."

"How long were they together?"

"Twenty some odd years."

"That's a long time to wind up leaving each other."

"I know the old bastard went crazy whore hopping. Mom got tired of it, I guess" Since Faye has no luck convincing him to stay she slips on some clothes.

"I guess I'll see what's happening downtown since you have to go home," She says with a snobbish attitude.

Jerry starts to go to the refrigerator and then changes his mind. He says he will just leave his beer in the box until tomorrow. After Jerry is at home Faye goes downtown. She is undecided about which side of the street to park on. It's a one way so it really does not matter. She walks in Ron's place first just to see who is around. Making conversation, she asks Ron if Oscar has been in there. Ron tells her no. She leaves and goes around the corner to Wilma's place.

There are several men gathered around a makeshift dice table next to a stair well that goes up to what use to be an old club. A lot of stories have originated from there. Now they are a bunch of rent-a- rooms, one or two that have a stove in them. The rooms are cheap and filthy. The stairwells and the hallway that divides them are excellent places for the winos to hide or for someone to urinate, discard trash, get high, or any number of misdeeds, and the smell and the condition indicate just that. Two of the men raise their head up to speak. The rest have their heads down shooting dice.

Wilma's place is a lot livelier than Ron's place. Ron's place is where the middle age clients hang out. You'll only find middle age men in Wilma's place when they are looking for some action one way or the other. To Fayes surprise, as she enters she sees James sitting alone at the table facing the door. He smiles and nods his head. Faye acknowledges him by going over to his table and sitting down.

"What are you doing here on a Monday night?" She asks.

"I was about to leave I came down here looking for you."

"You in an hurry?"

"Take your time."

Faye speaks to Wilma's husband Jed, whose running the place now that he is off from work. He loves to flirt.

He speaks back. "Hey, baby you're looking mighty good."

Faye flags him off and looks around to see if Charlene and Ann are around. She does not see them, so she goes back and tells James she is ready.

As they leave, he wants to know if there's any place special she needs to go first. Faye tells him yes–the liquor store. She has him buy her a pint of brandy and a couple of cokes. She forces herself to drink a swallow so that she can maintain a certain state of mind when it comes to dealing with her customers.

They arrived at her house, where Faye spreads another blanket over the bed before she and James proceed to take care of business. Afterwards they both clean up. Faye has already taken the money and put it in a plastic container in the refrigerator. Who would ever suspect it as being there. She never knows when one of her customers might decide to take leave of his senses.

When Faye steps out of the car, she hears someone calling her name. She looks up and sees Charlene and Ann opposite her coming across the parking lot. They are really laughing and snickering. Both proceed to tell Faye how they beat this guy out of his cocaine just because he was trying to be slick with them. Once they calm down, they say.

"We're surprised to see you."

"I told you I would be here." Faye says trying to indicate that she was running the relationship between her and Jerry.

"Girl we have been getting high as a kite every since you dropped us off." Says Ann.

"Who did you all beat out of their coke?"

"You remember when I took you over by the trailer and we went to that house but nobody was there at the time. This guy is suppose to be related to them. He calls himself trying to sell some dope for them. Girl we smoked all his dope, and that he didn't give us, we stole."

"He was mad at us. We didn't give him any pussy on top of that."

They start to giggle all over again.

"We see you're taking care of business." Mentions Charlene.

"You ought to have plenty money the way you are steady working. Or are you giving it to Jerry?" Ann asks, still being indignant.

Charlene and Ann start to giggle again. Faye walks off. They both stop giggling abruptly and tell her that they were just playing.

"It doesn't really bother me anyway." Faye adds.

Charlene and Ann hurry to catch up with her.

The other joints on the block have closed, except for Wilma's and Ron's. When they walk into Wilma's, Faye gets change for a dollar and goes to the juke box and plays "Secret Lovers." Charlene and Ann look at each other and shrug their shoulders.

They talk about what they are going to do in the morning.

"Did you see the news?" Asks Faye, interrogating them. "I don't know what I asked you for. I know you two didn't, but anyway, I saw Jenny and some other woman on there." Says Faye.

"You mean the punk Jenny?"

"Sure, but anyway they got busted for shoplifting out at the Mall."

They gossip on the subject for a while, talking about how they must have gotten caught. Ann gets up and signals them to follow her to the back of the club where she rolls a joint. Faye hits it once and does not want any more. She starts searching for her cigarettes and stops when she looks up and sees Charlene's pack lying on the table. They smoke the same brand.

"Faye, you sure are different since you have been trying to quit smoking dope." Says Ann. Charlene stops the conversation before it can get started.

"Just leave her alone, Ann. We both need to be doing the same thing."

Faye goes to the front and orders a Champale and a quart of beer. While the bartender is filling her order, she goes to the juke box and plays "Secret Lovers" again. The girls thank her for the beer, which has already been opened by Jed. It's part of the policy to open all beer sold, to keep people from walking out of the door with sealed beer. The permit is for on-premises consumption only.

It's almost time for closing, so they prepare to make a move.

Charlene says "Why don't we go to the Table Top."

The Table Top is a club designed out of an old house that was moved to its present location and has been added on to since then. Faye really goes for Charlene's and Ann's sake, since they don't have a car. They are sure they can get a ride home after they get there. Once they are there, drinks do not seem to be a problem. They have plenty of offers. Faye accepts, but when confronted about going to bed, she quickly throws a fifty dollar figure his way, to let him know she does not play games and refuses to go any lower. He doesn't leave her alone right away. Disgusted with the way things are developing, Faye decides that she will go home and try and get some rest. She tells Charlene and Ann she will see them in the morning.

"I'll be by your house first, Charlene."

At home, Faye fixes herself a drink and falls asleep before she can finish it.

The next day proves to be no different as far as associating with Charlene and Ann. After they finish shoplifting and sell what they have, they want Faye to take them to the dope house, which she does. However, they start to smoke it in the car. She stops them. This does little to change Ann's attitude.

Faye picks up Jerry and they are on their way home from going out to eat dinner. Faye gives Jerry a shopping bag. He opens it to find two pairs of slacks, some walking shorts with matching tops and some socks. He thanks her. When it is time to go home, he does not have the heart to say no to her tonight. They walk to the corner to use the telephone. Jerry calls his mother to let her know that he will not be at home tonight. She asks him what is he going to do about his lunch. He tells her not to worry.

"Your mother must really think a lot of you."

"Well it's a long story."

"You must have been a smart boy in school."

"I did fairly well in school. The old man really thought I should have gone to college. But when I got out of high school, I was so glad I didn't think about college. He kind of blames her for it."

"Do they still communicate with each other?"

"Yeah, they don't hate each other or anything like that. He moved up north after the divorce. I haven't heard from him in awhile."

"I hate to hear it's like that between you two."

"Oh, it's nothing I'm used to it now."

Faye spirits are uplifted. She is in a better mood now than she has been in a while. The next day Faye goes by the job and picks Jerry up for lunch. They eat at Wendy's. Faye goes over to her mother's house. This is another one of the many visits that Faye has paid to her mother and the boys in the past couple of weeks.

"Hello, baby."

"Hello, Mama."

"You sure look perkier than usual and sound better. If I weren't sure I'll say you seem to be filling back out. Someone or something is making you very happy."

Smiling, Faye fails to comment. Faye gives her mother four hundred and fifty dollars.

"Put this with the rest of my money before I forget to give it to you."

"This is the kind of money you used to bring before you and the boy's daddy broke up. What are you trying to do, get a new car or something?"

Faye politely ignores the statement.

"I'll be over to take you to lunch and go shopping for the boys Wednesday."

Faye's mother continues to talk to her while she gathers her things to go outside and fiddle around in her flower bed. Faye is used to her actions, so she just follows in behind her.

"Mama, have you been paying on our insurance policies like you are suppose to?"

"Yes that worrisome man was by here a couple of days ago. Why do you ask?"

"It just crossed my mind, that's all."

"I know I had some better tools to work with than these." Her mom says, going back into the house.

Faye cuts a piece of cake. She is use to the cake cover that is always on the table. Her mother keeps cake and cookies around for the boys.

"You want a piece of cake to take with you?" Her mother asks.

Faye starts to say no but thinks of Jerry. She cuts a piece and wraps it in aluminum foil.

"Well mama." She says as she gets a drink of water. "I guess I'll be going."

"All right. The boys will be here in about forty-five minutes. I'll work on my flowers when they get here, that way they can go outside and play."

"Don't let them ruin those new shoes, Mama. Speaking of something new, I have something for you."

Faye goes out to the car and opens the trunk, removing a shopping bag. When she returns she calls to her mother who is now digging in the closet for the shoes she wears when working outdoors.

"I'm in here." Faye waits until she comes out of the closet.

"Do you like this? It should match the shirt you got last week."

While her mother is looking at the blouse, Faye pulls some other shoes out of the bag.

"Oh, Child, this might be a bit too much for your mother to wear."

The blouse is a floral design with bright highlights accompanied with sky blue. The shoes are of a dark blue snake skin, to go with the blue skirt and jacket.

"I think you'll look great in it. Try the shoes on before I go."

It's getting close to three thirty. Faye does not want to be late.

"The shoes feel good Honey." She stands to get a better feel of them.

"Okay, Mama I've got to run."

She kisses her on the cheek and runs out of the door. Her mom pulls the shoes off and walks bare footed to the door. By the time she reaches it, Faye is pulling out of the driveway. Faye blows the horn and keeps going.

After Faye picks up Jerry and they are on the way back home, Jerry comments on how hungry he is.

"I'm kind of hungry myself" she seconds.

"It's amazing how you stay hungry when you're not smoking that pipe, isn't it? Where do you want to eat at? Or have you already started dinner?"

"No, I haven't started as of yet."

"Good, where do you want to go? I'm buying."

"Where do you get some money from?"

"I borrowed it from Richard at work."

"You could have asked me, you know."

"Yeah, but this is my treat."

"Well that is mighty sweet of you."

Faye chooses a soul food restaurant located in the downtown area.

"You want to go home first?" ask Faye. "I need to change clothes myself. I would like to go to a movie too since you are treating."

"That's fine with me."

All Jerry has to do is to pull off his green scrub suit covering his new shirt and jeans Faye has brought for him. But instead, he undresses all the way down to his shorts. Faye has gotten undressed also except for her under-garments. Jerry sneaks upon her from behind and grabs her by her breasts and starts sucking on her neck.

She lets him have his minute before she stops him. She tells him if he keeps it up they won't be through with dinner in time for the movie.

"I won't take long promise"

He continues to tease her. To her surprise when she turns around, he's completely naked and ready, which does not leave her much choice. He backs her toward the bed.

"Jerry you are something else, but I love it."

As she squirms to free herself of her underwear during the love making, Jerry asks Faye what makes him so much different from all the other guys she goes to bed with. A few seconds past as Faye tries to digest the question without overreacting.

"Uh, well it's like this." She flips him over so that she can be on top. Running her fingernails around the corners of his mouth. "It's rather difficult to explain. Every man I meet is different in his own way, but as far as he is concerned they are all the same. I know what they really feel about me so I limit my feelings. When I find someone I really like, it starts before we go to bed. That's part of the reason I try to stay high some kind of way when I deal with them. A lot of them I cannot stand. But they got what I need and that's money. Besides, you make me happy."

She slides her tongue into his inviting mouth. When they finish it is five fifteen. Faye rolls Jerry out of bed as he lies there exhausted. He has to catch himself before he hits the floor.

"Come on I told you before you got started but nooo, you had to have it right then. So come on, let's hit the shower."

Faye starts the shower, waiting a few minutes before Jerry makes it in. By the time they finish showering and get dressed it is six o'clock. That leaves the soul food restaurant off the agenda. Their second choice is to eat at Wyatts cafeteria at the mall so they will be right at the movies after they finish eating. Faye and Jerry enjoy the movie so much, they sit through it twice. Jerry nods periodically during the second showing. Faye drops him off at home.

She intentionally avoids Charlene and Ann. She does happen to see them at a distance. She is determined to make a hundred and fifty on this unenterprising Tuesday night. She stays out late but gets up early, so that she can take her mother shopping as she promised. When she arrives the boys are gone off to school already.

Her mother is not ready and it takes an hour. Faye cat naps in front of the television. This is only the second time they have been to the mall together since its grand opening. Her mother really enjoys the morning and part of the afternoon, especially eating the giant cinnamon rolls made at one of the delis. She even saves part of it and takes it home. They don't buy many clothes just odd and ends. Most of their clothes are provided by friends like Charlene and Ann. On the way back from the mall they stop at a few more elaborate furniture stores. Faye 's mother wants to know why she is interested in all of these new home furnishings.

"What's wrong with wanting something nice for a change?" She replies.

Time passes quickly. Faye has to rush off again, as always. When Faye picks up Jerry up from work, he is not as talkative as he normally is. He just stares out the front windshield.

Finally after cross examining him, he tells her he was just thinking about the letter he got from his lawyer.

"What did it say?"

"I've got to be in court in ten days from now."

"I thought he put it off another month."

"He said he needed to dispose of the case before he goes on vacation. He also needs the balance of his fee before that date."

"Well, if its the money that you are worried about, you know that you don't have a problem there. Did he mention anything else?"

"No. I tried to call him at work, but he was out all day."

"There's no need to worry. Everything will be okay. What do you want to do for dinner?"

"I'm not really all that hungry. What do you want?"

"I've got a taste for some tacos."

They go to Taco Bell. Faye orders six tacos for herself and two for Jerry. After they get home watching television and start to eat, Jerry's appetite comes back and he wants to eat up his tacos as well as hers. She breaks down and gives him two of hers.

Faye fixes herself an E&J and Coke and brings Jerry a beer.

"You're getting rather fond of that brandy aren't you?"

"Don't even try it. It's better than smoking cocaine."

"I guess you got a point there. It's cheaper anyway. I wonder if they have any good home movies on tonight?"

"I don't know but I'm going to check on that special that the cable TV people are running. I saw it this morning over at Mama's house."

"That would be nice."

"Jerry you did not ask me what I did today."

Jerry acts like he does not hear her talking to him. So she repeats it. Again he ignores her, until he cannot hold his laughter inside any longer. Faye throws a couch pillow at him.

"All right, how was your day?"

This time she reverses the role on him, but finally answers.

"It was great."

"Well what did you do?"

"Mama and I went shopping. We didn't really buy much but I looked at some furniture. It was really sharp. I loved it."

"Hey baby come here a minute." Faye eases over, he guides her down beside him, putting his arm around her neck.

"Let me ask you something. You stop smoking cocaine. Why?"

"Well, because I am happy now. I don't really feel that you want me smoking it. Furthermore, I don't believe you would smoke it, if you had another purpose in life. You really don't seem like the type. I think you just got mixed up with the wrong people like Duck for instance. Now don't get me wrong. I definitely crave it. But I want you more. Besides I really like having things. Especially if I have someone to share them with."

She kisses him on the corner of the mouth.

"You know, I kind of think you're right. I made a vow with God that I would do my best to quit if I got out of this mess I'm in."

"I don't see anything wrong with that. That's the problem with a lot of people. They don't want to commit themselves to doing something positive; it takes too much effort."

The next week and a half passes abruptly, with trips to the park and the movie and other forms of entertainment. Jerry and Faye pay the balance of the attorney fees. He assures Jerry that he has nothing to worry about. There may be a few stipulations he may not like, but otherwise everything else is in order. The court date is tomorrow morning.

Faye and Jerry enjoy a quiet evening at home alone. Jerry spends the night but goes home in the morning. He has already notified the job of his absence for the day. He gets dressed while Faye waits in the car. She declines to come in at this point of their relationship, even though Jerry's mother has gone to work.

Jerry is dressed in slacks, a dress shirt and a tie. The slacks are dark brown, the shirt is beige, and a blended tie. His low heel shoes are highly shined. He has shaven his beard completely off except for his mustache. Faye laughs when he returns to the car, but apologies when he looks at her with a stone face.

"You shaved! You look like a little boy now. But I think it looks nice." Rubbing his face.

They arrive at the courthouse thirty minutes early.

The courthouse sits at the beginning of Main street. The front is re-modeled, with beige bricks, and tall pillars face the river. A tall statue of some confederate soldier Jerry has never heard of is centered in front of the steps. The back of the courthouse itself consists of a combination of beige color bricks and a white wooden frame. Some people consider it poor remolding. The wings are brick and the middle section, including the steeple, is wood. This mix was done to reserve part of the original structure after the building withstood a fire several years ago. Inside, there are precious relics that pertain to Arkansas history, ranging from the Indians to the Civil War. The down stairs is where all the taxes are paid, and where licenses are obtained along with the sheriff's office. Upstairs is where the court rooms are. They take to elevator to the second floor; it is antique and slow. Jerry and Faye walk in the courtroom and sit down. There is no sign of his lawyer as of yet. There are approximately forty people seated in the courtroom. There are four or five whom Jerry recognizes. Faye knows a few more.

The judge is not on the bench yet, so the court room is rather noisy. Jerry sees his lawyer as he enters the court room, and rises to meet him. He and Jerry talk outside of the courtroom. They quickly go over the details. He also tells Jerry that he is glad that he shaved and reminds him to watch his manners. He tells Jerry that he will be around. He has to check on a few other things, so Jerry is not to worry.

Jerry re-enters the court room and sits down beside Faye. She whispers and asks him what the lawyer says.

"He was glad I had shaven and he said a few other things that's all."

The bailiff asks everyone to stand as the judge enters is seated. The prosecuting attorney sits to the left side of the room, facing the judge, with a stack of paper in front of him. While the stenographer takes the minutes, the judge's secretary runs back and forth making sure he has the appropriate paperwork. The only security is the bailiff. As the judge calls people to the stand and reviews their cases, some plead guilty, but nobody has been given any time so far. This is good sign for Jerry. The courtroom is nearly empty now.

"Jerry Collins." The judge calls.

Jerry approaches the stand and his lawyer does likewise. They stop in front of him and adjust the microphone so that he will be able to talk into it when the time comes.

"Jerry Collins you are before this court on charges of burglary. How do you plead?"

Jerry hesitates looks at his lawyer and says "guilty" as his lawyer nods his head.

The judge apparently looking over the case file takes a moment.

"Mr. Collins, I see that you have no prior convictions. Is that true?"

"Yes sir"

"Are you still working?"

"Yes your Honor."

"How long have you been working there?"

"Six years."

"Based on the facts presented, before me. I am going to recommend that you be placed on three years probation. You will also be made to pay restitution and probationary fees. Is that understood, Mr. Collins?"

"Yes sir." Says Jerry, his eyes blinking rapidly indicating a fraction of his nervousness.

"In the event that you fail to follow the rules of your probation, you will be bought back before me, and I will dispose of you as I see fit. Is that understood?"

"Yes sir."

"You and your attorney need to get together with my secretary. She will give you the necessary paperwork and the name of your probation officer."

The judge hands his secretary the folder containing Jerry's record. He calls the next person.

Faye gets up and leaves the court room smiling on the inside. She sits on one of the benches outside the door and waits for Jerry and his lawyer to exit the courtroom. Faye stands up and waits for them to finish talking. Jerry's lawyer tells him that he will be out of town for two weeks. If he needs anything, call him after that.

"Oh yeah." The lawyer says, "Remember to keep your nose clean. Probation is like having one foot out and one foot in the penitentiary." They shake hands before parting. A smile slowly spreads over Jerry's face.

Faye reaches out for Jerry's hand.

"You feel better now?"

"Can't you tell?" He laughs nervously.

The rest of the afternoon, they lounge around. Through all of the excitement of this morning ordeal, Faye almost forgets it's Thursday. She reminds Jerry. Jerry's dislike of the idea of Faye and her customers has become noticeable, despite his attempts to hide it. Faye reassures him it's all for a good cause.

Faye takes him home and stops on the way back at the Cable television office. She puts in a request for installation and pays for it. They will get it tomorrow, the woman tells her, after giving her a receipt.

She goes toward Third and State and waits for Oscar.

"Don't tell me it's Thursday again?" Asks Wilma.

"I don't know how you guessed it." Wilma and Faye both laugh.

"You're gaining weight, aren't you?"

"A little bit. Just trying to get back what I had." Oscar shows up as usual at Ron's place.

He also notices Faye's change in attitude and over all appearance, but he foolishly credits himself with being the one to add the real spice to Faye's life. He has been giving her more money than customary as he sees improvement around the house also.

"The last couple of times, I have been around. You haven't been smoking that stuff. You've been drinking and eating more though," he casually mentions

"I just decided to give it a rest. Besides it saves money."

Faye accommodates him but does not give him as much time as she once had previously done. He does not seem to notice. Between Oscar and a couple of other regular customers, Faye makes five hundred dollars easily. But she decides that since Jerry goes to work tomorrow, she will work most of the night, which proves to be fruitful.

The next day Faye wants to take Jerry to lunch but fears she will miss the cable television installer. So she calls him at work and tells him that she will pick him up this evening. The cable TV man comes right after lunch. It takes him a couple of hours since the house has never been wired for cable television. When he finishes it's almost time to pick up Jerry. Faye picks Jerry up and takes him to the bank so he can cash his check. He offers her a hundred dollars as part of his payment for helping him out on his lawyer fees. She declines and tells him to pay his probation officer. Faye asks him if he wants to go by the liquor store. She will catch up with him later.

He says. "I will probably be on the north side of town at Jay's if it's after ten o'clock."

He wants to go downtown but does not want to interfere with Faye's business.

Faye runs into Charlene, and she compliments Faye on how good she looks and asks about Jerry.

"You need to come by the house whenever you get a chance. We don't talk as much as we used to."

She can tell that Charlene is not as comfortable as she once was, but Faye tries to compensate by ordering her drinks, buying her marijuana or occasionally loaning her money. Even though she does not get it back, she gets a break when it comes to clothes and things of that nature. Faye ends to conversation when she sees one of her regulars.

Jerry gives his mother his receipt where he has paid his probationary fee and restitution fees for the month. She compliments him on his attire. He gives her some money to help out on the groceries and tells her to put up a hundred dollars. He also asks if he can use the car if she is not going anywhere. She hesitates and asks him a dozen questions before she gives in and tells him to be careful.

He does not go straight to the club because it is a little early. He goes over to a few friend's houses he knows from work. Richard decides he will ride with him. Jerry pays him the twenty dollars that he owes him. Richard wants to buy a bag of weed. Jerry takes him to a place called the hill. Jerry does not mind him smoking cigarettes or drinking, but he does not allow him to smoke marijuana in his mother's car. So they go over to Richard's house and smoke a couple of joints and Jerry decides he will go to Jay's lounge. The crowd is light because of the time. It is early by partying standards. He orders a forty ounce of beer.

As time passes he dances several times with several women. Pat comes over and sits at his table. She picks up an empty cup on the table, smells, blows in it and pours herself a cup of beer.

"What are you doing J.C.?" She calls him that instead of Jerry. She also knows it's payday for him. "You mean you are by yourself?"

"For right now, yes."

"Want to have some fun?"

"Like what?" Playing dumb.

"I guess you don't know? What's the matter with you?"

"Nothing. You look like you are already loaded."

" Hell, I'm just getting started. You know me. Let's get one."

"One of what?" He smiles sheepishly at her.

"Why are you playing dumb?" He stops smiling all at once.

"I don't smoke cocaine any more."

"Since when?"

"It doesn't matter."

"Well, buy me one."

"I just told you I don't smoke it anymore."

"You don't have to smoke an——."

Before she could finish the sentence Faye walks up and sits right under Jerry and kisses him on the mouth. Pat gets up, leaving her cup on the table.

"You bastard!"

"Look as though you had company." Faye says.

"Not really, what are you up to?"

"Nothing. I am through for tonight. What do you want to do?"

"Let's go downtown. It's boring here.

"Follow me over to mother's house so I can take the car home."

"You mean she let you have the car?"

"Yeah. She used to all the time, until I started messing up. She seems to think that I have improved lately."

"So do I. You ready? Wait Let me use the restroom first." Prancing in her steps.

Faye follows him to his mother's, where he parks the car and gets in the car with Faye.

"What about the keys?"

"She has a set."

They go downtown. Jerry is more comfortable now.

He's shooting pool for money and obviously is doing good, judging by the money sticking out of his top pocket. Faye walks up and takes it out of his pocket so he will not lose it, being he is somewhat intoxicated. She tells him it is getting close to closing time. He tells her this is his last game. After the game is finished, Jerry goes looking for Faye. He looks all over the club there is no sign of her. He then looks out the door. There, sitting on the hood of the car sits Faye.

"Why are you sitting outside?"

He walks up between her legs and puts his fingers through the belt loop of her jeans.

"Just waiting that's all."

"Got carried away, didn't I? Don't worry, I'll make it up to you." He takes her hand and leads her to the car door. "Let's go baby."

When they get home Faye turns on the television then proceeds to run some bath water. Jerry opens a beer and sits on the sofa. Despite the hour, he does not notice the TV until a break in the program indicates that he is watching HBO. He does not say anything.

He sneaks in the bathroom and is there for a few seconds before Faye notices him.

"How come you did not tell me you had got the cable installed?"

"I wanted to surprise you."

"Well you did that."

"Do you like it?"

"You know I do. You got all the extra too didn't you?"

"I want to make it comfortable for you when you make up your mind to move in."

"Uh, Oh!"

"What do you mean uh oh?" Slapping her hands into the bath water splashing water unto the floor. "You act as though you didn't expect it or don't want to. You promised to discuss it after you got all that court business out of the way. Didn't you?" Jerry does not answer. "Now I guess you cannot hear either?"

By this time she is standing in the living room with a towel wrapped around her. She is furious, going to the refrigerator pulling out the ice tray dropping a few cubes in a glass. She throws one at Jerry, then continues to fix her drink.

"Faye, there are a lot of responsibilities involved in living together as well as commitments. That may be something you have not thought about."

"I've thought about them. I've been married before, remember?"

"I'm aware of that."

"I assume that you are not satisfied with the way our relationship is going now." She does not answer, which is enough indication for anyone to know she is not satisfied.

"I don't make enough money to support the way I would like for us to live, if I did move in."

"That should not even worry you. I am capable of making money also."

"I know that. That's one of the problems. I'm not going to leave every time you have some trick come over."

"You should give me enough credit to know how to handle my business."

"I do, but when we live together it becomes part of my business also."

"Is that the only thing that keeps you from moving in with me?"

"That's the only one I see that would present a problem for us."

"So you do believe that I love you? Because I really do."

"Well I don't see anything wrong with trying it. I would like to, of course. I don't know how Mom will take it. Hell, you can never tell. It might make her happy."

Over the next several weeks, Jerry spends the night away from his mother's. He waits until his mother questions him a number of times before he tells her that he is going to move out for a while. He hopes she understands.

"Don't throw my bed away. You never can tell when I might be back."

The next day Jerry calls his probation officer from work and tells him that he has changed addresses. He would appreciate him making the necessary changes in his file. Mr. Dunn wants to know if he is doing all right, Jerry assures him that everything is just fine. He will be in to pay some more on his probation fees. He wants to pay it off in the very near future.

The future is looking brighter, as the house takes on an unprecedented undertaking of improvements. With the fluctuation of the weather from very warm to too hot, the house has become unbearable at times, even with all of the windows open and the fans going full speed. They are noisy at that. Faye decides to buy an air conditioner for the bedroom.

Jerry surprises her with a microwave oven.

"I know that it is hot in the kitchen."

He has gotten one with all the accessories. They are designed to enhance the flavor and the texture of the food, browning element and all, so that it will be as close to being cooked over a stove a possible.

The house begins to feel more like a private fortress to Faye. She has also chosen to show more respect to Jerry. She has become more discrete as far as her customers are concerned. They either go to a motel, which cuts down on the margin of profit, or she goes to the customer's house if she feels comfortable around him. A lot of times she has the room put into her name. Therefore, she can keep it for twenty-four, hours which sometimes adds to her pocket if she tells the customer the room needs to be paid for. All her customers, are required to use condoms. As for as Oscar, Faye tells him that her mother is living with her for a while because she is sick. They too go to a motel whenever the occasion arises.

Jerry does not complain when she is gone, for he trusts her judgment, regardless of the nature of her employment. He does show a slight discomfort sometime, but he seems to have adjusted to the situation quite gracefully.

Faye has stacked up on person hygiene items. She has always taken care of herself, but wants to be extra clean so that Jerry will at least feel unaware of what she does. She feels it is important to the way he treats her.

They have also devised a system where they jointly share the responsibility of paying the bills. Jerry is still never without money.

◇   ◇   ◇   ◇

"Mother, do you want to go shopping with me in the morning?" Faye asks her mom.

"Sure, child I don't have anything else to do."

"How are the boys?"

"They are fast asleep. I guess they played themselves down because they were glad to go to bed. What time are you going to be by here?"

"About nine o'clock."

"All right then, I'll try to be ready."

Faye hangs the telephone up and the dime comes back. Faye thinks to herself my luck is really improving.

After Faye takes Jerry to work, she goes over to her mother's. As usual, her mother is not ready.

"Mama, you're not ready. Why do you think I called you last night?"

"I know. After I talked to you, Mrs. Annie called and nearly talked me to death. I told her that you were taking me shopping. She wants us to come by and pick her up."

Faye lets out an inward sigh and rolls her eyes. But, she knows that Mrs. Annie takes her mother everywhere she wants to go.

"Well, you need to come on Mama."

"I'm coming. That's what wrong with you young folks, always in a hurry.

The first thing Faye does is stop by the telephone company and put in a request for a telephone and pays the deposit. The lady tells her it will probably be late this evening or first thing in the morning. Afterwards they manage to pay a few bills. It is convent to pay the gas and light bill, because they are right across the street from each other. But they are in the wrong place if you are driving. The line sometimes stretches for blocks, especially around the first of the month. The drive thrus are also close to a major intersection, which makes it even more hazardous.

On the way to one of smaller shopping centers, they pass by a vacant gas station lot were a peddler is selling Tupperware that is microwave safe at a decent price. Along with some nice looking china sets. Faye stop and buys a set of each. The gentleman accommodates them by putting the products in the trunk and thanks them. He says he will have some regular pots and pans one of these days soon.

Faye also goes by one of the local furniture stores and puts an application in for credit. With her mother as a cosigner and a substantial down payment, the man assures her that she should not have any problem obtaining the new bedroom set. Of course she has put down a false employment reference. She will have no problem being verified, since one of her tricks owns the company. She says she will check back tomorrow.

After they have eaten lunch, Faye takes them by her home.

"Girl, you've made some changes since the last time, I've been over here."

Her mother and Mrs. Annie go from room to room. They comment on every little item that appears to be new and practical. The air conditioner is the real topic. Oh, how they would love to have one, but the electric bill that comes afterwards is something they cannot afford to pay.

Her mother looks in the closet as always and notices the men's clothes and closes it back. She would comment but Mrs. Annie is with them she has no choice but to wait until a more appropriate time. Faye can tell by her facial expression what's on her mind. But as soon as they drop Mrs. Annie off at home, she immediately wants to know who is staying with her.

"You could have told me."

"I didn't have to tell you, you had an idea all along. I just wanted to satisfy you curiosity. That's part of the reason I took you by there."

"Well, who is he?"

"I'll bring him by one of these days."

"Does he work?"

"Sure he does."

"Where?"

"At the hospital."

"What kind of work does he do?"

"Something in surgery, technician or something."

"That's good."

"I've got to be going. Tell the boys I said hello. I'll probably be over to get them for awhile Sunday. It depends on what's going on."

"I better not tell them anything about it because if you don't show up, I'll never hear the last of it."

Faye arrives home as the telephone man is pulling out of the driveway. Faye blows her horn and flags him down. It is an easy hook up. Apparently a phone has been there before. Faye calls her mother and lets her know the phone is ready and gives her the number. She asks her to call her about four o'clock.

Faye goes over Charlene's house, but she is not at home. She goes downtown for a quick drink. Afterwards she picks Jerry up and is fixing some hamburgers, when the phone rings.

"What in the hell is that?" He looks around, trying to locate the source of the ringing. Faye walks over and picks up the telephone, which is virtually sitting under his nose. "I'll be damn!" He shakes his head, while Faye laughs and tells her mother how he is reacting. After Faye hangs up, he asks, "What else do you have around here that I don't know about?"

"Nothing yet."

Faye again surprises Jerry again the next day with a new bedroom suite. Jerry warns her that she may be moving to fast. He advises her to slow down. But he loves the Hibernation Series water bed.

"I went by Mother's today. Do you have any plans for the weekend?"

"In a way. I invited the fellows over for a card game and some dominoes."

"I'm surprised you're not going out."

"It's time we slowed down a bit, with all the bills and things."

"I'm glad they are friends from your job. Not some of those fellows out there still smoking that cocaine."

"Mama was asking me about some guys today, if I knew them. They were arrested for breaking into a store on twelfth street."

"What did they get?"

"Some meat and about thirty dollars."

"Speaking of friends, when is the last time you saw Charlene, Ann and the rest of them?"

"I went by Charlene's there wasn't anybody home so I left a note. I haven't heard from Ann at all."

"Say baby, why don't you change those curtains, they kind of drive me nuts. They remind me of that damn hospital."

"You sound as though you hate the place."

"No I like my job, but I hate that supervisor of mine. He gets on my nerves. I think, I will put in for a new position as soon as I can."

"Back to the question, since you have company this weekend. I would like to bring the boys over next Sunday for awhile."

"That's fine with me. They probably get tired of being around a woman all the time."

"What does that mean?"

"Just that all boys need to be around a real man like me to show them something every once and awhile."

"Well, speaking of a real man. Don't you think you need to fix that window? It will probably start getting cool before long." Jerry acts like he is interested in the television. "No comment." She asks.

"I heard you." Speaking harshly.

"You don't have to frown up about it."

"No I'll do it you'll never let me live it down if I don't."

Faye goes to the refrigerator and gets him a beer, opens it for him.

"This will make you feel better." She giggles at him.

CHAPTER 4

The cooler weather is a welcome relief from mosquitoes. Not only did summer bring a few deaths resulting from heat strokes, but a rise in the price of vegetables, beef, and so forth. With fall in the full swing, many of the animals and birds are preparing for hibernation. Jerry and Faye make it a habit to watch the flocks of birds flying over head.

The problem with cocaine is so minute that no one seems to notice. Those who do refuse to take it serious at all.

Tracy is one of those individuals who takes it serious. His attire has changed completely. The few insignificant rings he and Sheila had on earlier are no longer noticeable, for they are covered with more weighty diamond and gold necklaces. The junk cars are gone except for one. A newer model sport car occupies the driveway. It has no tags on it yet.

The only real complaint that Tracy has is that someone else has opened a cocaine house around the corner and is stealing some of his business. He tries to compensate for by giving bigger pieces and staying on his runner about bringing in more business. Rather than closing up early on the week night he stays available or has someone posted almost twenty four hours a day. A few customers refuse to buy from him unless they have no other choice do so because they say his attitude has changed. He talkes to people like they have tails on them.

◇   ◇   ◇   ◇

"When did you say you were throwing your girlfriend's birthday party?" Asks Richard.

"In about two weeks on the seventeenth." Jerry replies.

"She was born in October uh?"

"Yep."

"That makes her a Libra."

"I guess. I don't really know about all those signs."

"What all are you going to have at the party?" Ask Richard.

"Beer, wine, whiskey, cognac brandy and weed. I'm going to show some nude videos also."

"Who all have you invited so far?"

"All the cool people we work with; Jean, Sue, Mac, Tonya, Charles, Hudson, Riley, and a few others."

"Me and Sue are the only white ones."

"Damn Richard. It doesn't matter as long as you are cool with me. Hell you know everybody's not cool like you. Besides I'm going to invite some of her friends as well. The word will get out. I don't want too many people there."

"Well breaks about over. We better be getting back to work," suggests Richard

"Wait a minute. I wonder what Charlene's last name is."

"Who is Charlene?"

"One of Faye's friends."

"Hell this paper's a week old. Give me a dime." Richard fumbles to find a dime and only comes up with a nickel and some pennies.

"I think I have a nickel."

"You better come on. You know the supervisor has been on your ass lately."

Jerry quickly dials his home number. The phone rings several times before Faye answers.

"Hey baby what are you doing?" Asks Jerry.

"I was just washing my hair." Responds Faye.

"You need to be careful about that it's cool outdoors."

"Don't worry I'll have it covered up." Richard taps him on the shoulder and waves as he leaves the break room.

"Hey I've got to go. Listen, what's Charlene's last name?"

"Anderson Why?"

"I thought so. The reason you have not seen her is because she is in jail, or at least she was last week."

"For what?"

"What else? Shoplifting. I've gotta go. Bye."

After Jerry hangs up. Faye calls the police station.

"Do you have a Charlene Anderson in jail?"

"We sure do."

"How much is her bond?"

"Just a minute." Click, Click, putting her on hold and right back off again.

"It's fifteen hundred dollars. She will need one hundred and sixty dollars with a bondsman or you can go through the county."

"Okay, thanks."

Faye finishes washing her hair and rolls it. She sits under the dryer for about thirty minutes, gets dressed, and goes down to the police station. They tell her that she will have to go to the county. She attempts to post bail, but she does not meet the proper requirements. She in turn has to call a bondsman, finding the closest pay phone, which is located in one of the clubs on Third and State.

The county jail consist of a two story white frame house that has a certain peculiarity about it. A person can stand at Third and State and see it. From the outside it does not look like a jail but like a haunted house fixed especially for Halloween night. It has a high multi- pointed green shingled roof rusty bars on the windows, television antenna, barred doors and thin paint gives it all the appearance it needs for fright night. After walking from Second to Third to use the telephone, Faye chooses to have a drink, while waiting for the bondsman. She knows it will take at least an hour. She has parked her car in one of the deputy's parking places. The deputy is raising hell about it. Faye is not around. When Faye finishes her drink she walks back down to the county jail. The bondsman has not shown up yet. So she waits outside in the car. She has been advised to move it. The bondsman shows up about fifteen minutes later. He and Faye go through the proper paperwork. Now she has to wait for the deputy to go and get Charlene from the city jail.

The women are not kept in the same building as the men. Which takes another twenty minutes. When Charlene sees Faye she forces herself to smile. She looks terrible. Her hair is unkempt. The curl she has is dried out. It needs moisturizing badly. The clothes she has on are musty and need to be ironed. When they locked her up her clothes were put into the same locker as were a dozen others. Her breath is foul from the lack of brushing her teeth. After all the necessary papers are taken care of, the desk sergeant gives her a card notifying her of her court date.

Charlene and Faye hug each other. Water fills the wells of her eyes as she exits the building, walking to the car.

"How come you didn't call over mother's?"

"You're not going to believe this. I could not think of the number for nothing in this world and it's not in the phone book."

"How long have you been locked up?"

"About a week and a half. Oh girl I'm so glad you thought about my ass. Give me a cigarette."

"Where did you get busted at?" Faye asks. Rambling in her purse for her cigarette lighter.

"Out at the mall. I could not believe it. Girl, they had to run me down. I was running too!" Charlene giggled half heartedly. "I know I'm not going to smoke anymore cocaine. You look so good since you quit. Girl and I mean real good. I know Jerry is having a ball with that ass."

"I feel better too. You wouldn't believe it. You want to go over my house and get cleaned up?"

"It sure wouldn't hurt. I feel yuckie," she says, pulling hard off the cigarette, inhaling deeply.

They arrived at Faye's house and go inside. "Faye!" Charlene's outburst startles her. "Girl look at this house. You have really been doing it. Your house never looked so good. It's good you and Jerry got together. You guys make a good couple. You act like the old Faye I knew when we first met, we were fresh out of high school, remember?"

"Sure, we used to really have some good times."

Charlene looks around the house, admiring everything from the microwave oven to the bedroom suite.

"Girl this is one of those Hibernation Series water beds." She flops across it lazily to test the texture of it. "It feels so good. king size at that! I bet you and Jerry have some fun in this big old boy." They both giggle. "It sure feels better than that hard bed in the jail house. It's cold as hell in there and nasty. I saw Mildred and Tina while I was there. Mildred was doing thirty days for petty theft and Tina was fixing to go to court on a marijuana charge."

"Where is Ann?"

"I don't know. You haven't seen her? The last I heard I heard from she was pregnant."

"Girl, be for real."

"I am. She should be about four months pregnant now."

"You can't even tell either."

"She's still smoking cocaine that's why."

"Do you think she will quit?"

"I doubt, it the way she loves to smoke."

"I hate to see what the baby is going to look like."

"Why doesn't Stuart stop her?"

"Shit, Stuart says that it's not his baby. They broke up not too long ago."

"That's news to me." Faye looks at her watch. "Let me go and get Jerry before I'm late. You know how he is. You can go ahead and take a bath while I'm gone. Look in the closet and find you something to wear. I'll be back in a few."

Charlene goes into the bathroom and starts some bath water running. She goes to the stand up bar that sits in the corner to fix herself a drink, then goes to open the freezer to get a couple cubes of ice. She remembers Faye keeps her money in the refrigerator. She always has. More than likely in a Tupperware container or under the crisper. She finds it. It is a sizable amount. Charlene takes fifty dollars out of the container, trying to put it back as close to the way it was. She takes a large swallow from her drink and then refills it. Searching the closet for something to wear, she finds a skirt set that fits her, still being a bit too large. She settles for it anyway. After bathing and all, she moisturizes her hair with some of Jerry's hair activator. Turns on the television and relaxes on the couch until Faye and Jerry arrive home. Faye has informed Jerry of what she has done. Jerry speaks and continues on to the refrigerator to get a beer, returning to the couch to watch television. Faye and Charlene go into the kitchen and continue their little talk.

Meanwhile Faye fixes Jerry something to eat. When she finishes it's about six thirty. Faye apologies for taking so long with his dinner. When Faye goes to fix herself a drink, Jerry seizes the opportunity to tell Charlene about the party. He tells her to call him at work. He will fill her in on the details later. When Faye gets within hearing range they quickly change the subject.

"I would not have known you were in jail if it hadn't been for Jerry reading last weeks paper."

"By the way will you check on a subscription to the local paper for me?" Ask Jerry.

"A lot of things are going on now and I hate to hear it from someone else first. By then it's usually all twisted around."

"Jerry, you sure have changed. I was telling Faye how good you and her are doing since you all stopped smoking that cocaine."

"Yeah, I can take it easy now. I don't have to worry about trying to find some money to buy some more dope with. That shit will drive you crazy. I don't have to worry about getting into trouble either."

"I'm going to stop smoking cocaine too. I don't like going to jail."

"Did they charge you with a felony?"

"Yes because I had over two hundred dollars worth of clothes."

"Well I better go and check on a few things." Charlene mentions "I'm going to take Charlene home and I'll be back."

"All right." Jerry gets up and goes to the kitchen. He puts the dirty dishes in the sink that has already been filled full of water; the suds have all disappeared though. He gets another beer and returns to the sofa. He intends to watch the movie but falls fast asleep.

"Do you want me to take you home first so you can put on some jeans or something?" Faye asks.

"I guess I could change. I don't quite look right in this skirt set."

When they enter Charlene's apartment, she notes. "This place is a mess. I'll probably clean it up tomorrow." Charlene look through her closet that has no organization to it at all. Clothes are just thrown in there as well as on the bed. A few of the nicer outfits are laid across their hangers. Many of them still have price tags on them. Charlene eventually finds some jeans that fit tightly and has to iron them. She also finds a sweater to put on so Faye can have her skirt set back. Faye drops Charlene off downtown and goes back home.

Charlene goes into Ron's place to see what's going on. She buys a beer and sips on it while sitting at the bar, her attention is divided between watching the television and the doorway. After nothing significant happens she decides to go farther. She looks for a ride, which turns out to be relatively easy to acquire. She goes to the dope house and buys a quarter piece and returns back downtown. She goes into the ladies room. As she prepares to smoke the piece of cocaine she brought, she realizes that she does not have a cigarette lighter, luckily, she had a dope pipe at the house. She goes out and asks several people to borrow one Even then she has to leave the person a dollar deposit.

Jerry sleeps while Faye cleans up the kitchen and takes a bath. She rolls her hair. At ten o'clock she wakes him and asks him if he is going to watch the news. Sleepily he replies, and manages to sit up after a few minutes. They sit and watch the news together. Jerry stretches back out and lays his head in Faye's lap. She rubs her hand across his chest as he lays there in an attempt to go back to sleep.

"Jerry are you sleep?"

"No, I'm awake; what is it?"

"I've been doing some thinking."

"We know that you always do."

"No seriously. I'm been thinking about going to school."

"School, for what?"

"You know that career college that they have just opened up" Faye talks hesitantly, "I've been interested in the nurses program."

"Well, why don't you check into it then?"

"You don't mind?"

"Hell no, I'll be glad for you to go. Anything beats the streets. You sound as though you might be getting bored with it."

"No, I just want to make you proud of me, that's all."

"I'm already proud of you."

"You know what I mean Jerry."

"As long as it makes you happy. Let's go to bed."

The next day Faye puts in a subscription for the local newspaper. Then she checks on the schooling. But there's a lot more to it than just enrolling. She picks up the necessary papers and applications to fill out later. She decides to take care of some business, which she does. She returns home and separates her money on her way to the refrigerator, finding her hiding spot. Normally she would not count her money, she notices the twenty dollar bill she had on top is gone. She's pretty sure because of the ink that was splattered on the front bill. She fingers through the remaining bills, not really sure how much was really there. But she knows the twenty dollar bill with the ink on it is missing. She tries to remember if she had been back in there since placing the bill on top. She comes up with nothing. Jerry does not know anything about my hiding spot. Or at least he has never given any indication that he does. Besides if he needs any money, which he doesn't, he would ask. She knows he's not using cocaine again. She haunches her shoulders and puts the money back in the same hiding spot. This time she knows how much is there. She writes the balance on the last bill also.

She calls her mother to see if she is at home, then tells her mother she will be over in a short while. They sit down and watch the soap operas and talk about the boys and other things. Among them Faye tells her mother about getting Charlene out of jail, And about her money she feels may be missing.

"Well, why don't you ask Jerry? You all seem to have a good understanding. Or if you don't believe he got it, leave it alone and watch and see if any more comes up missing."

"You know, you maybe right."

"Charlene and I used to hide our money in the icebox when we stayed together but like you say, leave it alone and see what happens."

Faye continues on as if nothing has happened. That evening Jerry takes Faye out to dinner and to the movies. The next morning Faye tells Jerry that the paper should be delivered starting any day. She also reminds him that today is Thursday. He does not reply.

Jerry dresses for work.

"I believe you look better every day." Says Faye.

"So do you my dear." She walks up and adjusts his tie.

"I enjoyed dinner and the movie last night."

"I thought you might would like that. I don't want to bore you."

"You don't have to worry about that."

"Let's go. I don't want to be late."

That evening Faye picks up Jerry up as always. She has to go and take care of her business. Jerry calls his mother as he always does on Thursdays to see how she is doing. He was there the weekend so he knows she is all right. She is so proud of him. He has also managed to save up a couple hundred dollars, despite his probationary fees and the bills. His weight has accumulated again so she no longer fears that he may be on drugs. After a rather lengthy conversation, Jerry tells his mother he has to go because she has a tendency to talk all night. He knows she misses his company.

It is approximately six thirty now and Faye has dealt with Oscar. She feels somewhat relieved now that she has done so. He still pays exceptionally well. He is curious to know how her mother is doing. She assures him that they are all fine and that her mother will be well soon.

After mingling downtown for a while, Faye runs into Charlene.

"Hey you mean Jerry let you out this evening?"

"We have all of that squared away. So there's no problem there."

Despite the amount of activity at the hour, Charlene appears to be in a hurry. She is riding with Debbie.

"Are you going to be here awhile?" She asks, questioning Faye.

"Sure. I have some business to take care of."

"I'll be back after a while and buy us a drink." Walking off as she finishes the statement.

Knock! Knock! Jerry opens the door. "Hello, Charlene."

"Hi Jerry. I was going to call you."

"Come on in."

"But I got tied up so I decided I would stop by. Is Faye here?"

"No, she's gone out to take care of business."

"How are you going to do the party?"

They both sit down.

"Well, I have to get her away from the house first."

"When?"

"Not this Friday but next Friday. If you can come by here or call and ask her to take you somewhere and keep her out for awhile, I'll do the rest."

"Jerry, do you have a beer?"

"Yes, I'll get you one."

Charlene jumps up. "No, I can get it."

"All right then, bring me one too."

Charlene goes to the refrigerator and gets out two beers places them on top of the stove next to it, and listens for a moment. She hears no noise from Jerry. Charlene goes into the Tupperware again. She quickly takes off three twenties and puts the rubber band back around the rest of the money. Getting Jerry a glass she tries to compensate for the little access time.

"I didn't need a glass. As I was saying, if you can get her away I can take care of the rest."

"I can do that with no problem."

"I haven't seen Ann and some of the others. Put the word out for me. Don't tell anybody who's not cool."

"I'll call you again to make sure that everything is set."

"Good."

"I better be going. Debbie is waiting for me outside."

Jerry lets her out and runs some bath water, but lets it get cold, because he has gotten off into a movie. He has to redo his water all over again. While he is in the tub, Faye comes home. She calls his name. He answers and says that he is in the bathroom. Faye peeps in on him and tells him to stay in the tub. She is going to join him. She separates her money and goes to her hiding spot. Her mouth falls a gap when she pulls out the roll of money and there is no marked twenty. Counting it, sixty dollars is missing. She puts the money she's going to save with the other and marks it again. Entering the bedroom, she sheds her clothes and goes to the bathroom, easing into the tub with Jerry. She is silent. Instead of getting into the tub the way she usually does, she sits facing him.

"What's the matter with you?"

"Nothing."

"You have had a rough evening?"

"Not really."

Jerry has never been one to press the issue. So he finishes bathing and gets out of the tub, puts on his robe, gets a beer and fixes her a drink.

"Maybe this will make you feel better."

Still despondent, she manages a half smile. Jerry lights a cigarette. Faye asks him if he minds lighting one for her. He gives her his and lights another for himself. Faye is looking at him, observing his movements. She notices nothing in him that would indicate his using any cocaine.

"Why are you looking at me like that?"

"Just looking."

"You want to talk about it?"

"Nope."

"Okay."

He raises his hands into the air, deeming the present situation as hopeless, and leaves the bathroom.

After Faye gets out of the tub, he attempts to start another conversation but the answers are so bleak. he just remains quiet. Faye beats him to bed this night. After the news he joins her. She plays sleep. He knows better. He lies there for a moment before he reaches over her and pulls her to him. She snuggles closer but says nothing. Jerry wants to make love to her but thinks against it, since she seems to be preoccupied.

Morning comes, and her disposition has not changed much. He is about to let himself out of the car.

"Do you have any small bills loose? I don't want to have to break a fifty dollar bill. I have something else to do with it."

Faye gives him twenty dollars.

On the way in the door, Jerry mumbles to himself. "I wonder what's wrong with her."

Faye stops by her mother's.

"What brings you by so early? Oh Oh. Something not right, I can tell. What is it?"

"You're not going to believe this, but some more of my money came up missing again last night. Jerry was the only one there."

"Did you ask him?"

"No, but then he asked me for some money when I took him to work. He said he did not want to break his big bills."

"Well, honey there has to be an explanation. I would strongly suggest that you talk about it before it gets to far out of hand. It is no need for you to fall apart. The boys just left."

"I'm going to pick them up this weekend."

"That's good idea."

"You sure you do not want to come over for dinner?"

"I'm sure, you just have a good time with the boys and make sure you keep things together."

Faye cleans the house, goes to the grocery store and liquor store along a few other errands. Then she goes back home and rests until it is time to pick up Jerry.

"Hello baby, what's up? You feel any better than you did yesterday and this morning?"

"A little."

"I assume you still don't want to talk about it."

"I'll wait."

"Let's buy some chicken today, since today is Friday."

They stopped at Church's and buys a family size dinner.

Once at home. Jerry turns on the television, while Faye proceeds to bring out some china. She brings Jerry a beer and fixes herself a drink. Jerry is looking at TV She gets up and turns it off.

"What are you doing now?"

"I want to talk to you."

"Fine, shoot." He continues to eat.

"Jerry." He looks at her gazingly, while holding a piece of chicken with both hands. "I want to ask you something and please tell me the truth."

"I always do, I thought."

"I have some money missing."

Jerry put his chicken down and wipes his hands on the towel placed across his lap.

"Well didn't you find it?"

"No."

"Missing from where?"

"Wait let me finish. You remember when I got Charlene out of jail two days ago?"

"Go, on."

"I left her here by herself. She knows where I keep my money because we use to stay together."

"Where's that?" She ignores the question.

"Anyway, I could not prove how much was missing even though I know some was."

"Why didn't you approach her about it, or are you suggesting I got it?" Again she ignores part of his question.

"I was but."

"But what?"

"Will you let me finish?"

"Okay go ahead." Jerry reaches for his cigarettes. He has stopped eating all together.

"I was not sure, so I marked my money and counted it. Well, yesterday some more came up missing. There was no one here but you." Jerry drops his cigarette and has to jump up to get it because it has rolled between his legs.

"What the hell is that suppose to mean?"

"What else do you expect for me to do? Not say anything?"

"Wait. Let's go through this thing again. You left her here two days ago. Wait a minute, where are you talking about anyway?"

"In the refrigerator. I keep it in one of those Tupperware bowls."

"Well Charlene came by here yesterday. She asks if you were home. I told her no. She ask if I had a beer. I told her yes, that I would get her one but she refused and almost insisted that I let her get it. I stayed in here and was watching television."

"About what time was this?"

"I guess between six-thirty and seven maybe a little more. All I know is that it was somewhere in that time frame."

"I saw her downtown yesterday about that same time."

"She did not mention the fact she saw you. She just got a beer and cigarette and left."

"Well, that bitch!! I get her out of jail and she does me like this!"

"Why didn't you ask me yesterday, instead of walking around with your lips stuck out."

"I am sorry. I should have known better."

"You know I always ask you for what I want anyway."

"The first thing that crossed my mind was maybe you had started back smoking cocaine."

"I admit a good hit would be nice!" He laughs heartily.

"Don't even think about it."

"Just kidding. This chicken is just about cold now."

Jerry spreads his towel back over his lap so he does not get grease on his slacks Faye does the same. Jerry speaks with his mouth full.

"What are you going to do about it?"

"Most likely kick her ass."

"I have an idea."

"What?"

"If you don't say anything most likely she will do it again. So therefore I would take all of the money out and put a note in there that says something to this effect. 'What are you going to do the next time you go to jail Charlene?'"

"I would love to see the expression on her face."

"Then see what she does."

"I tell you another thing. Since she knows where you keep your money it's not a good idea to keep it in there. She could tell anybody for that matter. Have you thought about the bank?"

"I guess that would really be the best place if you really think about it." They finish eating. Faye states "I need to be going."

"I better call the fellas. We are supposed to play cards tonight. But first, I have some business. Come on I'll show you. You cheated me out of it last night." Just about the time they are thoroughly involved with each other the phone rings. "Hello."

"Hey, Jerry what's up man? We still gonna play cards tonight?" Hudson says, pushing to get the game going.

"Yeah. Have you talked to any of the other guys yet?"

"No."

"I'm kind of tied up why don't you give them a call. Then call me back."

"Will do."

Faye beats Jerry to the shower afterwards. The phone rings again.

"Are the guys still coming over?"

"Yes, they should be here in the hour."

"What time is it now anyway?"

"About six thirty. Where's your watch?"

"In there on the dresser. It stopped. I think I may have gotten some water in it or something."

"I'll look at it and see if I can fix it."

"It really doesn't matter, it's cheap anyway. I just bought it to be able to keep up with the time."

On her way out of the door. Richard walks in. "Hi Richard."

"Hello, Faye." Richard tells Jerry that Faye is looking good.

"Thanks Richard."

"Are you going to bring your girlfriend to the party?"

"I don't know. We've been on bad terms lately. You mean you can't tell? Do you think I would be over here every weekend if I wasn't?"

"Well, I guess that make sense. You got here quicker than I anticipated."

"You know how prompt I am."

"Yeah, sure."

"What do you have on VCR tonight?"

"Nothing special."

"What do you have there?"

"Just a few skin flicks. This one is a real sharp movie."

"We could check out the movie and save the nude movies for the party." Richard sits down and rolls himself a joint.

"I see you got some marijuana this time before you got here."

"It's good too. Smell it." He holds the bag up so Jerry can smell its contents.

"It smells like it might be pretty good." Richard lights up a joint and hits it a couple of times and passes it to Jerry. "I was thinking about getting half an ounce for the party."

"You better make sure you get all of the seeds out otherwise you will have seed burns all over the furniture."

"Don't worry. I'm going to cover it up anyway."

Mac and Hudson show up together. As they enter the house.

"Where's the smoke at? It smells good." Mac says, and continues on to the refrigerator. Hudson stops and wants to hit the joint. Mac puts the beer in the refrigerator and a fifth of whiskey on the table.

"You guys didn't finish the fifth you brought last week. I still have it over there on the bar."

"Save it for the party." Blurts Hudson breaking the seal on the new fifth. They are all sitting at the table, drinking and playing poker using poker chips.

There's a knock on the door. Hudson, slightly intoxicated, goes and just opens the door and just starts laughing. "Come on in." Hudson tells her. "You come to join the party?" Charlene looks at him but does not respond. "Well, I guess she can't talk. She ain't deaf is she?" Hudson sits back down.

"Is Faye here?" Charlene asks.

"Nope. You didn't run across her out there any where?"

"No. Not yet anyway."

"What are you guys doing?" She eases toward the table.

"I just told you to join the party, you act like you don't want to deal with a brother or something. What's the matter? You ain't use to a good looking man or something?" Says Hudson, finding his own statement overly hilarious.

"Is it busy out there tonight" Jerry asks.

"It's so-so" She replies. Jerry can tell she is high and nervous. Charlene reaches in her purse and gets a cigarette. Without asking she goes to the bar and fixes herself a drink. Then she drifts into the kitchen. Jerry acts as if he does not notice. Charlene opens the container.

Her face drains of blood when she reads the note. She fastens the lid back on the container and goes back to the living room area.

"There wasn't any ice in the box?" Asks Jerry. Startled she hesitates before answering.

"Uh, yes I forgot I need to tell my ride that I'll be out in a minute."

She exits the house and does not return. Jerry gets up and looks out the widow. The car has left. Jerry laughs and the guys turn around to see what Jerry is laughing at. Jerry tells them what has happened. They all laugh.

Hudson wanting to have the last say. "She ain't nothin but a tramp, then tryin' to ignore somebody. I started to tell that bitch something. She needs a good beaten down. I'll fuck the hell out of that bitch." Laughing again, having to close his mouth quickly, so he wouldn't slobber on himself.

Faye arrives sometime later to find the guys still there.

"Your friend was here earlier." Faye moves closer. "What did she say?"

"Nothing. She took the bait. She still didn't say anything. She said she was going to the car and never came back."

"I'll see her sooner or later."

Faye retreats to the bedroom. The men continue to play cards until three o'clock in the morning before dispersing. Faye is asleep when Jerry enters the bedroom, but is awaked when he attempts to get into bed.

"The fellas finally go home?"

"Yep."

" Good, I need to take a bath. Will you start the water running for me? I was so tired when I first walked in."

By the time she returns from her bathe Jerry is fast asleep. She tries to wake him so he can get out of his clothes. He sleeps harder than usual while he is under the influence.

In the morning Faye cleans the house. The boys are going to visit today. Jerry finally makes an effort to fix the broken window. When Faye returns with the boys, they are overfilled with enthusiasm. They spend the entire day exploring the house and it's contents. Jerry acts as chaperon all day because Faye has fallen asleep. She awakens about six o'clock. She fixes Jerry and the boys something to eat. Faye and Jerry take the boys home close to ten o'clock. Jerry gives them five dollars a piece before they depart.

After all is done, Faye and Jerry decide to go out. They go to one of the more sophisticated clubs on the north side of town. This particular one has a live band, which turns out to be soothing. The atmosphere is a whole lot more comfortable than downtown or the other clubs further up the street. They have the same type of clientele but are in a different part of town. After a satisfying day and a relaxing night, they refuse to leave the house the next day for any reason. Jerry anticipates that Charlene won't be around for the course of the week. Therefore he makes plans with Richard. Jerry is supposed to take Faye to dinner and to the movies, but he gets sick and insists that they come home. Richard is left in charge of the house. A few decorations will be appropriate. No one is supposed to park directly in front of the house.

The day comes . . .

At the movies, Jerry does a fairly good gob at play acting. When they make it home, Faye wonders what is going on next door, but is so wrapped up with trying to see after Jerry that she suspects nothing. She opens the door and turns on the light. She is so shocked. She nearly faints when everybody screams and starts to sing happy birthday. Faye beats Jerry in the chest with her fist. Not out of anger but out of being tricked.

"I thought that you were sick!"

Richard throws Jerry a bottle of chilled Champale. Jerry has to coach Faye as she opens it. Jerry is the first to give her a gift. It is a watch.

"I could not think of anything else."

A number of other gifts follow. Everyone is having a nice time with the music playing. The stereo they are using is Richard's. The videos are also playing. The crowd is slowly increasing. Jerry stands at the door and filters out those few strangers he does not want to attend.

Later, a young lady comes to the door. Jerry does not know her. He lets her in because she is a woman.

She asks the person standing closest to her. "Is there someone there by the name of Faye?"

"I think she is the one they are giving the party for." They reply. She approaches Faye and hands her a box that is wrapped in red wrapping paper, then turns around and leaves. Faye opens it but no card is attached to the outside. Inside is the dress that Faye, Charlene, and Ann saw at the mall. They were all crazy about it. Attached to it is an envelope. Faye tears it open. Inside is a note and a hundred dollar bill. The note reads, "I'm sorry that I could not make it. I hope you understand. Charlene." Faye breaks for the door. The car that Jerry says the woman got out of is gone.

"Look what Charlene brought me." She shows him the dress and the hundred dollar bill. "I don't know why she is acting this way. She's smoking that cocaine. I don't think she wants me to know."

"Enjoy you party. Worry about those things later."

Outside of Hudson getting totally smashed and having to be calmed down before he disrupts everything, the party goes smoothly. Of course, cleaning up afterwards is a different story. "I'm glad this is over with." Says Jerry. "Leave it alone. Let's go to bed. We'll clean up tomorrow."

Everyone is busy preparing for Thanksgiving and Christmas.

"Hello, Mama."

"Hello honey."

"What are you going to do for Thanksgiving?"

"I don't know I haven't quite made up my mind yet."

"Good, you can have dinner with Jerry and I."

"You finally gonna cook another Thanksgiving dinner? I'm so proud."

"Jerry is going to invite his mother also."

"That's wonderful. Just make sure you pick me up early so I can help you with the dinner."

"This is my project mama. Thanks anyway." Click, Click. "I've got to answer the other line hold on a minute."

"What are you doing?"

"I was just talking to Mama on the other line."

"I didn't want anything in particular. Just got a break. I thought I would call."

"So in other words you were just thinking about me, is that it?"

"I guess you could say that." She mimics him a kiss through the phone.

"You don't have to fix too big of a dinner. They're having a spread and I been eating like crazy."

"What's the occasion?"

"Some big shot is resigning or retiring, one or the two."

"I've got to talk to you later." Click.

"Hello, Mama."

"What kind of phone is that you've got?"

"Instead of giving a busy signal, it clicks to let me know some-one is trying to call. It rings on your end like it normally does. All I do is press the lever and it puts whoever I'm talking to on hold."

"I need that done to my phone." They chat awhile before hang-ing up.

Later...

Beep! Beep! Honk! Honk! Faye leans on the horn, trying to get Charlene attention before she enters her apartment. Charlene looks around and tries to pretend that she does not see who is blowing at her. Faye gets out of the car, waving at her.

"Charlene! Charlene!" They approach each other. Faye says, "You don't ever stay at home do you? You didn't get any of the notes I left under your door."

"I haven't been at home."

Charlene opens the door, Faye notices none of the notes are left on the floor. She already knew that Charlene had been avoiding her.

"You don't have to avoid me as long as we have been knowing each other. I think we should be able to talk."

"I know. I just don't feel up to it."

"I appreciate you paying the money back and I love the dress. The party was not as good as it would have been if you were there. You know if you ever need anything all you have to do is ask. I knew the day that you got out of jail that you were not going to stop smoking cocaine. I started to offer you some money but that would not have been right. You had me thinking that Jerry had gotten my money."

"I didn't think about that."

"I'm aware that we don't associate like we use to. Still that does not mean we are any less friends."

"I guess I felt so guilty and embarrassed until I did not think rationally. I'm sorry."

"I'm glad we finally got this out of the way. It has really been bugging me."

"Me too. You want a drink? I have some of your favorite brandy. I was going to bring it to the party. Ann and I stole some liquor out of the liquor store across the highway, while that old man was try-ing to flirt."

"How is Ann?" Asks Faye.

"She lost the baby I thought you knew." Says Charlene.

"What did Stuart say?"

"He didn't say too much. I think he was glad she did. They have started back talking last I saw."

"You been keeping track of your court date haven't you?"

"Yeah, I still have awhile to go yet. I have to go to plea and arraignment—sometime after Thanksgiving."

"I want to get him a couple pairs of cowboy boots and snakeskin if I can." Faye asks.

"What size?"

"About ten and a half to eleven."

"I know just the place to go. Let me show you some ladies boots."

"I love these. When did you get them?"

"The same day Ann and I got that dress. You can break them in for me if you want. I hate breaking in new shoes of any kind."

"What are you going to do for Thanksgiving?"

"I don't know. I would love to go home. But I don't feel like riding the bus to Michigan and I'm sure not going to fly."

"You can come over and eat with us if you want."

"I'll do my best to make it."

"I'll let you know what time and everything. I better get going. I have to turn in some papers at that school. I'm going to try and get in the upcoming semester."

"When is that?"

"In January."

"I need to go and get into something productive myself, to tell the truth about it."

"Here. Take this with you too."

Charlene hands her the fifth of E&J brandy. Faye picks up the boots.

"I'll catch up with you later."

The day before Thanksgiving, Faye hustles around the house doing this and that. Jerry is busy recording some movies he has borrowed from Richard. He has also borrowed Richard's VCR as well. The house smells of a variety of food. The turkey and dressing is in the oven. She has baked two cakes and is working on a sweet potato pie. The vegetables will be cooked in the morning. Faye's mother calls several times, to make sure that all is going well, since Faye refuses to come and get her.

The next day arrives quicker than normal, or so it seems to Faye. She goes and picks up her mother and the boys about ten o'clock. Jerry takes the car and goes to pick up his mother. Faye's mother helps set the table and finish with the odds and ends. The boys are dressed up and are practically on their best behavior, after a stern warning from Faye. An hour has left since Jerry has been gone. He returns with his mother. Faye has met Mrs. Collins before, but she has never been over. Jerry has talked to Mrs. Clark on the telephone but never in person. Mrs. Clark nor Mrs. Collins have ever met. They all pay their proper respects. Greeting, hugging and kissing each other, Mrs. Collins and Mrs. Clark seem to respond to each other rather well. They have to be quieted when Jerry prepares to say the blessing. Jerry carves the turkey while everyone else is busy serving themselves with other delicacies. The boys have been seated at the coffee table with a towel and newspaper spread over the immediate area to protect them and the furniture.

There is a knock at the door. Jerry answers it. It's Charlene and Ann. Debbie is sitting out in the car. She chooses not to get out until Faye beacons her. They of course are hesitant. They have been smoking cocaine. They only nibble at the cakes and pies. Mrs. Collins and Mrs. Clark volunteer to clean the table. While Faye entertains her guest, Jerry calls Richard and the rest of the guys to find out if they are coming over for the football game. The beer has been on ice since yesterday. After the guys arrive, the house becomes a bit noisy, with them cheering for their team to win. When night falls, Faye takes her mother and the boys home as, well as Jerry's mother. Charlene and the other girls have long been gone. Faye is gone until after nine o'clock. The guys have left and Jerry is asleep on the sofa. When Faye returns she too joins him on the sofa. They sleep until morning.

Ring! Ring! Faye climbs over Jerry to answer the phone.

"Hey, what are you doing?" Asks Charlene.

"Sleep."

"Still, sleep? I've got the package you said you wanted."

"Okay I'll be there in a few minutes."

"You don't even know where I am."

"Where are you?"

"We'll be over at Ann's."

Faye has an idea where she stays but wants to make sure, so Charlene gives her the directions.

"I'm on my way."

She hangs up the telephone and lies back down for a few minutes, nudges Jerry and tells him she will be back.

"I have to go and pick up Charlene."

She manages to wash her face and make it to the car thirty five minutes later. She finds the house more on recollection than on directions she was given. She pulls her jacket tight to guard herself from the cold.

She knocks on the door. Ann answers and tells her to come in. They go to the bedroom. The bed is loaded with new clothes. Charlene shows her the first pair of boots. They are made from boa constrictor from the toe all the way up. The second pair is a turquoise blue, reptile.

"Do you think he will like them?"

"He better."

The first pair has a price tag of three hundred and twelve dollars. The second pair had a tag that read three hundred and sixty-five dollars.

"How much do you want?"

"We'll take two hundred and seventy-five dollars. We would normally charge more than that for boots." Says Charlene. "But since its you." Debbie does not say anything. She just agrees. "I know you are not going to throw a party for Jerry are you?"

"No he doesn't want one anyway."

"He ought to like those boots. I started to keep a pair for Stuart, but Charlene talked me into selling them to you."

"What else do you all have?" They ramble throughout the other clothes. Faye buys a sweater out of the lot. "I guess I'll go, Jerry's off today."

Faye returns home. Jerry has gotten up and fixed a turkey sandwich and is drinking a glass of soda pop.

"What have you got there?"

"Charlene and them had some clothes. The only thing I liked out of the whole bunch was this sweater.

"I'm glad I didn't have to work today. I don't think I could have made it. Bring me some aspirin, will you?"

She brings him some aspirin and takes a bite of his sandwich. They lounge around all day. The phone rings. Jerry answers and they hang up.

"Who was that?" Faye asks.

"I don't know. They hung up."

Fifteen minutes later there's a knock on the door. It's the guys again, and they walk in one behind the other with sacks under their arms, chanting.

"Birthday boy, Oh, birthday boy!"

"It's not until Sunday." Exclaims Jerry.

"We know. We. intend to party until then. Comprehend?"

"You all are trying to kill me."

"Try?" Says Richard. "We are going to kill you."

They all have on the same type of blue jacket. They present Jerry with his. It has a big player's insignia on the back. They party until Saturday morning. Faye has long been sleep. Jerry crawls into the bed. He sleeps all day Saturday. Only to wake up and eat that night.

"I'll be so glad when all of these holidays and birthdays are over with." Says Jerry.

"So will I. By the way what did you get me?"

"It's rude to ask anybody what they got you for your birthday. Besides your birthday is not until tomorrow. This is part of it." She starts to seduce him.

After twelve o'clock, he convinces her that it is his birthday because it is Sunday morning. She gives in and tells him to look under the bed. He pulls out a pair of the boots and tries them on.

"I really like these boots."

"Look under there and get the rest." He retrieves a second pair.

"Boy, the guys are going to be jealous when I step in there Monday morning."

"I don't know if I should let you wear them to work. You might look too jazzy."

"For your eyes only baby."

"I bet."

"Let me finish getting the rest of my present."

CHAPTER 5

The Thanksgiving holiday is over and it's back to work for Jerry, who has had an extra long weekend. Jerry shows off his boots to his friends. Several other people comment on them as well. The day is rather laxed. Nobody seems to really be hyped up for work. "Hey, Jerry." He pauses to look around. Hudson approaches him. "You hear anything about a temporary lay off?"

"No, why do you ask?"

"I overheard some staff talking about one."

"Could be just a rumor anyway. You know there was a rumor going on to that effect once before, and nothing happened."

The week drags on with nothing out of the ordinary occurring. Friday's payday. At three o'clock Friday afternoon, Jerry, Hudson, and Sue are called to the office. The supervisor informs them there is a temporary lay off, effective today. Due to the depletion of funds it is mandatory that he cut back on employees. He assures them that it is nothing personal. As soon as all the money is allotted for the fiscal year, he will get in touch with them. He issues them their checks. Vacation time that has not already been taken is added to the checks as well. Jerry has no choice but to hang around until Faye arrives. He has mixed emotions. He finds Richard and tells him about what has just happened. Richard finds it hard to believe. He tells Jerry that he will be over tonight. Faye picks him up and they go to the bank.

"You're rather glum for a Friday evening, especially payday."

"You would be too."

He shows her his check stub, which indicates that his check is twice as much as it normally is.

"Why is that so much? That's good."

"No. It's not. Especially when it's my last one."

A chill runs down her spine, indicated by the chill bumps on her forearms.

"What happened?"

"They laid three of us off today."

"Well, you're not fired. You're just laid off. They will call you back before you know it."

The weekend is not as joyful as some of the past weekends have been. Jerry is not so upset about being laid off. He is mad because he had not been forewarned about it. Being able to draw unemployment is definitely no problem. He has definitely been employed long enough.

Monday he is up bright and early out job hunting. The unemployment office is his first stop. The application and the forms are frustrating enough, not to mention the long waiting periods that are involved as well. He spends all day every day for two weeks seeking employment. On Thursdays and Fridays he takes his mother to work and picks her up afterwards, so that he can use the car. Nothing materializes from his efforts and it is two weeks before Christmas. He has managed to save some money, thanks to his change in life style. This money is spent on Christmas gifts despite his being told by his mother and Faye that gifts would not be necessary. As Christmas nears, so does Jerry uneasiness. He is constantly being comforted by Faye, and reassured that everything is going to be all right. She also reminds him to always say his blessing before meals and at bedtime. She often prays with him.

"If something does not break after the holidays, I am going to have to do something different. You can't keep paying all the bills by yourself."

"I already know that if you were able to help you would do so. Therefore I don't mind."

"All I know is that something needs to break soon."

Christmas day is as if no problems exist. Gifts are plentiful and numerous. The families once again are invited to Faye's and Jerry's for dinner. The guys also show up over the holiday's. They refuse to let Jerry buy any beer and liquor, even though he is determined to prove to them he is doing okay financially. Jerry receives an extremely nice stereo with turntable, double cassette deck, compact disk player, amplifier with large speakers, along with a few clothes. Faye receives a few clothes and a really expensive gold necklace. The mothers receive their share of gifts also, and the boys get battery operated cars that are driveable and a quantity of clothes. Cards from distant and local relatives alike line the table tops.

New Year's marks the end of another year and the start of a new one. Jerry is becoming restless and irritable. It has gotten to the point where Jerry has become jealous of Faye's outings.

"What took you so long?"

"What do you mean? I wasn't gone that long."

"You act like you hate to stay at home with me."

"Baby you know that's not true. I'm just making sure that we have everything we need. It's no reflection on you. You should know that by now."

Faye gets him a beer and massages his neck.

"It's going to be all right. I'll stay here with you tomorrow if it makes you happy." She gives him a hundred dollars more tonight, even though she has given him money all along, especially since his layoff. Jerry stays at home. Faye does more than asked. He acts like she is not there. He spends most of his time fiddling around with his stereo, making tapes. He even sells a few to his friends for five dollars each. Hudson has moved to Little Rock and has obtained a job there at the hospital.

The next day Jerry's mother calls and asks if he has had any luck or received any kind of response in reference to a job. His reply is no. He has received his first unemployment check along with the ones that were being held during required waiting period. He feels relieved and offers to help with the bills. Faye seizes the opportunity to make some extra money herself while his mood has change and he's not feeling sorry for himself. She stops by her mother and discusses the situation with her.

"Well, it most likely from boredom and the lack of feeling useful. Some men feel that way. They have a tendency to become insecure and feel inferior at times like these. The only way that will change is something has to happen positive for him."

"Well he has money and everything. I don't see why."

"Men are strange creatures, Honey. Just remember that."

"Let me get back home. Kiss the boys for me."

Faye stops and gets some chicken and beer. Liquor is still plentiful from the holidays. They enjoy a peaceful dinner. Jerry decides to take a bath. In the meantime, Faye straightens up. There's a knock on the door. It's Richard.

"Come on in. Jerry is in the shower. He'll be out in a minute." Faye goes and tells him Richard is here.

"How is he doing?"

"As well as to be expected. You don't come over as much."

"I figured you and Jerry need more time."

Faye gives Richard an unorthodox look he changes his statement and says, "He hasn't been quite himself lately. I know being laid off has a lot to do with it."

"So you did notice." States Faye.

By this time Jerry is coming out of the bathroom dressed in his pants and robe.

"What's up Richard? I thought you had forgot about the old boy."

"No I haven't, I just been trying to work things out with the old lady, that's all."

"Making any progress?"

"Ah, a little bit. You know what I mean."

"Sure. Want a beer or something?"

"Yeah"

"Have a seat. I'll get it." Faye winks at Richard and leaves the room.

"So you're been tied up with the old lady uh?"

"Yeah, it's going to be all right. How about you?"

"I'm making it."

"No, I mean you and Faye. It must be rough on you, not working."

"You've got that right. I've got to do something. I feel like I'm going mad, sometimes. I really hate to hurt Faye's feelings sometimes. It just comes out. She's a good woman."

"Good looking too."

"Watch it buddy." They both laugh.

This is the first decent laugh Jerry has had in a while.

"Where all have you checked for a job?"

"I've been everywhere and no luck yet. I'm going to go again tomorrow. Enough crying. I got a tape for you. It's just your type of music. It's one of those live concerts that they play late at night with no interruptions."

"You need anything?"

"Naw, I'm fine."

"You sure? You wouldn't tell me if you did anyway."

Faye eases out the door while Jerry and Richard are engrossed in their conversation about the tape, that Jerry has put into the tape deck for Richard to hear.

She goes downtown but things are slow. She then continues to the north side, understanding that the holiday session just ended, and has put a damper on things. Still, there's always a willing party. They maybe difficult to spot, according to the untrained eye but not to Faye. She returns sometime after dark. Richard is gone.

"How come you didn't tell me you were leaving?"

"I thought you saw me when I left."

"You should have said something anyway!" He catches himself and lowers his pitch. "I didn't mean to shout. I have an idea."

"What might that be? If it makes you feel better I'm all for it."

"I was just thinking that maybe I could sell a little marijuana until something comes through."

"I don't know about that. Jerry something could . . . "

"I thought you were all for it if it made me feel better?" He says teasingly, cutting her off.

"You need to quit feeling sorry for yourself. Have you forgotten about your probation so soon?"

"No but I've got to live."

"We are living."

"To you maybe but not to me. I'll just sell enough to build a little bank account. Then I'll quit."

"I guess you are going to sell it out the house. I would prefer that you wouldn't."

"Okay, I won't. I'll sell it downtown then."

"I wish you would at least give it another week of looking for a job before you decide for sure." She backpedals, having a feeling she just put her foot in her mouth.

"You've got a deal" He snaps.

Faye does all she can to assist Jerry the following week in trying to obtain a job. Nothing happens. Jerry wins. He has already checked around town in the meantime trying to locate the best deal at the best price for the best quantity. He decides to use one of Richard's friends, who supposedly get his weed from the Ozarks. He buys a quarter of a pound. He takes some sandwich bags and divides the weed into dime bags. He counts how many bags he has. His profit only comes to one hundred and thirty dollars, over what he has invested.

Despite her unwillingness to cooperate. Faye has made a deal and must uphold her end of the bargain. Jerry asks if she needs to use the car for anything. He takes ten dime bags with him, wrapping them with rubber bands and tucks them inside his coat pocket. Downtown is one of the hottest places, for selling weed. The competition is fierce. The only distinction his has is the quality not the quantity. Once a person establishes the fact he always keeps a good quality of marijuana, it is easy to maintain a steady clientele.

Faye starts school the following week. The new undertaking that Jerry has gotten involved in has produced only minimum results. He is in luck if he can make two hundred dollars a week profit.

"How is school?"

"I like it. It's rather interesting as a matter of fact. How's business coming on your end?"

"It's doing fair not as well as I expected, nor is it going as good as I see some of the other people doing." Jerry does quiet a bit of drinking, smoking weed and shooting pool to keep from being bored. When he comes home his is rather loaded. "Another week of this and I'm going to be nuts. I think next week I'll try my hand at the unemployment office again."

The next week looks promising. Jerry has a couple of interviews for jobs that the unemployment office sets up for him. One of the interviews requires him to take a test. Then he will have to wait for the next term of employees to be hired if he does pass the test. The others consist of a number of people being screened for the same job. Jerry does not doubt his own qualifications, but being honest with himself, there are other people who are more qualified in this particular line of work. He does not have any success in seeking employment. Even so, he has made his mind up to stop selling weed, with a little coaxing from Faye. Little does she know, he is ready to quit anyway. She hopes this at least make him think about his situation and try to deal with it more maturely.

"What are you doing?"

"Trying to get my lesson done for tomorrow."

"Do you need any help?"

"If you don't mind you can look up the these words for me. Here you should be able to find them in this book. Just mark them for me."

There are some words in the book that Jerry is familiar with. He has either heard them at work or uses them himself.

"This might help me out some when I go back to work."

"That's a good way to look at it."

After Jerry has highlighted most of the words for her he stops and gets himself a beer and puts on his headphones to listen to his stereo.

The next night while sitting around doing nothing. Jerry tells Faye he needs to go downtown to pick up some money owed to him. After his arrival there, he seems to have more people asking him about marijuana than he did while he was selling it. While looking for Mike he physically bumps into Charlene coming out of the club.

"Hi Jerry where's Faye?"

"At home."

"Tell her I said hello. You still selling weed?"

" No."

"Damn I sure could use a bag."

"It's too slow, or maybe I just didn't have the patience."

"What you really need to sell is some cocaine. You would make a lot of money and everything." Charlene starts to walk off. Jerry stops her.

"Wait a minute. What are you fixing to do?"

"Nothing, what's up?"

"I want to talk to you a minute. You want a drink or something?" They go back into the club and sit down. "Say listen. About this cocaine deal. How do I go about getting hooked up with something like that. I mean, so I can sell it? What do I have to do?"

"You have to buy it, cook it if it is not already rocked up, cut it up into quarters or whatever size you plan to sell. It's not hard to do at all."

"First, I'll have to find someone to cook it for me. I don't know anything about any of that."

"I can get you hooked up with someone who will sell you what you want. I can also get it cooked for you. The best place to go and get it is Little Rock. You don't have to worry about the quality of dope."

"The only time I can go to Little Rock is when Faye goes to school. That will be the first thing in the morning. You think you can take care of that for me?"

" Sure I'll be at home."

"I'm trying to think where you stay at."

"On Liberty, you know those apartments on Liberty. The address is 405 Liberty Apartments, Ten C upstairs."

"Oh, yeah I know where that is. I'm going to get with you first thing in the morning. You think you can take care of it for me?"

"Yes, if you are going to come by."

"I'll see you in the morning about nine o'clock." They sit there for a few more minutes. As they start to separate, Jerry stops Charlene by touching her on the arm. "Do me a favor. Keep this to yourself. I don't want Faye to find out. I want to make enough money to surprise her."

"I will. Jerry loan me twelve dollars until in the morning?"

Jerry pulls out a sizable amount of money. He gives her fifteen dollars. He does not have any singles.

"Thanks. I'll see you in the morning."

"Later."

Jerry then concentrates on finding Mike. He finds him in another club shooting pool. He waits until he finishes and calls him to the side.

"What's up Mike?"

"Nothing much. You've been kind of scarce the last week or so haven't you?"

"I just been trying to keep a low profile."

"I guess you came to pick up that package?"

"Right."

Mike pats his pockets in an attempt to locate the money.

"Here it is. It's going to be about five dollars short. I had it all yesterday but ran short myself. I'll get it to you as soon as I can."

"Don't worry about it."

"You got any more? That sold pretty fast."

"No I'm thinking about trying something different. Weed is too much of a problem for me."

"All you have to do is get it. I'll continue to sell it for you."

"I may do just that. I'll get with you tomorrow."

Jerry goes back home. He walks in the door.

"I thought you might have gotten lost."

"No, not quite."

"You got through with your homework I see."

"I didn't have that much today."

"Good, let's take care of our homework."

"Your mother called. She wants you to call her."

"I better do it now before I forget." He says, locating the telephone. "Hello Mom, Faye told me that you called. What is it?"

"Your probation officer called today."

"What did he say?"

"He just wanted to let you know that you're paid up until next month. He doesn't want you to forget and fall behind. He also wants you to let him know if you have any luck in finding a job."

"I'll call him tomorrow. You doing okay?"

"You know your mother is always going to make it."

"What about you? You doing okay?"

"Yes, Mom."

"All right. I'm going to let you go. I'll talk to you later."

"Bye Mom." He says, acting somewhat annoyed at the fact his mother wants to know how he is doing. Jerry and Faye continue where they left off.

The next morning Jerry takes Faye to school. Then he goes directly over Charlene's house. He knocks several times before he finally gets an answer.

"Here I come!" Jerry can hear her yelling as she approaches the door. "Hi, come on in. Damn! What time is it?"

"It's after nine."

"I haven't been home long. Give me a minute to get ready."

Jerry waits in the front room while she gets ready.

Jerry stops at the gas station and fills the tank up with gas, checks the oil and water. He knocks on the car window. Charlene rolls it down.

"Do you have any cigarettes?"

"A couple. I could use a pack."

Even though Little Rock is only forty miles away, Jerry does not want any problems so he takes the necessary precautions, as far as the car is concerned.

They are on the way. Jerry knows his way to Little Rock so he doesn't need any directions until he gets there. Charlene gives good directions. They make it to the location without any problems. When Jerry pulls up into the huge driveway someone comes out of the house and watches the car until it stops. Jerry sits still. Charlene exits the car first. He meets her half way. She tells him what she wants. He points to a vacant house next to the one he just came out of. Charlene signals Jerry to follow her. They both go to the vacant house together. They are waiting on the steps. From their position they can not see the man approaching the back door. He startles them when he abruptly opens the door. They step inside. There is no furniture except for a table a couple of chairs. He pulls the shade down to the room they occupy at the moment. He goes into the kitchen and reaches into the bottom cabinet and pulls out a set of triple beam scales. When he re-enters the room, he reaches into his coat pocket and produces an ounce of cocaine. The guy speaks very little, almost none at all. The only thing he says is thanks when the transaction is finished. The rest is all nods and questioning eyes.

When they get to the car, Charlene ask to see the cocaine. She sticks her finger in it and rubs it across her gums.

"How is it?"

"It's real good. You are suppose to let me test it before you pay for it. How do you know it is some good?"

"I guess you got a point, at least that is what they do in the movies." He says, mildly joking about it.

"It won't be funny if you spend your money and get some bad shit."

She fastens the plastic bag back up and gives it back to Jerry.

On the way back home she is more talkative than she was on the way to Little Rock. Once back in Pine Bluff, she directs him to a house on the east side of town. It sits off into a semi rural area of the city. She checks to see if anybody is at home. After all of the introductions are made. Charlene tells Willie what they need done.

He says, "Hook me up when I get finished. You know the deal."

"That's no problem." Jerry says.

"Well, as long as we've got it understood. I don't want any problems," Willie responds.

The house is nice but sparsely furnished. Willie directs him to an almost vacant bedroom. Where he has a number of five gallon buckets for seats and an oversized glass table top. It is propped on top of two milk crates. He reaches into the walk in closet and gets a shoe box. Jerry is curious as to what is involved in the cooking process. Willie takes out his baking soda and an oversized test tube. He also has a glass pipe and pure grain alcohol. He tells Charlene to go to kitchen and bring him a glass of water and a glass of ice water. He proceeds to cook or rock it up. He is also overly anxious to smoke some, as is Charlene. The thought enters Jerry's mind, but only briefly.

After processing the first piece Willie fixes his pipe and asks for a piece to go in it. Jerry tells him that he would prefer he finish taking care of his business before they start to smoke. Willie is disappointed. He looks at Charlene who is stoned faced as well. Willie finishes, cutting the cocaine into smaller pieces, that are worth twenty five and fifty dollars a piece. Jerry counts a total of fourteen hundred dollars worth of cocaine. He only paid four hundred and fifty dollars for it. He smiles outwardly and then to himself and thinks of the money he is going to make. He is more than pleased with the potential profits the selling of cocaine than marijuana. He gives Willie two quarters plus the crumbs. He then gives Charlene two quarters. He then tells Charlene he is fixing to leave. Jerry does not want to be around them while they are smoking cocaine. Charlene asks Willie if he will take her home, when they are finished.

Willie says. "It's no problem."

Jerry bids farewell and leaves. He turns around and comes back. He tells Charlene he will be downtown tonight. If she brings him some business, he will compensate her for doing so.

Jerry returns home and recounts his product. He again smiles to himself. He looks around for a hiding spot. His stereo is the safest. Faye does not bother it at all. She considers it his personal play toy. Now that he has gotten the cocaine, he is uncertain as to how he is going to keep Faye from knowing exactly what he's doing. He reverts back to selling marijuana as a cover. He goes and buys an ounce. Not particularly concerned with the quality this time, he bags it up as before and leaves it laying on the coffee table.

After he has picked up Faye from school, he goes and cashes his unemployment check that has come in the mail.

"You hungry?" He asked

"I'm starved."

"Good, let's go eat."

There are places Jerry and Faye normally go to eat. Jerry passes them and is headed in an opposite direction.

"Where are you doing?"

"You'll see."

"You sure are acting strange. What are you up to now?"

"Who me?"

"Yes, you."

"Nothing. Can't I take you out to dinner?"

They stop and eat at a seafood place that is located close to the Mall. The advertisement sign located out front indicates all you can eat, six dollars and ninety nine cents. They enter the lobby and have to wait to be seated. After entering the dining area they are able to see the buffet, which has everything from frog legs, crab legs, lobster tails, shrimp and a few other seafood delights.

"Look at all that food." Faye whispers in Jerry's ear.

"You like this place?"

"How come we never ate here before?"

"Don't ask so many questions baby. Just enjoy your dinner."

She samples some of everything there is. She skips the frog legs at first, but, she finds they are really quite tasteful. After finishing their meal, Jerry leaves a dollar tip on the table.

"You're such a big tipper."

"Don't get cute." Faye laughs. Jerry pays the check on the way out.

"I'm so full." Says Faye.

"I'm rather full myself."

At home, Jerry gets a beer out the box, turns on the television, and props his feet on the table. Faye sits down beside him and is about to tell him what happened at school today when she spots the weed on the table. Jerry knows she has spotted it before she says anything.

"What is that?"

"What?"

"Don't play dumb with me, Jerry Collins."

"This!"

"It's called marijuana. What are you doing with it? I thought you had enough of trying to sell that stuff."

"Well, baby listen."

"Baby! Baby Hell! That's way you took me to dinner at that so called way out place. To soften the blow. Well, I'll be damn if it is going to work! I tell you what you go ahead and sell that shit. It' your baby. When something goes wrong or you wind up in trouble don't come whimpering to me."

"I wasn't trying to cover up anything." He says, trying to get a word in edgewise.

"I know. That's what you call being truthful."

"It's like this, I just reconsidered the whole thing. I may have given up on the project a little prematurely, that's all."

"Like I said it's your baby. That includes you coming in drunk also. I'm through with it."

"I can handle it. You'll see."

A little after night fall, Jerry tells Faye he going to take care of business. She hears him but chooses not to answer him. Jerry gathers his things and leaves. He's sure he can make her smile later. He makes it downtown just after seven thirty. He does not see Charlene. He makes himself comfortable and waits. She eventually shows and wants to buy a quarter piece.

"This is some damn good coke. I came earlier but you had not made it down here yet."

"By the way when you come and buy some coke. Come and get yourself. Do not send anyone to me. Understood?"

"I know how to do it." She frowns up at his face.

It's close to one o'clock. Jerry has sold six quarters and given Charlene one. He is not disappointed by the turn of events that have taken place tonight. It's more productive than a night of selling weed. Faye is asleep when he makes it home. He leaves the cocaine in the car. After getting ready for bed, he kisses Faye in her sleep. He has no difficulty in falling to sleep.

The next day while Faye is at school. Jerry rides to the west side of town to see how things look, particularly over by Tracy's, to see what business he can steal. Even though it is cold outside the runners that Tracy has posted outside linger about. They are ducking in and out of their hiding spots which include the old car in the yard. When Jerry walks up, they want to know what he wants. He says he is just waiting on somebody. So they don't pay him much attention. Jerry waits until he sees somebody he knows. He does his best to be discreet. He lets them know that he sells cocaine also. He promises satisfaction because of the quality and size. He walks them to the car and gets in before selling or showing them anything. He also asks them to keep it quiet.

"I will be downtown after eight o'clock if you want any more."

He talks to two more customers before he suspects the runner might be getting nosy or become suspicious of him. He decides it is time to go. It's cold anyway. He goes home. No sooner than he has lays down, there is a knock on the door. It's Charlene.

"Is Faye here?"

"No."

"Well, let me get two quarters."

"I told you not to come by the house!"

"You don't have to scream at me. If I thought Faye was at home then I wouldn't have come by."

"All right. Wait a minute."

"The next time, park down the street. Ask for weed if Faye is here. Unless it's absolutely necessary try not to come by at all when she is here. You know about what time that usually is. I'll be downtown about seven tonight."

Jerry thinks about the dumb statement he just made if it's not absolutely necessary when he knows it always is.

That evening while eating dinner.

Faye notes, "You seem to be in a better mood than usual."

"Yeah, I guess you could say that." They talk about several things.

"Well I better be going."

"Going where?"

"You know today is Thursday."

"I forgot all about that. I guess we better get going."

"We? Jerry, you know I can't work with you around."

"We'll have work around that. If everything works out the way I have planned it, you won't have to work at all." Faye is standing there somewhat bewildered. Jerry hugs her and kisses her lightly. He promises that it will not make a difference in the relationship. "Just drop me off and you can do whatever you have to do." Jerry understands what she means. It shows in her facial expression and in her body movement. "Believe me, I understand. Give me the chance to make you happy."

"But I–"

"Shhh" He gently puts his two fingers up to her lips. "Let's go."

Jerry goes to Ron's place and has a seat. He limits his movement from club to club, because he does not want to interfere with Faye. Faye runs into Charlene.

"Hey girl, is Jerry down here too."

"Yeah, why do you ask?"

"I just wanted to buy some weed is all."

"He's around here somewhere." She says, quickly glancing around.

Charlene gets a free twenty five dollar piece for every five she buys. She gets two of them before the night is through and almost gets a third. Jerry sells all of his weed. So he feels even better than the night before. He makes investment back the rest is profit.

It's twelve thirty when Faye comes in search of Jerry.

"Hello baby." She says and sits down beside him. "How's business?"

"Great, great." He says, then checking his own enthusiasm.

"You sound as if you are really enjoying yourself."

By the time Faye goes to the bar, orders, and returns the table is empty. She sets the drinks on the table and looks around before sitting down. Jerry returns from the back room proceeded by one of the guys he stopped at Tracy's place.

"How was your night?" He asks Faye.

"It was as well as to be expected. It gets better. I need a hot bath and some real loving."

"Sounds good to me. Let's go."

While Faye is running her bath water, Jerry is busy hiding the rest of his cocaine in the stereo, straining his ears to locate her whereabouts in the house.

"Jerry!" Her voice echoing from the bathroom. "You gonna bathe with me?"

"Yeah!" He yells back. "Be there in a second!"

Faye is pleased with his love making tonight. She just wants to be reassured of the relationship. She's not sure, but it might have been even a little better. She beats Jerry asleep.

He gets up and recounts his money. He has close to nine hundred dollars worth of cocaine left.

In the morning on the way to school, Faye asks Jerry if he called his probation officer yesterday.

"I'm glad you reminded me. I had forgotten. I'll do it as soon as I get home."

After returning home he calls his probation officer. Mr. Dunn tells him that there is no problem as long as he is caught up, or paid ahead, so not to worry. Jerry promises to bring him some money before the end of February. He also gives him his phone number so that Mr. Dunn can call him at home.

It's Friday and Jerry goes and buys two ounces of weed to make sure he does not run out. He is taking time to bag it up when then is knock on the door. It's Charlene.

"I know she's at school" She says, jumping to the defensive. She enters the house without Jerry saying a word. Jerry continues to bag up his weed.

"I want to get a half. That makes you owe me a quarter right?"

"You've got it. You make sure you keep up with what I owe you, don't you?"

"Has Faye suspected you of selling cocaine yet?"

"Nope, I hate to hide it from her, but one day she won't have work the streets."

"I wish I had a man to think of me that way. Everyone I come in contact with wants me to do everything. I can do bad by myself."

"That's true."

"I better go. Thanks."

"All right. I'll see you later."

Jerry rest until it is time to go and pick up Faye. She wants to go by her mother's house to check on the boys. Her mother wants to know how school is going. Faye has no complaints about it so far. She gives her mother some money for the boys and to purchase some groceries.

"I'll bring you the food stamps and the check as soon as I get them."

"I know, honey we are doing okay over here. I used some of your money to pay the insurance man. How's Jerry?"

"He's doing okay. He's out there in the car."

"Why didn't he come in?"

"I told him that I would not be long."

"Has he found a job yet?"

"Nope, but he's still drawing his unemployment and doing something else on the side."

"Well, that's good. As long as he keeps busy, he will be okay."

"I don't know about that." Faye mumbles.

"What did you say?"

"I just said you're right." Faye talks to the boys and gives them five dollars a piece that Jerry sent for them. "I am fixing to go, Mama. I'll be back over as soon as I can."

"All right. Tell Jerry hello and you be careful."

Jerry sells close to four hundred dollars worth of cocaine and two hundred dollars worth of weed before the night is through. Saturday night he sells the rest of the cocaine he has left. He leaves the weed with Mike. He tells him that he will see him Monday night.

He goes and finds Faye and tells her.

"Let's go have a good time. It's only eleven thirty. Tomorrow we will go to the movies and whatever else you want to do."

Faye smiles and scoots up under him while he drives. She rubs her hand between his legs. He teasingly presses the accelerator as if he is really excited.

"I'm so glad to get away from downtown. It's more relaxing over here on this side of town. I'll be glad when I finish school, maybe I can get a regular job. I would really like to become an RN."

"I'm glad to see that you are taking your schooling seriously."

"Why don't you call the hospital back and talk to your supervisor and see if he has heard anything about calling you back to work."

"I talked to Richard today, he said he had not heard anything. But calling him might not be such a bad idea."

The conversation ends as they enter the club.

"Come on, let's dance. I like that record." She informs him. The record is a slow song that has recently topped the charts.

"I've got that record on tape. I didn't know you liked it. You should tell me things like that."

"If it makes you hold me like this I will."

The light in the rear of the club comes on. It is close to closing time.

"Are you ready to go home?" Asks Jerry.

"Whatever you want to do."

The club next door is a private club and stays open until early hours of the morning.

"Let's go next door for awhile."

They talk and dance. Before they know it, it is time for this club to close also.

On the way to the house Faye tells Jerry she really enjoyed the night. The conversation and the dancing has made her feel better about the relationship and life in general. She manages to fall asleep before they make it home. Jerry carries her to the door, and she unlocks it while he holds her,

"I can walk, I know I'm heavy."

"If you were that heavy I would have put you down." He says, taking her to the bed room.

He runs her bathwater and counts his money before he wakes her up. He takes a bath with her as he does so many times.

"You must really be tired."

"I was, but that little nap seems to have done me some good. Besides, I'm not too tired, if that's what you mean."

"Well, I hadn't thought about it really."

"I can't tell judging by how hard you are. She splashes water in his face and laughs. He retaliates. She finally gives in.

It's Monday again and Jerry drops Faye off at school. He immediately goes over to Charlene's apartment.

"I see you made it this morning. I've been up all night." Says Charlene.

"You better slow it down, things can get out of hand."

"If I slowed down now it might affect your business, don't you think? I know you don't want that."

"Let's go." Says Jerry, somewhat embarrassed by his own remark.

On the way to Little Rock, Charlene is trying to nurse a beer that she has left in the freezer too long.

"You want another beer? You've been playing with that one every since you left the house."

The slurping noise getting on his nerve.

"I guess I could. If it's not too much trouble."

Jerry stops at one of the service stations on the side of the highway that has recently been built. He hopes that Willie is at home, thinking to himself before mentioning it to Charlene

"I should have told him that I would be through this morning."

"I already did."

"You've got a habit looking out for yours, don't you?"

Charlene laughs, "That's what it is all about. I'm just glad you went today instead of tomorrow."

Jerry opens one of his beers. Charlene has already done so.

This time, after the half ounce of cocaine has been rocked up it comes to a total of twenty seven hundred dollars. Jerry gives Willie seventy five dollars worth and some of the crumbs. Charlene gets fifty dollars worth and the rest of the crumbs. Jerry reinforces his operation by bringing his marijuana back up to par. He has been tied up all day and is still bagging up his weed when it's time to go and pick up Faye.

She looks at the marijuana on the table and does not comment. She slips into something more comfortable and asks Jerry if he is hungry. She makes preparations to cook the steak that has been thawing out in the sink all day.

The telephone rings.

"Jerry this is Charlene. Act like I'm someone else. I know Faye is home. I need two halves."

"Yeah sure, Richard. I'll be there in a few."

"Where do you want me to meet you at?"

"At the car wash at the end of Main Street."

"Bye"

"Who was that?"

"Nobody, just Richard."

"I'll be right back. I've got to take Richard to pick up his car."

"Don't take too long. Dinner will be ready in a little bit."

"I'll be back before then."

Jerry is gone about thirty minutes. The telephone rings.

"Hello, Faye is Jerry there?"

"No. He is suppose to be on his way to pick you up." She says, catching his voice right away.

"He is?"

"This is Richard isn't it?"

"Yes"

"That's what he said when he left."

"All right bye."

When Jerry returns. Faye asks, "Did you find Richard?"

"Yes, why do you ask?"

"I just wondered. He called after you left. I told him you had already left. He seemed apprehensive when I said you were on the way to pick him up."

"You know Richard. He can be so goofy at times."

"Dinner is about ready."

"In a minute."

Jerry picks up the receiver of the telephone. He calls Richard, but he's not at home. Jerry washes up and goes into the kitchen to eat. He is seating himself at the table.

"I was going to bring it to you." Faye says.

"It doesn't matter. I can eat in here."

"I noticed you had some more weed. So there is no need to ask you where you are going tonight."

Jerry looks up but does not reply. It's habit Faye does not like, but is getting use to.

"How was school today?"

"The same as usual."

"You got much homework?"

"No, I can handle it. That was fast. You must have really been hungry?" Jerry gets up and attempts to get a beer.

"Damn!"

"What's the matter?"

"Nothing, I just forgot to get some more beer, that's all."

"There should be some soft drink in there."

Jerry gets a drink and opens it and sets it down on the table. He goes and gets the newspaper. He's walking back in the door reading it.

"I see there have been three burglaries over the weekend and someone snatched a purse out at the Mall."

"Anybody you know get arrested over the weekend?"

"Not this time."

"Jerry we need to sit down and sort the bills out."

"Uh huh " He says absently, acknowledging her.

"You are going to have to go and pay them. So I won't have to miss a day in school. You check the mailbox?"

Jerry just shakes his head indicating no. He's reading the paper. Faye gets up and puts the dishes away and goes toward the door.

"I was going to go. I just wanted to finish reading this article."

"That's all right, I'll get it."

While she is doing so she wonders what he has done all day. He hasn't checked the mailbox and just got the newspaper. She dismisses it and attributes it to his little project. She glances through the mail finding nothing interesting. She lays it on the table. She continues to clean the kitchen. Jerry eventually glides toward the living room and turns on the television set to watch the news. Faye finishes the kitchen and starts on her homework. After one telecast of the news Jerry cuts the T. V. off and puts a tape in the stereo, which has the song that Faye likes. She stops doing her homework to listen.

"Just thought I would play it before I leave."

"You're going out early this evening."

"I need to be on top of things."

He gives her one hundred and fifty dollars toward the bills.

"You certainly must be doing better. You didn't gamble this time."

"No comment." He only gambles on rare occasions. He kisses her on the forehead and leaves.

It's cold outside so Jerry sits and observes things for a minute, with the car heater blowing full blast. He finally decides to go in the club. Jerry's first customer is one of the guys he stole from Tracy. He has twenty two dollars. Jerry tells him that he will let him go with it, but he needs to bring all of his business to him, not just when he is short. After a while Charlene shows up but it is way past dark.

"Things sure are slow tonight." Says Jerry.

"I know you need to be down here tomorrow after twelve o'clock noon. It's the first of the month, money will be everywhere. Give me a quarter. By the way Ann wants to know if she can come and cop from you? She likes your dope better than Tracy's too.

"Just explain the situation to her. So that she does not screw things up."

The night is so slow that Jerry decides to go home early. Faye is still up and talking on the telephone. She lowers the receiver.

"You're home early." He nods. She continues talking on the phone another few minutes before hanging up. "Things must be slow for you to come in this early?" She says it smiling.

"You like that, I see."

"Sure. I don't have to worry about you now. I can sleep in peace."

The next day Jerry goes and pays the bills. Faye has carefully taken time to organize them so he won't have any problems. He thinks about calling his job and talking to his former supervisor, but changes his mind. Instead, at twelve o'clock he goes by the school. He offers to take Faye to lunch. She is very surprised and inquires as to what honor she owes this privilege.

"I just thought it would be nice. Since I have to leave home early. It's the first of the month."

"Well, I knew it was something." She says, her voice losing some of its enthusiasm. "But this is still considerate of you."

They grab a quick lunch close to the school. When they finished he goes directly downtown and waits patiently. He is filled with anticipation. His persistence is justified. Charlene and Ann start off for him. The time has come to pick up Faye. The pace has been steady. He is already ten minutes late. Before Faye can say anything.

"I didn't mean to be late." He says. "Business is blooming right now. If you want to you can drop me off downtown. Then come back and get me, if necessary."

"Did you check the mailbox?"

"I'm afraid not. I haven't had time."

"I'll drop you off. Most likely I'll have to go to the post office and over to Mama's." Jerry arrives and he sees Willie fixing to get back into his car. He calls to him. Willie is approaching him, while he is telling Faye what to do. He finishes hurriedly before Willie has a chance to make it to him afraid he might say the wrong thing in front of Faye. Letting Faye leave.

"Surprised to see you out." Says Jerry.

"I was just about to leave. Let me have three quarters. That's some pretty good cane, you've got there." Jerry shuffles the rocks around in the match box, attempting to pick out some nice size pieces. "Another thing if you are going to get any more you need to get it rocked before Monday. I have to go back to work. Vacation is over. I'm glad in a way."

"Why?"

"So I can get a break from this fucking dope. This stuff will drive you crazy. I plan on borrowing some money from the credit union so I can get me a new truck. Let me run." cutting the conversation very short. "I've got a freak waiting for me."

"Say, chances are I will be over there Friday morning."

"I'll be there."

Meanwhile Faye has made it home and checked the mailbox. She has a slip indicating she needs to pick up something at the post office. She picks up her food stamps and cashes her check. Then she goes over her mother's. The boys are just getting home. "Hello Lil' Stevie, hello Tony." She says, kissing on each of them. "You both need a haircut. Tony get some tissue so I can clean your nose. You keep a cold."

"Hi Mama. What are you smiling about?"

"Just glad to see my baby in such shape is all."

"Thanks, Mama. Here's the stamps and their money."

"You don't have to rush and bring it over."

"I know, I just want to get it out of the way."

"How's Jerry?"

"He's doing fine."

"That's wonderful."

"What are you cooking for dinner?"

"Just some spaghetti."

Faye goes and looks in the refrigerator.

"When are you going to cook those pork chops?"

"I don't know you want some?"

"I'm going to cook a few if you don't mind. You want some?"

"No, baby, I got them for the boys. If I eat too much pork and it gives me a headache."

"Have you been taking your blood pressure medicine?"

"When I think about it."

Faye cooks a pork chop for the boys and gives them each spaghetti. After they have been fed, she bathes them.

"I better go Mom. I've got some homework to do."

"You must be enjoying that school. I see you are serious about it."

"I want to be something one of these days."

"You already are. You will always be my baby."

"Love you, Mama."

Faye goes downtown to look for Jerry. He is sitting in Ron's place, so is Oscar. She waves to Oscar and calls Jerry outside. She also noticed the anguish on Oscar face. There is little she can do at this point.

"I brought you some pork chops sandwiches. You really need more than this, but these ought to hold you for a minute."

"Thanks"

"You don't look like you have had too many drinks."

"No I've been too busy getting paid."

"Jerry, I want to talk to you for a minute before something is said or done. So you won't be offended. There's guy in here that I take care of business with. In fact, he brought the television. This was before we got serious. He's one of the few who spends two and three hundred dollars at a time. So I don't want to ignore him completely. But if you don't want me to say anything, I won't."

"No, I trust you. Go ahead."

"I won't be long anyway."

Jerry sits in the car and eats while Faye goes into Ron's place. Some of the tension has left Oscars face. She rubs him on the back and tells him that she will get him on Thursday. Right now she has to go. He acknowledges that fact. She returns to the car.

"That was quick."

"He's cool. I just don't want the old guy to think I'm just out and using him. He's really nice in his own way."

Faye and Jerry talk awhile.

"Well I better go. I've got homework to do. I should have went and washed. I'll wait until tomorrow."

"All right. Come and pick me up about one o'clock. No, that's all right. You get your rest, I can find a way."

"No. I will be here."

"OK bye."

Jerry goes back into the club. Oscar looks at him intensely. Jerry does not notice him or anybody else. A few people come and purchase weed. The majority buy cocaine. Undoubtedly Charlene and Ann have spent their checks on cocaine, considering the number of times they have been back including this one.

"I was intending to ask you, Charlene, what happen when you went to court?" Inquires Jerry.

"I went but they put it off until next month."

Charlene and Ann have put their money together so they can get a free rock. It's going on seven o'clock and Jerry has sold forty quarters and twenty three bags of weed.

By the time Faye comes and picks him up he has sold sixty-nine quarters and the rest of the weed he has on him, bringing his net total to slightly over two thousand dollars.

The next night is not quite as productive, but Jerry does not complain. He has sold nearly all of the half ounce that he had purchased on Monday. He only has ten quarters left and is trying to make up his mind whether or not he is going to Little Rock in the morning. He figures some of the break in business is due to a fight that has broken out inside Wilma's place. There were several police down there, including detectives.

The next day Jerry decides to go to Little Rock anyway. He goes by Charlene's place, but she is not there. He hopes the guy remembers him without her. Upon arriving, he has no problem getting what he wants.

"I'm gonna let you have an ounce for eleven hundred since you've been coming regular."

"I sure appreciate it." Answers Jerry. "You wouldn't know anybody that sells weed do you?" Asks Jerry.

"How much?"

"About a quarter pound."

"You should have ask before, home boy. I have some."

"How much is it a quarter?"

"Two hundred and fifty dollars."

"You will have to trust me with the money for a second. Sit tight in your car."

Jerry sits in the car. The man he is dealing with hops on a ten speed bicycle and rides out of sight. Jerry lights a cigarette, slightly nervous. He returns fifteen minutes later. He reaches down in the front his pants and hands Jerry the weed. Jerry looks at it, opens the plastic re-sealable bag and smells it. He does not question the quality. It is not a full of stems or seeds, either. The man that serviced him has gone, getting out of sight quickly.

Jerry takes a minute to get situated. He takes his time getting back home, being careful not to take any chances on getting caught for speeding. Once back in town he buys a six pack of beer and some chicken and goes toward Willie's house. He is no further than four blocks from his house and he passes him. He blows and blows his horn and pulls over. Willie obliges and turns around. Willie pulls up beside him.

"What's up?"

"I was just headed your way."

"You must have some business you want me to take care of." Willie says, smiling.

"Yes"

"All right. I was going to take this girl home but I guess she will have to wait."

He leads the way, with Jerry following.

Once at the house, Willie asks, "What do we have today!"

"Nothing but an ounce."

"An ounce! Man you're not playing are you?" They are seated in the room, that Willie uses just for smoking purposes. "This is Angela, Jerry. She's cool."

"What's happening?"

"Hi"

"You don't mind if I eat, do you?"

"No, go ahead."

"You want a beer?" Jerry asks.

Offering one to Willie and Angela. Jerry eats his chicken, keeping an eye on Willie while doing so.

"Where's Charlene?"

"I don't know. I had to make the run without her."

"I know she is going to hate that when I tell her."

Angela's eyes on Willie are filled with expectancy.

"Can I talk to you for a minute?" Says Angela.

Jerry leans in her direction. He is still watching Willie. She whispers in his ear. Jerry shakes his head, meaning no. She rubs him on the leg.

"I would but I don't indulged myself."

"You don't have to. Just let me, I'll take care of you."

"I tell you what. I'll just leave you a piece when I get ready to leave. Just look me up when you want to buy some good dope."

"I will, I promise."

"I'm always downtown after six in the evening, sometimes before then."

After Willie finishes, Jerry has a total of fifty-six hundred dollars worth of cocaine, excluding the gram he has given to Willie and the crumbs he gives to Angela.

"It will probably take me a while, before I sell all of this."

"I doubt it, at the rate you are going."

"I guess I better get out of here. This being the third of the month, they ought to be cashing those checks about now."

"Wait a minute. I want to show you something. Take off your clothes, Angela."

"Aw, man, I've got to go."

"No, wait you may never get a chance to see this again." While she is pulling off her clothes, Willie fixes the pipe. He picks up a nice piece of cocaine that is close to a quarter. He gives the pipe to Angela and lights her a torch. "Don't look at the pipe Jerry. Watch between her legs." Angela is standing with her legs wide apart. After she hits the pipe, Jerry notices a milky substance running down her legs.

"I know that's not what I think it is, is it?"

"Hell yes, it's cum. Ain't that something else?"

Jerry's nature stirs in his pants, forcing him to use his brain in this situation.

"You have fun Willie. I've got to run." Willie follows him to the door laughing "Man you are something else, Willie. I'll see you later."

As Jerry gets ready to pull out of the driveway, Willie hollers "Hey," stopping him. He hands Jerry a piece of paper with his work number on it. "Give me a call." Jerry forgets his beer but declines to go back and get it. He is pressed for time. He wants some sleep but he fears he will miss out on some business. He fixes a number of bags of weed and goes back downtown, anticipating another prosperous evening.

CHAPTER 6

The new year has gotten well under way. Spring has not quite made it here. The city is already stir. Cocaine begins to appear everywhere. Along with its presence comes a flare of transgressions. The city is encountering a display of outrage that it has never endured before. Like a gold strike, there are prospectors everywhere in search of a quick solution to their string of poverty. They come in all age groups. To be frank about it, no one actually escapes its vehemence. Some are just able to negotiate it better than others. Some get poorer, some get richer.

Jerry has managed to accumulate sixty four hundred dollars. He is content with his current source of income. Despite Faye's numerous reminders to contact his former job, he does not do so. But he refuses to let Faye know. He promises himself that he will tell Faye about his selling cocaine. He fails to stay in touch with Richard and the other former co-workers. They call in an attempt to reach him especially on the weekends. He does manage to leave Richard a bag or two of weed at the house occasionally. Faye is the go between for them at this point. Jerry manages to pay his probation officer this month.

"Jerry, there is someone at the door for you."

"Who is it? What do they want? What time is it anyway?" He asks, being awaken from a hard sleep.

"About two thirty." He lets out a heavy sigh, sliding out of bed.

"What is it?"

"It's Willie. I don't mean to bother you. Charlene is out in the car. She didn't want to come to the door because of your old lady. But anyway we need to get two halves."

"I told her never at home." His face showing displeasure.

"Well we could not find any place else."

"Wait a minute." Jerry goes to get his shoes.

"What does he want?" Asks Faye, yawning.

"He thinks he lost his ring in the car the other day, when I dropped him off at his house."

"Who is he?"

"He buys a lot of weed from me. Go back to sleep. I won't be but a minute." Willie has already given him the money. Jerry completes the transaction outside in Faye's car.

"Tell Charlene I will talk to her tomorrow."

"Thanks bro for showing us some love."

"Did he find it?"

"Yeah, it was down in the seat."

"Good." She snuggles up under him and is fast asleep.

Jerry has purchased a couple of gifts for Faye. Such as a diamond ring and a diamond pendant. He attempts to pacify her since he has not been able to take her to the movies on Sundays. He is and essentially sleeps all day.

The next day while Jerry is performing his daily tasks, he runs into his most faithful customers Charlene.

"I'm glad you came by. Why did you bring Willie over my house?"

"We could not find any coke anywhere else. That's the only reason."

"I don't give a damn what the reason was. First of all I did not want him to know where I stayed at. The second reason is I hate to lie to Faye. I don't want the police over there trying to kick the fuckin door in. It's already to the point where I don't like sneaking and selling cocaine without letting her know. What in the world am I going to tell her if they did kick it in. Hell, anything could happen."

"I hear you, Jerry. You don't have to get crazy. It won't happen again. I promise I need to ask you for a favor."

"What is it?'

"Can I get a quarter until later on? I'll pay you between now and the first"

Jerry refuses but Charlene is persistent. Jerry also knows how she is so he allows her to credit one this time. Charlene is not the only one who is in need of credit. A few other people Jerry is less familiar with request credit also. They are quickly turned down.

"It is dull this time of the month. I can't afford it right now." He quickly tells them

"You not going out tonight?" Asks Faye

"No, tomorrow is the first. Everybody's begging now. I'll just wait until tomorrow."

"If that's the case, I'm going to finish fixing those beans. By the time I'm finished with you they might be ready." Faye says, sitting down beside him. "When is the last time you talked to you mom?"

"She hasn't called, has she?"

"No, but it would be nice for you to call her."

"Let me call her now before I forget." Faye dials the number for him. "Hello Mom,"

"Hello Son. How are you doing?"

"Just fine."

"I figured you must be doing well, you hadn't called."

"It's not that. I've just been busy. You know how that is. You're doing okay, aren't you?"

"Just fine, son." They talk several minutes before Jerry hangs up.

"Faye bring me a beer will you? He takes the beer and just holds it, appearing to be lost in thought.

"What are you thinking about?"

"Nothing much. Let me ask you something. What do you want the most out of life right now?"

"To be happy, like now. To be with you. And like I said once before. To be something out of life. Other than that, I would like to raise my boys and possibly have another child someday. What do you want out of life?"

"That goes two ways. I want to be financially stable. To be rich would be nice. A family to share it with."

"I can tell that money means quite bit to you. You are a lot more cheerful when you are prospering."

"Do you believe there is a right way and a wrong way to make money?"

"Well I can't really talk because of the way I make mine but I would definitely like to change it. If it's about you selling weed, I don't particularly like the idea of you selling weed or any other drugs for that matter. Mostly because you are taking a chance on going to the penitentiary."

"Well, that kills that opportunity." Says Jerry to himself. "I'll have to figure out another way to tell her.

"I bought a game the other day." Says Faye.

"What kind of game?"

"Monopoly. You should like playing that it deals with money."

"Can you stand to lose?"

"If you can stand to win." They become so involved in the game that Faye forgets about the beans, until she smells them scorching. She runs into the kitchen and transfers them into another pot. They still have that scorched taste.

"I'll tell you what we can play one more game. Whoever loses buys dinner." Says Jerry.

Jerry loses and tries to make Faye think he has lost on purpose. She will not accept it as being fact. They settle on some chicken and potatoes with jalapeno peppers.

Tomorrow's the first. Jerry anticipates a good day, possibly even better than the first of last month. He has acquire a few more steady customers. He is pretty well stocked up. He fears he will run short before the third. He makes a mental note to call Willie at work. His intuition is correct business is excellent by his standards. Three thousand dollars in cash makes him a slight bit nervous. He would like to have a gun, but he's on probation. People have begun to talk about how much money he has been making.

"You are Jerry, aren't you? Faye's old man." Asks Debbie. Jerry nods his head, confirming her suspicion.

"I've heard about you. Ann and Charlene have mentioned you a couple of times. They said you are particular about who you deal with."

"They usually buy my dope, but I know when I get it most of the time it has been tampered with you know how they do it. I do not like them to know all my business. I have one hundred and thirty dollars worth of food stamps. I was wondering what I could get for them?"

"What do you normally get for them cash wise?"

"About seventy dollars."

"I tell you what. I will give you three quarters for the hundred and thirty dollars worth of stamps."

She discretely hands him the two books of food stamps.

"Thank you. I'll be back to deal with you, if you don't mind."

"Who have you been dealing with?"

"You know, Tracy don't you? His cousin has a dope house around the corner from Tracy. I've also been to that club on Second Street."

"You mean The Markers?"

"Yes"

"I've seen it. Even though I have never been inside."

"He just started selling cocaine. He has always sold weed."

"Is his cocaine any good?"

"It's about the same as yours. Your pieces might be a little bigger."

"Okay. Thanks. Come back and see me."

Faye comes to pick Jerry up. She goes in Wilma's place first. She does not see him. "What's going on, Faye?" Says Sammy. Faye does not hear him.

"You can't speak now? You think you're hot shit since your man started selling those rocks?"

"What are you talking about? My man does not sell cocaine."

Sammy tells the guy next to him. "Do you hear that shit? She doesn't know that he sells cocaine." Faye walks off.

She goes into Ron's place. Jerry is at the table talking to Ron. Faye walks up.

"Hello."

"Hey, Faye." Ron speaks.

"Well, let me go, Jerry. I'll talk to you later."

Ron makes an attempt to blow ashes off a table, retreating behind the bar.

"Are you ready?"

"Let me find Mike first."

"I saw him in Wilma's."

"I'll be right back."

Jerry takes care of some last minute business before going home. Mike has proven to be faithful as well as dependable. By the time Jerry is finished, Faye has already made it to the car.

"You know Sammie don't you?" Ask Faye. "The one who drinks wine all the time."

"I think so. I don't pay those guys to much attention."

"He got mad because I didn't speak. He said I thought I was hot shit now that you were selling cocaine."

Jerry is in an awe for a split moment almost giving himself away.

"What the hell does he mean, selling cocaine?"

"You know how people talk when they wish they had something you've got. Don't let it get you upset. He's just talking. He's just speculating. Nothing to worry about."

"I know that if you were, you would have told me anyway. You hungry? I got some steak and potatoes in the oven."

"I sure could use something to eat. By the way Charlene told me to tell you she has to go to court in the morning. She doesn't seemed to be worried about it."

"She'll come out okay. How did things go tonight?"

"Great, I'll take time to tally up after the third."

"You sound as if you are making thousands."

"Ha, ha, you never know."

The next day Jerry calls Willie at work.

"This is Willie." He says, finally coming to the telephone after five minutes.

"Willie, this is Jerry. Can you talk?"

"So, so what's up?"

"I need to holler at you this evening after work."

"I'll be home about four."

"I'll see you then."

Meanwhile. Jerry makes his run to Little Rock and checks a few spots around town when he returns. "The Marker" is one of those stops. The club is built like a house. The parking space around it is limited. Jerry goes inside. It's clean on the inside, especially compared to downtown. The floor is a lot cleaner. It's also hot. The heater in the corner is on high. There are two women running the bar. One of them has on a noticeable amount of jewelry. They both appear to be clean and well dressed.

"Can I help you?"

"Yes, I would like to have a beer and change for a dollar."

He is given his beer and change. He goes to the pac-man video game in the corner. He sits on the stool in front of it. He plays the game reasonably well. A dollar is more than enough. Business is at a crawl, so one of the ladies comes from behind the bar and watches Jerry play the game. She asks him if he wants to play doubles. Jerry declines but offers her the seat and says he will watch her play. She strikes up a conversation.

"So what's your name?" She asks.

"Jerry. What's yours?"

"Jo Ann. You're a fine, man. You got an old lady?"

"Yeah you could say that."

"I already knew what your name was. I see you downtown all the time. You know Mike don't you?"

"Yeah, seems like you've been watching me."

"You drink Colt forty-five and you smoke More menthol cigarettes."

"What else do you know?"

"I know you sell dope."

"Don't you know it is against the law to spy on people? What else do you know about me?"

"I'll tell you if you come and pick me up after I lock up."

"Who else will be here?"

"Nobody."

"What about the man who owns this place?"

"Oh, he won't be here tonight. That's the reason he gave me the key."

"I don't know. I'm kind of leery of people who watch me."

"I can assure you I'm not the police, just an interested party is all."

"Well, I guess I better be going. Just in case I get away. What time are you going to be closing?"

"Probably about one o'clock."

Jerry is on his way out the door, he glances back. Jo Ann winks at him and licks her lips.

Jerry's real purpose for being there is to see what kind of set up they have at the club. Yet he has not seen anything that pertains to what he is looking for. He decides they could not be getting too much business selling cocaine.

He returns home. He pulls the stereo out of the rack it sits on. He has devised a much better method of hiding his property. He has gotten a tape deck that looks workable. He removes a couple of screws and there is his money and cocaine. He counts ten stacks of thousand dollars, not allowing for the three hundred in his pocket. He sets the alarm clock and takes a nap. It turns out to be a short one. He picks up Faye and rushes off to Willie's house. He wants to finish before the evening flow of traffic. Willie has a brand new truck parked in the driveway. It is parked the long way, no one else can get in the driveway. Jerry blows his horn allowing Willie time to get to the door. Jerry does not want to hang around outside waiting for him to come to the door.

"I see you got that new truck like you said."

"Yes, I just got it yesterday evening. Do you want to look inside?"

They both go and examine its features. Digitized instrument panel, AM and FM stereo, bucket seats, power window and locks.

"They have really come along way with trucks. I noticed you have it parked the long way in the driveway."

"I don't want anybody to pull up beside it. You know how jealous some people are. They are liable to scratch it for the hell of it."

"How long have you been working for this company?"

"About twelve years."

"That's a long time."

They re-enter the house and are taking care of the business at hand. While doing so Jerry hears a telephone ringing.

"Just a minute."

Willie goes into the bedroom and brings the telephone into the room where they are. Whoever it was he told them that he was busy. He will call them back.

"Remind me to give you the phone number before you go. Only one or two people have it. It's an unlisted number."

"You have really been taking care of business lately, haven't you? I've always wanted a telephone, so when I had the money I decided to go ahead and get it. If you don't do things as soon as you are able, you'll miss out. I'm glad you came by today, that way I won't have to spend any money to get high at least today anyway."

"When you do spend it spend it with me. I'll give you a better deal."

"I know yours is good. I just hate having to go down town."

"I'm going to get a place to sell out of soon."

"That's a good thing to have bro."

"I wish I had this place. It's out of the way and everything."

"At the rate you are going you will need a place. Otherwise you'll attract too much attention downtown and you'll wind up getting busted."

"Have you ever bought any from that club 'The Markers'?"

"Yeah, this broad took me there one night last week. Before then, I didn't even know that he sold any."

"How is it?"

"It's about the same as yours. You may have him beat in size that's all."

"That's what someone else said too."

Upon arriving downtown, the first person he sees is Mike.

"I thought you might not make it. You're running late, considering the day."

"I had some business to take care of. You out already?"

"Yes"

They head toward the car. Jerry counts his money. It is all there. He supplies Mike with weed and pays him for what he has sold. Mike asks him if he can he get paid in weed.

"Why is that?"

"I can stretch it a little further."

"You haven't been messing with my bags have you?"

"No, you know better than that."

"I make them the size I want for a reason."

"I understand. You have some people looking for you. I told them that I had the package, but they wanted to deal with you. I guess they'll will be back."

"Okay, thanks." As Mike starts to get out of the car, Jerry says, "Say Mike, By the way, in the future, if anybody comes to you looking for me, you haven't seen me. Always let them call the first shot. Especially if you are not sure of them, and in that case, tell them, you don't sell anything. All money in not good money. If you happen to go to jail for being real I won't have any reservations about getting you out."

"I've got you covered. Anything else I should know?"

"No, that's it. Say, before I forget, do you know a woman named Jo Ann?"

Mike starts to laugh, "Yeah she's a real freak, she's got some fire head too. Head so mother fuckin' good it'll make your toes curl. Get you some and tell me how good she is. I'll catch you later."

Mike starts to cross the street and a car approaches. He breaks into a trot to keep from getting hit.

Ann approaches the car while Jerry is in the process of organizing things. She taps on the window. Jerry motions for her to come around to the passenger side of the car. He reaches over and unlocks the door. Ann gets in. Jerry notices the odor her body gives off. He rolls the window down and spits.

"What's up?" Asks Jerry.

"I've got some matching his and her jeans. See, they're black."

"What size are they?"

"They will fit you and Faye."

"How do you know?"

"As many clothes as I have gotten for Faye, I know."

"What do you want for them?"

"They cost sixty dollars a pair."

"That makes no difference. What's your price?"

"Three quarters."

"I'll give you two big one's. That's the best I can do."

"But..."

"I can't do anything other than that right now."

"I get the edge next time, right?"

"Maybe. It depends on what it is. I haven't seen Charlene today. What did they do in court?"

"She got thirty days in jail and a fine."

"Thirty days?"

"Yes, the judge gave her credit for the week she had already been locked up. If I get a chance. I'm going to take her some cigarettes and money down there. My rides waiting on me. I've got to go. Make sure you tell Faye."

Jerry watches Ann as she makes for a car. He thinks to himself that it must be Stuart. Then he notices how much weight Ann has lost compared to the first time he remembers seeing her. She needs to take a bath and comb her hair. He unconsciously shakes his head. He puts the jeans back into the sack and puts them on the floor of the car. He lingers around taking care of business. He glances at his watch, having to look at it twice. It's one thirty.

"Damn" He says, cursing slightly to himself.

Briskly crossing the street, he jumps into the car, taking a chance on Jo Ann still being there. Five minutes later, Jo Ann is locking the outside bars on the door. Jerry turns the motor off. She stares at him really unsure of who he is until he gets completely out of the car.

"I didn't know who you were. I didn't think you were coming."

"I got so wrapped up taking care of business that I did not realize what time it was." In the mean time she unlocks the door, inviting Jerry inside.

"Do you want a beer?"

"I guess one wouldn't hurt."

She manages to get herself one also.

"So what else do you know about me?"

Jerry asks, having a seat on one of the bar stools at the bar. She sits on the one beside him.

"You're kind of shy aren't you?"

"A little bit." He says.

She slides off the bar stool and faces him the look she gives him is an indication of something going on inside her. With half a step she has found her way between his legs, her hands already tugging at his belt buckle. Not a word is spoken. Jerry finds his nature being caressed by her hot mouth. He stands up and lets his pants fall to the floor. She is already on her knees, forcing him to sit back down again. Thinking about what Mike said and the pleasure he feels, he grins. His arms straddle his side. He offers no assistance. Mike was right. The stirring inside him will not let him hold his own juices. He explodes, releasing them into her mouth. She relishes every drop. A smirk eases across her face. She gets up, hands him a few bar napkins, and proceeds to the ladies restroom.

"That's just a sample you can get the rest any time."

Jerry's needs has been satisfied. He is ready to go, straining his eyes to see what time it is in the dim light. He thinks about Faye.

Faye is asleep when Jerry makes it home.

In the morning while she is getting ready for school she does not bother to wake him until the very last moment before it's time to go.

On the way to school, Faye says, "You're mighty quiet this morning,"

"I'm dead tired."

"I need to go and make some money this evening. It's bill time again."

"We'll talk about it this evening."

Jerry goes back home and gets into the bed. He lays there a minute thinking before falling back off to sleep.

In the evening, the subject has risen again about the bills.

"You're not broke are you?" Asks Jerry

"No, I never get broke anything could happen. I thought you knew that."

"Here."

Jerry gives Faye three hundred and fifty dollars. He tells her that they will definitely sit down and talk tomorrow. Today is one of his big days. He does not have time.

"Pass me that sack on the dresser in there will you?" Faye retrieves the sack. "See if those jeans are the right size for us."

"Who did you get these from?"

"I got them from Ann. She said that they were the correct size. She also said that Charlene got thirty days in jail minus the days she already spent plus a fine."

"I guess I'll go down there to see her."

"There are some food stamps in the glove box. I had forgotten I had them in there. You can buy grocery with them instead of using up the cash."

"Are you sure that you aren't selling cocaine, with all these bargains you have been getting lately?"

"What's for dinner?" Ignoring her.

"There's some steak still in there. Do you want some? It won't take long to fix. Here read the paper and relax."

Faye goes into the kitchen. As she takes the steak out of the refrigerator, she pauses with the door open and drifts off into thought, wondering if Jerry is really selling cocaine.

"Oh, you startled me."

"What are you thinking about?"

"Nothing, I was just thinking."

"How was school today?"

"We didn't really do a whole lot today. I miss you helping me with my homework."

"It's all been for a good cause. You'll see."

"When?"

"Tomorrow for sure."

Jerry kisses Faye and gets a beer out of the box. It takes Faye's longer to cook than she anticipated.

"Fix me a couple of steak sandwiches. I need to be going."

Faye does what he wants, but she wishes he would slow down enough to eat properly.

"If you are going to go grocery shopping, you need to come on."

Faye puts her food into the oven. She is not accustomed to eating in a hurry. She has always taken her time no matter where she has to eat.

Jerry gets out of the car with his paper sack. Faye comments on the condition of the bag. He really needs to get another one. That's the excuse, she uses to come back after she has finished shopping for groceries.

Faye walks into Ron's place. The crowd is sparse. Ron is shooting pool. She does not have to ask where Jerry is. Ron points her in the right direction. Without hesitation she goes into the back room. Jerry is back there with several rocks of cocaine in his hand. Ann is back there along with two other customers. Ann is the first to see Faye enter. Jerry looks up and there she is. Her mouth is wide open.

Before he thinks he blunts out "What in the hell are you doing back here?"

Faye shakes her head from side to side, trying to get out some sort of response. Ann squeezes out past her in the process. Faye leaves the club. She sees Ann getting into a car.

"Ann!" She screams.

Ann turns around. Faye and Ann meet half way, in the parking lot. Faye is shouting at Ann.

"How come you didn't tell me that Jerry was selling cocaine?"

"It's not my business to tell you, but to tell you the truth, I wish my man had enough sense to sell some cocaine and not use it. Besides he's doing it for you. So if I were you, I would be cool." Gesturing with her hands, she says, "Stuarts waiting for me."

"Does Charlene know about it too?"

"Everybody knows about it except for you."

Jerry has come out of the back and asks Ron, "Which way did Faye go?"

"All I know is that she went running out the door. She dropped this sack."

Jerry ignores the sack and goes out the door. By the time Jerry makes it outside, Faye is gone. Jerry is filled with rage. He goes to Wilma's place and uses the telephone, knowing Faye has not made it home. He goes back to Ron's place.

"Did you see her?"

"Hell no."

"You must have made her mad." Meddles Ron.

"I'm the one who is mad. Women just won't let well enough alone. They always have to ruin things."

"Hey."

Jerry calls one of the older guys who usually hang around drinking wine or anything else they can get.

"Go to the liquor store and get us a fifth of vodka."

A smile broadens over his face. He nods to the other fellas hanging in front of the heater. They began to whisper and react among themselves to the situation. He returns promptly with the fifth covered by his jacket. Ron does not allow liquor in his place. Since he does not have liquor license. He acts as if he does not see the bottle if they make an attempt to keep it hidden. Jerry takes the fifth and tells the man to keep the change. The man acts as though he is disappointed until his partners tell him he has enough to get a drink. Jerry offers Ron a dollar for a cup of ice. Ron turns it down

"You don't intend to drink all of that, I know. It's none of my business but as much money as you carry you don't need to get loaded."

"I can handle it."

Jerry pours himself a four ounce cup of vodka and turns it up. He pours himself a second when Faye taps him on the shoulder. He turns around and the bottle slips out of his hand and burst on the concrete floor.

"Can I talk to you for a minute?"

He does not answer. He attempts to help Ron with cleaning the floor. Ron tells him not to worry about it. He signals the guys around the heater to come and help him. The man whom Jerry gave the money to, takes the bottle from one of his drinking buddies and puts it in his pocket, then assists Ron with cleaning up. Faye takes the same cup of vodka. Jerry just poured and hands it to the same guy, who stops what he is doing and hurriedly downs it.

Faye wraps her arm in Jerry's arms. It's cold outside. Jerry strikes a pose next to the car, despite the cold. Jerry is the first to speak.

"You just weren't satisfied!"

Faye silences him by putting two fingers up to his lips and pressing them softly.

"Wait before you go on." She says in a low concerned voice. "I understand what you are doing. But there is only one thing. Don't do this for me and don't do this to yourself. There is a harsh reality behind all of this and that is. You made a vow to God to stop using cocaine if you were spared. Which is worse? Selling it or using it? That's for only you to decide. If you can handle all the consequences, when it all falls apart, so can I. I can't help but stay because I'm in love with you. I really could not stand for you to be unhappy no matter which way you choose."

By now Jerry is at a loss for words. He lights a cigarette.

"Faye, you know, you're right. A man does what a man has to do to make his dreams a reality. Whether it is done consciously or not, there are things in this world that I want to feel at least once. That's one of the choices, that has been given to all of us. The compassion and love you feel for me shows. Let me show mine in anyway I see fit. That's the real reality. Can you deal with that?" She does not answer. She just nods her head.

"Let's go. It's kinda cool." She says.

"Your blood is so thin. It's spring"

When they pull up in the driveway. Jerry tells her to wait in the car, until he flicks the light twice. He wants to show her something. He goes to his hiding spot. He hides his other cocaine but takes out the money. He breaks the thousand dollars bundle apart, and scatters them all over the sofa. He then flicks the lights. Faye enters, curiously looking around to see what Jerry has to show her. When her eyes reach the couch. her astonishment shows. Pointing at the money she approaches it slowly.

"How much is it?"

"Let's count it and see."

"Jerry you should be ashamed of yourself. Look at all this money."

Jerry goes and gets a beer. He just sits and watches her count.

"You're not going to help me count?"

"I know how much is there."

She is separating the hundred dollars from the rest of the money first. Then she counts the money in stacks of one thousand dollars. Jerry sees the glow in her eyes. She continues to count.

"How long have you been selling cocaine? Forget it. I already know. There is one thing I can say honestly. I am proud of you. It makes me happy to see that you are strong enough not to use it. It takes some kind of will power to do that. That still doesn't change the fact about you selling. The only thing I ask is to keep the coke away from me. I don't know if I'm that strong."

"Sure you are. You have a special strength that a lot of women don't have."

After close to thirty minutes, Faye asks, "You said you know how much is there. How could you keep a secret like that from me?"

"It was not easy, believe me."

"There's almost fourteen thousand dollars here." He reaches into his sock.

"This should make it an even fourteen thousand dollars."

"Well, I have a small surprise myself."

Faye goes to the refrigerator and looks in the freezer. She removes a piece of aluminum foil. She throws him a wad of bills held together by a rubber band.

"This is what you call cold cash. How much is this?"

"Count and see."

"It's twenty-five hundred dollars." He finally says after several minutes. "How could you keep this from me?"

"I haven't. It's been in there whenever you needed it. I was, really, saving it just in case you ever went to jail. I could hurry and get you out before your probation officer found out."

Jerry wraps the rubber band back around it and hands it back to her.

"That's an excellent idea. Put it back where you had it."

After putting the money back up they are sitting on the couch talking.

"What are you going to do now?" Ask Faye.

"What do you mean by that? Nothing's changed. Except for the fact that I will eventually have to rent an apartment to take care of things. I do not know how much longer I can contain the situation the way it is. Especially downtown. People talk and it won't be long before the wrong set of ears hears it if they haven't already."

"You know, I was just wondering how could Charlene keep it from me all this time?"

"There's one thing you should always remember. Very few people cannot be bought for a price, especially when it comes to drugs."

"I sure hate that. Charlene didn't use to be that way. I'm going to take her some cigarettes and some personal things."

"You know, that's another one of the things I admire about you that kindness that you show, particularly when a person is in trouble. I guess that is what makes genuine friends."

Faye blushes at the complement, something she has a habit of doing when Jerry pushes the right button. Sometimes chill bumps cover her arms. Secretly, Jerry flatters himself for being able to make her glow at will.

"What was that you were saying about an apartment?"

"Don't worry, I'll let you know it's just a thought. I haven't really put a whole lot of emphasis on it yet."

"Let's go to bed." Says Faye.

Jerry picks up the money and puts it under the bed until the next morning. Then he puts it back in its original hiding spot.

Things change, Jerry does not allow Faye to work the streets anymore. Faye see to it that he eats no matter what time of day or night.

"I saw a truck the other day. I am thinking about buying it. They only want sixteen hundred dollars for it. That way, you will be able to maneuver when you get ready."

Less than two days afterwards. Jerry comes to pick up Faye in his truck. He has already put new tires and rims on it.

"How do you like my truck?"

"It's kind of old isn't it?"

"That's the idea! The motor is what counts. I can always get it painted when I get ready."

"Since tomorrow's Saturday, I'm going to jail and see Charlene."

"Tell her I said hello."

Friday night is a busy night. Jerry can tell that Charlene is not around. Willie asks if he can get some credit until pay day. He knows Jerry is not going to turn him down at this point. Jerry goes to his truck to get some more dope. He observes something he has not seen before downtown. A detective car and two squad cars arrive on the scene. They first go to Wilma's place and then to every other club. Jerry stays in his truck and observes only to find out later someone had broken into one of the stores downtown and were seen running toward this area. The police searched a good number of people and arrested one man, for possession of marijuana. Those who are outside shooting dice quickly disassembled their makeshift tables, making an effort to hide them. This of course shakes Jerry up. He mumbles to himself, warning himself to be careful and to be aware of his surrounding more than he has been. He carries as little dope on him as possible. He will make numerous trips to his truck rather than catch a charge for possession with the intent to deliver.

When Jerry comes in early Saturday morning, Faye is still up watching television. "How was your night?"

"Fair, but nothing spectacular." Says Jerry.

"I started to come down there and keep you company, but I changed my mind. I wasn't sure how you would feel about it."

"I would not have mind. If it got busy you know how to stay clear."

"I made a peach cobbler if you want some."

"That would be nice."

He rubs his hand together briskly as a sign of readiness. Faye brings him some vanilla ice cream to go along with it.

"How much drinking have you done tonight?"

"I doubt it I drank a full can of beer tonight with all the excitement going on."

"I would hate for you to get sick with all this sweetness. I know that if you eat peach cobbler and ice cream and have been drinking you'd regret it later. You mentioned excitement. What kind of excitement?"

"They just had a few guys break into the clothes store at the corner of Third and Main. They still did not catch them. It's brings unnecessary heat down there."

"You definitely need to be careful."

"I think I may slack up on the weed. Then again I may let Mike handle it if he wants to. I can hide the cocaine a lot better than I can the weed."

"That's something to think about."

"I tell you what I want you to do something for me tomorrow I mean today. You know those magnetic key holders that you stick under your fender? They are called Hide-A-Key. Go to the auto parts place on Main and get me a couple I have something in mind."

"I'm going over to Mother's at lunch break. I'll do it then. You like the pie? He shakes his head indicating yes with his mouth full.

"While you are running errands buy some balloons. Make sure they are the good kind. Not the ones that tear up easy."

"Balloons? What's the purpose of balloons?"

"They are water tight which makes them good for storage. What do you know about that club they call Markers?"

That's on Second Street. Some guy name Waters runs that club now. From what I understand he's pretty well off. He owns another business or two around town. He does not stay in Pine Bluff. He stays in one of those small towns around here somewhere."

"You know anything about him selling cocaine?"

"Not unless he just recently started."

"Tonight I want you to go down there for a while and see what kind of business he's getting.

"Any particular time?"

"Any time after dark."

"How is your money situation?"

"Low. I took care of all the bills. I see you didn't have time to do so."

"Anything special you need?"

"No, not really."

"If you do, don't hesitate to ask. Here." He gives her one hundred and thirty odd dollars. It consist of all small bills. "Don't mind the small bill do you? They get in my way."

"You got any more small bills big shot?"

"I didn't mean it like that."

"I know. Just kidding."

"Give me a cigarette." She lights one and gives it to him.

"There are some more in the refrigerator if you're out."

"What's the purpose of keeping them in the refrigerator?"

"It keeps them fresh."

"Where did you get that outfit?" Faye pulls off her housecoat. Underneath she has on a red negligee, very skimpy and made of silk and lace.

"You like it?" She asks, turning around so he can get a full view.

"Looks nice. I like what's in it better."

"You really think so? You better like what's in it I've got to firm up a little." Pinching her waist to grab the slight layer of fat. "I've been thinking about going to the spa. What do you think?" Jerry is nodding and does not hear her. She sits on his lap and places a hand on each of his cheeks and kisses him. "Am I that boring or are you just tired?"

"Just tired you know that."

"I'm going to get a membership at the spa. They have a special rate. Three months for sixty nine dollars. Come on. Let's go to bed."

She pulls him up and leads him to the bedroom, helping him undress. By the time she finishes putting his clothes up and cutting out the lights in the house, Jerry is fast asleep.

He awakens in the morning about ten. Faye is already gone. She has left a note on top of his cigarettes. "Running errands will be back soon. V-8 juice in the refrigerator. Drink one it's good for you. Love Faye."

He stumbles into the kitchen. He opens a can of V-8 juice and pours it into a glass. He adds salt and pepper before he drinks it. Then he makes his way to the shower. Faye is just walking in the door.

"You're awake, I see."

"Sorry about last night didn't mean to go to sleep on you."

"That's okay you can make up for it now if you want."

"Now? You're a mess you know it."

"Are these the magnets you were talking about?"

"These are the newer style, but they should work."

"I brought you an Air fresher to go in your truck. I don't like the ones that dangle from the mirror."

Faye takes off all of her clothes and joins him in the shower.

"Where are you going?"

"To see if you drank your vegetable juice this morning before I give you any."

"You don't have to check. I honestly forced it down."

"Well, if that's the case I really wish you did not have to go today."

"We will do something you like tomorrow."

"I know it's not quite the same as Saturday."

"Where are those jeans I got from Ann?"

"I washed them. They wear better after a washing first. If you want, I'll iron them right quick if you want to wear them."

Jerry is dressed and ready to go.

"I'll see you tonight sometime. Gotta go."

"Take care."

Jerry gets the sack from the auto parts store, separates his money and he's gone.

It is one o'clock in the afternoon.

"I'd like to see a Charlene Anderson, please."

The officer at the window checks the listing.

"Do you have any identification?" He asks.

Faye has already taken out her driver's license. She hands it to him. He enters her name into the computer and runs a check on it.

"Have a seat over there. It will be a minute or two."

Faye is directed down the hallway to a flight of stairs that goes downward and ends at a black painted door. To the left is a small window about the size of a floor tile with a small grill like plate at the bottom. Faye looks in the window. She sees the guard opening the door to the small waiting room. Charlene walks in. Faye knocks on the glass, talking through the grill.

"Hey girl!"

"Hello, Faye."

"You got some jail time I see."

"That sorry ass judge. He must have been mad because his old lady wouldn't give him any the night before or something." Faye laughs.

"He gave a couple of people some jail time. He ask me what I did for a living. I said the same thing I was in there for. I think that is what really did it."

"You should have known better than to make a remark like that."

"When I went in there that morning I was loaded."

"I'm mad at you. I really want you to know that."

"For what?"

"How come you did not tell me what Jerry was doing?"

Charlene covers her mouth showing her surprise.

"You found out!" Faye gives her a brief description of what happened that night. "I'll tell you all about it when you get out. I don't want to talk too much. I brought you some cigarettes and some personal things. I'll put you ten on the books if you want."

"I don't know what I would do with a friend like you."

"You've got three minutes left." Informs the guard.

"How much longer do you have left?"

"About sixteen days."

"Well, I better go."

"Thanks for coming to see me. I can say one thing I got plenty of company this time."

"Time is up." Advises the officer

"Can I get my cigarettes and personal hygiene products?" Charlene asks.

"As soon as visitation hours are finished and we get organized."

Faye goes down town.

"I see you made it." Says Jerry.

"How late is it? I left my watch in the house."

"It's nine o'clock." Answers Faye. "I just came from the Markers."

"What did you find out?"

"I saw Waters there tonight. He pretty well has his act together. He has two girls to handle all the business. One of those women sure has a nasty attitude, I don't know what her problem is. Jerry ignores that part of the statement. "But anyway, Waters plays pool and helps at the bar, but basically he acts like he does not know what's going on."

"What about the traffic?"

"Apparently, it's pretty good. I counted fifteen people in a short time. The lady that wears all the jewelry? She leads them to the back and they come right back out again. It's quiet as far as the police are concerned. Also, if I'm not mistaken, I think that area is out of the city's jurisdiction."

"Yeah, that falls under the Sheriff's department. I think I better get something to eat before everything closes. This town is dead after ten o'clock as far as eating establishments being open. You want to drive?"

"Sure. Any particular place you have in mind?"

"How about some catfish?"

"I think the one on the west side on Carter Street is the best. What did you do with those hide-a-keys I bought today?"

"Damn! Turn around. No that's all right. Nobody knows about them anyway. I put some of my rocks in each one and hid them under the hood of the truck."

"Suppose they fall from under there while you are out somewhere?"

"I doubt it. That magnet on the back is pretty strong. They are made for that sort of thing. What's that noise? It sounds like metal rubbing."

"I don't know. It normally would have stopped by now."

"Remind me on Monday and I will take it to Johnny's garage."

"Where is that?"

"If you keep going out second past the Markers, its across the railroad tracks."

"That's a little out of the way, don't you think?"

"A little, but bit he does good work."

The idea comes to mind buy Faye a new car.

"How much fish do you want?"

"Order a pound for me. Then whatever you want."

"Are we going to eat it here?"

"No, I have to get back this is Saturday."

"Where are you going to eat at downtown?"

"Probably in Ron's place."

"That smell ruins my appetite. It won't take us that long to eat."

"No, Faye." Jerry said, bluntly.

Faye sighs, she nibbles at her food until she is tired of it. Jerry's appetite is not affected by his surroundings. He eats his and part of hers.

"This place smells like a pig sty."

"Oink, Oink." Says Jerry mockingly. "What do you want to drink?"

"A Champale as usual." Faye says snobbishly.

Ann approaches. "Ann have you been to see Charlene?" Asks Faye.

"I'm not going down there. They will probably lock me up, as much money as I owe them in fines."

After Ann takes care of her business with Jerry. Faye calls Ann to the side.

"When are you going back to the store?"

"What do you need?"

"Some women's sports wear. Something that looks good, but not too revealing, I'm going to start going to the spa."

Ann acknowledges Faye's request but is moving toward the door at the same time.

"I'll see what I can do. When I do something I'll tell Jerry."

Faye sees Jerry is busy with someone else. She takes the opportunity to go around to Wilma's. She turns the corner and there is Oscar.

"Hello, Oscar, how are you doing?"

"Fine and you?"

"I'm making it."

"How are things at home?"

"They're just great."

"How is your mother doing now?"

"She's getting better."

"I thought we had a better understanding than that?"

"What do you––?" She knows Oscar is no fool, so she squares up. "I was going to tell, you but I didn't want to hurt your feelings. I really do like you. Did you really get back together with your wife."

"No, we went ahead and called it quits."

"I'm sorry to hear that. If you need your television you can get it."

"No, I'm not that type of person. Can I buy you a drink?"

"Not tonight, maybe some other time. You're sweet. I can't imagine why your wife would want to leave you." Faye squeezes his hand and kisses him on the jaw." See you sometime."

Faye walks into Wilma's. Wilma is there wiping the bar with one hand and emptying an ashtray with the other.

"Well, look whose here!" They laugh and lean over the half door that leads behind the bar. They hug each other. "Where have you been?" Asks Wilma. Faye tells Wilma that she is going to school and how she is trying to settle down.

"I knew it was something. Nobody hardly sees you anymore. I think some of those guys you used to date figured you left town or something. They've been looking, though, you can believe that. It's doing you good. You look so well."

"Thanks, I feel better. I just wanted to say hi. I'll see you later."

"All right then."

When Faye walks back into Ron's place, Robert is coming from the back room. Jerry is behind him. She knows what Robert is up to.

"Hello Sweetie."

"Hi Robert."

"You want to go and have some fun?"

"No, I'll pass." Faye starts to walk off, but Robert grabs her by the arm.

"Why not?"

"I don't do that any more."

"Why, you finally found some trick to settle down with or something?"

"You're being stupid as usual." She snatches her arm away.

"I'm not finished talking to you."

"I think you are." A voice says. Robert turns around.

"Ho, Ho. No wonder you turned into miss goodie two shoes all of a sudden."

"I think you need to leave, punk, before you overload your ass."

"You are lucky me and you old boyfriend are cool, otherwise it wouldn't be this easy."

"Fuck you" Says Faye.

"Come on, let's leave it alone. We don't need to attract a whole lot of attention."

"I can't stand him."

"You are gonna have fools no matter where you go."

It is past the middle of the month and things have slowed down considerably. Jerry again has more pleas for credit than normal. He wants to keep his budget balanced. He only allows so much credit and property the rest has to be cash regardless of who it is.

The following Tuesday . . .

Faye says. "Jerry, you know Mama's house got broken into Sunday. She says that it must have been part of a gang. She said she sees them out all times of the night."

"What did she have missing?"

"Her old wedding set and the boy's portable television."

"What kind of TV was it?"

"A Zenith thirteen inch color. It was in good condition, because she does not allow them to touch it."

"Skeet came to me Monday with a television. I know it was hot because of the amount of money he wanted for it. I can't be sure what kind it was."

"I wouldn't be surprised if it was the same one."

"I'll check on it when I see him. He'll be downtown sooner or later, you can believe that. What kind of outfit is that?"

"It's an exercise outfit."

"So, that's where you have been going lately."

"Jerry, I can't believe you. Lately you have become so involved with yourself that you don't see anything."

"Don't say that. It's all for you baby. It looks nice."

CHAPTER 7

Jerry is sitting across the street from Ron's place in his freshly painted truck. The sun is blocked by the darkly tinted windows. With the air conditioner blowing full blast, he is listening to his stereo, which consists of an expensive radio, graphic equalizer, disk player, cassette player and capable speakers.

The club owners are complaining about all of the activity outside. They say they are not making any money because everyone is outside drinking. Either they bring the beer or liquor with them or it is purchased from the liquor store across the street. The patrons complain about the atmosphere in the clubs, saying it was too hot inside and the owners are too cheap to put air conditioning in them.

Honk, honk, honk. A car is slowly making its way through the ample crowd gathered on the parking lot. Jerry squints his eyes. He tries to focus in on what his is actually seeing. An Oldsmobile, an early eighties model, is occupied with four males. All seem to be in their late teens and early twenties. They are waving what looks like bags of cocaine in ounce packages. They leave out of the parking lot and turn left onto Main Street, traveling at an unreasonable rate of speed They slide to a stop at every red light, hanging out of the windows. Jerry follows them all the way to the end of Main. He manages to get into the outer lane next to them. He waves a stack of bills at them and beckons for them to follow. They take the back road away from the immediate city traffic, to some apartments.

They pull into the parking lot where they get out of the car. They have guns in their belts. The presence of other people does not seem to matter to them. Jerry asks one of the two youngsters.

"Wasn't that cocaine you all were waving all over the place like that?"

"Of course. What did you think it was baby powder?" They all laugh.

"Don't you know you can't come here waving dope all over the place like you're crazy. The police here don't stand for that."

"Yo! Bro." Snatching the pistol out of his belt. It appeared to be a forty five automatic. "I got something for them if they fuck with me and my boys. We come to take over this country ass town."

Jerry is slightly nervous. He has his pistol lying in the seat.

"What do you want for the drugs? Let me check it out.?" Ask Jerry

The one who appears to be leading, tears open a bag. Jerry moistens his finger and sticks it into the white powder. He then rubs his fingers across his upper gum. They become numb instantly.

"What kind of price did you say?"

"I didn't. How many do you want to buy?"

"That depends." They huddle for a quick conference.

"Six hundred an ounce."

It is difficult for Jerry to hide his disbelief, but he manages to display an air of coolness.

"Give me six."

"Six? What do you do for a living?"

"The same thing you guys do." He reaches behind the seat and reveals a Cown Royal bag. He takes a five thousand dollar bundle and breaks it down. "Where can I reach you guys, if I want some more?"

"You will be downtown as you call it, won't you?"

"I should be."

"Well, we will keep an eye out for you."

Jerry puts the truck in gear and starts to pull off. He stops and waves at them with a chrome plated, long barrel 357 magnum. They point and wave back at him with theirs.

Faye has not made it home yet. After another phone call Willie has not either. Jerry returns home, checks each package, and hides them outside in a steel box he has buried in the ground outside the back door. He gets out his calculator and sits down to figures out his margin of profit. He would make his money back and an additional twenty five grand or so compared to the usual. Jerry laughs out loud, wondering where did those fools come from. They must have stolen that dope from some dealer up north. They were sporting some out-of-state tags.

Two days later while watching some guys at the dice table, outside under a stairwell downtown Mark walks up to Jerry and asks if he can speak with him in private. Jerry obliges by standing away from the crowd.

"You interested in buying some cocaine at a good price?"

"What kind of price are you talking about?"

"How about an ounce for nine hundred dollars? I've got some home boys in from out of town."

Jerry does not acknowledge the fact he has already brought six ounces at a cheaper price, he just politely declines.

"You're not going to find a better price anywhere."

"No, thanks."

Mark goes to the west side of town. He proposes the same proposition to Tracy. Tracy is interested. He does not make a commitment until Mark tells him that if he buys three ounces he can get them for eight hundred an ounce. Mark tells Tracy that he will be back and to stay put. Forty-five minutes later, Mark returns with two of the out-of-towners. Mark makes the transaction. He has twenty four hundred dollars. He gets four ounces. He only gives Tracy three. He stashes one in his pants. Mark starts to sell cocaine as well. He also smokes more than he sells. He struggles to makes a thousand dollars off of the ounce. His grandstanding last two weeks before he is back where he started. By then the trick he has played on Tracy has been done and attempted by several others.

There are some new dealers on the scene. Downtown is the starting point for many of them. Jerry has a monopoly, but is losing ground to the newcomers. They have quarters as big as halves. Mark manages to get a line of credit with the out-of-towers, since he has sold some for them. He has promised to pay, but he has smoked it all up. He is downtown hustling, trying to get the money on the gambling table.

The out-of-towners appear one evening. Mark tries to beg for some more time. They are tired of his games. Two of them stand with their guns ready, one behind the wheel of the car, while the fourth whips Mark unmercifully.

"If you don't come up with my money, we will be back!"

Jerry leaves the area because his name is already in the air. He does not want to be seen by the police. He tells Mike to lay low until everything is cleaned up.

Another day, while at a gas station on the west side of town, Jerry bumps into Tracy. Tracy is the first to speak.

"You're rolling, I heard."

"A little bit."

"That's hardly the case. They say you are worth fifty thousand cash easy." Blushingly, Jerry laughs him off.

"As long as you have been rolling you should be worth two or three times that much in cash alone, not counting assets. Look at the jewelry you've got on. Jerry pointing at two rings in particular. Tracy holds them so Jerry can get a better look.

Tracy says. "I've got some business to talk with you. Maybe we can hook up."

"That sounds good to me."

As they depart in their respected automobiles. Their automobiles facing the opposite direction side by side. Tracy leans out the driver's side window.

"Say Jerry, did you happen to do any business with those dudes from out of town?"

"Yes, it's a pretty good deal they've got going on."

"What are you fixing to do right now?"

"Nothing urgent."

"Follow me."

Tracy goes to his trailer. He pulls far enough into the driveway to accommodate Jerry's truck. Tracy's runners come toward him. He waves them off. They check out Jerry's truck, trying to peep in the windows.

One of them asks. "Mind if we take a look?" Jerry bobs his head.

As they enter the trailer, Jerry notices quite a few changes concerning the interior. It is in bad need of cleaning. Someone apparently is in the process of doing so. A deodorized carpet cleaner is sprinkled all over the thick plush carpet. Sheila comes from the back room. Jerry speaks. Her appearance has changed. Jerry has trouble figuring out who she is at first. Is it her hair cut or the tint in her hair? No, she has lost some weight. By this time his thoughts are interrupted when Tracy states.

"I bought several ounces from those out-of-towners."

"I bought six for thirty six hundred myself." Jerry responds.

"That's six hundred dollars an ounce. Was Mark with them?"

"No, I stopped them going down main street. Why do you ask?"

"No reason, I was just wondering was all. You wouldn't be interested in going in with me on a kilo would you?"

"I don't know. It depends on what a kilo cost."

"Roughly twenty-two thousand dollars."

" I don't know if I am ready for a step like that."

"Do you know what kind of return you would get off of a kilo? You probably would clear well over seventy thousand dollars. Plus what you put into it, you could make your quarters as big as halfs and still clear that much. Sheila, bring me and Jerry a beer."

"There's not any more."

"What in the hell do you mean there's not any more? I just bought a case last night."

"I guess the guys drank them all up."

"They were here this morning."

"Well, they must have come in here and got them."

"I thought I told you not to let anybody in the house while I was gone?"

"Well I __"

"Shut up and get one of the fuckers to go to the store and get us a case." He throws a waded up bills in her direction "Got damn bitch, can't do shit right."

"I've got to be going anyway,"

"It won't be but a minute before they get back."

"I'll get back with you on that business proposition."

As Jerry makes a right hand turn after leaving Tracy's trailer, there are some more guys standing at the corner. They flag him down.

One asks. "You need any thing?"

Jerry plays dumb. "Like what?"

"He doesn't want anything. Hell, he don't even know what we got to sell."

Jerry chuckles and drives off. He is curious to know whom they are selling for. His mind drifts back to Sheila. She has changed. There was a time when she made his nature stir just by looking at her. He has tried on several accounts to talk to her but she never took him seriously.

Jerry is sitting downtown when he is approached by an older woman.

"Is your name Jerry?"

" I beg your pardon?"

"Your name is Jerry. I'm not here to play games. You're the one who sells dope. My son was just fine until he started smoking cocaine. If I catch you selling anymore to my son. I'm going to call, the police on you!"

"Can I ask you who your son is?"

"His name is Rodney but he calls himself Skeet."

"You have my word lady,"

Jerry shuts down for the night, after the little side show is over. He does not want to press his luck. He looks for Mike but when he does not see him right away, he goes home.

When he walks in Faye is doing some aerobic exercises. There are papers scattered all over the coffee table and the couch.

"What's the matter? You can't make up your mind to do your homework or exercise can you?"

"Sure. The exercise relaxes me. Speaking of relaxing , you look tired."

"I don't know if I'm tired or if I just had a rough day."

"It must be something. You're home early. You want me to rub your back?"

"No, I just want to talk. I need your input on this. I talked to Tracy. He wants me to purchase some cocaine with him."

"How much is he talking about?"

"A kilo."

"How much is that?"

"I think it weighs, two pounds and four ounces. It costs twenty two-thousand dollars."

"I'm not trying to sound negative right away but, he should be able to buy that much by himself. Why would he offer to bring you in on this? There is one other thing. Most of the time in cases like this one somebody gets screwed. I'm afraid it will be you."

"I kind of think about it the same way you do."

"I don't know how true it is, but Charlene says that Sheila is smoking now herself. I have not seen her in a while. So I can't say for sure."

"I don't know, but, the profit margin is excellent."

Jerry and Faye sit down and calculate the possibilities.

Faye says. "If you are so determined to buy a kilo why don't you buy a kilo and then sell him half if he wants to buy it? If not, then his loss is your gain."

"With all of the pop up cocaine dealers, I could sell a little weight myself and still come out ahead."

"That's not a bad idea."

"Here, before I forget. Here's a little something before I forget." Jerry hands her a ring. "Try it on. If it does not fit then you can have it sized."

"I really like this. Where did you get this?"

"Some lady I talked to today who worked in a jewelry store in the mall."

The ring is a mixture of jade and diamonds, approximately a carat and a half each. After trying the ring on as many fingers as possible, she finally settles for one, kissing on Jerry and thanking him.

Jerry says. "I am suppose to meet her tomorrow, she said she would have some more items."

Jerry's next step is to locate the out-of-towners. After much red tape he is directed to them. They have failed to make an appearance downtown since the beating incident. They have negotiated themselves into an apartment on the east side of town. It is well secluded. Jerry recognizes their car. He is sure that this is the apartment, at which their automobile is parked. He knocks on the door several times before he detects a slight movement in the curtains. The barrel of a gun is pointed at the door. His body shivers slightly at the thought. He starts to back up when the door opens. He still does not see a face but a hand beckons him in. Jerry has his hand on his piece. By this time he approaches the door with caution.

The inside of the apartment is scarcely furnished. It is arranged on an efficiency apartment style. There is a microwave oven and baby bottles. Jerry notices that they are all sweating with the air conditioner blowing full blast. Cocaine is everywhere, on the table, on plates, in bags. There is also a big glass pipe and a sealing machine that individually packages each piece of cocaine.

"What's up? We didn't mean to scare you. We didn't know who you were"

"Do you have any more drugs left?"

"We have some ounces left. You know you got a heck of a deal."

"How's that?"

"We didn't know that you paid twelve hundred dollars for an ounce down here."

"What's the price, now?"

"Eleven hundred dollars an ounce."

"Whew. I came to talk about buying a kilo."

"If you are willing to make a trip up North, we can hook you up for eighteen thousand dollars. Maybe less."

"I'll let you know. What are you doing by putting coke in a baby bottle and then in the microwave oven?" Jerry asks.

"It cooks the same way. This is just faster. If you leave it in there too long the bottle will crack, like these over here. It's really makes no difference. You let it cool and have to break the bottle anyway.

"Who are you guys rocking it up for anyway?"

"We might as well make us some of this money. What you people sell for a quarter, we sell for ten dollars. So we are going to take all the business. Put that pipe up!" The leader says interrupting his conversation with Jerry talking to one of his colleague. "I told you not to smoke that shit around me. You act like you can't do without that shit." Directing his attention back to Jerry. "This is what a quarter looks like."

Jerry knows if they start selling pieces that big for twenty five dollars, his business is going to take a turn for the worse.

"If I did decide to make that run up North. How long would we be gone?"

"We could fly up there and rent a car coming back. It would be less than twenty four hours"

"That sounds good. I'll get with you."

Jerry tells Faye about the meeting.

"No way Jerry. You are not going up north with those fools, especially by yourself. Next thing you know you'll be in the damn river somewhere."

"Settle down I hear you. Let's go looking for an apartment. Downtown has gotten so outlandish that I almost refuse to go down there. Where's my phone book?" Faye hands him his phone book. "Say Mike what's up?

"Wait. I've got the phone Mom." He says, being careful not to let his mother hear any of their conversation.

"What are you doing? I need to talk to you"

"I'm ready. Meet me at the IGA store in fifteen minutes."

Mike gets out of the car when he sees Jerry's truck enter the lot.

"I wanted to meet you here because Mom acts kind of funny sometimes. Hello Faye." Mike says, making it a point to speak to her.

"Hi Mike."

"What's on your mind, big shot.?"

"I'm going to cut the weeds out downtown. You don't have to look like that. I've got another deal you may like even better." Mike's facial expression shows a sign of relief. "You interested in selling cocaine?"

"I was just about to wonder what was going on."

"It's getting hard to sell weed these days."

"I'm going to be downtown with you for a while until I can get set up somewhere else."

"Here's your money off the last batch of weed." Mike says, handing Jerry a small wad of bills. "I'll get with you tonight."

"Fine with me."

Over a period of the next couple of weeks Jerry comes across a suitable apartment. On numerous occasions Jerry spends the night. So does Mike, who is still holding onto his business downtown, doing his best to inform his clientele of his new location. Some are relieved, saying it is getting hot downtown. It will not be long before the police are going to start busting people. Faye makes it a point to at least have a phone put in so that she can stay in touch.

Jerry makes another connection with the lady at the jewelry store. During the noon lunch hour he drops in to see what she has for him. Without hesitation, she slides him a tray of diamond rings containing approximately sixteen rings, none of them less than a carat weight in diamonds. Hesitant at first, fearing it might be a set up, he pushes it back to her. She insists it is okay, because security is laid back during the lunch hour. He takes a chance, walking out of the store with them all. He compensates her with an ounce of cocaine.

"I thought that you were not going to sell dope on Sunday?" Faye asks, reconfirming his promise.

"I have to now. The demands has gotten so big that I would miss out."

"I don't care. You do that, and you will eventually wind up in trouble. Besides that's our day!"

"Why are you screaming?"

"You know you promised."

"Well, I'm sorry things have changed."

"They sure in the fuck have."

"All that jewelry and things you have gotten you should not be complaining."

"You can take all this jewelry and stick it." She is pulling the rings off frantically and dropping them on the floor. "You know what I want."

She goes into the bedroom and slams the door and locks it. Jerry picks up the jewelry and places it in a candy bowl on the table he gets a couple of beers out of the refrigerator and leaves.

Faye comes out of the bedroom and stares out the front window watching the truck as it disappears down the street, tears rolling down her face. This the first time she has cried in a long time. Thoughts enter her head. She dismisses them and fixes herself a drink. She sits on the couch and takes the rings out of the bowl one by one and slowly places them on her fingers. As if to compromise the situation, she turns on Jerry's stereo and puts in the tape he made for her a while back.

She falls asleep on the sofa, only to be awakened by a knock on the door. She peeps out the window. She opens the door and the first thing she sees is roses, a lot of them. Red and white. She thanks the delivery man and reads the card. "To my dearest, nothing can ever come between us. For nothing else matters. Please try and understand. I am in too deep to quit now. I love you. Jerry." She calls the apartment, Mike answers the phone.

"Hi Mike, is Jerry there?"

"No he just left here. He had to make a run."

First thing in the morning, Jerry and Mike make a trip to Little Rock. They have tried to get in contact with the out-of-towners. They of have no luck. They make a deal for several ounces. On the way back, they spot a state trooper on the side of the highway. The Trooper turns on his blue lights.

Mike says. "Aw man! You're not speeding are you?"

"No, don't worry. I Know him. He is just speaking."

Jerry waves and keeps on going.

"I didn't know what was going on. I thought he was going to stop us."

Jerry laughs and opens another beer. So does Mike. When they return to the apartment the telephone is ringing constantly.

"Hello?"

"Hey baby."

"What's going on?"

"Tracy was over at the house early this morning. He said that he needs to see you as quickly as possible. He acted nervous."

"Where are you?"

"At school."

"Okay, I'll see what he wants. Bye."

Jerry eases his truck down the street towards Tracy's house, looming cautiously after noticing numerous blue flashing lights in the proximity of Tracy's trailer. Jerry makes a block, stops, and parks his truck, deciding to walk. There is a crowd gathered. Jerry asks the nearest person what has happened.

"Some guys came down here and started shooting." One man volunteers information readily.

"Was anybody hurt?"

"I don't think so. The police won't let anybody close. They haven't called the ambulance so apparently not." Jerry leaves.

◇　　　◇　　　◇　　　◇

"You know any thing about cooking cocaine in a microwave oven?" Asks Jerry.

"No, the only way I know is the way I have been trying to teach you." Says Willie

"I've almost gotten it down." Comments Jerry "I've got some more I need done, so I can get some more practice."

"You know, they busted a couple of guys downtown the other day for possession of cocaine."

"I heard but I never found out who they were. They have been riding through kind of regular since that incident with those out of town boys."

"Where are those boys from anyway?" Ask Willie.

"Somewhere from up north Michigan or Chicago one of the two. They have practically taken over downtown. They've got a bunch of younger guys down there selling Crack."

"Crack? Is that that new shit? It tastes awful, but it gets you high though. You know, I wondered what the hell was going on. Man, this dope situation is getting out of hand."

"I tell you what. Crack is not the same as this or does not appear to be. It's kind of beige in color, not white like this, and not as good, but bigger pieces."

"That's probably why they can cook it in a microwave like that. I don't think that this real shit would stand up to something like that. What are they cutting it with?"

"I really could not say. All I know is that it is different."

Finishing up, Jerry says. "Well I guess I better go. When is the last time you saw Angela?"

"She was here the other day. You need to get you a shot of that, man. That pussy is on fire. Man she'll fuck your brains out for a hit of dope. That head ain't no fuckin' joke either."

"I can imagine, I'm gone. I'll see you later."

◇　　　◇　　　◇　　　◇

"Mike I need you to be downtown. I hate to send you, but we need the business. There will be a little something extra in it for you. If you think it's too hot, give me a call and I will put you back over here."

Faye comes over and brings Jerry something to eat and some beer.

"You don't have to worry about this apartment,"

"I know. Still it wouldn't hurt to clean up. Where's Mike? There's enough in there for him to eat also."

"I sent him downtown things have slowed some."

"Did you ever see what Tracy wanted or what happened should I say?"

"No. The place was crawling with cops, so you know I didn't hang around."

"When you get through eating, I want you to make love to me if you don't mind"

"You know I don't. You know I have been busy lately is all. You don't have to sound so pitiful."

"I didn't mean to." She says, her eyes telling a different story.

"I promise I will be home around ten tonight." Jerry apologizes with his eyes

"You sure about that?"

"Yes, I am."

Jerry goes downtown and picks up Mike.

"Things are slow. I'm going home tonight. I'll leave you enough to take you through the night."

The next day . . .

Jerry goes over to Tracy's before he goes to the apartment.

"I came by the other day. There were police everywhere." Mentions Jerry.

"Yeah, we had a minor disagreement around here. Did you come to a conclusion on buying the kilo?" Asks Jerry.

"Things have been so funny lately until I've decided to wait."

"I was hoping that you would come through. I checked with Waters. He acts so funny sometimes. He tries to play everybody for a fool. Everybody knows that he is selling cocaine by now. He even keeps it from his wife. She's one of those, uh, what do you call those religious women? What do you call them?" Thinking for a moment "Sanctified women."

"Yeah that's it."

"Why is it so important that you buy a kilo? If I knew the real reason Tracy I might be willing."

"All right, I'm going to give it to you straight. You can see things have slowed down considerably. I've got these renegade crack dealers all around the block. Man, they are taking up all the business. I guess it'll be a war around here after a while."

"I noticed that the other day." Says Jerry, agreeing with Tracy. He notices that Tracy does not have on his rings today. "How soon do you absolutely need to make the deal."

"That's what all the commotion was about the other day. I've managed to get part of the money together."

"Oh one of those deals, huh? How is two days?"

"That will have to work."

Jerry makes the necessary arrangements. He rents a car. Jerry and Mike make the trip with two of the guys from out of town. He decides not to fly so they can go well armed. They make the trip in just under thirty hours.

Jerry presents Tracy with half a kilo for eleven thousand dollars.

"I don't quite have that much."

"What do you mean? I thought you were ready to buy half a key?" Jerry asks. his voice higher than usual. "How, much do you have?"

"Six"

"I will let you have a quarter key for the six."

"I would rather have the half a kilo."

"What does that mean? You don't have the money, so there's no other way. I'm not fronting a damn thing. That's the best I can do." His voice somewhat hostile.

"I guess I will have to settle for that, then."

"You got the money now?"

"I'll have it in a minute."

"Well, when you get it, you know where to find me." Jerry says, wasting no more time.

Later . . .

Jerry asks, "Is Waters here?"

"Wait a minute. If it is important, I can call him."

"Yes, very."

The woman attending the bar dials the number for him and hands Jerry the phone. "Hello, Waters? This is Jerry."

"Jerry who?"

"That's beside the point. I have a deal for you, if you want it."

"What is it?"

"I'm not at liberty to discuss it oven the phone."

"Do you know where Johnny's garage is?"

"Sure"

"Give me an hour."

After hanging up the woman strikes up a conversation up with Jerry.

"Is your name Jerry?"

"Yeah."

"Jo Ann told me to tell you to get in touch with her. She said it was important."

"You don't have any idea what she wants?"

"I'm not sure, but I do know she mentioned something about you and her."

"Yeah, right." Jerry leaves out the door without saying another word, mumbling to himself once he's outside "Fuck that freak."

A big Lincoln Town Car pulls up. Jerry is already talking to Johnny. Johnny tells him who Waters is. They shake hands "I know you." Advises Waters. "I've seen you several times before. Besides, I've heard a lot about you."

"Oh yeah, how's that.?"

"I understand you been dealing with one of my colleagues."

"Who?"

"A female. One of my gals she told me about it. You want me to tell you what she said?" He laughs, easing the tension in the air. "Ain't much go on there I don't know about." He says, cackling again. Jerry can tell he is a jokester by his demeanor.

"Well I might as well get straight to the point." Says Jerry, his tone abruptly grim.

"You interested in buying a quarter ki?"

"What's the price?"

"Six G's."

"When can I look at it?"

"Now if you want."

"You mean you're carrying that kind of merchandise around with you.? Man I don't know. You ain't the fed's are you?" Chuckling.

"Be serious."

"Hell, I am." Waters says, sniggling, clapping his hands together once.

Johnny allows them pull inside the garage, letting the large bay doors down. Jerry allows Waters to pick whichever quarter he wants. Waters returns to the car. Unsure, Jerry has his weapon within reach. Waters is holding a brief case. Tossing it onto the trunk of the car, Waters pops the two locks concurrently. The briefcase is almost full of money.

"Looks likes you been taking care of business."

"I try." He counts Jerry off a stack of bills, and sets them in thousand dollar piles. Jerry does not touch them until he has finished counting Waters sees that Jerry is satisfied with the count. "I'm out of here. Maybe we can do business again sometime." Waters says, wasting no time, signaling Johnny to open the doors. The car disappears in the dust from the gravel road.

Jerry stops at a car lot on the way home to inquire about a car he is thinking about getting for Faye. The dealer is busy discussing options with a customer standing in front of the car he is interested in. Jerry tries to be discrete in getting his attention because he does not want the car sold out from under him.

"Sir, excuse me sir."

"Just a minute, son. I'll be right with you, I'm trying to sell a car here." Jerry hastily steps to his truck, gathering his money bag. Bag in hand, easing the stack of bills into view. Jerry says again. "Excuse me sir."

"Excuse me, good people. This young man has a problem. Don't you___ Lord will you look, here look here. Yawl excuse me. Look at the money in that man's hand. Yawl excuse me. This man wants to buy a car."

The salesman leaves the couple standing there, escorting Jerry inside. Jerry returns with the keys to the Cadillac and a receipt for the money. "Hey yawl fells. Come here make sure this car is clean and everything for this young man. This man came to spend some money. Hell, them other folks wasn't gonna buy nothin' anyhow. You just ride until you get tired son. Keep it till next week. You ain't got be in no hurry, the paper work will be here whenever you come back." Jerry parks his truck outside the gates of the car lot and drives the car he just purchased.

Over at Willie's . . .

Willie asks. "Where did you get this at?"

"I went up north and bought it." Jerry brags.

"You must have gotten it from those out of town boys." Willie says. Still shaking the test tube over the flame. "Why is it taking so long to cook? I still don't think it is as good as what you have had."

"Get your pipe and try it." Jerry suggests. Willie tries it. "Well, what do you think?"

"It's different. It has a different taste, that is for sure. See the residue in the bowl? It is not the same color as your other coke was."

"I'm talking about the high." Jerry asks.

"It gets you high, but I don't feel numb like I usually do."

"Do you think it will sell?"

"It should. It is the same thing as what everybody else is selling."

"I'm selling weight now, if anybody wants it."

"What kind?" Willie asks.

"Anything from a gram to an eight ball to an ounce."

"I heard that. You must have pick up a hell of a package."

"I did all right."

"I've got some plastic scales if you don't have any."

"I bought a set of triple beams from Tracy."

"Let's finish up. I need to go and relieve Mike."

Walking into the house, he finds that Faye is busy rearranging furniture.

"You must not have anything to do."

"Why do you say that?"

"Because you're redoing the furniture and all."

"Women do these kind of things, darling. What do you think?"

"It looks nice. Come here. I want to see how nice you look in your new car."

"Jerry, I know you must be joking." Jerry holds up the keys.

Faye gasps loudly when she sees the car.

"Is this mine for real?"

"Have you ever known me to play? Come on. Let's take it around the block."

"This car rides so good. Wait until I show Mama."

"I tell you what, you take me back to the car lot so I can get my truck. I am supposed to meet Mike."

"I thought you were going to ride around with me."

"I've got to pay for this, you know. Money don't grow on trees."

Suddenly most of the exultation is gone. She dares not let him know how she feels at the moment.

Three weeks later . . .

Jerry pulls up as a car is leaving the apartment. After Jerry makes it inside the drug house.

He asks. "Wasn't that Sheila?"

"Yes."

"What did she want?"

"She wanted a quarter ounce. When I told her that she had to buy two eight balls she said she would wait and talk to you. I'm surprised she did not see you on the way out. Charlene came by with these clothes. She left them and said that she would get with you on them later."

"Anybody else?"

"One more thing. What about food stamps?"

"They get half of the dollar value. If they have a hundred dollars worth, they get fifty dollars worth of dope. As far as merchandise, I don't need any. I've got shit stored everywhere. I need to sell some of it. I'm going home. If any thing arises, call me. Give this to Charlene when she comes back. You need anything?"

"No, I'm fine."

"I'm home Faye." She does not answer. "I'm home!" Still no answer. He looks all through the house. He thinks that maybe she could have left with someone else. Her cars are in the driveway. He turns on the stereo and turns it back off. He turns on the television. He hears the back door opening. He pulls his pistol from his belt, easing it back once he sees who it is. Faye staggers in with a bottle and a glass in her hand. "Faye you're drunk." Jumping to help her negotiate her steps. Tears are streaming down her face. "What's the matter?"

"Nothing."

"Why are you crying?"

"I'm not."

"It sure looks like it to me."

"Come on. Let's sit down. Are you unhappy or what? Answer me truthfully."

"If you must know, yes."

"How can you be? You have everything that you could want."

"Can't you get it through your head that just because I have material things, I don't have to be happy. I felt better when we were struggling. At least I had you."

"You still do. You're going to school and to the spa. I thought you were happy. You have to make a sacrifice somewhere. I wish I was at home many a night, but I know what has to be done. Besides, I'm going to let it go after a while anyway."

"Don't lie to yourself. You will never quit until you are made to quit. One way or the other. I really hated to say that. I will do anything for you, even if it means I have to die." Jerry makes an attempt to quiet her. "I'm just being honest. There is no such thing as taking it all. You take and never give anything in return. It won't last."

"I'll quit, you'll see." Jerry is thinking about what his mother once told him. A drunk person never lies. Unless the person is an alcoholic. "Let's take a shower baby."

"What are these?"

"Just some clothes I got from Charlene. Look at them later. Come on."

As they lay in bed.

Jerry promises. "At the end of the month, we are going to go somewhere—just me and you.".

"Shhh" Faye puts two fingers on his lips. "Just wait until the times comes."

Jerry feeling some remorse about the situation. "I mean it. At least for a couple of days."

"I know you do."

The phone rings.

"Jerry, this is Mike. Skeet is here."

"Let me talk to him."

"Skeet, this is Jerry. First I want to ask you about a television and wedding ring set. Do you know anything about those items."

"What kind of ring?"

"It's an old wedding set. I was wondering, they belong to a friend of mine. Their house was broken into a while back. Anyway you get out of my dope house. Your mother threatened to call the police on me and I will fuck you up and her too if she does. So don't come back. Buy your shit some fuckin' where else. Let me talk to Mike. Mike, get him out of there. He is not allowed around there period. So don't sell him anything ever, no where." Jerry growls, slamming the phone down.

Jerry goes to the ice box and gets a beer. When he returns, Faye is asleep. He kisses her on her forehead. Little does he know it has been a while since she has slept peacefully. He falls asleep thinking about what she said.

"What time is it?" Jerry asks, waking up.

"Eleven-thirty" Faye tells him

"Let me call Mike. Forget it. I'll go over there. I've been thinking about someone else to work with Mike."

"Why is that?"

"I don't feel comfortable leaving him there by himself, the way people have been gunning to rob people. You look pretty this morning." He says, stroking her softly. "Do you feel better?"

"Sure."

"That's good. Next time you decide to feel sorry about things, call me before you get drunk."

"I will. I'm sorry baby."

"No. I'm sorry. I should pay more attention."

"I still have a slight headache. I took some aspirin. It should go away. I looked at the clothes you got from Charlene. They are nice."

"I better go check on Mike. There are some clothes laid out over there for you to wear."

"Thanks."

"I'm gone. I can still get in on the second half of the day at school. I wasn't going today, but anyway."

"Is school going to last throughout the summer?"

"It depends on if I want to go on or not. I think I will. See you later."

Jerry walks in to the apartment unannounced. Mike jumps up.

"Who is that?" Jerry asks. "Just this chic I know."

"Wake her up. I don't want anybody in here spending any amount of time, especially spending the night. If you need a break let me know. How was business last night?"

"Pretty good. Not bad for this time of the month. They said the police were downtown again last night. That may account for some of it. I almost forgot. Waters called. I would have called you, but he said it was not urgent. He said he would be at the club after eleven."

"Have you eaten yet?"

"No."

"Call a cab and go get yourself something to eat." Jerry hands him forty dollars. "Take her with you."

Mike has been gone about twenty minutes when Sheila comes in and asks Jerry if he will hold her rings for an eight ball.

"Does Tracy know about this?"

"No, and I would prefer if he didn't."

"I'll tell you what. I'll give you a sixteenth. You just make sure you pay me back. Keep the ring on your finger. Say, let me asks you something, when we gonna do some fuckin'?"

"Whenever you get ready." Jerry eases over and locks the door.

"Let me see what kind of head you got?" Jerry unzips his pants.

"I'll give you a sample right quick, I've got to go."

Five minutes later . . .

"Thank you, Jerry. I owe you one."

Jerry calls the club about eleven forty five.

"Let me talk to Waters."

"This is he."

"This is Jerry. I understand you called yesterday."

"You got time to come over?"

"Sure."

"I'll be there in about twenty-five minutes."

When Jerry gets there no one is at the club but Waters.

"What's going on?"

"Not too much. You want a beer? Let me find you a cold one. I just finished re-packing this box."

"Where are your girls?"

"I fired both of them bitches."

"For what?"

"They came up three thousand dollars short last night and sixteen hundred a few nights ago."

"How did they manage that?"

"Hell, I don't know."

"They say they got beat. I think Louise is the one behind it all. Jo Ann is just going along with it. I'm not really prepared to let anyone else take over."

"They are not smoking, are they?"

"They say they're not. Hell you never know though. Anyway, that is not what I called you over here for. You heard anything about some new dudes? They are suppose to have been sent down from up north they are working with a guy who lives here."

"I don't know the guy they are working with, but I met some fells a while back. They seem to be cool. Just wild and crazy as hell."

"I understand they are handling some pretty big weights."

"I know they mentioned they might send somebody else down in place of them. I didn't know they had. They may be the same ones you already met."

"I don't think so. I don't know what's going on with those fellas."

"Me either. That dope you sold me is not the same as what I've been getting."

"I was told that myself."

"You haven't tried it?"

"No, I don't smoke. Do you?"

"Uh, no."

"I checked around. It's the same thing almost everybody else has. I would like to get another quarter or a half a kilo, if you can stand it."

"I haven't got it right at the moment. Just some loose ounces. If you need something to hold you over until I get some, I'll give you an ounce or two and collect later."

"You shoot pool?"

"You any good?"

"So-so."

"Shoot you a game for a hundred."

"Bet."

Jerry wins the flip. Waters has to rack the balls. Jerry runs three balls and misses the next shot. Waters misses after his second shot. Two shots later, Jerry wins the game.

"I tell you what. I'll give you a chance to get even. How about two out of three?"

"Bet."

Waters barely wins the second. Jerry wins the third.

"I think I'll buy my girl lunch tomorrow with this." He chuckles and turns up his beer. "You want those ounces now?"

"Meet me at Johnny's. I'll lock the door and I'll be right behind you."

Johnny has a lot of business going on from the looks of it. There is more going on than what meets the eye. A few people Jerry recognizes. He puts two and two together. This must be where Waters peddles some of his dope. Further observation indicates that one of Johnny mechanics actually does the selling. Waters arrives. Jerry hands him the package and tells him he will let him know tomorrow evening if he can get a hold of another package.

Jerry goes by Tracy's. No one is there. That seems odd. The dealers on the other corners are going strong. Jerry then goes to the apartment where he last dealt with the men from up north. They are gone. Further, investigation leads him to a larger set of apartments, where he deals with someone all together different.

"What happen to the other guys?"

"They got called back. They were fucking up too much money. What do you need?"

"I'm interested in a kilo."

"I'll have to make a call or two first. Here's my beeper number. Call me in a couple of hours."

"How does it work?" He explains to Jerry the process of using the beeper. That's pretty neat. I may get me one of those."

Jerry goes home and eats dinner with Faye. He tells her of the day's events. He calls the out-of-towers and waits for their call. They finally return it.

"I can have it for you by tomorrow evening." The out-of-tower says, "Twenty grand"

"No way. Eighteen."

"Nineteen is the best we can do."

"That will work." Jerry calls Waters and tells him twelve grand for a half a kilo. "Tomorrow evening."

"Great, I'll be ready." Says Waters.

"Hello" Faye answers the telephone.

"Hi, Faye."

"Who is this?"

"Charlene."

"You sound funny. I didn't not recognize your voice. What's up?"

"I need you to do me a favor."

"It's depends."

"I'm in jail again. Do you think you can help me?"

"How much is it?"

"Three hundred and sixty dollars."

"What did you do this time?"

"The same thing, just a little more happened."

"Let me talk to Jerry first. I'll let you know. Bye."

"What's the matter now?" Jerry asks.

"Charlene is in jail again."

"I guess you are going to get her out?"

"Yes, if you let me have the money."

"You know how she did you the last time."

"As much dope as she buys from you, you ought to rush down to the jail and bail her out."

"Don't get started with that all over again. Do what you want."

CHAPTER 8

The weather is not the only thing hot these days. So are the police. There are enough crack dealers and runners to take care of the present population. The more elite crack dealers have beepers. One or two even have telephones in their cars. People line up at the crack houses like they were in the process of buying tickets to a sold out concert.

The police are everywhere downtown. All exits to the parking lots are block. The police want information and are determined to get it. They had secretly set up on top of a vacant three story building and film the activities going on outside the downtown clubs. They arrest any and everybody suspected of selling drugs of any kind. They use the film and snitches to entrap unsuspecting drug dealers. Arresting the people who are outside gambling. Those who were just looking go to jail, also. They might not stay but they went. The information the cops got tonight is just the beginning of what is to come.

"You really need to give me my money. There are people that I owe and they don't play when it comes to their money." Threatens Scarver.

"You give me a day or so and I will have it." Says Thomas.

The guys from up north are determined to monopolize all of the crack business that they can staking any and everybody interested in selling. When they have trouble collecting, they do it the rough way.

Three cars enter the large, government-subsidized apartment complex, located on the east side of town. They stop in front of an apartment. Several young men get out of the cars while Scarver and another watch. The door is kicked in. There is screaming, breaking of glass, and the slamming of furniture. Kids are pushed aside. Thomas is beaten and cut in several places that require stitches. This action by outsiders causes an outrage within the neighborhood. Action is taken to prevent it from happening again.

Later . . .

Jerry tells Scarver that they needed to stop all of the violence.

"Besides, you are from here you should know better." Jerry chastises him.

"If a son-of-a-bitch made money like you do, then we wouldn't have to kick his ass to get paid."

"All I can say is suit yourself."

"How is business?"

"It's doing great right now."

"Why don't you let us in with you. We could give you some nice deals on some cocaine. On top of that you would have the protection you need."

"Why would I want to do that? I'm going good by myself."

"The higher-ups were just talking about giving you dope for a piece of the action."

"We might as well stop discussing that issue. It's dead. No way. You really need to lay low. The police are looking for you and your buddies."

"It really doesn't matter. I'll be out of jail faster than they can blink."

"What is that little gadget you got there?"

"It seals each piece of crack individually. It's nothing more than a seal-a-meal for food. It keeps people from fucking with the pieces."

"See how much each one of these pieces weighs?" Inquires Jerry looking at the scales closely.

"These scales are slightly off." Indicates Scarver.

"I know I've got two sets anyway. Let me ask you something about this dope. "What is the deal on it?"

"What do you mean?"

"It's not the same dope you had at first."

"I don't know exactly how they prepare it. All I know is they do something to it before I get it. I know that it can not be used in a needle like regular cocaine. If one of the runners get sprung on this stuff, they automatically call him back up north for re-schooling."

"Those guys, have got their program together."

"I hate to cut the conversation short but I've got to run."

"You have my beeper number, right?"

"I got it."

At the house . . .

Faye says to Charlene. "What did they do today in court?"

"They appointed me a public defender. I go back to court in two weeks." Says Charlene. "He said if I pleaded guilty, he would get me five years probation."

"I'll tell you what you need to take heed." Warns Faye. "Your luck is going to run out sooner or later. You know they are catching people left and right out at the mall. They have a lot more security than they use to."

"I'm not the only one. They caught Ann a couple of weeks ago. She went to crying, talking about how she was pregnant."

"Pregnant? Again?"

"Yeah, girl. She won't go to the clinic and get her pills, but she can go get some crack all day and night long. I know I don't have any room to talk, but that girl's thighs are not as big as your neck."

"Aw, girl, she's not that small."

"That's what you think. The baby is due in about three or four months and you can hardly tell that she's pregnant."

"Whatever happened to Debbie?"

"Her folks sent her to a rehab center. You know her folks have a little money. She went to stealing from them, so they hurried up and got her away from here. She used to work out at the arsenal before she started smoking. There is no way I would have lost that good job. How are you and Jerry getting along?"

"Sometimes I don't know. He treats me good and all that, but he's not at home like he used to be. He's always at that damn dope house."

"Why don't you go over there?"

"I do every, now and then to clean up. He really doesn't want me around when he's trying to take care of business. I have over five-thousand dollars in the bank and some more over Mothers."

"Does she knows what Jerry does?"

"Girl, no. There is no way that I'm going to tell her, either. I went to church with her and the boys last Sunday."

"All I can say is, if I were you, I would not complain too much. It's a lot of women out there who wish they were in your place."

"When is the last time you went downtown?"

"I hardly go down there. The police are down there almost every night. They took Wilma's husband to jail the other night, just because, somebody walked out with a can of beer in their hand . Now he watches everybody who goes in and out. Let me get another drink. I might as well get drunk. I don't have any money to buy dope."

"Why don't we get together and go out like we used to?"

"We ought to go out this Friday."

"You hungry?"

"Some food wouldn't hurt."

"Let's go to that yogurt place over by Taco Bell."

"Yogurt?"

"Yes, it good. It tastes like ice-cream."

At the apartment . . .

Bates asks. "Say Mike is Jerry here?"

"What do you need?"

"Ask him if he will hold a stereo until Friday? I get paid them."

"Say Jerry, Bates wants to know if you will hold a stereo until Friday?"

"Stereo?" Jerry exits the bedroom zipping his pants. "What kind of stereo?"

"I have it out in the car. Is it yours?"

"Yes."

"And you don't know what kind it is? Let me see it" Jerry goes out to the car and looks at the stereo. There is another man in the car as well. He never turns around. "Bring it in and let me see what it sounds like. What do you want on it?"

"A sixteenth."

"I'll tell you what. I'll give you a gram. You make sure you come back and get it." The two guys look at each other and haunch their shoulders.

"You want it or what?"

"I guess so."

"Put the stereo in the back room, Mike. Tell Angela to get her ass out of here unless you want to get you a shot."

Mike laughs "You got the front. It wont take long if that pussy's any good." He says, laughing again.

"Don't forget to put the stereo in the back room. I don't want anybody to come in and see it and say it is theirs. We've got enough shit in here already."

Jerry has managed to accumulate quite a bit of merchandise being traded for crack.

"If Paul does not come back and get that television by the week-end, you can have it. I don't need another one."

"You know, Shirley brought a rabbit coat by here the other day and wanted me to hold it for a half."

"She must be crazy, as hot as this weather it is." Jerry and Mike both laugh.

"You know this dope is driving people crazy. You would be surprised what they come through here with. You know Pat?" Mike asks.

"I can't place her right off the bat." Jerry is trying his best to remember.

"The short fine one. At least she use to be fine. Well anyway, I remember when she used to act all stuck up and thought she was too good to even speak."

"What did she do?"

"She came in here and offered to give me some head for a quarter. I started to do it just because of the way she used to act. I told her no and she almost cried. I had to run her out of here."

"You have to watch the way you do some of those women. Some of them will get mad and snitch on us."

"I really feel sorry for some of those broads sometimes, though. Well let me take care of the business at hand." Mike says, unzipping his pants. "They know they can beg."

Ten minutes later . . .

"Tracy has not called today has he?" Jerry asks Mike.

"No."

"I wonder if he has my money yet? If he doesn't, he should. I'll just wait until tomorrow. I wish you had a car so you could go and get us something to eat. Why don't you buy yourself a car?"

"I am shortly. My mother was way behind on her mortgage and bills. So I have been helping her out a lot. She want's to know where I am getting my money from. I told her that I work. That's the reason I put on those dirty clothes sometimes when you take me by the house."

"I was wondering what you were doing with your money."

Jerry also knows that Mike is a womanizer and will spend his money on any woman he likes.

Elsewhere in the city . . .

Is the sound of a siren blasting. Paramedics rush frantically to get vital signs. A young man suffers from respiratory failure caused by smoking crack. The friends he was getting high with abandon him from the fear of being harassed by the police. The ambulance rushes away to the hospital.

"What do you mean, you don't have any money? I gave you an ounce and you can't even come up with a lousy thousand dollars?" While Jerry is chastising Tracy, Sheila stands there hoping that he does not say anything to him about the money she owes. "It's none of my business, but since you owe me, it has become my business. I heard you are smoking. Have you gotten so strung out that you can't make any money?"

"Not really. I owe so much that's it's hard for me to get out of debt." Tracy says, looking for sympathy.

"I'm not going to let you use me in order to pay somebody else. What are you doing now as far as business if you are out of dope?"

"I'll shut down until I can get some more money together."

"I'll tell you what. I've got a new man I would like to try out. You let me use your establishment to work out of." Jerry tells him. "We can work out a deal in the meantime. I'll get with you first thing in the morning."

Sometime later . . .

"What's up Jerry?"

"I see that you got your girls back in the club again." Teasing Waters

"Yeah I had to. Business went into a slump. I don't have the time to be at the club in the daytime."

"Do they still handle your crack for you?"

"Hell no! You must think I'm crazy." They laugh. "I'm letting one of Johnny's boys handle that. I just opened another place on the east side."

"Did you ever find out what happened to your money?"

"You know, you never get it straight of things, but I heard they were somewhere smoking and got so high, they got beat for the rest. I heard that you have taken over Tracy's place." Laughing, Waters says. "Boy you're a motherfucker."

"Not really."

"Naw, you're hell all right. I see you bought your gal a Caddie. How come you didn't buy her a Lincoln.?'

"A Lincoln? Man, I wouldn't drive a Lincoln if they gave me one."

"I wouldn't buy a Cadillac, no sir. You buy the best or walk the rest. That's the way I feel about it."

"As far as Tracy's place, the way it's going I'm going to bail out. That place is more trouble than it's worth. The police have started riding real heavy on that side of town."

"You know it's not wise to stay in one place too long. After a while, somebody's going to snitch. As soon as one of those crackheads get into trouble, they tell everything they know and half they don't know in order to get out of jail. Half the time the charges they are in jail for are bunk in the first place. I got some information from a pretty reliable source. The police are plotting to bust a few. I will let you know in a day or two what's really going on."

"You do that for sure. Your beeper number is still the same isn't it?"

"Yeah. Why don't you get a beeper?"

"I don't want to be able to be located like that. Besides, so many people have them cops automatically notice them. They know you are selling dope or think so anyway. You know Mark Green? He owns a clothes store on the north side. I saw him with a beeper the other day. Otherwise I would have never known that he was in the business. It's bad to be stereotyped but right now that's the way it is."

"He was in the business way before you or me."

Over at Tracy's place . . .

Jerry says, "Ralph I want you to work with Mike. It's too hot on this side of town. From now on I don't want the door opened unless you look out the peep hole on the window. If they look suspicious don't answer. I don't want you and Mike laying around watching television. I want you to keep a look out at all times."

"Do you have anything planned for this afternoon?" Ask, Faye when Jerry gets home.

"Nothing in particular."

"Can I ride with you?"

"Sure. I could use some real company for a change."

They go to Water's place, the crowd is light this time of evening. Louise is the only one attending the bar. She speaks when Jerry walks up to the bar. He orders two drinks.

"Where is Waters?"

"He should be here any minute. I just talked to him on the phone." Jerry returns to the booth where Faye is sitting.

"Don't look right now. There's a guy sitting at the bar drinking in a red shirt and some slacks. He's the police."

"How do you know?"

"I just know." Talking in a loud whisper. When Jerry looks up Waters is there. Apparently he came in through the back door. After surveying the crowd, he walks in Jerry's direction.

"Hey my man, what's up?" He sits down in the booth across from them.

"Who is this?"

"Faye this is Waters, Waters, this is Faye."

"You've been keeping her hid haven't you?"

"Not really."

"I wouldn't blame you if you had. She's pretty." Faye returns the complement with a smile.

"That guy over there. Who is he?"

"He's cool."

"Isn't he a cop?"

"Boy you can smell them can't you? Gotta nose like a hound, don't you. Yes he's the one I told you about. I give him a little coke and he's good to go. You want to meet him?"

"No way. If he sings to you, he will sing to them."

"He will let you know when things get warm in your direction."

"I would prefer if he was not able to associate my name with my face."

"How do you think I am able to move so rapidly?"

"What does he charge."

"I usually give him a forth of an ounce a month, Hell, he's just going to smoke it up."

"Will you pay him for me and I will reimburse you? He can keep me informed through you. Let's go baby."

"You leaving? I thought maybe you would allow me a chance to get even on my money."

"Sure, some other time."

Once they are in the truck . . .

Faye says. "Settle down baby. You've been so jumpy lately."

"I'm going over to Scarver's. You are going to have to sit in the truck. I won't be but a minute. Jerry knocks on the door in code and waits for an answer. Three minutes later the door opens.

"What's up?"

"Let me have a word with you."

"Can you come back later?"

"Hell, he doesn't have to come back! Come on in!"

Jerry looks around Scarver to see who is talking.

"You Jerry?"

Jerry notices the gun lying in the man's lap, and another man standing to his left. Jerry pays closer attention to the man standing up, for his appearance merits focus. He is very muscular, thick hair, heavy eyebrows almost joining together, eyes dark and slanted. His look is intense and intimidating. The gun in his hand is a large caliber automatic.

"You know we were just talking about you."

"Oh yeah? What about?"

"When are you going to pay the money you owe me and my man here?"

"What did he say?" Jerry asks.

The man standing up takes a step forward. Jerry looks at Scarver and points at him in a threating gesture.

"What the hell is he talking about?"

The man stands up.

"My man Scarver says that you owe him close to two grand. As of now he's another three grand short. To be honest, I'm sick and tired of this shit. If you guys can't pay up, then you don't need to get any dope from here. So far I'm over twelve grand short. Just this week alone." His voice deep and thick.

"Now that you are finished, I think I better leave. It seems that you got me fucked up with someone else. I don't have to borrow any money from you or anyone else. You must not know who I am."

"Is this the man you are talking about?"

Scarver shakes his head indicating no. Jerry slams the door on his way out. He hears Scarver and the man in a shouting match.

"What's the matter with you?" Faye asks as he gets back in the automobile.

Jerry contemplates on going back in there and confronting Scarver with his pistol.

"Nothing. Lets go some place quiet and have a drink.

They go to a club on the north side of town. When he enters, the owner of the club is at the door. He notices the amount of jewelry Jerry and Faye have on.

"That's some nice jewelry you've got on. You wouldn't be interested in selling some of it, would you?"

"No, sure wouldn't."

"If you ever decide to sell any of it, I would be interested."

The owner lets them in free of charge. He accompanies them to the table, telling the waitress to give them a run of drinks on the house. Faye and Jerry dance several times. The lights on the dance floor reflect off on their jewelry. Several people comment and want to know if it is real. Jerry tells Faye he is not thrilled about all the attention right now.

After leaving the club, Jerry and Faye go by the apartment. Jerry collects the money that has been made. He makes sure to leave have enough crack, before retreating to the house.

"I don't mean to sing the same old song. But you need to take a break. Shut down for a week. You can afford it." Faye says.

"I know you only say what you think is best. I need to, I really do. I just can't right now."

"How much have you saved up so far?"

"At last count, eighty-five thousand. Pass me the phone"

"Yes, this is Jerry. You get your business straight?"

"Yeah, I'm sorry you got caught in the middle. I can handle those fellas. They get a little carried away sometimes."

"It didn't look like you could handle them to me. You need to keep me out of your got damn business. I don't like being set up like that a motherfucker could wind up dead like you're going to be if you don't get those fools their money. I hope we have that understood. Another thing. You need to clean up that mess you've got laying all over the place. If the police come in, you won't have a leg to stand on."

Scarver has remnants of crack everywhere, in broken bottles, broken plates, scales, and sandwiches bags. Not counting all the crack he has hidden around the place.

"What makes you so cautious all of a sudden?"

"I'm just playing a hunch. I got some bad vibes."

"I appreciate your concern. Later."

"Do me a favor, will you baby?" Jerry asks when he's off the phone.

"Sure."

"Fix me a drink. Any orange juice in the box? I think so. Good. Gin and orange juice."

"What's the occasion? You haven't drank hard liquor in a while."

"Just trying to unwind so I can get some rest."

The phone rings. Charlene is back in jail again. She asks Faye to please come get her before her probation officer finds out and puts a hold on her. Faye tells her she will be down as soon as she can.

"Who was that?"

"That was Mama. She wants me to come to the house. Something about one of the boys."

"If I am asleep when you get back, wake me up."

It is September . . .

The police have secretly been staking out different businesses, houses, apartments and other places suspected of selling crack. They have set up temporary pawn shops to retrieve some of the stolen goods taken in a multitude of unsolved crimes involving property.

"Hello, this is Waters. Is Jerry there?"

"Hold on a minute."

Mike hands Jerry the telephone.

"You busy?"

"In a way."

"It's important. Can you can meet me at the club?"

"Be there in a few." Before Jerry can put the phone on the hook, someone knocks at the door. "I'll get the door." Jerry says, getting up from the couch.

"Hey." Angela speaks on her way in.

"Get that bitch out of here. I'm not selling her shit." Says Mike.

"What do you mean you not selling her nothing?" Ask Jerry.

"Man that whore burnt me." Mike says.

"Wait. I'll serve her and I'll talk to you about it later." Angela's nervousness is obvious. She leaves.

"When did she burn you?" Jerry asks. "Hell ain't nothing wrong with me."

"Man, I fucked that tramp about a week ago up in here one night. Two days later, I was in trouble like a mother fucker, dick on fire like a son-of-bitch."

"How come you didn't use a rubber like you were supposed to?"

"I did. I used one of yours. It busted and I kept on strokin'. The shit got good I guess."

"I bet you will wear your hard hat the next time." Jerry says, teasing. "Mike, hold everything down. If Faye calls tell her I will be back shortly."

Jerry drives to Water's place.

"I've got some information that you might be interested in." Says Waters. "The police have been watching this place off and on." Jerry shifts on the bar stool. "It's cool right now though. It's my understanding that they have a couple of undercover cops, going around buying dope. Mostly quantities like sixteenths on up to an ounce."

"You just now found out about it? What have we been paying that crack head ass cop for? The information you got I already know. I'm going to make it a point to go and sit in the courtrooms a few days just to familiarize myself with some of these detectives I haven't seen yet."

"I know. I talked to him. He said that he was out for a week. When he came back the investigation was already underway. That's a slick move, talkin' about sitting in those courtrooms. I told you man you're a motherfucker."

"The word I get is that it has been going on for a couple of months now. I don't know about the police buying, but the investigation has been going on."

"Any idea who the cops are or what they look like?"

"I think the car they are riding around in is a newer model sports car. As for the rest, I don't know. They should not be too hard to spot. Undoubtedly they will probably pay whatever you want for the dope, so that's one way of figuring out who they are."

Three days later . . .

Jerry reaches Scarver.

"What's the matter? Your beeper not working? I've been trying to get in touch with you."

"I've been leaving it at home."

"What's up?" Scarver asks.

"Have you sold anything to some strange guys in a red sports car? A new model?" "When?"

"In the last couple of days maybe."

"Fred brought two guys over yesterday twice. He said that they were his cousin, from out of town. I did not get a look at the license plate but I know I hadn't seen them before."

"What did he buy?"

"They bought a half ounce each time."

"Well, you need to watch yourself. My sources says that they are the police."

"The police? Are you kidding?"

"I'm afraid not. I'll talk to you later."

Knock! Knock! Knock!

"Who in the hell is that this time of the morning?" Jerry mumbles.

Faye answers the door

"It's Waters. He says, it's important."

"You're out mighty early."

"I left your number at the club. It was easier for me to come by. They found Scarver dead."

"Come on in. Dead? What happened?"

"Somebody shot him in the head, execution style. The police are questioning any and everybody who they suspect of having any dealings with him. Whoever did it also tried to burn the car up, but it was just smoldering when they found it."

"What are you going to do?"

"Nothing. I'm not handling any dope anyway. Johnny and his boys are."

"I'm going to shut down for a week or so. Maybe things will cool off a little."

"That may not be such a bad idea. Well, I'm out of here. I'll be in touch."

"Faye, get some clothes and things together. Enough for a week. We're taking a vacation."

"Where are we going?"

"I don't know just pack. I'll be back after a while."

Jerry drives to the apartment.

"Mike, how much dope do you have left?"

"Not too much."

"Count it. up. Let me know. Ralph, get this place cleaned up. I want all of this excess stuff our of here. Load it up on the truck."

"Where are we going to take it?"

"I don't know. I'm going to store it in one of those rent-a-rooms across the highway, until I get back."

"Get back?" Ask Mike.

"What's going on?"

"There has been a murder and I don't want the police finding anything by accident. Mike, I want you to stay here. I do not want any dope sold out of here, period. Is that understood? Bring your girlfriend over and relax for a week. Furthermore, you don't know where I am or anything else."

"Put this in your pocket."

Jerry gives Mike ten one hundred dollar bills. He pays Ralph and leaves.

On the other side of town . . .

A bystander asks. "Whose house is that?"

The police escort some people out of a government-funded apartment.

"That's pitiful that they put that woman's clothes and kids outdoors like that." Says a lady compassionately.

"At least it is not winter time. She should have paid her rent. It's not but fifteen dollars a month. And with those guys she has coming and going, from what I understand she has the money, but it's too late now. Besides she raised so much hell, they want her to leave anyway." Reveals another woman.

Ten days later . . .

Jerry tells Faye. "You heard that Charlene got four years, didn't you? You should have let her stay in there the last time. When she got out the last time, she told me and everybody you came and got her. I just didn't say anything because she's your friend."

"Thank you for understanding, baby. We just go along way back. I didn't even know she had gone to court. I guess I will go and see her for the last time for a while."

"Don't let it get you down. You did everything that a real friend could do."

"It really might help her. Maybe she will straighten out after this."

"I know. I just wish there was a better way."

"Did you get the telephone transferred to the other apartment?"

"Yes."

"Good. I'm going to start moving tomorrow."

"What name did you get the apartment in? That's all right I don't want to know."

"I guess the guy who works for the cable television place will be there this evening. I gave him some dope yesterday. He promised he would show."

"How do you keep running across all of those deals?"

"Did you forget what I told you already?"

"No, I remember."

"What was it?"

"Everybody has a price, especially if they smoke crack."

"Do you think business will be the same at the new place?"

"Not really. I don't want it to be."

"You're strange. One minute you want all the money, the next minute you don't care."

"Sure, I do. I just told the ones I wanted to know, because of with all this snitching going on. I think things have gotten too wide open, I'll move again. Give me a kiss. I've got to go." Faye puts her arms around Jerry's neck.

"You know, I think we should get away more often. I never thought I would ever get the chance to go to the Bahamas."

"Too many vacations like that and you are liable to wind up pregnant. I know your birthday is tomorrow, but with everything going on, I am going to have to stay close."

"I understand." Faye says, kissing him on the lips.

"Gotta go."

Jerry manages to send Faye two dozen roses and two dozen carnations. He also buys her a gold bracelet with an inscription on it that reads. "Faye and Jerry forever 1989. Love you."

"Ralph, you're short a hundred dollars."

"I don't know how."

"The next time it comes out of your money. How's everything on your end Mike?"

"The same as usual."

"I take it you mean everything is fine? Whose car is that parked in front of the door?"

"I'm holding it for a guy. I didn't want to, but he begged so hard that I went ahead and did it."

"I want it moved from in front of the door. Remember, it's your baby. Any calls?"

"Nope."

"Mike, get yourself some rest I'll take over for a while."

"Hi Jerry."

"What's up Sheila? How's Tracy?"

"I don't know. I haven't seen him in a week or so."

"What do you need?"

"What did you say you wanted?" Sheila asks, the gentleman with her.

"What do you want?" He asks her in return.

"It's up to you." He replies.

"Give me a forth of an ounce." The gentleman has the exact amount already counted out. Jerry recounts the money, then lays the package on the table.

"When are you going to pay your bill, Sheila?"

"I'll pay it the next time I come. I promise."

After Sheila and the man leaves a thought enters Jerry's head. He wonders who that man is with Sheila. Then he dismisses it, knowing Sheila.

"Ralph, bring me a beer." There is no answer. Jerry gets up and goes to the box himself. Then he walks throughout the rest of the apartment. Mike is asleep. Ralph is in the bath room.

"Ralph, you in here?" Jerry asks tapping on the door.

"Yeah."

"You need to hurry up so you can watch the front."

Five minutes later Ralph comes out of the bathroom, gets a beer and sits by the window as usual. A customer comes in. Jerry is busy doing some figuring and tells Ralph to take care of him.

"You don't have a bigger one than this?"

"They are all the same."

"That's all right. I'll go somewhere else." Jerry puts down his pen.

"Wait a minute. What's the problem?"

"He just doesn't want the dope is all."

"Why?"

"They're too small." The customer complains.

"Too small? Got damn! Let me see what you've got there Ralph. What happened to these pieces here? Go wake up Mike. Mike, what the hell is going on here?"

"What do you mean?"

"Why are these pieces so small?"

"Let me see I don't know."

"Where are yours at?"

Mike goes and gets his pill bottle. Jerry takes a piece out.

"How's this one my man?"

"I'll take that one." The customer's attitude changes.

"Come back, you hear. This won't happen again." As the man leaves, Jerry turns to Ralph. "You have got some explaining to do and it better be quick." He says thumping Ralph sharply on the head with his pen.

"Uh Uh"

"Empty your pockets and socks too. How much money is this? Mike, go and check out the bathroom and see what you can find."

"I don't know whose this is." Contends Mike.

"Is this your pipe?" Ralph shakes his head. Jerry slaps him with the barrel of his pistol.

"How long have you been doing this?" Ralph mumbles something. Jerry snatches off the gold that Ralph has on, and makes him take off his brand new British Knight tennis shoes. "Now get out you damn crackhead." He yells, kicking him in the seat of his pants. "Here Mike. Sell these for fifteen dollars a piece."

"I never paid too much attention." Mike says after Ralph leaves. "I knew that he went to the bathroom a lot. He says it was his stomach. I never thought he was smoking that stuff. I knew he smoked weed."

"We won't have to worry about him any more. Go on and finished getting your nap out."

The telephone rings.

"What are you doing?" Asks Faye, sounding sexy.

"Nothing too much?"

"Did you get a chance to watch the news?"

"No, I had to fire that dog gone Ralph."

"Why?"

"Come to find out, he had started smoking the damn merchandise."

"Did Mike know?"

"No, I don't think so. Mike has never been short."

"They had a shooting on the west side. They did not say who it was. Then they had another incident at the mall. Some guys snatched a couple of things and ran."

"Did they catch 'em?"

"Yes. One thing I can say is that these country ass police always get you sooner or later."

"Anything else about Scarver?"

"No, not tonight. They will eventually come up with something sooner or later."

At the jail . . .

Faye asks. "When are you leaving for the penitentiary?" She and Charlene both have a stream of tears running down their faces.

"I don't know. It shouldn't be long." Sniffs Charlene.

"We'll, I won't say I told you so. It won't help the situation any." Faye says, trying to take a sober attitude.

"I know Faye, I won't be gone that long. The lawyer said that I would probably be back on the street in about four or five months."

"That's no time at all."

"I just hope I can leave that crack alone when I get out."

"Sure you can."

"I don't know. Do you remember when we used to smoke?"

"Sure I do."

"It's not the same. They've done something else to this dope. I notice a lot of people who use to smoke it occasionally are really strung out now. That crack as they call it makes you do some weird stuff."

"You may be on to something there. It definitely makes a whole lot of sense."

"You and Jerry are lucky you quit before now."

"I'm going to leave you a couple hundred dollars on the books to take with you. You've got my address? Write me and let me know how you are."

"Thanks Faye, I love you."

"I didn't know that you had moved." States a customer back at the apartment. "I thought that you were still operating from the other place. There were some guys selling out of the same place last night. They hang outside during the day. The police came and caught them in the apartment. The ones they took to jail were charged with trespassing, breaking and entering, and possession with intent to deliver."

"Who were they?"

"I don't know. They said they were selling for you."

"If you don't see Mike or myself around, you can bet they are not selling for me."

"Didn't you have two guys work for you at one tine?"

"Yep."

"I know you did, but the other guy. What's his name?"

"Ralph."

"He was one of those who got arrested. How long have you been here any way?"

"A little while."

"It seems to be a lot quieter than the other place."

"I believe so myself." Jerry agrees, smashing his cigarette out on top of the beer can.

After Don leaves. Jerry calls the house. Jerry has Faye call the police station to see why they are holding Ralph Peters.

"All right. I'll call you back."

Ten minutes later . . .

Faye says. "I called like you asked."

"What did they say?"

"They dropped the charges on him. He's out."

"Just like I thought. Thanks."

"Any thing wrong?"

"No, just staying on top of what's going on."

"You hungry?" She asks, but Jerry is too preoccupied to notice his stomach.

"I'll cook some pork chops for you and Mike, if you like."

"Sounds good. Bye."

Mike is peering out the blinds. "Here comes Faye" He says, opening the door before she gets to it.

"That was quick." Notes Jerry.

"I already had them on when you called."

Ann is the next customer at the door.

"Hello Ann."

"Hello Faye."

" I haven't seen you in a while."

"I've been staying at home. Have you heard from Charlene?"

"I just got a letter the other day."

"I thought that you were pregnant."

"I was."

"What happened?" Faye asks, showing more concern.

"I had the baby, two days ago."

"Two days and you are up and around already?"

"You know the way they do things now."

"What was it? A boy or a girl?"

"A girl."

"How much did she weigh?"

"Two pounds and six ounces."

"Girl, you for real?" Ask Faye, Ann counts her money quickly.

"She is still in the hospital. I got to go. My ride is waiting. See you later."

"Slow down Mike, you're acting like you are starving to death." Jerry tells him.

"I am." Mike responds, speaking with his mouth full.

"I don't know why you didn't speak up. You could have gone and got something. You might as well drive the car you got from the old boy. He hasn't come back to get it yet."

"What can I do for you, Peggy?" Ask Jerry.

"I've got some clothes for sale." She has a grocery bag that's seen better days. She pulls out some clothes that are badly wrinkled.

"Peggy, those clothes are used."

"I only wore them one time." She says, her eyes wanting Faye to save her.

"No, I'm afraid I can't use them." Jerry insists.

Ten minutes later . . .

She is back again. This time she has an ironing board and iron they are practically brand new.

"Peggy what are you doing?" Jerry asks, almost irritated.

He pulls her out of the doorway into the apartment and slamming the door.

"I know I can get something for this."

"You should have ask me about it when you left. I can't—"

"Jerry, I can take them over to Mama. She needs another ironing board and steam iron."

"All right, give her a quarter so she can go."

"Here Mike, give her two." Faye taking an extra piece out of Jerry's hand.

"Thank you, miss lady."

"Faye, do me a favor?" Asks Jerry. "Go and get me a carton of cigarettes. Bring Mike a carton also. I've almost smoke all of his up."

"No luck on finding you a car yet Mike?"

"I saw one I liked but I need a cosigner."

"What, is it brand new or something?"

"No, it costs forty five hundred dollars. It's an eighty-four Riviera."

"How much do you have, already?"

"Three Thousand."

"I'll tell you what. I will loan you the rest and you can work it off."

The next day Mike has his car. He lets Jerry drive it to see what kind of deal he got.

"It's nice Mike. I really like it. I was thinking about getting me another car but I think I'll wait. I've spent so much money getting the truck and the Cadillac, plus we still have Faye's old car. I have to fix it up because she won't trade it."

They go back in to the apartment.

"Turn on the news Mike." Jerry insist.

"In the news tonight police are again investigating still another murder. They are not sure if the killing of James Scarver and this one is related. They both appear to be execution style killings. The unidentified, partially decomposed body of a man was found at a dump site. His hand and feet were bound with barbed wire. The police are not sure what the victim actually died from.

"Well I'll be damn. This city has gone nuts. I haven't heard anything else from those guys up north." Says Jerry, Commenting on the situation.

"Maybe they've decided to lay low."

"Or maybe can't find anybody to take Scarver's place." Jerry proposes.

November is no different than the two previous months. Another man is found dead. Police dismiss it as a suicide.

Faye wants to throw a surprise party for Jerry but she is reluctant to have it at the house. She talks to Jerry about having it at the apartment.

Faye concentrates on Thanksgiving dinner at the house.

"What are we going to do with all this food?" Asks Jerry. "We didn't have all this the last time. There still was plenty left over."

"You wouldn't want your mother to think you are doing bad, would you?"

"No, but I don't want her to think I robbed a bank either."

"Just be glad we've got it. Everybody is not as fortunate. You are staying home Thanksgiving aren't you?"

"Sure, as you always say."

"I'm not playing with you Jerry, you are going to take time out for Thanksgiving, or else! I'm going to pick up your mom and my mom first thing in the morning. So you need to be here. Your mother ask how come you didn't call yourself and invite her to dinner. I said that you were working. She said you never worked so much since she knew you."

Jerry starts to laugh. "My mother said that?"

"She also said at least you were staying out of trouble. If she only knew. If you stay for dinner I won't tell."

"You wouldn't."

"Don't try me." Faye says.

Jerry shuts down and allows Mike to go home for Thanksgiving. Dinner is a big success. They take pictures, play the blues, and drink champagne.

"I'm glad to see that you have decided to do something constructive with your life Son. I always knew you had it in you. It just took the right woman other than me to bring it out." Brags Jerry's mother.

After things have settled down somewhat Jerry decides to leave the house.

"See you all later."

He kisses both mothers and gives the boys some money. He attempts to kiss Faye. She turns her head and gives him a nasty look. Jerry leaves anyway. Their mothers notice even though they act as though they don't see.

"I'm glad to see that you and Jerry are getting along."

"He can be impossible at times."

"Is he still working for that private contractor?" His mother probes.

"All the time. He spends more time on the job than he does at home. I'm not complaining though. Some men won't work at all."

The party starts at nine o'clock.

Jerry tells Mike to only sell to the regular customers, and to be very discreet and take them to the back room. There is plenty of liquor, beer and marijuana. The crowd gathers quickly. Some of them are expecting a crack party.

"Richard! What the hell are you doing here?" They shake hands and hug each other. "How long has it been?" Asks Jerry.

"Just a year."

"You still at the hospital?"

"Yeah"

"How is everybody else?"

"They have quiet a few new people there."

"Faye must have called you?"

"Yes, she did. You have got a good woman. I guess you know that by now. What are you doing these days?"

"Just taking care of business."

" How come you never came back to the hospital?"

"I just didn't."

"You still selling that good weed?"

"No it got to be to much of a problem."

"Say, I got something for you to check out." He offers Jerry a joint. Jerry declines. "It's your birthday. Fire it up."

Jerry does, and he coughs after a couple of tokes.

"What do you have in this joint?"

"Nothing but a little cocaine."

Jerry is really insulted, but he refuses to get angry. He blames himself for smoking it anyway.

"When did you start smoking cocaine?"

"Try it, You will like it."

"I already know what it is all about."

"How do you know?"

"I sell it, Richard, but I don't use it. Let me show you something."

He shows Richard a couple of ounces and a sizable amount of money.

"No wonder you didn't bother to come back."

"Richard, you are my friend, and you will always be. But it's not healthy for you to smoke that stuff. It gets to be a terrible habit after a while."

"Is that why you sell it?"

"I may be wrong for selling it, but that does note make it right for you to smoke it."

"Don't worry. I can handle it. I know when to quit." But his weight loss is

considerable.

"Come on. Are we going to debate or are we going to enjoy the party?"

"I guess you're right."

Faye gives Jerry a matching bracelet but it is wider than hers. It is engraved with the inscription, 'Happy Birthday Jerry and Faye 1989'.

"What's wrong with you?" She asks, affected by his mood. She clutches his hand.

"Nothing. I'll tell you about it later."

"Let's propose a toast." Encourages Faye. They stop the music and propose a toast.

"May our relationship be as good and as long as life itself."

Faye gives Jerry a big kiss. Everybody cheers.

The party is going great until the police stop in and look around. Jerry asks "What business do you have here?"

They reply. "We had a disturbance call. Some one called and said the music was too loud."

"It's turned down, so you can leave now. Good bye."

The crowd slowly disappears afterwards. Those who remain party until the break of dawn. Some sit in their cars and smoke primos and smoke crack out of cans or their homemade pipes. In the darkness one can see the flicker of the lighters in the cars. When the party is over Jerry, hires a couple of begging crackheads to help clean up.

"I really enjoyed the party, baby."

"Did you really?"

"Something is on your mind."

"Yeah, Richard. He's smoking primos."

"Where did he get it?"

"He brought that he had with him. I think I made a mistake telling him I sold it. I reacted too quickly. I was trying to prove a point."

The only thing you can do is tell him about it. Nobody could tell you anything at one point and time."

"You're right. Let's get some rest."

"Are we going home?"

"Yes, this place stinks."

At the house while laying in bed . . .

Jerry says, "You know, its not too late to help him. He still has his job and all."

"Jerry, can I say something? Maybe you're feeling guilty."

"How?"

"You can't be for it one way and against it the other. It really won't let you rest."

"Go to sleep."

"The truth hurts." Faye says, having to get the last word in.

When Jerry awakes the next morning breakfast is right by his bed side.

"Is this part of my birthday hospitality?"

"Yes and no. You could get the same treatment everyday, If you stayed at home."

"I know."

"You tossed and turned all night, like you have something on your mind."

The phone rings.

"It's Mike."

"Yeah"

"Need something to work with."

"Be there in a minute." Jerry gobbles down his food. "Fix up some of that turkey salad you fixed last time."

"Sure."

"I'll be back."

"How did you manage to sell all of that I left earlier?" Jerry asks Mike when he gets in the apartment door.

"It appears that we are the only ones who have any at the moment."

"If that's the case, don't sell anything bigger than a half. Maybe we can make up for lost time."

"There was a white boy at the party last night. Is he cool or what?"

"Yes, why do you ask?"

"I noticed he was setting out in the car with another guy. The other guy came in and bought some dope."

"From now on, when you see him do not sell anybody with him anything. Tell him you're out."

" He's not the police is he?"

"No, he's a personal friend of mine."

Christmas Time . . .

During this time Jerry and Mike turn down more stolen goods than they can possibly keep track of. Some customers bring gifts that are still wrapped to trade for crack. In several cases, they are stolen in burglaries or from under friends and relative's Christmas Trees. Christmas is good to Jerry and Faye. For them it is like any other Christmas.

The streets are extra quiet. Bicycles do not clutter the streets and impair traffic. All these things were noticeable to the non users and users alike. While the streets were extra quiet the police station is bombarded with calls of theft. People are hurt and angry.

The only thing the police could say is. "We are working on the problem."

CHAPTER 9

The phone is ringing early this morning. Faye thinks to herself. Faye gives it to Jerry.

"Stay at the house. I will be there after a while."

"I wonder what that was all about?" Jerry mutters, questioning himself.

"Who was it?"

"That was Mike. He said to hold still and he would be over." Jerry calls the apartment but there is no answer. A couple of hours later, Mike shows up.

"What's going on."

"I just got out of jail."

"They had a warrant for me and you."

"For what?"

"Dope."

"Did they catch you with something?"

"No. I hid the dope when I saw them coming. They say I sold some dope twice to an undercover cop, back in November."

"This is April. They can't do that!" Jerry protest.

"They surrounded the apartment. They had state troopers, detectives, and regular police. They asked where you were. I told them I didn't know you. They said I was a damn lie."

"Did they search the apartment ?" Jerry asks, lighting a cigarette.

"No, they just had personal warrants."

Faye lights one also, fear evident in her eyes.

"How much did it cost you to get out?"

"Five hundred dollars. They are still bringing in people. They had so many they took us over to the park." Responding to this, Jerry pulls on the cigarette so hard it glows bright red. "They made a makeshift jail out of the recreation building."

"I better call the bondsman before I go. I don't want my probation officer to find out just yet. I would rather be the one to tell him.

"Stay here with Faye until I call. Faye, if I don't show back up or call within the hour, call and find out what's going on. Then get in touch with the lawyer."

The bondsman is already there when Jerry arrives. During all the commotion. Jerry manages to post his bond and walk out.

Jerry goes directly to see his probation officer. He explains the situation to him.

"Well, Jerry I really don't know what to say. If you beat the charges you may have a chance. If they don't violate your probation, they can revoke your probation if they so choose. If you hadn't posted bond I would have had to put a hold on you. It's nothing personal. It's just my job. Are you in a position to pay the rest of your fees and restitution?"

"I could."

"That might help if they try to violate you." He makes Jerry a receipt for the remaining amount. "What's this for?" He says, accepting the five one hundred dollar bills.

"That's just in case things get a little hairy. I'll be in touch. Thanks, Mr. Reynolds." A sigh of relief is in order, still finding it hard to believe.

"Faye did you call the lawyer?" Jerry asks.

"I called and left word. His secretary says that she will have him call just as soon as he gets in."

Faye hands Jerry a beer. He gives it to Mike who is already drinking one.

"I need something a little stronger than that." Faye returns with a gin and orange juice. "That's more like it. Thanks."

Jerry looks Faye directly in the eyes. He can see the apprehension in them. She dares not to speak it.

"What now?" Ask Mike

"I don't know. I need to talk to the lawyer first to see what's going on."

Jerry reimburses Mike the money he spent out on paying bail. "If the lawyer calls, call me at the apartment. We are going to go and get the dope out. You never know what these police will do next."

Jerry and Mike makes a thorough search of the apartment to make sure all crack is found.

"Say something, Mike."

"I don't know what to say."

"Any ideas who the undercover cop was?"

"Not really. It could have been anybody to be honest."

"Once we talk to the lawyer, he can find out for sure who it was."

"I thought I was extra careful. I know it wasn't anybody white, that's for sure."

"Wait a minute. Let me call Waters." The telephone rings several times before someone finally answer. "This is Jerry, is Waters in?

"If it's importan–

Yes, it is important. Call him at home and tell him to call me right back at this number. If he's not there, call me back and let me know."

"This is Waters. How is it going Jerry?"

"Man, you are not going to believe what went on this morning."

"What's that?"

"The police are picking up everybody." Jerry exclaims.

"What do you mean everybody?"

"They are arresting people who they say sold dope to the police. Apparently it is part of the operation that was talked about some months ago. Some kind of sting operation."

"Did they pick you up."

"I went and posted bond. They picked up Mike. I didn't know until he called me. I was shocked."

"Give me the number again, and I'll call right back. I need to call Johnny." Says Waters.

"Take this dope and put it out in the truck. Here is my pistol also." Jerry orders Mike.

The phone rings again. "What did you find out?" Jerry asks.

"I talked to Johnny's wife. She said they just came and got him from home. She was trying to call me then. I guess I better check and see if they have a warrant out for me." Waters says.

"What ever happened to that cop friend of yours?" Jerry asks.

"He quit a while back. I think they were fixing to fire him any-way. This lady friend of mine said she had some information. But I haven't heard any thing else from her."

"If she's anything like the other information you had, you need to put a bullet in her head."

"Speaking of bullets in the head, any idea yet on who shot Scarver?

"That's a matter for delicate ears."

"Well, I'm headed for the house."

"That sounds like a good ideal."

"I'll talk to you later."

"Well Mike, lets go get some rest. There's nothing else we can do right now."

Jerry enters the driveway. Faye is sitting on the porch with the telephone beside her. Jerry walks up.

"Nothing yet?" Jerry asks.

"Not yet."

Jerry sits down besides her, then notices that her eyes are blood shot.

"You've been crying?"

"Of course not." Clearing her throat. Jerry puts his arm around her. She lays her head on his shoulder. They are silent for a num-ber of minutes. Faye asks "What are you thinking about?"

"I don't know. What are you thinking?"

"I'm scared are you?"

"I don't know yet. Look, let's go do something until this evening. I want to get back and catch the news."

"I would really just like to stay here. Besides, the lawyer is liable to call anytime. I'll fix you a drink if you want. Take the phone out back. Let's sit in the back yard."

The five o'clock news main topic is the city undergoing a major drug bust.

"More than ninety people are arrested in today's sting opera-tion." The reporter notes.

They show the detective and state troopers along with the pros-ecuting attorney. At one particular apartment, the prosecuting attor-ney states. "We intend to take our city back."

They show the gathering of people arrested at the make shift jail out at the park.

The news reporter goes on to say, "Not all warrants have been served. Several more turned up at the police station and turned themselves in, while some are still at large. Bonds were kept low, so that those who were able to make bond immediately could. Those who could not were transported to the county jail.

"Whew, they've really got some kind of mess on their hands." Jerry says after the broadcast. "I recognize a lot of the people they just showed. Tracy was one of them. I'm glad that didn't get me on television. Mom would have a fit. Damn!" Jumping up from his seat, Jerry says, "You know what. My name will probably be in the newspaper tomorrow."

The morning paper headline is about the sting operation, with a color picture of one or two individuals on the front page. It is taken at St. Luke apartment complex. Many of the people who are arrested, are over night dealers or runners for someone else. The paper has a full story of when the sting operation first started, which was nine months ago. A list of names accompany the column. The prosecuting attorney states that everyone implicated in the recent sting will undoubtedly get some time. This starts a panic among the crack dealers. Jerry makes an appointment with his lawyer.

Jerry is guaranteed that his case can be properly disposed of for about ten thousand dollars. This is of course, no problem for Jerry unlike some of the other dealers arrested in the sting.

"Mike, it's going to cost a lot of money to beat those drug charges. I talked to my lawyer. He has agreed to handle both of our cases as part of a package deal."

"How much is he talking about?"

"Ten grand."

"Wow. There's no way I can afford to pay that kind of money."

"We'll sell as much as we can."

Faye knocks on the door. Mike opens it.

Surprised, Jerry says. "I see you didn't go to school today."

"No I wanted to wait and see what the lawyer had to say."

"Well, you know how it works. Money speaks for itself."

"So you really don't have anything to worry about then. Am I right?"

"I'm pretty sure the lawyer can handle it."

"You are not going to sell any more dope, are you?"

"What do you think I'm going to do with he rest of the dope I have? Beside they've already had the sting. They aren't thinking about us now."

The crack situation only escalates. Many people think on the same lines as Jerry. If they do not have the money for their lawyers, the only way that they can get it is to sell more crack, with the hope of not getting caught. Many dealers move their operations. They all eventually move from the west side to the east side of town. Nightclubs become a popular place to distribute crack. Dealers have a tendency to sell there, since the traffic could go unnoticed.

Faye is at home . . .

"Charlene, you have gained so much weight! You look like your old self." Faye says, and they hug each other.

"You still look the same, Faye." They laugh about the clothes Charlene has on.

"I still have the clothes you packed up and asked me to keep."

"I need to take a bath, so I can wash the penitentiary smell off of me."

"I talked to Jerry. He said it was okay for you to stay for a little while."

"What do you have to drink? It won't take much and I will be high as a kite."

"How does it feel to be off of crack?"

"Honey, it feels so good. Yes!" Charlene shakes her fist as an expression of how she really feels. "The first thing I need to do is get my hair fixed. There's too many things I need to do or want to do. I don't really know where to start. What I really need right now is some dick." She says, giggling.

"I know that's right."

"There were so many women in there that I know and you know from the street. You'd think that they have left the state, and all the time they are in the penitentiary."

Both are sitting on the sofa, using the end table to support their drinks.

"How was it?" Asks Faye.

"It's not as bad as some people say. It's no fun either, so don't get me wrong. You would not believe all the bulldagging going on in that place either. To top it off they have all kinds of dope there also. Crack, weed, all the same things as in the free world."

"I'm not surprised. It has gotten so bad out here that it is ridiculous."

"I saw in the paper about the sting. They got Jerry, too, didn't they?"

"Unfortunately so."

"You think he will get some time?" Charlene asks, picking up another cigarette, using the butt off of the one she just smoked to light another.

"Not really. He's paying that lawyer enough."

"I could not believe all the people they picked up."

"It surprised us all."

"You want to go over and see Jerry after you bathe and everything?"

"That's fine."

An hour or so later, the two go to the apartment.

"He went over to Willie's to take care of some business." Says Mike.

"Come on Charlene. We will come back. I don't want to hang around here. Jerry will be furious."

Jerry and Willie are at their usual spot in Willie's house. They talk about several things including the sting operation. Upon returning from the bathroom.

Jerry asks, "What happened to the rest of that piece?"

"That's it."

"I can tell you cut a piece off, by the way the dope looks ."

"I don't know what you are talking about. You don't think I would steal from you, do you?"

"Ain't this some shit. I always give you what you want. I will fuck you up about trying to take something from me."

Willie still does not want to own up to stealing some of Jerry's crack. Jerry gathers his property and most of Willie's cooking tools.

"That's my stuff you got there. You can't just take my shit."

"That's the same way I feel." Jerry says.

Willie realizes that he cannot make any money or get drugs for rocking up other people's drugs if he does not have the equipment. He confesses.

"Shit, man. Here's your shit." Willie says, raising up the bucket he is sitting on and coming up with a piece no bigger than a half.

"You are fuckin' stupid. You fucked up your shit with me for that little extra piece? Now I'm not going to give you a damn thing for today."

"Aw, man. Don't do me like that."

"Man, fuck you. Ain't no tellin' how much dope you've stolen from me."

"That's the first time I swear."

"It doesn't matter!" Jerry yells, still keeping Willie's property.

Jerry leaves and goes to the apartment. Faye arrives shortly afterwards.

"What are you doing?" Asks Faye.

"Well look whose here! Hello Charlene."

"Hi Jerry."

Charlene hugs Jerry.

"I almost did not know who you were." He comments, noticing her eyes, how clean and bright the whites are.

"I don't look that much different, do I, Faye?"

"Not quite. But you look good and that's for real." Interjects Jerry.

"Why thank you Jerry." She says posing. They all started to laugh.

"Jerry, what are you doing in the kitchen?"

"Cooking up this crack."

"You haven't been cooking it up have you?"

"No, Willie has been doing it. I caught him stealing some of it today, so I will do it until I find someone to cook it for me. I'm pretty good at it myself now, but not as good as Willie." Charlene is in the front room talking to Mike.

"How much more dope do you have left?" Faye asks, really nervous and scared for Jerry's freedom and selfishly thinking about the two of them.

"I don't know. Not much."

"I will be glad when it is gone." Quarrels Faye. "We are fixing to get out a bit. I just wanted you to see Charlene."

"She looks good when she stays away from this stuff. Do you think she will?"

"I don't know. I hope so."

"Speaking of friends. Have you see Richard?"

"No, not lately."

"Remind me to call him later on."

"Are you coming home for dinner?"

"I'll probably send Mike at something, after a while."

"Okay. We will see you later." She promises, kissing him on the jaw.

"You know." Charlene comments as they get to the door. "I didn't know that Mike looked that good."

"He's all right. But I think you might be more horny than anything."

"Well that too. I could go for a good fucking about now. Do you think Jerry will let him off tonight?"

"I don't know. I will call him and let him know what is going on."

The next morning Jerry arrives at the apartment. He calls out loud for Mike, as he enters the door.

"I'll be out in a minute." Mike yells from the back.

After Mike has come forward, Jerry talks to Charlene through the bedroom door. "Charlene, Faye has to go to school this morning. I'm going to take you to the house or wherever else you want to go. Faye probably told you, I don't like people hanging around here."

"Okay, I'll be ready in a minute."

"Some guy came by here last night. He wanted your home phone number." Advises Mike.

"Who was he?"

"I don't know. He said that you had given him the number, but he had misplaced it. He acted like he really got mad because I wouldn't not give him the number."

"What did he look like?"

"Tall, slender, with some gray in his hair, dark complexion."

"Was he in a truck?"

" I think so. It was dark color. I can't be sure of that either. It was dark."

"I know who you are talking about. The next time he comes and I'm not here, give him my home phone number. He's cool. Kind of crazy, but he's cool."

"You have a good time last night?" Jerry asks whispering.

"Lord have mercy. That bitch was hot, cumming like a pet coon. Man I'm tired than a motherfucker. I thought I was suppose to be fuckin her, shit. I think it was the other way around."

"I know she did, as long as it has been since she had some real dick."

"Hell, I'm still tired."

"I'll be back in a little while. Come on Charlene."

On the way to the house, just out of making conversation, Jerry asked Charlene. "How was business last night?"

"It was good until he shutdown at one."

"Are you going to leave that crack alone this time?"

"I sure am."

"You can make yourself at home. Just don't take advantage of the situation." "Don't worry, I won't. You really gonna stop selling dope?"

"Who told you that?"

"Faye mentioned it casually, that's all."

"Yes, for the record only."

"What does that mean? I'm not going to tell Faye, you can be sure of that."

"That's for the record. Here's the key. Don't touch my stereo. Bye."

◈　　　◈　　　◈　　　◈

"Business is kind of slow by the looks of it." Jerry says, seeking information from Mike.

"Yeah, I guess everybody must be staying in. We need to keep them coming if we intend to be able to pay that lawyer. You know what I mean?"

"No problem."

There's a knock at the door.

"Come on in, Rick. You can be rather difficult to get a hold of at times."

"Just part of the process." His accent makes him sound capricious.

"You still got that package?"

"That package and some."

"What do you have it in?"

"I've got it covered. Be right back." Says Rick, reentering the apartment with an army style duffel bag.

"Boy, I really like this one!" Exclaims Jerry.

"This particular one has six extra clips to go with it." Indicates Rick, his eyes gleaming.

"What does it shoot?"

"Nine millimeter shells. Forty some odd rounds per clips. This is the real kicker. See this switch? Semi or fully automatic and this forty five has one extra clip. It also come with this shoulder holster. I have a few others. I figured these would be the ones that would interest you."

"What kind of price are we talking here?"

"Half an ounce maybe."

"How do you want it?"

"Anyway is fine."

"I'll give it to you in powder. I'll add a little extra. I had to fire my man that cooks all the dope. He got greedy."

"You need for him to be taught a lesson?" Asks Rick rotating his shoulders.

"No, he's a crackhead. It's punishment enough now that he has to buy all his dope from here on out."

"You' the man. I've got some more artillery coming in from the coast. I'll check with you in a couple weeks. Next time, I might be able to give you a better price. What about your main man here. You interested in anything in particular?"

"I'd like to get a forty-five if you can get one."

"You hear that shit? Jerry. If I can get one!" Flexing, "I'll get with you when I come back. Your order is as good as filled. Next time."

"Thanks, Rick."

◇　　　◇　　　◇　　　◇

"Hi Faye." Charlene says, as Faye struggles to get in the door, carrying books and several bags.

"Did you find everything okay, Charlene?"

"Yes, I called myself cleaning up a bit, it didn't take much. I left everything pretty much the way it was."

Any messages from Jerry?"

"No but Richard called."

"I better call Jerry then."

The telephone rings several times.

"Hello baby"

"What's up?"

"I was just checking on you. I have to make sure everything is all right."

"I'll be home in a few. I have to drop off a package anyway."

"By the way Charlene said Richard called."

"Maybe he will be at home today. All right, I will see you in a little bit."

"Bye."

Jerry calls Richard and again there is no answer. "I'll be back in a few, Mike." As Jerry approaches his truck to leave the apartment a man walks up to him and ask if he will hold his car. "I don't hold cars."

"Would you be interested in buying it?"

"Where is it?"

"Over there."

"Pull it up here. Let me take a look." The car is in the late seventies, and appears to be in good shape. "What do you want for it?"

"Two eight balls."

The drug has really taken its toll on this young man. Jerry thinking to himself, he is terribly underweight, his shoulders are slumped, his teeth are dingy and his body odor is repulsive.

"Do you have the title?"

"Not with me."

"How do you expect to sell the damn thing without the title?"

"I can get it."

"I may be interested but I will have to get it done in front of a notary. I don't need any more problems. You check back if it's not too late."

"I will do it today. Can I get a quarter until I come back?"

"No, I don't do that either. If you hurry you might be able to make a deal today."

"I'll be right back."

As Jerry fumbles with his keys to find the one to open his truck door he spots a beer can by the wheel. Picking it up, he notices the pin holes in it and the burnt area surrounding the holes. Someone has been smoking crack and discarded it. He shakes his head and flips it into the back of the truck.

"What's in the bag?" Faye asks as he comes in the door. Jerry has transferred his guns into a paper bag.

"Just something I bought today."

He heads to the bedroom. Faye follows. Pulling it out of the bag, he begins to examine it further.

"What are you going to do with that?"

"Keep it."

"I know that. You never can tell when those funky ass police will come kicking in the door. They won't kick in another one if I can help it."

The firearm gives him a sense of power.

"Jerry Collins" Faye says, her voice firm. "You must be going crazy! The only thing that gun will do is get you killed!" Jerry holds two fingers up to her lips. "Shhh! It won't happen." She snatches his hand down.

"Don't start. Do you have a V-8 juice in the box?"

"At least you are doing something good to yourself these days."

"Not as good as you are to me."

"I know that. It won't soften the blow, it won't work."

"I do need you to do me a favor."

"What?"

"I need you to go to the gun store and buy me some nine millimeter shells and some forty-fives."

"Now, I know you have lost your mind. I'm not going to do that, regardless of how mad you get."

"Whose mad? I've got to go."

Faye lights a cigarette. Jerry takes it for himself. She lights another one, tapping her foot.

When Jerry gets back, the same man is waiting outside in the parking lot.

"You got the title?"

"Is this what you are talking about?"

"Where is the registration and the rest of your papers?"

"In the car. I'll ride with you. If we hurry, I know a lawyer who can do it. He works until late anyway. What was the deal now?"

"Two eight balls."

"I thought it was an eight ball and a sixteenth."

"No, I really need two eight balls."

Once at the lawyers office, Jerry places the value at which he buys the car at six hundred dollars. The lawyers takes care of the necessary paperwork.

"How's my case coming?"

"Get in touch with me Friday."

They leave the lawyers office, both laughing.

"Can I get you to drop me off at home afterwards?" The young man asks.

"That's no problem."

Jerry goes to his apartment and gets the man two eight balls.

"You really got a good deal." Blows Mike.

"I couldn't pass it up. Everybody knows my truck now. I can fix this car the way I want it and go anywhere without being noticed. Isn't that the telephone ringing?"

Mike runs to answer it.

"It's Charlene!" Yelling so Jerry can here him.

"What does she want?" Mike hunches his shoulders. Jerry grabbing the telephone receiver.

"Your lawyer called. He wants you to come see him Friday."

"Yeah right, tell Faye when she gets home to call me."

"Tell Mike to call me when he gets a chance."

"Charlene says call her when you get a chance." Relaying the message right away. "Don't forget to tell Faye like I said."

"I won't."

❖   ❖   ❖   ❖

Later at the hospital . . .

"What room is Richard Thorton in?"

"Room two forty-five, west hall." The cute lady says nicely.

"Thank you."

"What's going on Richard?"

"Hello Jerry. How did you know I was in here?"

"I called your house several times and I never got an answer. So I called the job. They told me what was going on. What happen to you?"

"I just had a small accident."

"It couldn't have been that small. They have got you bandaged from your head to the middle of you chest. What happened?"

"One of those butane lighters blew up in my face."

"Should I ask what you were doing with the lighter?"

"Me and some guys were getting high and it just blew."

"I told you that night at the party about that damn crack."

"I know. I wish I would have listened now."

"How bad it?"

"Not too bad. Third and second degree burns. It caught my hair and my shirt. It would not have gotten that bad if I had not been high. It still could have been worse."

"That's one way to look at it. I bought you something to put around your arm." Handing him a watch. "Remember, never forget what time it is. You've been off from work. You need any cash?"

"No."

"I don't know why I ask, you wouldn't tell me if you did."

Jerry hands him a sealed envelope.

"Thanks."

Richard lays it down on the bed without opening it.

"I may not get by here tomorrow, but Faye may come by."

"How is she?"

"She's doing okay."

"What about you? I read the papers."

"From one friend to another, I'm scared."

"Why don't you back out?"

"To be honest, I'm in too deep. If I'm going to the joint, I might as well go for the gusto. I'm making a final decision as soon as I talk to my lawyer Friday."

"I wish you would back out anyway. This maybe more serious than you may be willing to admit."

"That may be true, right now at least."

"You know how Faye really feels, don't you?"

Jerry says, hanging his head. "She will be all right, she's strong."

"Don't push her to far Jerry. The strongest of them will crack under pressure. Especially the ones that are in love."

"I'll take it easy on her. Enough of my problems. You hurry up and get out of here. This place has a smell of its own. If you need anything call me."

Jerry gets back to the apartment as the phone is ringing.

"Charlene told me you wanted me to call." Says Faye.

"I finally got in touch with Richard."

"Good, how is he?"

"He'll make it. He's in the hospital."

"What happened?"

"He was smoking crack with somebody and the lighter blew up in his face."

"Poor Richard."

"I went to see him. I told him you probably would show up tomorrow. When you do, take him a snack pack of chicken. He says the food is terrible. Beside he could use it. How was you day?"

"Same as usual. Is Charlene at the house?"

"Yes."

"I want her to do something for me. I'll be there in about an hour."

Jerry makes it home about two hours later.

"Charlene, I want you to do me a favor. I suspect some foul play on Mike's end. Call him after I am back to the apartment. Ask him if you can spend the night with him."

"Is that all?" She asks, her hormones raging.

"Let me finish. From the time I leave, stick close to him as you can. Don't act like you are watching him. Count how many customers come between then and one o'clock. Try to keep track of what they buy."

"Why are you doing that?" Asks Faye.

"I suspected foul play on his end the other day. I just been too busy to investigate."

The next morning . . .

Charlene hands Jerry a piece of paper.

"I wrote it down so I could be sure. It may not be exact, but it's close. From eight last night to one this morning, you had sixty three customers buy quarters, fifteen buy halves, and two buy grams. From one until three he sold twelve quarters and three halves."

"From one to three! I specifically told him to shut down at one every night except for the weekend. If my money is not right, I'm going to whip the shit out of him."

"Jerry wait. I did you a favor, now do one for me. I know it's your money and all. Will you check it and wait until tomorrow tip up on him, that way he will not suspect me of telling on him. He's not a bad guy."

"I assume you kind of like him. I hate to say he may be on this way out after this."

The next night Jerry set a trap of a different sort.

"It's two in the morning. Mike, I thought I told you to shut down at one." After sending a customer inside to buy some drugs. "Let me have all the dope and the money. Is that all you have sold since I left?"

"That's it."

Jerry pulls out his forty-five.

"Empty the rest of your pockets and socks." Mike produces another pill bottle and another fold of money with a rubber band around it. "Well kiss my ass. Whose is this?" Mike doesn't answer. "I don't intend to ask you again." Jerry cocks the hammer on his pistol and starts to raise it. "It's Tracy's! It's Tracy's!"

"You know what ? I ought to kill you, as much as I do for you and pay you. You sell me out for some punk who can't even sell his own dope because he smokes it all. I suspect his girlfriend of setting us up anyway. I will find that out for sure, too. But you! Off with the jewelry."

"This is mine."

Jerry hits Mike with pistol, overreacting. Jerry almost strikes him again, but the trickle of blood on Mike forehead stops him.

"Off with it. When does Tracy get his money and his dope?"

"He will be here about three."

"Good, we are going to wait. I've got a big surprise for him."

During the forty-five minute wait, Mike tries to talk to Jerry. Jerry refuses to hear any of it.

"You really need to shut up before I change my mind." Jerry slings the empty beer can up against the wall. Wiping his mouth with his sleeve. Tracy finally shows up. Jerry is behind the door. Mike opens the door as always. Jerry slams it shut. With his pistol on Tracy, he locks the door. Get up against the wall." He orders. He snatches the clutch bag out of Tracy's hand and pats him down. "Have a seat with your buddy there." Kicking him in the behind. The first thing he pulls out of Tracy's clutch bag is a snub nose thirty-eight, then a pill bottle with pieces of crack and a small gathering of bills.

"What the hell are you doing?" Tracy demands.

"Shut up. I'll ask the questions in this place." Jerry compares the dope. "It was not good enough for you to mess up your own business. You want to come over here and fuck up mine. Get up."

"Hold it! It was not my idea. It was Mike's. We just split all the money down the middle." He slaps Tracy across the mouth with the pistol, which immediately draws blood. Then he kicks him in the balls. Tracy doubles over in pain. "That was for that bitch of yours. If I find out she set me up, I'm going to have her taken care of. Both of you get out of here. If anything happens, you better not be in town. If you didn't do it you might as well have. I'm going to kill you." Tracy reaches for his bag. Jerry kicks him in the side. "Without the bag!" Jerry takes all the dope and puts it in the bag and goes home.

Faye and Charlene are both awaked.

Faye asks. "What's going on in here?"

"Nothing. Go back to bed."

"What's wrong?" Faye asks again.

Rubbing the back of his neck.

"I caught Mike and Tracy trying to cut into the business, the slick way."

"I was hoping that you were wrong about Mike."

"I did too, but I wasn't."

"Whose is that?" Talking about the thirty eight caliber revolver and the drugs.

"I took it from Tracy and Mike."

"They were trying to get it, weren't they?"

"There is no telling how much they have beat me for. Well, Mike can kiss it good bye. He can pay the lawyer the best way he can. I refuse to help him regardless."

The next night . . .

Faye asks. "Do you want me to sit up with you at the place?"

"No, I handle it. I'll be home about one thirty."

"Baby, please be careful."

Faye notices the stress that Jerry has been under lately. He is not the same. He has become irritable and temperamental. Mike comes by and wants to talk. Jerry tells him there is no need for a conversation and closes the door.

Jerry arrives at the lawyer's office.

"Hello Mr. Collins. Mr. Morgan will be with you in a minute."

"Thank you."

"Come on in Jerry." The lawyer says, stepping aside so Jerry can enter his office first. "How is everything?"

"That's what I've come to find out."

"Well, Mr. Collins, I ___"

"Hold it Mr. Morgan. Give it to me straight."

"All right. The prosecutor won't budge, neither will the judge. They insist everyone involved with the selling of crack be sent to the pen."

Jerry scoots to the edge of his seat.

"What do they want, more money?"

"No, I tried that. I've got a couple more things I need to try, but the chances look slim. All the judges have been pumped up on the situation." Mr. Morgan is also sitting on the edge of his seat. Jerry lowers his head for a minute. "The only thing I can do right away is to keep it out of court for a while and hope things cool off a little."

"That package deal we talked about? Cancel it. Just work on mine. I do mean work on it. We will straighten out the finances later."

"Okay Jerry. If anything develops, I'll let you know immediately."

"Thanks."

Jerry walks out without saying another word.

When Jerry gets to the car, he just sits there for a moment with his head on the steering wheel to collect his thoughts. They are running wild at the moment. He thinks about a few of the others who have already gone to the joint. Everybody said that nobody would get out of the sting without some time. It has finally started to sink in. He starts the car. He stops by the liquor store on the way to the apartment. He buys a twelve pack of beer, a pint of gin and a quart of orange juice. When he gets to the apartment, he just sits there and drinks. He does not answer the door, at least not right away. He finally reaches a level of intoxication where he does not have to think of what the lawyer or anybody else has said. The only thought going through his head now is. Run with it. Winner takes all. That is exactly what he intends to do.

Faye arrives that evening after school.

"It stinks in here."

She goes around opening windows.

"Have you forgotten where you are?" Faye turns around to face him. She can read through him. She knows how he acts when he's hurt. So she does not dwell on the fact that he is drunk.

"What did the lawyer say?"

"Everything will be all right."

"What did he really say?"

"I just told you, so leave it at that."

"When you get ready to tell me I'll be here for you."

A couple days later . . .

Jerry says. "Say, Waters. I haven't heard from you since the big party. Any news from your lady friend?"

"No, I haven't heard a thing."

"You still taking care of business?"

"No, I'm through. Everybody is either smoking it or selling it for themselves."

"What about Johnny?"

"He's out. He's selling it still. Last I heard he had started smoking. What about you?"

"I'm still at it."

"If I hear anything, I'll let you know. Good luck."

"Yeah."

Jerry slams down the receiver.

Over the next couple of weeks Jerry diligently works his own crackhouse, from nine a.m. to one p.m. during the week days and almost twenty-four hours on Friday and Saturday.

While at the gas station early in the morning pumping gas, a young lady drives up beside him. She blows her horn. Jerry looks but he does not recognize her. She rolls down the window and ask him when he gets through can she have a word with him.

"Aren't you Jerry Collins?"

"That depends."

"My name is Vanessa. This is confidential. I deal with the police everyday, so you can believe what I tell you. They were talking about your place the other day. So you need to watch your step. I don't know for sure what they were going to do. I will let you know as soon as I find out something."

"What's it going to cost me?"

"This is from one friend to another." She says, and drives away.

❖   ❖   ❖   ❖

"Faye, I notice that Jerry does not have a whole lot to say since he lost Mike." "That's part of it."

"I'm going to try and find an apartment. I don't want to interfere with everything going on."

"Did you ever check on the secretarial job you were talking about? As good as you can type, you should not have any problems."

"I did. I just haven't heard anything yet."

"You are not part of the problem through. I was thinking maybe we could do something special for him."

"Like what."

"I don't know. He's not responding to much of anything these days. I'm not going to school today. Let's fix him something to eat. I don't see his truck. We can go inside and wait. I have the key he took from Mike."

"Maybe we ought to wait. You know it's hot around here."

"He won't be gone that long. Come on."

They enter the apartment and Faye goes directly to the kitchen. Charlene goes toward the bathroom. She runs back to the kitchen and grabs Faye by the arm.

"Come on Faye, let's get out of here."

"What's wrong with you?"

"Just come on. I'll explain later."

"What did you see?"

"Nothing, just come on!"

Charlene gets Faye as far as the front door before Faye hears a noise and insist on going to see what is going on. There is Jerry, putting on his clothes.

"Who the hell is this bitch?" Faye screams.

"Get your clothes on and get out." Jerry tells her.

Faye rushes the woman. Grabbing her hair, she slams her to the floor, scratching at her face fiercely. The woman has no time to react or properly defend herself. Jerry and Charlene pull the two apart. Jerry grabs Faye and wrestles her to the floor. Charlene grabs the other woman's clothes and ushers her toward the door. The woman not taking care to put her clothes on, runs out half naked.

"Let me go. Get the fuck off me you no good son-of-a-bitch. Let me up got damit!" Jerry loosens his restraint on Faye, he tries to talk to Faye, but she is slamming things on her way out. Charlene follows her.

When Faye gets home she hasn't cooled off any. She goes to the closet and grabs Jerry's oozy. Charlene stops her at the door. She is trying to reason with her.

"What are you doing? You don't know how to operate all that gun."

"How could he?" Shrieks Faye.

"Just be realistic for a minute and think. You know how men are. Besides if you would have listened to me in the first place, it would not have happened." Charlene fixes her a drink and gets her to sit down. "Will you stop shaking?"

"You sound as though you know something I don't."

"I do. Men are men regardless of who they are with. It's such a thing as taking the bitter with the sweet. He must not care about the bitch. He told her to get out."

Charlene and Faye sit up all night drinking and talking. Jerry does not come home. Faye refuses to call the apartment.

"You need to call and at least check on him." Suggest Charlene.

"He knows how to call the house."

Jerry on the other hand has no one to talk to. This is only one in the number of incidents that has been haunting him lately. It just seems to be another drop in the bucket. Out of all the customers he has served though out the night only one really seems to show any real concern. Maybe it's because he realizes he has some real problems also. They start to talk. Jerry spills his story and Eddie spills his.

"I think a lot of times about the way things would have been." Eddie says, having flash backs. "More than I do about how they could be. It seems like I'm trapped. I don't know which way to go. I remember when I first got out of high school. I was a real good looking young man. I played football. Even had a scholarship. I got married and the old lady started having kids. I became steadily unhappy. I wasn't what I thought I should have been. Now I'm smoking this shit."

"What does your wife do now?" Solicits Jerry

"Smokes like I do. I have honestly grown to resent her. She was the reason I didn't take the scholarship. She gave me the money to get this. Do you think she is going to be happy when I get back? After being gone this long. I wish I was in your shoes. I'd tell her to get lost." Eddie remarks, guzzling the beer Jerry gives him and belching loudly afterwards.

"I had a job making seven dollars an hour, working at night. Then I started hearing things about my wife fucking other men for crack while the kids were there. I've got all boys. The oldest one can talk. He tells me anything I want to know and some I don't. He's smart for his age. When I got paid she wasn't happy until I smoked up all of my paycheck with her. Then we would have to go and beg for money to get baby diapers and milk. It's a damn shame. She walks around now without her hair combed. She won't half bathe. It makes me sick. I ain't no king myself but shi__ man I don't even know."

"What would you do different if you could do it all over again?"

"I would follow my mind and not my heart. I would be more of a man. If she loves me she will be with me either way. I just wish I would have known that a long time ago."

"It's not too late to change."

"Well, I better get going. It's past day break."

"Here, take this with you." Jerry gives him a gram. "Maybe you can be in charge for a minute and thanks for listening."

Jerry calls Faye. "Have you cooled down enough to talk sensibly."

"What do you mean talk sensibly?"

"I want you to come over here, so we can get things straight." Faye hangs up the telephone with no reply.

"Where are you going?"

"That was Jerry. He wants to talk to me."

"You may be mad, but you are not that unreasonable. There was a time when you sold yourself for money and he put up with you."

"That's different."

"Ha. Not hardly. When you sell dope you can't help but run into a real freak every once in a while."

"Shut up Charlene. You act like you're on his side."

"You going dressed like that?"

"Sure, I might even get fucked while I'm there."

"That's the spirit."

Jerry keeps an eye out for her, opening the door before she has a chance to knock.

"Let me say one thing before you get started, I was wrong. I can't change that, understand? Whatever you decide to do, do it today and I will accept it. If you don't do anything, I don't want to hear about it next week or the week after."

"You got your nerve." She slaps him twice.

"You feel better now?"

"Not really. The first one was for not letting me kick the bitches ass and the second one was for getting caught. I thought you were going to stop selling dope anyway."

"Are we back on that again."

From the sounds of it I'm just wasting my time talking about it." Probably."

"You have become so impossible to reach these days. Do you think you are going to the joint?"

"Probably."

Faye comes out of her gown.

"Can I get mine or did you get satisfied? You better make love to me like you used to. Otherwise it's going to really be some shit." She threatens, pinching him very hard. Someone knocks on the door. Faye spins him back in the direction of the bedroom. "You can forget about the door, mister." He does not argue.

Afterwards, while in bed . . .

Faye asks. "Are you going to call your mother? Mother's Day is in a couple of days."

"I don't know. She hasn't had too much to say after she read my name in the paper. You know, people on the job commented on it too. She even refused to keep any more of my money."

"Can you blame her? The last time Mama and I went to church she lectured me the whole time. Jerry?"

"Yeah."

"Do something for me."

"What's that?"

"Don't do what you did again."

"Sure. I apologize baby. You know sometimes a man can get so wrapped up in himself that sometimes he doesn't know how to face home. If you know what I mean. You probably wouldn't understand."

"I might, if you would explain some things to me sometimes."

"Well sometimes I just don't want to burden you with some things."

"I want you to burden me. Two heads are better than one."

"Let's go home."

Charlene and Faye are having one of their casual conversations.

"I saw Mike today. We messed around for awhile. I think he and Tracy are still selling partners. He did not act the same. He really acted like he was high. I started to ask him if he was smoking but I changed my mind."

"Why. Were you afraid he might have said yes?"

"You know, Faye, I can't figure you out. You can be so smart when you want to be. The other day you were ready to kill Jerry."

"Well, I can say, I would rather he fooled around than start smoking crack."

"That makes sense."

"I'm suppose to go back over there tomorrow and see Mike."

"You want to help me fix dinner?"

"At this hour?"

"Jerry should be home."

"Okay, just kidding."

"You know I can't understand Mike. He had it made. Jerry would have given him anything he wanted. I know he never gave Jerry a dime of the money he owed him on the car."

"Do you think Jerry will let him come back to work for him?"

"I don't know. Once you blow it with Jerry, he's rather reluctant to come around unless he really likes you. I think it's really going to depend on Mike."

The phone rings.

"Charlene, will you get that?"

"It's Jerry." Charlene says, giving her the receiver.

"It's me. Listen to me and listen good. First, call my lawyer, tell him not to waste any time. He knows what to do. We already talked about it. Second, taped to the bottom of the microwave, there's an envelope. When the probation office opens be there. The instructions are in the envelope."

"Where are you?"

"In jail"

"What happened?"

"The police stopped me on the way home. They don't have a bond set as of yet. So there is nothing you can do. Don't worry. I'll be out first thing in the morning."

"Do you know what they are charging you with?"

"Possession of a firearm and possession with the intent to deliver. They got fifteen thousand out of the truck."

"Oh—"

"I got to go. Talk to you later."

"Jerry's in jail again?" Charlene asks, reading the conversation.

"Yes, they stopped him on the way home. If he gets out of this and does not quit, I'm leaving. It's driving me crazy." She reflexively lights a cigarette and fixes a drink. "Apparently he knows what he is doing."

"We will see in the morning. Faye goes in the kitchen and turns the fire out under the rice on the stove."

First thing in the morning, Faye is at the probation office. She got in touch with the lawyer last night. She has Charlene calling him still to make sure he does not drag his feet. By eleven o'clock, Jerry is out of jail. He has posted a ten thousand cash bond.

"You know the prosecutor is real upset about you making bail." Suggest Mr. Morgan.

"That's his tough luck. I'll bring you some more money later this evening. First I have to go see my probation officer."

"You and he must be pretty tight."

"I have no problem with him. I'm not suppose to."

"What was that?"

"Nothing, see you this evening."

At the house . . .

Faye says. "Jerry's out. They say that he had been released. He should be home any minute." Says Faye.

"Well, you can relax now." They tap glasses.

"Girl, if I'm not careful, I'm going to be a full-blown alcoholic after a while. Jerry already says that I need to slow down. I don't know what he expects me to do especially at the rate he's going."

Jerry walks in the door. Faye rushs to him. She hugs him with a quick kiss.

"You got out hours ago. Where have you been?"

"I had some things to take care of. We need to talk, but not right now. I've been up all night. Fix me a drink, a tall one, and wake me in a couple of hours."

Jerry and Faye exit to the bedroom.

Ten minutes later . . .

Faye comes out.

"He's asleep already?" Asks Charlene.

"Yes, and we need to get some sleep too. This is the third night I've been up."

"I can tell. You've got bags under your eyes."

"Charlene, you know what your problem is?"

What?"

"You notice too much."

"Don't get off on me. As much crack as I smoked, it feels good to notice things." They both fall asleep on the couch.

Jerry wakes up first. Charlene hears him and is awaked also. She curses silently to herself. She's late. She was suppose to meet Mike a couple of hours ago. Jerry is easing out the door. Charlene stops him.

"Will you take me somewhere?"

"You better come on. Where are you trying to go?"

"I'm suppose to meet Mike."

"Mike?"

"Yes."

"What's he doing now?"

"He's still selling."

"That's good."

"You know, you are about to drive Faye crazy. She drinks like a fish."

"I'm the one about to go crazy. That little deal last night cost me over twenty-five grand."

"Where are you going now? If I'm not intruding."

"Back to work. I've got to make up the loss."

"Jerry, think about this. You are way ahead. There is no way you could have made all that money and saved it up working a regular job. Take what you've got and run."

"I'm going to explain this to you one more time, Charlene, just like I told Faye. There is a big damn chance that I will wind up in prison. Any amount of time is too much. If I give up now, I will not have been true to the game."

"Being true to the game is either going to get you dead or broke and in the pen."

"If you did go with a hundred grand stashed when you get out just imagine what you could do."

"It just doesn't work like that. Is this where you want to go?"

"Yes, this is fine. Thank you. Jerry remember Faye is my best friend."

"Yeah, sure."

Charlene knocks on the door. Sheila answers.

"Is Mike here?"

"Come on in."

Charlene walks in. Mike and Tracy are sitting at the table getting high. Mike looks up and slams his hand on the table.

"Why didn't you tell me who it was at the door?"

"I didn't know that you didn't want her to know."

"It looks like I may be interrupting something."

"No problem." Mike says, trying to pacify the situation. "I didn't think you were coming."

"I overslept."

"Come on. Join the party." Tracy never blinks an eye, not recognizing the awkwardness of the situation.

"No, I think I'll pass."

"Sheila, get her a beer. You smoke weed don't you?"

"Yes."

"Here, roll yourself a joint."

Mike hands her a twenty-five dollar bag of weed. Charlene smokes a joint but is not saying too much.

"Why are you so quiet?" He finally asks.

"Just enjoying the high is all."

"You sure you don't want to hit this? Once or twice won't hurt."

"No, I'd rather not."

"Well, let me put a piece in a joint. I know you aren't worried about a primo. It's the best way really. Bring it with you. We are going to the use the back room for a while. If you need anything, holler."

Mike gets his crack, his pipe and a couple cans of beer.

It's the next evening before Faye sees Charlene again.

"You must have enjoyed yourself yesterday?"

"Yeah." Her voice lacking real enthusiasm.

"You don't sound like you did. You okay?"

"Just tired is all."

"All right, I'm going to see Jerry. I'll talk to you later."

"I'm going to have to go out of town to take care of some business. I won't be but a day." Jerry tells Faye.

"Does that mean I can't go?" Faye asks, he pulls her to him, butting heads.

"I would love for you to go but it's strictly business. Besides, I need someone to look after the store while I'm gone."

"I don't know much about it."

"You don't have to do it but one day. Get Charlene to help you. I will go over everything with you before I leave." Faye just stares at him. "I would really appreciate it. I'll leave in the morning and be back the next day or before."

Before leaving, he advises Faye, "Don't keep it all in the apartment. Only keep ten pieces at a time. Keep the rest in the car. You don't have to look like that. Everything will be okay. I promise."

"Where are you going?"

"To Texas. Me and Nick are going. I won't even be driving."

"Who is Nick?"

"You know that new club that just opened? The one that everyone hangs at now?"

"Why are you fooling with him? Charlene and I went into the club several nights ago. They were smoking crack and everything right there in the club. Every stranger who sells dope now hangs out there since they stopped them from selling downtown. All they do is sell to those young kids."

"Well I can't help what they do. I have to go where the money is. See you when I get back."

Faye does not know what she feels, but she decides to keep quiet for the moment.

"You act like you are nervous." Implies Charlene when they open up at the apartment.

"I am." Faye counters, not hesitating to admit it. "I don't know why he didn't just close down until he got back. Do you want to go out to the car or should I?" Asks Faye.

"I'll go. You watch from the door. Make sure you lock the door back Charlene."

"This package only has nine pieces in it." Warns Charlene.

"That's okay. Jerry was in a hurry. He may have miscounted."

"It's not even two o'clock and I'm already bored." Charlene says complaining.

"Don't make this any harder than it has to be, Charlene. Who is that blowing out there?"

"That's Mike. Let me go and see what he wants."

Forty-five minutes later . . .

Charlene returns.

"Where did you go?" Faye asks frustrated.

"I just went around the block."

"Around the block? How could you do me like that? You know how I feel about being in here already. What did you do? You look like you are as high as a kite. I sure hope that you didn't tell Mike that Jerry was gone."

"No."

"Yeah, I bet you didn't."

"No, I did not I promise."

"I noticed yesterday that you were acting funny. I sure hope you haven't let Mike get you started smoking again."

"No, he hasn't. Mike is cool. He wouldn't do that anyway."

"I would not put anything past him as long as he is dealing with Tracy. I really didn't think that you were going to fall for him. I just don't want you to get yourself back into something that you can't handle."

There are plenty more occasions when Jerry has to leave, not necessary to go out of town, but in the course of taking care of business. He does so more often than Faye really cares for. Charlene, of course, does not mind.

"What happened to the rest of the pieces I gave you?" Asks Jerry.

"Isn't that all of them?" Faye asks honestly.

"No. You are short six pieces." Forcing himself not to argue with her, he asks. "Where's Charlene?"

"She's gone with Mike."

"Again? This is the third time that this has happened. She has run off somewhere each time you take up with her. The next time I'm going to get on her ass regardless. Just watch her, or after a while things will start to leave the house. Then you will be walking around with tears in your eyes, raising hell. Then I don't want to hear it."

"I'll talk to her." promises Faye.

"You better."

The next time that Faye sees Charlene is almost a week later.

"I see you finally decided to show up." Faye says, not giving Charlene a chance to cover herself. "I've tried to stand up for you but you are on the same road as before. Somebody told me that you had started back stealing again. I hate to tell you but Jerry wants you to move out."

"I don't have anywhere yet."

"I can't help that. I'm sorry. I can hold Jerry off a day or two, that's all."

Charlene starts to cry.

The next day Faye comes home and Charlene is gone. A note is on the table. It reads. 'I really appreciate you trying to help me. If there is anything that I can ever do for you never hesitate to contact me. Love you, Charlene. I got most of my clothes. I didn't have room for the rest. Please hold on to them.'

The next evening Faye is arrested for a D.W.I. She calls Jerry and he is furious. "How in the hell did you get stopped and get a D.W.I. in the first place?"

"I'm not drunk." She declares. "I had a couple of drinks before I left the house. I think what really made the policeman's mind up was I had a half pint of brandy in my purse."

"Do you have enough money to make bail?"

"I have enough money, but the only way I can get out right away is for someone to come and get me. Or I will have to remain here for twelve hours at least."

"I'll be there in a few minutes."

"Thanks for coming so soon."

"You know I was not going to leave you in jail and you do look like you are drunk."

"Very funny." Faye says, trying to put some humor into the situation. "The only thing that I can say is call the lawyer and explain to him who you are and see what he can do."

"What happened to your hand?"

"You know Bryon, don't you?"

"I think so. He kept on begging for some dope and I wouldn't give him any. That's no reason to jump on him was it?"

"No, not until he asked to suck my dick for some. Then I tried to knock his teeth out."

"What is in that crack? Cocaine didn't make us act that bad, did it?" She wonders.

"No, I really don't think so."

They drive together back to the apartment.

"It looks like someone is getting a new washer and dryer." Jerry noticing first.

"That looks like Perry driving that truck." Observes Faye.

Jerry and Faye approach the apartment. Perry whistles for Jerry to come to the truck. Jerry eases his hand off of Faye as if his is unsure about her condition.

"I'm fine." She assures him.

"What do you have going on now, Perry?" Jerry asks.

"You in the market for a washer and dryer?"

"Not really."

"Come on man. They both are brand new."

"Let me talk to the old lady. Come on in. Faye, are you interested in a washer and dryer?"

"What does he want for them?"

"I don't know much about those things. If you want to you can go out there and look at them." Then changing his mind, he says "You stay here. I'll do it."

"You can tell they're still new. They are still in the cartons." Byron says, pleading his case.

"If I get them, you will have to deliver them to the house."

"You're calling the shots boss. You want them?"

"Yeah I guess so." Re-entering the apartment, Jerry has to wake up Faye.

"You haven't been to get your car yet. Come on. Let's go before they realize I've come back. Otherwise I'll never get a chance to leave."

CHAPTER 10

R ichard makes a visit to Jerry's apartment.
"Hello Richard."

"Hello Jerry."

"It's good to see you up and around. Your face is coming along great."

"It's going pretty good. I'm suppose to go for a skin graft right here. That's the only spot that does not want to heal right. How are things with you?"

"About as well as to be expected."

"How's Faye?"

"She's doing about the same. I bought a six pack. Care to indulge?"

"You off from work today?" Asks Jerry.

"Yeah, I've been off." Answers Richard.

"What do you mean by that?"

"I got fired about a week after I came out of the hospital."

"I sure hate to hear that."

"How come you didn't call me or something?"

"This may sound contradictory, but I want you to hook me up in the business."

"What business is that?"

"The same one you are in."

"Are you crazy? It has me climbing the walls, and you want to get into some shit like this? Hell, I lost close to thirty grand last month and caught some new charges to top it off."

"I could make a fortune. Half the people at the hospital are smoking now."

"What about you? Have you stopped completely."

"I'm going to be honest. I've smoked since I got out of the hospital."

You can't smoke and sell it. It just won't work."

"I don't see why not as long as you use your head."

"There's no such thing as using your head when it's full of crack, Richard."

"You used to smoke and you quit. So what makes you think that I can't?"

"I'm not saying that you can't quit. I was just lucky. I had someone and something to help me. I don't think that I could have done it any other way. Believe it or not, I still have flashes. It's a whole lot worse than trying to put these cigarettes down. Sometime even they remind me of when I used to smoke. The smell of it burning produces cramps in my stomach. Sometimes I can smell certain chemicals in the air and I have flashbacks. If it was not for the money among other things, I probably would still be smoking. Besides, this crack is a whole lot different than what I smoked. It has people doing things that I never thought that I would see or hear about them doing. Things like women having sex with dogs. Men you and I grew up with sucking dicks to get high. Stealing, robbing. Look at the women all around you. They look like shit now. They use to look like angels, and now they are suckin' and fuckin' for five dollars. They are going days and weeks without taking a bath. Fuck it. I really hate that I sell it sometimes. It makes me feel low down."

"If you don't help me get started, somebody else will."

"As smart as you are, you can get a job anywhere you want."

"When you ask me to help you get started selling weed, I helped you."

"That's totally different. I'm sorry Richard, I can't."

"All right, if that's the way you want it. I've got to go. I'll get with you later."

"What about the beer?"

"You drink it."

"Whenever you need anything, call me Richard." Richard slams the door on his way out. "Fuck it." Says Jerry opening a beer.

◇ ◇ ◇ ◇

Meanwhile . . .

On the other side of town. Several plain police cars and squad cars surround Tracy's house. Four people are escorted to jail. Among them are Tracy, Sheila, Mike, and Tracy's sister (Marilyn).

Sheila is released immediately.

"I understand that you use to work for Jerry Collins." Detective Stone asks Mike.

"I don't know a Jerry Collins."

"You don't realize what you are being charged with, do you?"

"Yes, I do."

"Looking at your previous record, I see that you have two prior charges. You were with Jerry then weren't you?"

"What difference does it make?"

"I might get this possession with intent to deliver charge thrown in the trash if you tell me where he gets his dope and from whom."

"In other words, you want me to snitch."

"Not exactly in those words."

"Forget it. Lock me up and set my bond."

"I understand that he has dumped you. Don't you realize that you are going to the joint? You might as well make it easy on yourself. Just because he bought you a car, I wouldn't go to the slammer for him."

"I really don't need to hear anymore of this crap. You need to get your information where you got the rest from."

Detective Stone picks up the telephone.

"Come and get this trash out of here."

Three days later . . .

Mike is released with no other charges pending. Marilyn is charged with possession. Tracy is charge with possession with the intent to deliver.

When Mike gets out, he goes to Tracy's place.

"Sheila, are you going to help Tracy get out?"

Sheila needs a bath. Her hair, the little she has left, has not been combed in days.

"He didn't say anything to me about it."

She says, trying to get another hit off of her pipe.

"He said he called and talked to you. He also said that you should have most of the money. I told him that I would help you get the rest."

"When I got here, someone had been in the house. I didn't find any money."

"How much was Tracy charging you a week to sell out of here?"

"Why?"

"He told me to collect from you."

"He didn't say anything to me about that when I left the jail."

"Well, I'm in charge until Marilyn gets out."

"If I have to pay rent then I'm not going to help get him out."

"You just let me worry about that."

"No wonder you don't have any money. From the looks of this pipe, it looks like you smoked it all up. Well, I tell you what, don't expect me to support your habit."

"I don't need you to. I'm not completely broke."

"At this rate you will be before tomorrow."

Once again Jerry is arrested.

"I can't talk on the telephone but I need for you to come down here tomorrow."

"Can't the lawyer get you out today?"

"No, he said that he is having trouble getting a bond set. The judge won't comply."

Faye sets up all night. Her drinking has not tapered off.

The next day . . .

He says. "You don't look like you got much rest."

"I'm fine." Her eyes telling a different story. "Have you heard from the lawyer?"

"He said to hang tight. The prosecutor wants to put a hold on me. The probation officer said he would stall as long as he could. Don't start crying." Tears flowing freely now. "Listen I'll get out. It just takes time that's all. You know where everything is in the apartment. Call Richard. I don't want you at the apartment by yourself. Just sell what I have already fixed up. It should be close to five thousand dollars worth. Use your own discretion as far as Richard is concerned. Keep an eye on him. I think he's still smoking but he's the only one I can trust at the moment besides you."

"I would rather put it all up until you get out. I don't care to be around that stuff at the moment."

"You can never tell what might happen so I would prefer that you take care if it for me."

"What do you mean, there's no telling what might happen?"

"Don't get all blown up. I'll be out in a day or two. If I need anything else. I'll have the lawyer get in touch with you if they don't let me call."

"Time is up, Mrs. Collins." Informs the officer.

"Mrs. Collins?" Asks Jerry.

"I told them that was my name. Otherwise they wouldn't have let me see you. Be careful. I love you."

They both kiss the screen that divides them.

"I love you too, baby. Don't worry. I'll get out."

The next day . . .

Faye makes it a point to call the lawyer repeatedly.

"Ma'am, I understand how you feel. I am doing what I can."

"Evidently you're not. He's still locked up. All the money he's paying you and you still can't get him out!" She yells at him, hysterical at this point.

"Mrs. Collins. Mrs. Collins, if you calm down a minute. I am in the process of getting his cases in another court. Therefore, I can handle the judge. So if you will be patient, I will get him out. I'm almost sure of it."

"I'll be looking to hear from you. Bye." Claming down for a minute, Faye hangs up the telephone rather roughly.

Then turning her attention to Richard, who has volunteered to help her.

"I'm going to see Jerry. So you can either leave now or keep the door locked and don't answer it for anybody."

"Tell him I said hello and to keep the faith." Richard offers as Faye departs.

"Hi baby."

They both place their hands up to the glass, mock touching.

"Hello. I talked to the lawyer. He said he could almost guarantee that he would get you out. He's trying another judge or something."

"First of all. How are you?"

"I'm fine."

She forces herself to smile.

"Did you get some rest last night?"

"Yes, a little bit."

"How's everything at the apartment?"

"Everything's okay."

"Is Richard giving you any problems?"

"No, he said hello. Jerry, when you get out this time, will you promise me that you will quit?"

"Faye, this is not the time or place, okay."

"We will discuss it later." She says, her voice very sober. "I cannot keep going through this. It's about to turn me into a nervous wreck."

Faye returns to the apartment. It's vacant.

"I wonder where Richard is?" She says partially out loud.

She assumes that he may have had something to do and used the opportunity to do so. She goes to where she hides the crack. She stops to think a minute. Then she ponders over the situation before she actually realizes that some of it is missing. She attempts to run a tally to see exactly how much is gone. The closest that she can figure is fifty pieces, which amounts to a little over a grand. She calls Richard's apartment. She gets no answer.

The following day . . .

Faye goes to see Jerry.

"I had to work the apartment by myself yesterday after I left here."

"What happened to Richard?"

"You have to promise me that you won't go flying off the handle. I'll take care of it because it was my fault. I should have know better."

"Will you stop talking in circles and get to the point."

"Richard left with some of the dope. He was gone when I got back. I haven't been able to reach him."

"Well, I'll be damn!! Hell, how is it your fault? Everything is falling apart. He better have a fucking good explanation."

"Let's talk about you. What did the lawyer say?"

"I haven't heard anything from him today. How about you?"

"I called. His secretary said he was out."

"Have you been to school?"

"No, I'll catch up. What do you want me to do about the apartment."

"I really don't want you there by yourself, especially at night, so just lock it up. I'll deal with it when I get out."

The following day . . .

Faye notices there are a few renegade crack dealers hanging around the apartment. It hasn't taken long for word to get out about Jerry's whereabouts. She checks the apartment and leaves.

Upon her arrival at home, the telephone rings.

"It's Mike. Hello Faye. I just called to check up on you. I understand Jerry is in jail. Is there anything I can help you with?"

"No, I can manage."

"You wouldn't need any help getting rid of some of the merchandise would you?"

"What happened to Tracy?"

"He's still in jail. Jerry didn't mention it to you?"

"No, he didn't."

"Well, maybe he doesn't know. They may be in different jails."

"I don't know. If he is not out by Friday, I might need your help then. Check with me Friday about three."

"Okay, I'll see you then."

Friday rolls around and Jerry is still not out. Mike shows up like he said he would. "I appreciate your help Mike."

"You want me to follow you home? You don't look so well."

"No thanks. I can make it."

"I don't know how much Jerry would have paid you but here's one hundred and fifty dollars."

"Thanks, do you want me to come over and work this evening?"

"I don't know. Call me about two o'clock."

"I can see you are upset, but don't worry, Jerry will get out. He knows his business."

"I know."

It's three o'clock in the morning.

Faye sits up listening to the tape Jerry made for her. She goes to the closet and gets her nightgown. She looks up and there's a shoe box. She knows what is in it. She hesitates before she takes it off the shelf. She works the rubber band partially off before it breaks. She lifts the lid. It's been a long time. The pipe stills looks the same. She take it into the living room and puts it together. Just one little hit will make me feel better. The pure grain alcohol is on the bar. She wipes the dust off the bottle.

This is not the same high that Faye was accustom to. She cannot believe the after taste that this stuff leaves in her mouth. She cleans the pipe and puts it back up. She is unable to rest afterwards. She drinks some more alcohol to help sedate her. Finally she falls asleep.

Faye visits Jerry the next day in jail.

"Why are you so nervous?"

"I'm not nervous."

"You may not realize it, but you act like it."

"I went ahead and sold some last night."

"You mean you worked by your self?"

"No. Mike stayed there with me."

"Mike!"

"Yes, I started to tell you yesterday that I might let him help. He called before and asked me if he could. I ask him where Tracy was. He said in jail."

"I heard one of the guys mention his name today. How did it go?"

"It went fine. Each time a customer came in I let Mike sell to them. I just watched."

"That's a real smart move. That's what I should have done. Maybe I wouldn't have the first charge I got."

"How much did you get rid of last night?"

"Close to seventeen hundred."

"Any other problems?"

"No, I missed you last night."

"I miss you too. These kind of days make a man wish he'd spent more time a home."

"Maybe you will. I sure hope so."

"Did you hear anything from Richard?"

"Not as of yet."

"I can't believe he would do you like that."

"He's been through a lot lately. He wasn't quite himself anyway. There is no telling what was on his mind. You know there is no visitation tomorrow, don't you?"

"I guess I'll have to see you Monday. Hopefully, I'll be out by then."

This time Faye hits the pipe before she goes to the apartment, placing the shoe box in the trunk of the car afterwards. During the course of the evening, she goes into the bedroom of the apartment and locks the door. When she exits the room she feels paranoid. She attempts to eat some chicken. She just nibbles at it before putting it into the refrigerator.

"Has Tracy got out yet?" She asks, making conversation with Mike.

"No. His brother is supposed to be coming from out of town to get him out."

"What about Sheila? How come she didn't get him out?"

"She's too busy smoking to be of any use. The only reason that his brother is coming is because Tracy is going to pawn his car to him for getting him out."

"What happened to all that money he had?"

"A fool and his money does not last long."

"What about you?"

"What do you mean?"

"I know that you are smoking."

"How do you figure that?"

"Don't you think I know what you are doing when you keep running to the bathroom? It shows. You have lost weight and everything. Come to think of it, I don't know why I let you work after the way you did Charlene."

Faye is intoxicated and apprehensive herself.

"I thought we had that settled yesterday."

"Drop it."

"She was going to start back smoking anyway." Urges Mike.

"When do you go to court?"

"Next month."

"Have you gotten a lawyer yet?"

"Yeah, Mary Briggs."

Faye looks at him in a peculiar manner.

"Do you know her?"

"Everybody does. She can't sit still in the courtroom for thinking about another hit of the pipe."

"She said she wouldn't charge me that much. I've already paid her seven hundred and fifty dollars. I owe her four hundred and fifty more."

"Well, I wish you all the luck in the world."

"She's not the only lawyer walking in and out of the courtroom in a daze. Charles Mason has been all out in the projects smoking. He's charging five hundred dollars and an eight ball to handle cases."

"They need to take his license. I know he smokes for sure myself."

"You know David Parks?"

"Not really."

He got twenty years for selling two rocks. Johnny got the same thing, but he's out on appeal."

"Did they go to jury trial?"

"Yeah."

"What about you? Are you going to a jury?"

"It depends on whether or not my lawyer can reach a decent plea bargain."

"It's really best to try and plea bargain. If you go to a jury, you are going to be found guilty anyway. You can't beat these white folks."

"What about Jerry?"

"I don't know yet. We are going to close at twelve tonight."

"That's when they really start coming."

"That's too bad. Not on Sunday."

"Can I buy a sixteenth before I leave?".

"I don't have any packages that size. If you want dope instead of cash, I will give you ten quarters rather than money."

When the night is over, Mike assists Faye in leaving. He doubles back to sell what she has given him. He takes three pieces out to smoke and sits on the steps of the apartments to get rid of the rest. This is hampered by the police who ride through and shine their spotlight. After seeing they are going to make the block, he rushs to his car and lays down in the seat until he is sure they have gone on about their business. He leaves and goes over to Tracy's. Sheila is still up. She inquires as to how much crack Mike has and talks him into not selling it, in return for a good time.

Faye goes home, and hides the money she has made. The shoe box has become her companion for the night once again. Daybreak has edged its way in before she realizes it. She decides it is time to quit. She takes a shower and observers herself in the mirror. For the first time, she notices the effect the alcohol is taking on her. Eating is just a passing thought at the moment. She will make up for it tomorrow for sure. She can't sleep so she decides to go to the church with her mother.

"Is Jerry still in jail?"

"Yes, Mama."

"Why don't you spend the night over here rather than staying cooped up in that house all by yourself?"

"Thanks, Mama, but I'd rather stay at home."

"Don't worry yourself honey. Just believe and it will be all right. You get some rest, too. You look tired."

Upon returning to the house, she sleeps until ten o'clock that night to be awaken by a knock on the door.

"Were you asleep?" Charlene asks Faye.

"A little bit.

"I didn't mean to wake you."

"Come on in. I could use some company anyway."

The shoe box is still sitting on the table.

"Want a drink?" Offers Faye.

"I guess I could. I heard about Jerry. I'm sorry."

"Oh, he'll be all right."

"What about you?"

"Everything's fine."

"When is the last time you saw Mike?"

"I haven't. He acts too funny at times. I've been staying with Debbie."

"I didn't know she was back in town. How is she?"

"She's doing okay."

"No, I mean as far as her rehabilitation."

"She doing good. She's back at the arsenal making good money. She goes to counseling once a week. I make it a point to keep everything away from her. I'm so glad for her. She appears to really be happy too."

"What's this? Some new shoes?" Faye's reflexes are too slow. Charlene raises the lid.

"What are you doing with this? You haven't gone back to smoking have you?"

"It's just something to do until Jerry gets home."

"Jerry would have a fit if he knew you smoked any at all."

"When he gets out, I'll stop like I did before. It's all in your mind anyway."

"I sure could use a good bump about now."

"If you want you can. I don't mind."

"Make sure you are not short on Jerry's money."

"I'm not broke, remember. If I smoked all this, I could pay for it easily."

"Don't get any ideals." Faye warns Charlene

"I don't plan to."

Before the night is done, they manage to smoke three hundred dollars worth of crack. Charlene smoking the majority.

"I'm tired of smoking." Complains Faye "Let's clean this mess up. My chest has started to feeling funny."

Faye is cleaning the pipe out with alcohol and starts to pour it down the drain. Charlene asks.

"You are not going to pour that residue out are you?"

"Why not?"

"That's another two or three good hits."

"Here you clean it then. I want a drink."

Jerry's lawyer comes to see him Tuesday.

"Sorry it took so long. I just came from seeing the judge."

"What did he say?"

"He agreed to set you a bond at ten thousand dollars. This is the last time he is going to set a bond for you. He said strictly cash."

Jerry heart leaps, but then he sighs heavily.

"If you can get me a phone call, I can arrange to have the money brought down here."

That evening Jerry is released. He doesn't worry about the apartment. He only goes by and checks on it.

"Jerry?" Faye asks after a number hours in bed.

"Yeah."

"I want to ask you something."

"Shoot."

"Uh, there's nobody here but me and you, right?"

"I hope so I'd hate to think there's a spy in the house, but then you can't never tell about them folks."

"Stop it. I'm serious. Let's get high and relax."

"That's fine with me. You want to fix the drinks or should I?"

"I'm not talking about getting drunk."

"You don't smoke weed so that's out. Well maybe you do once in a while."

Faye has gets up and gets the shoe box.

"This is what I am talking about." She says,

"You have got to be kidding!"

Jerry comes out of his relaxed position.

"If I was, I would not have asked. I'm trying to be as honest as I possibly can in this relationship."

"No, Faye."

"There come a time when I want to do things. I want to do them with you."

"I said No!"

"Well here. I can pay for it. Is that what you want?"

"Is that it!" Slap. He raps her across the head. "What in the hell has gotten into you?" He grabs her, pinning her arms up against the wall and trying to restrain her physical efforts.

"Let me go. I tell you one thing. If you don't, I am going to do it anyway!"

Jerry slaps her several more times.

"You been smoking this shit while I have been locked up."

"No, I have not. You just think I do everything to make you happy. So far you have only thought of yourself. Day in and day out I drink myself in to a stupor. Well, tonight I refuse to do that. To top it off I have to face the realization that you are going to the penitentiary. Well that's something I just can't do!"

"Shut the hell up!"

"I'm not finished. You can kick my ass if you want. It's time you woke up and realized this is not a game. What in the fuck do you figure I'm going to do when you are gone? Tell me that!" She yells, whisking the hair from her face. "You have an answer for everything else. Answer that!" Jerry does not answer, she has tears running down her face. "Damit! What am I suppose to do?" She cries.

"Faye, I want you to understand one thing. I love you. I always have. I never intended for things to happen this way."

"Well if you love me, understand just this once, will you? You don't have to get hooked. We quit before. We can quit anytime we get ready."

Jerry lights a cigarette. He puffs on it nervously as he ties his robe.

"I really wish you would stop crying. It makes me nervous."

"Something needs to make you respond."

"How come you didn't tell me how you felt earlier?"

"You have got to be deaf and blind. What do you think I've been saying."

"I tell you what. You can do what you want. Get as high as you want."

"So now it's do what I want. Kick me out of the car. What's the matter? You afraid that you can't handle it? As money hungry as you are you wouldn't dare smoke it all up. I'm sure of that."

"Come on. Let's do this so I don't have to listen to this shit all damn night." He says watching her smoke a minute before taking it himself. "This shit is as nasty as hell."

"It's what you sell."

"What's up with you, resentment or what?"

"What do you think?"

Jerry goes and gets a beer.

"What are you peeping out of the window for?"

"I don't know. I just am." Replies Jerry. "I thought I heard something."

"It's your imagination. Sit down and relax."

"Doesn't this crack make have you nervous?"

"A little. I just recognize it as a part of the high." After a couple more hits, Jerry says. "I've had enough you can smoke the rest of that piece."

"I'm putting up the rest." Faye acts as though she does not hear him. It really doesn't matter. She has another piece anyway.

Twenty minutes later . . .

He asks. "You still not finished yet?"

"Be through in a minute."

A strange thought flashes in Jerry's his head. He feels he has been compromised.

"You feel better now?" He asks, as Faye climbs in the bed beside Jerry.

"Thank you." She says as she starts kissing on him.

"I really don't care for that shit. I feel like a fuckin rabbit." Jerry says, still uncomfortable.

"Let me fix you a drink. It will mellow you out."

After half of his drink is finished.

She asks. "You okay now?"

"Sure, I'm not sleepy though."

"You will be when I get finished." She promises, fondling him.

"Either that stay in jail made you extra horny or that pipe did." Faye says after their lovemaking.

"Why do you say that?"

"You haven't made love to me like that in a long time."

"I don't know whether to take that as a complement or an insult."

"Don't worry. It's a complement." She says, kissing him on the shoulder. "What are you going to do tomorrow?"

"Take care of some business probably."

The next day Charlene comes by.

"Did Jerry get out yet?"

"Yes, honey. I'm so glad. I'm also glad you came by. I want you to do something for me. Come on."

Faye stops around the corner from the apartment and lets Charlene out.

"Get a sixteenth already rocked up. If it's not rocked up get as many quarters as you can."

A few minutes later . . .

Faye asks Charlene. "Who was there with Jerry?"

"Nick and some other guy. They were drinking beer and talking."

"Where are we going now?"

"Where do you think? Home."

"Suppose Jerry comes home?"

"He won't. I'll call and see what's up. Jerry and I smoked some last night."

"How did you manage that?"

"We just did it."

"I know Nick smokes. I smoked some with him last week."

Later that night . . .

Jerry says. "Faye put me some hot water on the stove. I have to cook up some. I ran out." Jerry gets the large mirror and a couple of single edged razor blades.

"Do you know what you are doing?"

"Yep. By cooking it in hot water you really don't have to worry about catching anything on fire."

After cooking and cutting the crack into the correct sizes, there are some crumbled pieces left over. "Where is that pipe at?" Asks Jerry. Faye quickly goes and gets it "We might as well smoke up the crumbs. There is no use in wasting them. Willie would love to have these."

"When is the last time you saw him anyway?"

"I haven't. He doesn't even buy from me. If he does, he sends someone else to buy it. This is the last time we are going to smoke any of this for a while. I don't need a habit right now for sure."

"I understand."

"You sure have settled down since last night. You're not drunk either."

"I like that part for sure."

"Don't start peeping all out the windows all over again. All you have to do is relax when you smoke."

"This stuff won't let me relax. Save some of it. Don't smoke it all. I have to get back to the apartment."

"You don't have that long before one o'clock. You'd be surprised what you could do in that length of time."

Well this is not the last time Jerry smokes and certainly not Fayes. With the help of Charlene and a few others, Faye's bank account begins to dwindle.

"I've got to go to Little Rock. I'll be back shortly." Says Jerry, instead he goes over to Nick's, there a couple of younger girls, the oldest being nineteen.

Nick tells him. "You don't have to worry about anything over here and certainly not your old lady. Here, take this to the back room." Nick gives Jerry the pipe and the alcohol. "Pick either one of those young freaks you want or we can switch up. It makes no difference to me."

Meanwhile . . .

Faye is having a party of her own at one of the motels in a secluded part of town.

"This sort of reminds me of the old times we use to have." Says Ann.

"It sure does. I remember we used to get high as a kite." Adds Faye.

"I feel a lot better smoking here at the motel than I do at your house." Says Charlene. "If Jerry showed up there would be hell to pay."

"He doesn't mind if he and I smoke, but he doesn't want me smoking it with anybody else."

"Well that's understandable." Seconds Ann.

"Don't forget, Ann. I want an outfit like the one you have on."

"No problem. Charlene and I are going first thing in the morning."

"We have to go as soon as the mall opens while they are still trying to get organized. The security has really been heavy since that old woman and her daughter got robbed on the parking lot."

"Did they catch the people who robbed them?" Asks Faye.

"Yeah and you know them too. It was two boys and a girl. The girl was Kenny Smith's sister. I know the boys when I see them."

"I want the outfit but don't get caught in the process. I don't have the money to get you out."

"You've got the money it just depends on if you want to spend it or not."

"Don't bet on it. That reminds me. I have not paid that D.W.I. fine I got."

"I bet you won't get another one, will you?" Mocks Charlene.

"That one scared me to death, just going to jail."

After leaving the motel, they get in the car.

"Drive straight Faye! The police are behind us!" Nervously yells Charlene.

"I am driving straight! Shit."

"Both of you settle down." Ann says, calmer than either of them. "Make the next right turn Faye. I'll throw the pipe out."

Ann throws the pipe out of the car and the police keeps going.

"Jerry is going to kill me." Cries Faye. "Did the pipe break?"

"You know it did the way Ann threw it out." Snaps Charlene.

"What are you doing now?" Ann wants to know.

"I'm going back to see. What do you think?"

The only thing that is left are the two stems. The bowl is shattered.

"That's what I say about this crack. It has you paranoid for no reason." Regretfully states Charlene.

"Do either of you know anybody who sells them in town?" Charnel and Ann both shake their heads no.

Faye drops them off. She is trying to think of something to tell Jerry that won't arouse his suspension.

Meanwhile . . .

Jerry goes by the house and knows the pipe is missing. He leaves and goes back to the apartment. As he sits there, his thoughts wander. He wonders if he has opened a can of worms that he can't handle or whether they were already opened. Was that big display of emotion the other night a build up to what she wanted anyway? He had thoughts of what she might have been doing while he was in jail. His thoughts are more intense now. The action he wants to take is hampered by the guilt he feels himself.

A loud knock at the door interrupts his thoughts.

"You made it back I see." Faye says.

"Why didn't you come by the house?"

Jerry does not answer.

"What's wrong with you?"

"Nothing. I was just thinking."

"I just wanted to check on you."

"I'm okay."

"Did you get your business taken care of."

"I guess you could say that. We started to go to Little Rock but we changed our minds."

"It may have been the best that you did. I dropped the pipe while I was cleaning it. I thought that I would tell you so you wouldn't be mad."

"How did that happen?"

"I just dropped it on the floor."

"Good. Now I don't have to worry about it."

"I saved the stems and put the rest in the trash. If you're hungry I'll go home and cook."

"I'll be there after a while."

"You sure you're okay?"

"I said yes!" He says irritably now. He knows she is lying to him. He also knows that the only thing that can make her lie to him is the crack.

While Faye is on her way to the house, she wonders if Jerry knows anything. Had he been by the house and not mentioned it? She hopes she did not sell herself short. The last thing she needs is for him to mistrust her.

"I really need to stop smoking." She says out loud.

She calls Jerry and asks him if he wants her to bring his food to him. He says that he will be home. Faye has fallen asleep and wakes up before he makes it home.

It's two o'clock in the morning.

"I thought you were coming home to eat."

"I got tied up."

"You want me to warm it up in the microwave?"

"If you want."

"You don't sound well."

"Just tired, that's all."

"Are you sure?"

He does not answer right away.

"Why do you keep asking me if I'm okay. Should I be or what."
She knows he knows something is up, he's just not saying. "Did you
go to school this morning?" He asks harshly.

"No".

" And why not?"

"I just decided to wait until everything__."

"Everything what?"

"Everything settles down. Why are you snapping at me?"

"Well, it's settled. Make sure you go in the morning."

He chooses not to say anything else the rest of the night.

Faye gets ready for school the next morning. She looks in the
mirror and notices her complexion. She has a few unwarranted
pimples. Knowing how bad her skin had gotten at one time while
she was using drugs before, she applies some medicated cream on
her face and leaves it while she finishes getting ready.

"Hey Jerry, you coming down to the club again tonight?" Asks
Nick, while they are sitting around the apartment drinking beer.
"Business was pretty good last night."

"I might."

"What's the matter with you?"

"You act like you just lost your best friend." Says Nick.

Drake butts in. "Speaking of best friends, Mike got eighteen
years this morning."

"Whew! Eighteen! I don't know if selling this shit is worth all the
time they give you or not." Blurts out Jerry.

"It's not, you can believe that." Replies Nick. "Tracy goes to
court tomorrow."

"I thought he just got out again."

"He did, but he has to go to court tomorrow on the first charge.
He said something about trying to get all of them condensed into
one charge. That's the only way they let him. In fact, what they
actually do is run all of the time you get, concurrent instead of con-
secutive."

Drake seems knowledgeable about the proceedings.

"So much for jail talk. I don't want to hear it." Jerry interrupts, wanting to cut the conversation short.

"What's the matter with you, J.C.?"

"I know it's not Mike. You were acting weird last night."

"Nothing that I can't handle."

"Here hit this. It will make you feel better."

"No that's all right Nick."

"Go ahead. This is the real deal, not like that junk we sell."

Jerry hits the pipe several times before he loosens up.

"Say, Nick, you are not going to believe this."

"What's that?"

"Faye thinks she has gotten slick. I allowed her the smoke the pipe with me. She thinks I don't know that she is steady smoking with whom I don't know. I intend to find out."

"Drake, go and check the front." Nick says. "Let me tell you something Jerry. Don't take it personal but from one man to another. You can't allow your feelings to get in your way, especially in this business. Otherwise it will drive you insane. You get what you can and let it go at that. That includes women and all. As far as your main lady is concerned, keep her at a safe distance at all times. She doesn't need to smoke at all. A woman on crack ain't shit. You see how Sheila did Tracy. She used to be a good girl. Now she's a real bitch. A man has to know how to handle a good woman when he has one. You see, I don't allow mine to come around at all. If she wants something she calls. I'll get there when I can. You better wise up."

It's lunch time at school . . .

Faye leaves. She parks in a secluded area and fulfills her desire. She is high. She also chastises herself as she looks in the rear view mirror to gather herself. She knows that she is headed down the same road at a higher rate of speed than she was before.

"This is the last time." She speaks out loud. This time she really means it.

At home . . .

The phone rings. "Faye, what are you doing?"

"Nothing in particular."

"Will you come over to Ann's house and pick me up?"

"I really don't have time, Charlene."

"We've got that outfit you wanted."

"I'll be there as soon as I talk to Jerry."

Minutes later . . .

She is at their door.

"That didn't take long."

"I told Jerry I wouldn't be long, so come on. What's Ann's problem?"

"I think the neighbors called the police. The neighbors told them that the kids were left at home all night by themselves. Next thing we know, S.C.A.N. is here. They were mad, too. The baby is real sick. They may press charges on her. I hope not."

"You can just give me fifty dollars for the outfit. I already paid Ann. Take me over to the west side. I have to take these over to Marilyn's."

"What's she doing now?"

"She's selling crack. Her and Sheila got to fighting the other night. Sheila stole some of her dope. As soon as Tracy goes to the joint, Marilyn is going to put her out."

As soon as Charlene gets the dope, she puts it in her homemade pipe.

"Don't smoke it in the car. You know the police are bad around here." Says Faye.

"Make a left turn here. Stop at the corner. We can go in here and finish." Charlene says.

"We are going to have to hurry. Remember what I told you."

It is after nine o'clock when they finish.

Faye is worried about how Jerry is going to react.

"Do you want me to go with you? I will tell Jerry that it was my fault."

"No, I'll handle it. I'll just tell him about Ann. I don't want to get you mixed up in it. I should have left when I started to."

"I thought you were coming right back?" Says Jerry.

"I was, but when I got over to Ann's the police were there. They took the kids." "So what did you have to hang around for?"

"I couldn't just leave."

"That's no excuse. You could have called. I might as well say what's on my mind. I don't know which you value the most at this point, our relationship or that damn crack. But I refuse to put up with this shit."

"What are you talking about? I don't say anything when you come in all times of the night."

"It's not for you to say. I've been doing this as long as we have been together. So if you can't handle it, you certainly don't have to."

"What is that suppose to mean?"

"Exactly what you think it means. If you can't control yourself, you need to tell me now. We can end this relationship in a heart-beat."

"If you are looking for an excuse to leave, don't look for me to give you one."

"I'm not into playing head games, Faye Clark. Just because you know I care does not mean you can play me for a fool. Case closed. I don't care to discuss it anymore. Clean this house up. It's a mess. What time does school normally get out anyway?"

"About three thirty. I usually make it home at four."

"Jerry must really be mad at you." Says Charlene a few days later.

"This is the only time I get a chance to get high with you."

"The only thing he's doing is making sure you stay at home so he can freak those young girls without getting caught."

"Charlene, I resent that statement. You don't have any right to say something like that."

"I don't know why in the hell not. I heard Drake talking about how they freaked JoAnn."

"When was that?"

"Forget it. I should not have said that. I don't know for sure."

"It's to late now. When was it?"

"I don't know. It's been a couple of weeks, I guess."

Faye puts on a pair of jeans she hasn't worn in a while. She closes the bathroom door to get a look in the full length mirror. There was a time these pants fitted perfectly, but now they hang on her. She drinks a V-8 to ease her conscience.

"Jerry."

"What is it?"

"You don't have to sound like that."

"I didn't mean to. Excuse me."

"Yes you did."

"What do you mean? Yes you did."

"Nothing Jerry. I want you to get me pregnant."

"What brought that on?"

"I just want a child by you."

"Can't you pick a better time to discuss that than now?'

"What better time would you suggest?"

"Let's talk about it tomorrow."

"Do you love me?"

"Faye, listen. Just because we have our difficulties doesn't mean I don't."

"Do I satisfy you in bed?"

"Yes. Can we discuss this tomorrow?"

Faye fixes herself a drink and settles down to watch television.

"Charlene, I want you to do something for me."

"What?"

"Don't come around for a while, okay? It's nothing personal, but I need some air. I have to quit smoking. I want Jerry to get me pregnant so that I will quit."

"You don't have to get pregnant to quit."

"I know, but it will give me a purpose."

"You've got two purposes already. You don't need another."

"I need some kind of purpose. I can't quit like I thought I could."

"Sure, you can. It's all in your mind."

"I mean it Charlene, Stay away."

"If you feel things are that far gone, why don't you go to a rehab center?"

"I can't afford to leave right now, especially with everything going the way it is." "If Jerry needs you he can call. Do it for yourself, not for Jerry or anyone else."

"I don't need a lecture. I know what needs to be done."

"Jerry can we talk now?" Asks Faye.

"Let me say this. I've been doing some thinking on the subject. There are a lot of things that you need to take into consideration. For one, I have a good chance of going to the joint. I don't want my kids to have to do without me or you. Or without anything for that matter. I wasn't raised on welfare. I don't want my kids raised that way."

"When I finish school and get a job, I will be making good money."

"That's another thing. It would be wise to get your career in the proper prospective before setting up any obstacles, that will inevitably slow you down or stop you from accomplishing these goals. Having a child will not broaden this relationship. The relationship needs to be steady."

"What are you saying? That it's not steady?"

"Quit being on the defensive all the time. You didn't used to be like that. Last but not lease, bringing a child into the world on dope of any kind is out. That goes for Mama and Daddy both."

"The baby won't be born on dope. Don't you think I have enough sense to quit at a time like that?"

"Sure. I believe you can do anything you really want when you want it. But it seems to me that you have given up as far as the stability of the relationship and the future are concerned."

"Well I don't. You'll see."

For the next two and half days Faye is determined to show what she is made of. She can quit smoking crack. She drinks really to compensate, despite her unconscious willingness to be honest with herself. Finally, she allows herself to smoking just one piece which she obtains by buying someone else a piece in order to go and get hers. Her excuse is there is no use in stopping all at once. If she can smoke in intervals, then she is not addicted.

Jerry's new ring of associates are determine to show him what life is all about. In turn he spends much more time showing off and enjoying himself he does taking care of business. Foolishly he looses several thousand dollars shooting dice and making senseless bets.

"Lisa is rather fond of you. Every time I look around she want to know more about you." Nick tells him.

"Well, Nick, she can just get uninterested. I don't need anyone who wants to get attached. I've got enough problems. All I want is a good fuck and a fast good-bye."

"Hey hey, that's my boy. What she needs is to get something constructive going for herself. If she keeps hanging around a dog like you, she won't look good for long."

"Wait, home boy. That's a low blow. I'm not that bad, Jerry. I just give them what they need. You would not believe, I went though the projects the other day and these young girls tried to proposition me for some crack. They couldn't have been no older than fifteen at the most. You'd be surprised. A lot of times, their moms put them up to do things like that by threatening to kick them out of the house."

"You're right. I better get to the apartment. You guys are making all the money."

"We will be over to kick it with you later."

On the way to the apartment, Jerry stops at the liquor store.

"Hi Jerry."

"What's up, Tricia? What are you doing way on this side of town?"

"Just out. I saw your mother the other night. Well I see her every day, but you might need to check on her."

"Is she all right or what?"

She was doing okay, but she was walking at two o'clock in the morning. I was on my way in. I stopped and we had a long talk. She is really worried about you. She really doesn't know what to do. She looked as if she had been crying but tried to straighten up when I stopped to talk. You should at least call her to check on her. It might make her feel better."

"I'll give her a call."

"I've known your mother a long time, Jerry. She's a good woman. I'll tell her I saw you."

"Thanks Tricia. Can I get you something?"

"No, I can get it."

Patricia attempts to pay for her purchase. Jerry reaches over her in an effort to take care of it himself.

"I insist."

"Thanks, I'll see you later."

Jerry calls his mother's house after reaching the apartment and he receives no answer. He knows she is at work. It eases his conscious for a moment though.

After he returns home, he calls again.

"Hello, Mom."

"Hi Son. How are you?"

Before he can answer that question, she starts talking.

"You finally decided to call your mother. What's the matter? Did you receive any of my messages?"

"Yes, Mom, I got them. I've just been busy. That's all."

"You should never get to busy to call your mother."

"I know. I saw Patricia earlier today. She told me that she saw you. What are you doing out at that time of morning?"

"Fresh air never hurt anyone."

"That's true. But at two o'clock in the morning, that's a little too much fresh air. Besides the way things are going on in this town you really need to stop it."

"I had my pistol in my purse."

"That's beside the point. How about dinner Sunday evening?"

"I thought you would never ask. I could fix you dinner at home. You probably could use a good meal."

"We are going out to eat."

"Save your money, son. I know how expensive these lawyers and things are."

"I still can afford dinner. That won't change the situation any."

"How's Faye?"

"She's fine."

"That's good. She doesn't call me like she use to."

"Well, you know how school and trying to look after me can be. Listen I've got to go. I'll see you Sunday. Don't forget! Bye."

"What is that I smell?"

"Weed."

"You must have had company."

"No, I just smoked a joint."

"You don't know what you want to do, do you?" Jerry asks, fussing at Faye.

"I figured I could smoke it in place of crack."

"I'm not contradicting you at all. I'm glad to see that you are making some type of effort to quit, even though you should not substitute one for the other. You were not born with any of these mind blowers. So you can do without them if you want to."

"How are you coming along?"

"Not as well as I would like."

"You still having trouble maintaining around Nick and the others?"

"That plays a part. I believe I could do better if I didn't have to look at it every day."

"You know the funny thing about this crack is, I don't really like the high it's fucked up. But I go to it when I feel down, disgusted, angry, or whatever."

"I'm glad you recognize it as being that sort of drug. Maybe we can do something that will fill those voids in our lives."

"We don't do the things we once did. I really miss them."

"So do I. How much time do you have left in school?"

"Maybe close to three months."

"Maybe then we can take a vacation on the coast."

"We could do that now." She says, wanting to get away.

"Don't even try it. You will be finished with school before you know it."

"I though you would be ready, Mom. I told you I would be here."

"I know how things are right now. I thought maybe you got tied up or something. You didn't bring Faye with you?"

"No, I wanted to spend this evening with you."

"That's nice to here. Come on in here where it's light so I can get a good look at you. I knew I should have cooked you a good meal. Faye is not feeding you or you're just not eating."

"It's not her fault Mom."

"You're not worrying yourself, are you?"

"No, I just kind of let things take their own course."

"Well, that's good. Are you praying?"

"Yes, Mother."

"I know you don't want to hear it but prayer helps. You never get to big for Him."

"Mom, you need to come on. It's getting late."

"Be ready in a minute."

CHAPTER 11

Knock, Knock, Knock.

"Hello Mr. Collins Did you receive your notices?" Ask the landlord.

"Yes."

"Either you are going to have to pay your rent or I am going to have to ask you to leave. I haven't said much to you even though you sell dope all times of the night. So I do expect you to pay your rent."

"How far behind am I?"

"The last time I received any rent was back in May. And it's was late then if I remember correctly. This is August. I can't wait any longer."

"I will get with you tomorrow."

"I'll be looking for you."

The middle aged woman with graying hair smiles forcefully and walks off.

The next day Jerry goes by the office and pays one month's rent and promises to pay the rest.

❖　　　❖　　　❖　　　❖

"I sure wish you would comb your hair." Pleads Jerry.

"It's combed." Answers Faye.

"Well, comb it again."

"I don't know why you are still walking around here raising hell. If you're still mad about that ounce and a half of dope, I would appreciate it if you would take it out on somebody else instead of me. If you think about it hard enough, you will realize that you didn't bring it home. Between all those buddies of yours, there's no telling who picked it up. If you're accusing me of getting it, you might as well say so."

"Did I say you got it?"

"You might as well. What I don't understand is why you have to carry so much at one time anyway. This is not the first time you have lost a considerable amount of crack or money for that matter."

"When I want some advice on how much dope and money to carry I will ask. Until then just shut up."

"I'll shut up all right the next time you go to jail and need someone to play messenger. I want you to remember that! Where are you going?" Faye asks as Jerry exits the door, following behind him. "That's all you know to do is run. You're not man enough to stand up and face things." Jerry ignores her. He starts the car and burns rubber.

Once at the apartment, he raises the bottom of the cabinet under the sink and retrieves his pipe. He takes a hit and peeps out the windows constantly. The telephone has been disconnected for a while now. It serves as a hiding spot for crack. Jerry sits up and smokes for hours at a time. On several occasions he has invited not only just women to join him but men as well. Sometimes he knows little or nothing about them at all. It beats smoking alone when he's not at home. Business has long since dwindled to a mere trickle. At times it is completely at a stand still. No matter. Jerry still goes there every day as if business is normal.

"Your mother called again." Faye says when he gets home. "I wish you would return her calls. I get tired of lying to her."

"Will you just do as I ask?"

"When you get time, I need to talk to you. It's very important."

"What is it? You can tell me now."

"Okay then. I think I'm pregnant."

"Have you been to the doctor?"

"No."

"Well, go to the doctor and then let me know."

"Oh, I can't stand you, Jerry Collins."

"I've been told worst."

Faye rolls a joint and adds some pieces of crack to it.

"You must not be pregnant. You haven't slacked up on smoking that shit."

"At least I'm not smoking the pipe."

"That's just as bad or worse. Tony smokes primos, one right after the other and he's as crazy as hell. He stays paranoid. Even when he's not high or smoking. Its taking it's toll on you whether you want to admit it or not. I admit I smoke and it's not doing me a bit of good."

"That's the first sensible thing that I've heard you say in a long time."

"I have slacked up on the beer but you drink alcohol, smoke weed and crack. What's next? You never seem to get high. Your body can't take that kind of abuse on a constant basis. You may not want to listen, but I really wish you would."

"I didn't think you cared anymore."

"Crap! I didn't make you pay for your dope to get the money. I did it in an effort to try and get you to stop."

"You're the reason I'm the way I am now."

"Don't you think that's being a bit unfair?"

"No, not at all."

"This is not the first time I've told you that. If I am pregnant, do you want me to have the child?"

"I hope that you are not. We discussed that some months ago."

"Well if I am, I'm not going to have an abortion. I'll just quit using drugs period."

"That would be the only good thing about it. Still, I don't want a child."

On the other side of town in St. Luke's apartments . . .

Several eviction notices are being served. Not because the small amount of rent that is required has not been paid, but because there is too much traffic going in and out of the apartments. They have received several warnings. Two or three crack dealers at a time operate out of an apartment. Disturbances throughout the night are not uncommon. Guns in the hands of youngsters are like mere toys. Target practice at street lights and road signs is evident. Small gangs always occupy the breeze ways and stairwells of these apartments, no matter what time of day or night it is.

"What did the doctor say today?" Jerry asks.

Faye, as she reaches into her pocket and hands Jerry some folded papers. Then she walks off.

"Wait a minute."

"I don't want to talk about it."

"I think we need to. The only way I don't talk about it is if it's not mine." Faye stops abruptly.

"What in the hell does that mean?" She raises her hand to slap Jerry but he catches her by the wrist. "Why?"

"Why what? We discussed this several times. So I know it was not an accident."

"Those pills are not one hundred percent effective."

"As long as we've been going together they have been. So what's wrong with them now?"

"You really don't want a baby do you?"

"No, I sure don't."

"You might as well accept the idea because I am not going to get rid of it and that's for sure."

"If that's the way you want it, but I don't have to accept it."

"Where are you going?" She asks him as he storms around the house. Jerry does not answer. He just gathers a few things and starts to leave. "You think, I'm a toy or something don't you? Well, you will see."

"We sure will you bastard. Why don't you take all of your clothes with you?"

"Pack them. I'll be back."

"No, you won't. Go stay with that other bitch you've been fucking!!"

"Have it your way."

Jerry storms out. Faye slams the door.

It's two o'clock in the morning.

Faye is sitting up listening to the stereo, smoking crack out of a homemade pipe and drinking brandy. The pipe is made out of a piece of radio antenna.

Jerry is at a motel room and does not seem to be disturbed by the current situation. He and two other women sit naked on the plush carpeted floor. A mirror lies on the floor between them. An ice chest sits near the bed. It is full of beer and liquor.

At three-thirty in the morning, Faye is depressed and frustrated she decides to go by the apartment. She has her own key. To her surprise, no one is there. She looks around for evidence that might indicate if Jerry was recently there. There is none. She searches the apartment for crack. She again comes up with nothing. It only adds to her depressed disposition. She has some crack at the house, but it is not enough to carry her through the night. How she would love to have someone to talk to. She checks her pockets for some money and comes up with only a few bills. She opens the glove box and produces her money card. Going to the automatic teller machine posted outside the bank, she draws a hundred dollars from her almost exhausted bank account.

After not having any luck on the west side where she knows some drugs should be. She chastises herself for not going to the east in the first place, but she uses the opportunity to look for Jerry's truck. As she drives into the projects, a young man quickly approaches her.

"What do you need?" He says.

"You don't look like you sell dope."

"I can get it for you though."

"Forget it."

Faye gets out of the car and walks toward a group of young men who at least look like they might sell crack.

"What do you need baby?"

"I know what she needs." One of them replies.

"I don't mess with babies." Faye says sarcastically.

"What I got you'd love." He laughs, grabbing his crotch.

Faye ignores him and asks if any one of them might have a gram.

"I don't have a gram but I can give you these five pieces for ninety dollars." One of them quickly offers.

She hands him five twenty dollar bills. Faye wraps the crack in the ten dollar bill she receives as change. She starts to drive off when a woman she recognizes waves at her.

The woman approaches the car, and they speak casually.

"I haven't seen you around in a awhile."

"I stay at home a lot now."

"What are you getting high on?"

"I've got a little something if you have a place around here close." She gets in the car and directs Faye to the back of the apartment complex. They get out of the car and go to an apartment. The woman pushes the door open. There are no lights. The smell is the first thing that Faye notices. The woman flicks her lighter and lights a candle. "You don't have any lights in here?" Faye asks

"No, they've been shut off."

"Who stays here?"

"I use to. I got evicted."

"I'm fixing to go. I don't want to get caught in here."

"No, don't leave." She begs. "It's cool. I promise." She lights another candle. Faye can see better now. Beer cans clutter the floor as well as trash, garbage and baby diapers. The table is decorated with candle wax, cigarette butts, ashes, and burnt matches. The furniture is ripped up.

"Do you sleep here?"

"Yeah, when I can't find any where else."

"It so hot in here. I'm sorry, I can't stay."

"Will you give me one piece before you go."

"Come out to the car." Faye turns on the interior light. The woman has her homemade pipe in her hand already. Faye starts to ask to use it. She thinks about the condition of the apartment and the smell of her clothes. She dismisses the idea. "I wish I could help you but I don't have any extra cash. Wait I might have—" Faye takes her crack and wraps it in a kleenex else and gives the woman the ten dollars plus a piece of the crack. The woman thanks Faye and goes back to the apartment to smoke the crack.

Then the woman goes and asks one of the crack dealers if she can get a piece for ten dollars. They all refuse to sell her a piece. She searches for someone who has an additional ten dollars. After not having any luck, she again approaches the cracksellers who are tired of her begging.

"That's not ten dollars worth." She complains when one young man finally gives her a piece.

"You can take it or leave it." He tells her.

She takes it and returns to her apartment.

Faye has made it home after once again driving by the apartment to check for Jerry's presence. She piddles around until daybreak with her pipe and her brandy. Then she calls his mother's house, knowing that he is not there, but hoping so. When his mother answers the phone she disguises her voice and asks if Jerry is there.

"No, he's not. Can I take a message?" Faye hangs up.

She is in a drunken stupor, topped by a system saturated by crack. She goes to the kitchen and finds the sharpest knife. She lays it on the table beside her. She gets a good hit of crack, followed by a large swallow of brandy. Faye takes the knife and slashes her ankle. Terrified at the sight of her own blood, she panics. She then tries to stop the blood from pumping out in spurts on to the floor. She manages with some success by applying a tourniquet around her leg. She picks up the telephone and calls her mother.

"What the matter?" Her mother asks.

"I'm hurt."

"Where is Jerry?"

"He's gone. I don't know."

"Are you hurt bad."

"I'm bleeding and I can't stop it."

"Just remain calm. I'll call you right back."

Her mother calls the paramedics.

"Just keep talking to me until the ambulance arrives. You'll be just fine."

Faye hobbles to the coffee table. She hides her pipe and the knife under the sofa. The paramedics arrive and slow the bleeding. The police arrive a few minutes later. They to want to know what has happened. They can also tell that Faye is intoxicated. The two police officers whisper among themselves. They contemplate an attempted suicide.

"Your name is Mrs. Moore, but you still use your maiden name Miss Clark. Is that correct?"

"Yes."

"You must be divorced I presume."

"Why else would I use my maiden name?"

"Did you have an accident or is that wound self-inflicted?"

"An accident."

"Have you been drinking?"

"Yes."

"Do you use any kind of drugs?"

"Why do you want to know all of that for? I didn't call you in the first place."

"We have to fill out a report."

"The only report you are going to get is outside. Get out of my house!" She yells at them.

"Lady, you don't understand."

Faye screams to the top of her voice. "Get out! Get out of my house!"

The ambulance drivers take Faye to the hospital, were she is stitched and released. She refuses any further treatment.

"Why don't you come and stay with me and the boys for a while?" Her mom asks her.

"No Mom."

"At least for a day or two. Maybe you and Jerry can get things back together by then."

"I just need some rest is all."

"Well, at least let me help you clean up."

Afterwards she cooks Faye a meal. Faye has eaten and is asleep when her mother has to leave so she can meet the boys. She leaves telling her not to hesitate to call if she needs her.

When Faye awakens she is surprised at how late it is. The first thing she does is roll herself a primo and fix herself a drink. Her thoughts have drifted back to Jerry. She wonders if he has called and she didn't hear the phone ring.

Getting dressed, she goes back to the apartment.

"Where have you been?" She asks.

"What difference does it make?"

"Jerry, we need to talk."

"It won't—What happen to your foot?"

"I fell and cut it. I had to go to the emergency room. You weren't around. I could have died."

"It's not that bad. Let me see." Jerry removes the bandages. "What in the hell did you fall on?"

"A can."

"Don't bullshit me."

"As you were going to say a minute ago. It won't matter. Well, I happen to think it does."

"Faye, lets get one thing straightened out otherwise we might as well squash the conversation right now. You fail to realize that you do not run a damn thing. I do. I give you the benefit of the doubt or should I say the benefit of being my woman. That in turn does not mean I am weak."

"I never said you were."

"You don't have to say certain things. They are automatic. I told you when you first ask me about getting pregnant. I said no. That is the way it should have stayed. You know the situation. The only reason I have not gone to the joint already is because the lawyer has kept my case out of court. He will do so as long as I continue to pay him. I have come to realize that no matter how much I pay him. I'm going anyway. So therefore I intend to enjoy myself regardless."

"Is that what you call enjoying yourself? Smoking crack and staying out till all times of night."

"Ha! And who suggested that we smoke some crack one night? When we were doing so well."

"If you're blaming me. I don't feel that you are justified. If I thought that it would lead to this I would have never suggested that we do it."

"If Eve knew that eating the apple would have caused all of this, do you think she would have eaten it?"

"That still does not mean that it would not have happened anyway."

"So now you want to put everything on the odds. Everyone else is smoking it, so we have to become a statistic like them."

"So that's the real problem you think I'm the cause of you being hooked. You're so macho why don't you quit? If you quit so will I."

"Wrong, sweetie. You are going to quit anyway. No child of mine is coming into this world with a habit."

"You act like I don't have enough sense to know better than to keep smoking. "When are you coming home?"

"I might come home when I'm finish."

"Jerry please come home."

A couple of days later when Jerry returns to the apartment from home, there is an eviction notice taped on the door. He has twenty-four hours to vacate the premises. Jerry does not debate with himself about the notice. He feels now as though he can sell as much crack on the street as he can out of the apartment. He borrows the services of the next male customer to come on the scene to help him load his truck.

"Why are you moving all of this stuff home?" Inquires Faye.

"I'm giving the apartment up."

"I saw one of the notices saying that you were behind on the rent. You do have the money to pay it if you wanted to right?"

"Of course."

"You could have left that old couch where it was. We don't need it."

"It's too late now. I'll just set it in the back yard until I can haul it off."

Faye smiles to herself. She is glad that the apartment is vacated. She never truly trusted the idea anyway. After all of the contents are moved from the apartment, Jerry relaxes at home in front of the television.

"Jerry, why don't we leave here?"

"Where would we go?" Faye is on her knees beside him.

"We could go anywhere. It won't matter. Any place is better than here. We could go to Texas. You could get a job, a good job, and so could I."

"Naw, that won't work."

"Please Jerry. Lets do it for the both of us. Baby don't make me beg, please."

"No, I have to see what the outcome is going to be. If I do go to the joint, I've paid over twenty-five thousand in cash for bonds. They have to give it back."

"The desperado has finally come to his senses. You can't be serious? Now you want to think logically. You have had five times that much in front of you. Don't be foolish."

"I'll be back shortly." Jerry storms out of the house.

On his way to the projects, Jerry sees Nick. They pull into a vacant parking lot and converse for a while.

"I haven't seen you around. You must be staying at the crib a lot."

"Well, not exactly." Admits Jerry.

"Say, we've been having a ball over at the club after closing. New girls show up every day." Nick notices Jerry's favorite ring is missing. It is an oversized lion's head with very large diamonds in the eyes and mouth. "Where's that ring you're so crazy about?"

"I left it at home. I was cleaning it."

"You coming by the club anytime soon?"

"Yeah, I'll see what I can do. I hate to run, but I'm on a mission."

"Page me when you're through." Nick says.

Jerry makes it to the projects. He wonders what's going on. People are standing around, sitting on cars, chairs on the lawns, there are a lot of people who stay in the projects, but they have never gathered in masses like this before. Some people are also from different parts of the city.

The West side is so infested with police that the boldest crack dealers retreat. Those who worked against each other decided to work together. The police would never ride into such a concentration of people, not here anyway.

Jerry parks his truck and gets out. Several people whom he has dealt with notice him and come to ask if he to is going to be selling out here. They want to be runners and get paid for their services. He selects just one out of the bunch to be his runner. He will be paid in dope depending on how much business he can muster. Jerry won't have to pay him much. He's a smoker.

Despite Jerry's demand that Faye quit smoking due to her pregnancy, she's not deterred. Her weight does not indicate her being pregnant. She has reverted back to wearing some of her clothes that she wore almost two years ago. Before she quit. Her hair has started to break off from the lack of proper care. Her eyes tell the tale of what's going on inside her. Obtaining a high is the only comfort she seeks. Jerry is like a worn out pacifier to her. He's there but he fails to meet the qualifications he once met with ease.

A cab pulls up in the front of the house and blows. Faye opens the door. To her surprise, her mother and the boys get out. The boys run to meet their mother's embrace.

"Hello Tony and Lil Stevie." They both have a 'Thinking of you' card in their hands. Taped inside is a five dollar bill. "Oh, thank you." She hugs them both at the same time. They are filled with excitement.

"Hi Mama."

"Hello Honey. We decided to come see how you are doing. Why don't you get your telephone turned back on? I have the money if you need it."

"No, the boys need that money. Besides, I'm okay now."

"That's good to know."

Her mother looks in the freezer. A lot of the meat is freezer burned.

"Why are you letting this meat ruin?"

"When you get ready to leave, take what you want with you."

"I'll do that, but first I've come to fix my little girl a good meal."

"I'm really not all that hungry Mama."

"It's no trouble honey. I don't mind it at all. I like it better when you had some real meat on your bones."

"I haven't lost that much weight."

"Let's put it this way you can 't stand to lose anymore. Where's Jerry?"

"He's out taking care of some business."

"How is he coming along?"

"As well as to be expected."

"I know how that can be sometimes."

"I've been intending to ask you, Mom. Have you been paying on the insurance?"

"I don't like it when you ask about it, but yes. I always try and keep it up."

"Hello Jerry."

"What's up Charlene? I haven't seen you in a while."

"What are you doing out here?"

"The same thing as every body else, selling dope."

"You still got your apartment?"

"If I did, I sure wouldn't be out here."

"How's Faye?"

"She's okay."

"That's good. You gonna be out here long?"

"Not too much longer. Why?"

"I would like for you to take me home."

"If I have time. I'll get back with you."

Night approaches and the crowds start to thin. Jerry has not done nearly as well as he once had. The competition is too ferocious. Besides in order to maintain a steady clientele, you have to be available, which is something Jerry fails to do.

Jerry gets into his truck and cranks it up, really not caring if Charlene gets a ride home or not. Evidently she has her eye on him. She hollers down at someone standing near by the truck who stops Jerry and points at the window. Jerry waits for Charlene to make it to the truck.

"You better come on if you are going to go."

Charlene directs him to her place.

"When did you move over here?"

"I've been here about a month."

"Is this good enough?" He asks, stopping to let her out.

"Come on in for a minute."

"No, I better go."

"I've got some beer in the box."

"Well, I–"

"Come on."

"All right. Just one."

"Have a seat." Charlene says and brings Jerry a beer. "Care for a cigarette?"

"'No, I've got some. How much do you pay a month here, if I 'm not being too nosy?"

"One hundred and sixty dollars plus lights."

Charlene pulls out twenty dollars and asks Jerry for a piece of crack.

"I haven't sold this much all day. Kind of slow."

"You have to get established out there first. There are so many people out there. You remember when you first started selling coke."

"Yeah, it was something else then."

Charlene sets her glass pipe on the table. She gets Jerry involved in a conversation. He begins to reminisce.

"You were so scared when you first got started. You did 't want Faye to find out."

"She didn't for a long time either."

"No, but when she did she was mad."

Charlene passes Jerry the pipe with a small piece of crack she has just brought. Jerry hesitates for a minute but accepts.

"You can relax here. There's nothing to worry about." She assures him. Charlene gets up and slips into something more comfortable. Jerry accepts another beer. While Charlene is getting dressed he takes out his own dope and places a couple of pieces on the table. "I have a razor blade if you want one." Charlene volunteers.

"No, that's all right." Charlene brings it anyway.

Jerry cuts her a piece.

"Why don't you relax?"

She unbuttons his shirt.

"I think I better go."

"Why? You not enjoying the company?"

"Sure."

Jerry finds himself using Fayes favorite word.

"You don't have to be nervous. Nobody would suspect you of being here."

It is three o'clock in the morning.

The two of them sit undressed on the sofa, still smoking. The beer is gone.

"It's late. I better be headed toward the house." Jerry says.

"I have ten dollars left. If you don't mind I would like to get a piece before you go." Jerry is somewhat mad with himself. He feels guilty especially after he begins to tally in his mind how much he and Charlene have smoked. "What's the matter?"

"Nothing. I was just thinking."

"Don't worry. You will never hear a word of this anywhere."

Somewhat contented by those words, he hands her a quarter size rock of crack. He declines the money.

"You can come here any time you need a place to relax." She invites.

"Thanks."

Little does he know Faye has been through the projects. She has asked of his whereabouts. Word has it he has been gone since dark.

"Oh, you startled me." Faye says when he walks in the door.

"Why are you sitting up at this time of morning?"

"The question is where have you been?"

"Taking care of business as usual."

"I know that. Where?"

"In the projects."

"The east, side I presume?"

"Why the twenty questions?"

"You need to take a shower, You stink."

"I don't stink."

"That's a matter of opinion."

Faye goes and gets into the bed. She lays there until Jerry has fallen asleep. She finds his dope and his money. She is surprised that there is no more that it is. Still, she takes part of it. She sits in the dining room and smokes while he is asleep.

When he awakens, Faye is again playing sleep. He counts his money and checks his dope. He thinks before he speaks.

"Wake up. Have you been in my money?"

"Don't brother me with stupid questions. I don't even know where you keep it."

"I know what I had when I came home."

"You were so high when you came in, I'm surprised you knew where you lived."

Jerry is not one hundred percent sure. He has not been sure of anything every since he started smoking. Jerry has lost a considerable amount of weight. His skin is darker and his complexion is rough. The clothes he wears do not fit at all. He's no longer as interested in sex as he once was. He only indulges at random because he does not want to just give his dope away. Even then he fails to get a proper erection.

"I'll probably go over Mama's today."

"I'm going back to the projects."

Faye leaves first. Jerry gets high before he leaves. He keeps looking out of the window to make sure Faye doesn't double back. After he has gone she does just that. She takes the microwave, television and a few other appliances. The television she takes to the pawn shop, along with the microwave. The other she takes over to her mothers. She remains at her mother's until Jerry calls.

"You take the television and things out of the house?"

"Of course not. What are you talking about?"

"If you didn't, someone has broken into the house."

"I'll be there in a minute."

After she arrives . . .

She asks. "Aren't you going to call the police."

"Are you crazy? I don't need them in my business."

"Well, what are we going to do about the things that are missing?"

"What I can't understand is why they took part of the stereo and left the speakers."

Faye goes into the bedroom.

"Jerry, they have been in my jewelry box."

"What did you have in there?"

"My rings. I cleaned then last night."

"Undoubtedly whoever got this stuff is on crack. I'll keep my eyes open for any signs of it."

"You need to call the police."

"No way."

"As many people who are selling crack, how do you think you are going to find out anything?"

"People talk. Flash a little crack here and there, someone will come up with something. I'll be back."

"Where are you going now?"

"To the projects, unless you have a better idea,"

Jerry again goes over Charlene's apartment.

"What's wrong now?"

"Someone broke into the house and stole quite a bit of merchandise."

"When?"

"Today sometime."

"In broad daylight? What did Faye say when you got home this morning?"

"She said that I needed a bath."

Before you leave the next time you need to take a shower. A woman, can smell another woman especially if she's been around a man a while. I wouldn't be surprised if Faye set that little burglary up."

"She wouldn't do all that." Jerry protest, defending her.

"If you say so. You should never under estimate the fury of a woman."

During the next couple of weeks. Jerry smokes so much crack he is nauseous all the time. He has severe stomach cramps and radical bowel movements. He can't hold anything on his stomach. Even a glass of water sends him running to the rest room. His body needs water. His skin is so dry it is flaky.

"Faye, will you go to the store and bring me something? God, I'm sick."

"You're so sick now that you can't get out of bed. Now you expect me to run here and there. I'm not going to get you well so you can run off and lay up with some bitch. To be honest, you could go over there now. I really wouldn't care."

"What's wrong with you?"

"You're so smart, you figure it out."

Faye slams the door on the way out. Jerry crawls out of bed in search of his pipe. Every time he hits it he cramps severely. He throws it down in disgust.

He again goes to Charlene's house. She is glad. She runs errands for him. She rubs him down and with hand feeds him. He stays for three days. Finally, he gains enough strength to get out. Out of the fear that he may relapse, he is reluctant to smoke any crack. He stops in the projects on his way to the house.

Nick is one of the first faces he sees.

"What's up Jerry? You're just the man I need to see. Park your truck and come with me."

"I really don't feel like it."

"You have got to see this."

He leads Jerry up a flight stairs.

"I'm really not into all this Nick."

"This may make you come to your senses." When they enter the apartment, the guys just stop and look. Nick does not lead him directly to the bedroom but points that way. "Go ahead."

"What the__. You lousy bitch."

Faye lies on the bed totally naked. She attempts to cover herself when she realizes it is Jerry.

Jerry turns and walks out of the room, pauses and looks at Nick, then leaves. Nick is trailing in behind him.

"Why? Nick Why?"

"It is the only way Jerry. I could not stand it myself. I knew if I told you that you wouldn't believe me. She has been up there for two days."

"I really ought to go up there and kill that bitch, but she's not worth it. I've got a better way."

Jerry tells Charlene that he needs to use some of her space for a while. He goes home and starts packing. He throws his things in the truck. He gets what he can in two loads. Charlene drives his other car away for him.

"You don't think you'll get sick all over again, do you?" Charlene asks.

"It won't matter." Jerry smokes until he feels some sign of sickness and stops for the moment. "You can smoke this, I have had enough."

"You're really mad, aren't you? You knew what she was before you started a steady relationship with her."

"That's beside the point."

"You look at everything wrong. The world is a stage. You're just another actor like everybody else."

"That's probably not my baby she's pregnant with either."

"No, I think you maybe wrong there. That's usually the last trick a woman will use to hold her man. She's probably really hurt because it didn't work."

Faye finally decides to go home. Tears fill her eyes as she looks at a nearly empty house. Her heart is what's really empty. She wishes she were dead. She hates the crack that has cause her so much agony. However, it is the only thing that comforts her. She needs to get high again. She wonders if Jerry may have been right about her being the reason for their downfall. Did it happen prematurely or was it going to happen anyway?

Jerry continues to go to the projects. He panics when he sees the police ride through. They are in patrol cars. They look but they do not stop.

Jerry starts to leave his truck quits. He has some guys who consider themselves mechanics to look at it. He offers them some crack if they can fix it. Unfortunately they are unable to do so. He has to leave it in the projects. When he returns the inside is stripped. Nobody has seen anything. He leaves it there for a couple of days before he has it towed to a garage. He is informed that the transmission needs to be replaced. The fixing price is approximately four hundred dollars.

"When are you going to get your truck?" Ask Charlene.

"I don't know. I guess whenever Mac gets it ready. I need to find some dope. I'm completely out. I've check in the projects. Nobody wants to sell any quantity."

"We can go to the west side." Charlene suggests. "Marilyn sales quantities."

"I really don't want to go to the west side as bad as the police are."

"You got a better idea?"

"No, let's go."

Charlene and Jerry both notice the Cadillac being towed by the wrecker.

"Isn't that your car?" Charlene blurts.

"Fuck yeah."

"What are they doing with it? You must be behind on the note, you know he'll come and get your shit in a minute."

Jerry's disposition fails him further now, he can't believe all this is happening to him. He curses to himself.

At the trailer . . .

"Marilyn, I want to get a fourth ounce." Says Charlene.

"I don't have that much Charlene." From the looks of Marilyn and everybody else, it looks as though they have smoked it up. "Do you want a sixteenth instead?"

"I guess so."

Charlene makes the purchase and attempts to hand the dope to Jerry.

"No, you hold it until we get to the other side. The last thing I need is another charge of any kind."

Rather than sell the dope as planned, Charlene and Jerry smoke it up. Jerry is mad at himself for doing so. He does not want Charlene to know how low his money really is.

"I thought you were going to come by the house honey."

"No, Mama. I've been busy."

"Why don't you move home with me and the boys. That way you can still pay for all this furniture you owe for."

"I just need some time to think."

"Sit down a minute Faye. I'm you mother but I'm also a woman. I know that you are hurt. Whether or not you want to tell me the rest now is up to you. You don't need to keep things bottled up inside you. I have never seen you look this bad. I really would like for you to see a doctor."

"I already have."

"What did he say?"

"Nothing."

"Faye, look at me. Are you pregnant?"

"What makes you think that?"

"You don't have to shout. I just asked. Your weight does not indicate that you are. I was just following my intuition."

"Well your intuition is wrong."

"Okay, fine. Is there anything that I can do for you?"

"No."

"Here's a few dollars. I know you need them."

"Thanks Mama."

"Well I must be going. Mrs. Annie is waiting on me. Promise me that you will come by tomorrow."

"I will."

Faye's mother kisses her on the cheek and hugs her. Faye counts the money the her mother has given her. It's one hundred and twenty-five dollars.

Faye goes to the projects. She sees Jerry, who acts as if he does not see her. When Faye approaches him he turns and walks off.

"Jerry!" He keeps walking. "Jerry, I need to talk to you!"

"What in the hell do you want? You're lucky I don't kick your ass all over this parking lot." Faye touches his arm. "Keep your hands off of me." He brushes where she has touched his arm.

"I just want you to know that I'm sorry."

"You're damn right you're sorry. You've said it. Now, good-bye!"

"Where are you staying now?"

"You have got a lot of nerve. None of your business. Furthermore, before I forget, you need to go to the doctor and get yourself checked. The word is out on you."

Faye stares with her mouth open. Jerry walks off. Tears run down her cheeks. She runs to the car. When she sits down in the car, she bangs her fist on the steering wheel as she cries.

"Can I help you lady?" Ask a young man walking past.

"Get the hell away from my car!"

Faye starts the engine and almost runs over the young man in the process.

"You must be crazy lady!"

Before Faye makes it home it starts to rain. She pulls the car over to the side of the road and leaves it. She walks home in the rain. The rain is cool and feels good to her. Besides, it hides the tears she cries. Upon arrival at home she searches the medicine cabinet. She finds a partial bottle of turpentine and drinks it. She wants to kill the baby so badly now.

"Mrs. Clark, you are about four months pregnant by records. Your baby's size does not show it. Are you on any kinds of drugs?" Faye just looks at him. "Well if you don't want to answer I will tell you this. You are not only endangering your own life but the life of your unborn child. I'm going to prescribe you some iron and vitamins along with a dietary supplement. I want you to come back and see me in three weeks. Do you have any questions?"

"No."

"Okay. You take care of yourself and I'll see you then."

Faye does not go by the store to have the prescriptions filled. She throws them out the window.

"Hi Honey."

"Hello Mom. I hate to rush but I need some money. I've got a bill to pay."

"How much is it?"

"Seventy-five dollars."

"Aren't you glad I saved some of that money you gave me?"

"Sure. I'll see you later."

"Your boy Willie sure is buying a lot of dope. You know why don't you? He quit his job and drew all of this retirement money at one time." Says Nick to Jerry, while standing around talking in the projects.

"How much was it?"

"Twelve thousand dollars. He owed Bobby three thousand of it for dope when he first got it."

"Get serious Nick."

"I am, dog. I doubt right now if he has a thousand dollars left."

"When did he get the money?"

"About a month ago, if it's been that lo—Oh shit!".

"What?"

"Here comes the police. Come on."

Jerry and Nick run into a nearby apartment. They send a couple of the kids outside to see if the police are gone.

"I think they are taking some people to jail." One of them comes back and tells them.

"It's getting so hot out here that it's hard to make money anywhere." says Jerry. "I heard they are going to have another sting. When I don't know, but it should be soon from what I understand. I've really been thinking about leaving town."

"What's holding you?"

"I don't know any more."

"If you want my advice, I would go. You won't be so lucky the next time they lock you up. I saw your truck today. Some white guy was driving it."

"Yeah, I know."

"Are you going to go and get it?"

"No."

"What happened to your Cadillac? I know you didn't let them reposes it."

"Why are you asking so many questions?"

"Just curious."

"It's really none of your business."

"The rent is due tomorrow. Are you going to help me pay it?" Asks Charlene.

"As much dope as you smoke up and you want me to help you pay the rent!" Jerry asks venomously. "I don't have the money. I might as well have my own place. You're reaping all the benefits."

"What do you call it when you're fucking the shit out of me?"

"Oh, that's it. Let me clear the air here. I don't buy pussy. If I did, I wouldn't buy it from you."

"Who do you think you're talking to?"

"You! I can leave here anytime you deem necessary."

"Hello Mama."

"Hi baby. Where are you calling from?"

"I need you to come and get me."

"Why are you crying?"

"What's wrong?"

"I'm in jail."

"Oh my goodness. How much is it?"

"Two hundred and fifty dollars."

"I'll be there as soon as I can. Will you be all right?"

"I guess so."

Faye's mother arrives, pulling the boys along, one on each hand.

"Why is Mama here with all these police?" Asks Lil Stevie.

"She's in jail that's why." Says Tony.

"Hush the both of you. Don't let your mama hear you say that."

On the way to Faye's car her mother asks.

"Do you want to talk about it?"

"Not really."

"Honey, you can't keep going on like this. You use to talk to me about anything. I'm afraid that if you don't get some type of peace of mind, you are going to lose it." Meanwhile . . .

Jerry has gotten a cheap motel room. He rents it for a week. Without any company, Jerry has time to think. So many things cross his mind. He thinks about Faye, the money he has lost and the fact that he is going to prison. The repercussion proves to be too great. He stays high. He adds alcohol to his list. It maintains him when he is not smoking. Company is relatively easy to find, especially when crack is part of the proposition. He looks at himself in the mirror, trying to convince himself he is still in control. He wears the same clothes for days at a time. His car is dirty. Cigarette butts, beer cans, pieces of broken hangers, shoes, clothes, dirt and paper clutter the inside.

Faye sits in the house. The lights are turned off now. She has gotten the money to pay the bill several times. Still she has failed to do so. She uses candles at night to find her way through the near empty house. The furniture that has not been repossessed she has sold. The bed she sleeps on is ragged and very unstable. Rather than iron her clothes she hangs them up, hoping the wrinkles will fall out.

"What kind of washer and dryer is this?" The man from the used appliance store asks Faye.

"They are new. I've only had them a few months."

"I don't really need them. I'll give you a bill for the both of them."

"They are worth a lot more than that." Pleads Faye.

"Like I said. I have more than I can handle now. I really don't need them. That's the best I can offer."

Faye accepts. He pays her. He and his helper haul them away.

Faye immediately goes to the crack dealer. Only after she has smoked up all of her money does she realize that she is out of cigarettes. She looks around the house for something that might be worth a few dollars to the crack dealer. She finds nothing. Shaken by her recent arrest for prostitution, she is reluctant to proposition anybody whom she does not know. In turn she it treated badly by her customers.

"I don't have but fifteen dollars."

"I can't do anything with that."

"You're the one that needs it, not I."

"Where are we going to take care of business at?" Jake asks Faye.

"We can't go to my place. My girlfriend might be around. What about your place?"

Minutes later . . .

Faye lights a candle.

Jake asks. "Where are the lights? I remember when you used to walk around and would not speak to me. I can't believe you are living like this. Why don't you get some help?"

"Are you going to fuck me or give me a damn lecture?"

"I want some head first."

"You don't have enough money for all of that."

"Like I said, you need the money, not me. What's it gonna be?"

After they finish . . .

He says. "I remember when you use to turn down anything less than fifty dollars."

"Listen, Jake get dressed and get the hell out!"

The little money she makes only wets her appetite. She spends days on end giving herself away for ten dollars at a time or for a bump of crack. If she is lucky, she will run into somebody who is willing to spend all of their money with her because they smoke crack themselves.

It's three o'clock in the morning . . .

She is at an all night gas station and convenient store. Faye has just bought herself a new cigarette lighter. She walks out of the store.

"Hi Richard."

"Faye, is that you?" Not meaning to insult her. "I haven't seen you in a while. How's Jerry?"

"He's okay I guess."

"What are you doing out at this hour?"

"Just out and about."

"You know you didn't have to steal the drugs I left you with."

"I came back by the apartment nobody was there."

"You did not forget where the house was, did you?"

"Well, I'm sorry I guess, you know how it is."

"You still getting high?"

"Yes, I sell a little bit here and there."

"You in the mood for some company?"

"I guess so."

"Why don't I leave my car and ride with you?"

Faye and Richard go to his place. He has moved to a cheaper apartment. It is sparsely furnished. Evidence of crack smoking is all over the place.

"I notice that you don't sound too thrilled when I ask you about Jerry."

"We're not together anymore."

"I didn't think so when I saw you. You don't look the same at all."

"Neither do you." Feeling insulted again.

Richard takes out a pill bottle that contains about twenty pieces of crack.

"Can I ask you something Richard?"

"Go ahead."

"I really would like to take a bath."

"No problem." Richard finds her a towel and makes sure she has everything that she needs. "One more thing. I need a shirt, if you have one. A large one will do." Faye hurriedly takes a bath. She is glad to feel the warm water embrace her body. Richard is in the room smoking when she exits the bathroom. "I used some of your deodorant and cologne."

"That's all right." Pausing a moment. "Faye?"

"Yes."

"Are you pregnant?"

"No, I just have a little stomach is all."

"Oh, I just thought that you might have been. I know if you were you couldn't be to far along. Tell me what happened between you and Jerry."

"I really don't care to discuss him."

"I really hate that I messed up our friendship."

"I don't think you messed it up. You just didn't come back around was all."

"Here. Get yourself a good hit."

"Do you have anything to drink?"

"Look in the kitchen cabinet."

Faye returns with a fifth of whiskey.

"This is all I found in there."

"That's all I drink."

"I like brandy, of course you already know that."

"You drink brandy, you can handle that. After the first swallow you've got it licked. Be careful with it though. You will be drunk before you know it."

"That's the idea, isn't it? Whatever happened between you and your girlfriend?"

"We never quite got things back together. I had the accident and lost my job. You know when you're down, you're down. Faye, can I ask you something?"

"Sure."

"Have you ever made it with a white man before?"

"Sure. What about you and a black woman? Or is that the reason you asked?"

"I guess you could say that. I have always thought of you as being attractive. Even now."

"Huh? Yes. Your the one whose drunk."

"Don't ever put yourself down like that."

Faye unbuttons the shirt that she has on.

"What are you waiting on?" Richard nervously fumbles with his clothes. "Here, let me help you. Now you won't have to go through life wondering how it is to make it with a black chick."

It's daybreak . . .

Jerry pawns the last of his jewelry. On the way out the door he stops when he notices a familiar piece of jewelry.

"Can I see that woman's bracelet?"

Water fills his eyes as he reads the inscription on the back. Faye had pawned it. He wish he had the money to get. He promises himself that he will come back and get his and hers.

With the thought of making it big again, he knows he can sell crack again. He also knows the only thing preventing him from doing so is his smoking. He tries to stay away from people who once knew him as a profitable crack dealer. He is embarrassed in their presence. They believe he still has part of his prior fortune stashed away. So now that know he is smoking, they try to hang close to him.

Jerry stops at the store and buys a pack of cigarettes. He has suffered through the night without any. I've got to get something to eat, Jerry's thinks. After he and his new found friends have managed to smoke up all the crack again.

Jerry asks. "Where are you going now?"

"We are going to the store and get something to eat."

"Like what? I thought you didn't have anymore money."

"I have a couple of dollars if that's what you want to call money."

"What are we going to buy to eat with a couple of dollars?"

"I see you don't know anything about surviving. A bag of potatoes. I'm sure you have eaten fried potatoes. All you want is something to satisfy your appetite, right?" "You have got a point there." Admits Jerry.

Jerry buys the potatoes and steals a block of butter.

While they are eating . . .

Eddie says. "Pretty good, wouldn't you say?"

"Yeah, at least I'm not hungry anymore." Jerry is pleased.

"I told you. It works every time." Brags Eddie "Now we can hustle a little better. We don't have to worry about our stomachs."

"Let's go back to my place and see what we can find." Suggests Jerry.

Jerry finds his boots. They are worn but are in good shape. He also has a few pieces of clothes that still have tags on them.

"You think we can get anything for this stuff?"

"What size are the boots?"

"Size ten and a half."

"I know someone who might be able to wear the clothes and the boots too."

Urges Eddie. When the transaction is finished, Jerry trades two pairs of snake skin boots, a pair of slacks and a sweater. They manage to get two quarters and a twenty dollar piece. They are pacified for the moment.

Jerry thinks about the rent for his room being due tomorrow. He casually mentions it to Eddie while they are smoking.

"You can come stay with me and the old lady. She won't mind."

"I don't know you know how women are."

"Listen, I run the house, not her."

When Faye awakens, Richard is up and already smoking.

"You finally awake up sleeping beauty?"

"I guess."

"Here. This should wake you up." He hands he the pipe. "I started to wake you but you were sleeping so hard until I decided against it. You know, Faye, I was just sitting here thinking."

"About what?"

"The way things were when we first met each other. I use to tell Jerry how beautiful you were. I always told him not to restrict you. Otherwise you would crack under the pressure."

"It was really better when we did not have much. At least he was working a real job."

"I miss the working atmosphere myself."

"Jerry was furious when he found out you were smoking."

"I know. We discussed it once or twice."

"What about your schooling?"

"I'll eventually go back and finish. I only have a couple of months left before I become LPN."

"That would be great. I remember Jerry used to be so proud of you. I don't know whether he ever indicated to you how proud he was. But he use to brag to us all the time." Tears fill Faye's eyes, and she sniffles. "I'm sorry. I didn't mean to bring up bitter memories. I looked at you this morning while you were sleep. You are pregnant, aren't you?"

"I think I better go."

"You don't have to leave. I didn't mean anything by what I said."

"I know you didn't."

"Here. Take this with you."

Richard gives Faye a couple pieces of crack and a few dollars.

"I forgot I didn't drive."

"That's right. I'll take you."

Richard puts on his shoes and shirt.

They are silent on the way back to Faye's car.

"I hope to see you again." Says Richard.

Faye does not acknowledge. She gets into her car. She notices a note on the window. "Customer Parking Only. Car will be towed away at your expense." Faye turns on the windshield wipers so that the note will blow off.

She returned to the house, which only brings her despair whenever she enters it. There is no use in cleaning up she decides. It's getting close to Thanksgiving. It won't be as pleasant as it was for the past two years.

"Say Jerry, I hate to say this, but my old lady is talking shit."

"Got damn it! She doesn't bitch when I'm smoking crack with you and her at all times of the day and night."

"I know, but she doesn't want a stranger around the kids."

"I guess it will be all right if I leave my clothes here until I can relocate?"

"I can handle that."

Jerry sits in his car and smokes a cigarette. Giving it a chance to warm up, he thinks about going home again. His pride, guilt, and shame won't let him. So for the next couple of days, he sits on the parking lot of the projects. When night falls and he feels the need for some sleep, he wants to cry, but the tears won't come. Besides, they wouldn't do any good anyway. All of his options have run out. He dresses himself as presentably as he can. He goes into the grocery store and gets a shopping basket full of meat along with a couple cases of beer. He writes a check. He had his doubts that his ideal will work. It proves to be fruitful after all.

He goes back over Eddie's house.

"Where did you get all of these groceries?"

"At the store. Do you have any idea where we can get rid of the meat?"

"We need some of that." Says Eddie's wife. "You can rest here if you don't have any other place to go."

Jerry is offended as well as pleased. Even though he tries to hide it, he is in bad need of some decent rest. Jerry and Eddie sell the meat to a few of the local businesses owners at half price.

They buy crack with the money, returning to Eddie's house.

"Do I get a piece?" Begs Eddies wife.

"You just had a piece, woman!"

"If I don't get anymore, both of you can leave!"

"You must be crazy." Says Eddie.

"No. You forget whose name this place is in." Jerry has no choice but to oblige her. In turn, Eddie has to do without.

When night fall approaches, Eddie tells Jerry that he has to leave.

"No he doesn't. We made a deal today and I'm not going to go back on it. At least he bought some diapers and milk. The kids have eaten. If anybody goes tonight, it's going to be you!"

"I don't want to start any confusion. I'll just leave."

Jerry sleeps on a pallet made on the floor. Eddie gets mad and leaves.

"Don't worry about Eddie. He'll be back. It's too cold for him to go any where else."

Jerry leaves first thing in the morning. The cashing of checks has worked so well that he decides to do it a couple more times.

"Mr. Collins, your bank account is closed. I am going to have to call the police."

Jerry nods his head and quickly leaves the store. Influenced by the moment, he tears up his checkbook to avoid further temptation.

CHAPTER 12

The situation had become desperate. The police are carrying assault rifles in an attempt to match the fire power of the crack dealers. Being shot at is not their idea of being a policeman in Pine Bluff. Little does everyone know that a second sting is underway and began as soon as the first one ended.

Faye walks into the club. Business is extremely slow. Wilma does not notice her at first. Faye goes directly into the ladies room. On her way out Wilma says

"Hello Faye. You can still speak to me."

"I know, girl. I'm sorry."

She is too ashamed to hold her head upright.

"Don't worry honey. We all go through these sorts of things. It will be over before you know it. Just be patient."

"Thanks Wilma. You have always been a help."

"You still drink Champale?"

"It's been a long time."

"Here, this one is on the house."

Looking Wilma in the eye for a split second.

Faye says. "I'm going to go back here if you don't mind."

"Go ahead honey."

Faye slowly walks to the back of the club. She sits alone and drinks. She drifts off into a daydream. She remembers the way things used to be when she came here on a daily basis. How easy it was for her then. She comes back to reality and hurriedly finishes her drink. She waves to Wilma on her way out. As Faye starts to cross the street, she is stopped.

"You're Faye, aren't you? I've been trying to catch up with you?"

"For what?"

"You may not know me, but my name is Calvin."

"I know who you are."

"Let me get straight to the point then. I want to know if you are interested in selling you house?"

"Of course not! What make you ask that?!"

"I just thought you might."

"I'm sorry. You're wrong."

"Here. Let me write my name and number down, just in case you change your mind."

Faye takes the piece of paper that has his name and number and lays it on the car seat, thinking to herself that he must be crazy if he thinks she's going to sell her house to some crack dealer.

"I don't need it that bad." She says to herself, talking out loud.

On the west side of town . . .

A customer asks Jerry. "You're all over town selling, aren't you?"

"It pays to move around."

"Let me get a quarter piece." Jerry produces a match box with several pieces of crack. He lets the customer pick his own piece. Jerry sells two more pieces almost immediately. He gets in his car and leaves.

A few minutes later . . .

The customer returns and asks another man who was standing around.

"Did you see that skinny guy who was standing here a few minutes ago selling this bullshit?"

"What's the matter with it?"

"Look. It's nothing but soap!" He says, tasting it again with his tongue.

"I don't know him. He just got in his car and left."

"If you see that son-of-a-bitch before I do, you tell him that I am going to kill him!"

It's Thanksgiving . . .

The cold wind is howling gently. Jerry sits in his car without the motor running. The gas hand indicates empty. He never knows when someone he has sold some bunk dope to may come looking for him or run into him by accident. He does not know all the people he has deceived. When he does fall asleep, he is terrified when he wakes up. He gets mad at himself for falling asleep, knowing what could happen.

The house is dark and cold. Faye lays huddled in the bed despite the desperate knocks at the door. She talked to her mother a few days ago and promised that she would be home to at least eat dinner. She is in no mood to socialize with anyone, not even her own family. She wants to cry but she's tired. She has never dealt with such a wide array of emotions before.

Jerry calls Mrs. Clark house.

"Hello Mrs. Clark. Is Faye there?"

"No, she's not. May I ask whose calling?"

"Yes Ma'am, this is Jerry."

"How are you doing?"

"As well as to be expected."

"Have you seen Faye lately?"

"No Ma'am."

"Do you have any idea where I might find her?"

"There are a couple of places."

"Where are you?"

"I'm just out and around."

"Would you care to come to dinner?"

Despite his intense hunger.

He says. "No Ma'am, I'm fine."

"Do you think you could find Faye for me?"

"Mrs. Clark, I must be honest with you. I don't have any gas in my car, otherwise I would do it myself."

"Can you make it over here?"

"I'll try."

"If you run out before you get here, call me back and I'll get it to you."

Jerry nurses his car to Mrs. Clark's house. She is waiting for him and opens the door as soon as he enters the driveway.

"Where is your coat?"

"In the car."

"Come on. Let me fix you something to eat. You look like you could use a good meal." Jerry fills the emptiness within his stomach. The boys stare at him. They hardly speak a word, as if they could sense something was wrong. "Have you had enough?"

"Yes Ma'am."

"Here's ten dollars. I hope that will help. If you find her, please bring her home. I really would appreciate it." She hugs him. "Thing will get better all you have to do is pray."

"I'll remember that."

Jerry runs out of gas about a mile from the nearest gas station that is open. He curses but there's an empty antifreeze jug in the trunk. Jerry makes up his mind to brave the cold. His luck improves as he catches a ride on the way back.

"It's a bad day to run out of gas son." The older man says."

"Yes sir, you're right."

The man waits until he is sure that his car will start.

"I see you got one of those good old cars." He says.

"Yes sir, you're right."

The gentleman waves as he drives off.

Jerry goes by the house. He doesn't see Faye's car in the driveway. He backs up, remembering that he still has a key to the door. He looks around. He walks into the house, flicks the light switch by the door. Then he realizes how cold and empty and smelly the place is. He walks softly even though he does not suspect anyone of being in the house. The light from the windows allows some amount of visibility. He looks in the kitchen and sees cans, dirty dishes, and garbage littering the place. Proceeding to the bedroom, he walks up to the bed. It looks like a pile of blankets and rags. It moves, and he stops daring not to move.

"What are you doing in my house?" Half startled, he hesitates.

"I was sent by your mother to find you."

"Now that you have done so, get out!"

"Where is your car?"

"None of your business!"

She chooses not to tell him that she has sold it for some crack.

"Why don't you go home?"

"This is home!"

"You need to get out of this dump." Jerry proclaims.

Faye rushes him, throwing her fists wildly.

"It's your fault!"

"No it's not. Besides, it's a little late for laying the blame anyway." She tries once again to fight back the tears. This time she's unsuccessful. They flow freely. Jerry walks up behind her. As he puts his arms around her, she trembles and sobs out loud. "I don't know what to say, but I'm sorry for the both of us. It wasn't suppose to happen like this." He whispers. Tears finds their way down his unkept face. Faye shakes her head indicating that she agrees with him. "There's nothing I can do for you now. I can't even help myself." Jerry admits.

"You just don't get it, do you? The real meaning of life is not money, it's happiness. Real happiness."

"Do you want me to take you over your mother's?" Jerry asks.

"Do you really want to help me?"

"Sure." Jerry says, Faye breaks a half smile. He stills uses her favorite words.

"Make love to me. I'll never ask you this again if you don't want me to." Jerry looks around.

She says. "The accommodations may not be the best, but they are not really what counts."

"I will under one condition."

"What?"

"That you let me take you home to your mother when we are finished?"

"Sure."

"This is a far cry from what it once was, isn't it." Jerry whispers as they both ease into bed. Faye puts two fingers up to his lips and presses hers against them.

"I'm glad you decided to move in with me and the boys." Says her mother while she fixes Faye's hair. "Maybe you and Jerry can try and get things together again."

"You're asking for too much Mama."

"You can never tell, honey, what might happen."

The warm house, comfortable bed and fresh clothing feels good to Faye. She looks out the window at the severely overcast skies. Her mind focuses on Jerry.

Jerry now sleeps in the empty house, being careful to hide his car. He comes in late at night and leaves first thing in the morning. He needs more rest that what he's getting. He also thinks about the checks he has written and whether they have issued a warrant for him yet. He refuses to go home to his mother's.

A couple of days pass . . .

Faye is well rested and certainly well fed. Jerry said he would come back by. Somehow, Faye knew that he was lying. Her mood has saddened. She thinks about her car.

"Where are you going as cold as it is outside?" Her mother asks concerned.

"I have something to do. I'll be back."

"Just be careful." Her mother says.

She walks the streets. As always someone stops.

"Where are you going?" A man asks.

"That depends on where you are."

"Do you get high?"

"Yes, do you?"

"Yeah, I've got to go and pick up someone else. You're welcome to come along." They stop at a rather nice looking house. "I'll be right back."

A lady accompanies him when he comes back out. Faye gets into the back seat.

"You can still sit in the front." The lady tells her. Faye declines

They stop at the crack house. Neither Faye nor the other woman offers any money to him. He doesn't ask.

"Do you drink?" He asks Faye.

"Yes."

He buys a pint of brandy and some gin. They pull up to a motel where he pays for a room. He opens the trunk of the car, he retrieves a leather bag. They enter the room and shed their coats. He carefully unwraps the glass pipe, then puts it together like a professional. The anticipation builds within Faye as she watches. Taking out what appears to be an eight ball, he cuts off several pieces. He lights a torch and passes the pipe to the other woman first. Faye's heart skips a beat as she watches the smoke fill the glass bowl. It's now her turn. She slowly inhales the dust colored smoke. When she exhales, her head rings and her heart pounds. The woman starts to shed her clothes. Faye just watches, not particularly moved by it.

"You shame to take off your clothes, baby?"

"I know that you're pregnant. It doesn't matter." Faye slowly undresses. When she is finished, she sits back down on the bed. "Show her what to do." He says to the other woman.

The other woman reaches over and starts to slowly move her hand along Faye's thighs. Faye's first reflex is to jump. Chill bumps cover her entire body.

"You act as it you have never did this before. Relax, it's fun. Trust me." The woman says reassuringly.

"Here Mickie, let her get a good bump. Maybe she'll relax some." Faye hits the pipe again, followed by a double shot of brandy. Faye quickly refills the glass and downs part of it. Mickie runs her hands between Faye's legs. "Get on with it Mickie." He is naked. He sits in a chair next to the bed masturbating.

The next day late in the evening.

Faye mother scolds her.

"Where have you been? Faye doesn't answer her mother. "You could have at least called."

"I really don't feel like being questioned like I'm still a little girl."

Faye goes to the boys bedroom and slams the door. She looks in the mirror at herself. She grabs her hair with both hands and screams as loud as she can.

"Open the door, Faye." Her mother hollers.

"I'm alright. Go away!" She vows to herself to never be involved with another woman again. She cries herself to sleep.

"It's been a while, but I finally found you!" Before Jerry can respond he is hit in the mouth with a pistol. He is tripped from behind. When he falls he is repeatedly kicked in the ribs, stomach, and head. "I ought to kill you for selling me that damn soap! If I hear of you selling some more to anybody, I will kill you!" Jerry feels pain everywhere. He touches his face to find that his mouth is bleeding. Two of his teeth are broken. There are people standing around looking, but nobody bothers to assist him. Jerry crawls to his car and manages to drive away.

"Faye, breakfast is ready." Says her mom. Faye comes out of the room. She has been asleep all night in her clothes. She washes her face. She sits at the table. "You all right this morning?"

"Sure."

"You must have really been tired. You slept all evening and all night."

"Where are Lil Stevie and Tony?"

"They have already gone to school."

"You could have awaken me. I would have helped get them ready for school."

"I'm so used to it that it really didn't matter. Faye, you are grown and I know you know the difference between right and wrong. I could smell the liquor on you when you came in yesterday. You are not thinking about that baby at all. It's too late to get rid of it, so you might as well bring the baby into this world healthy."

"I know you are trying to help Mama. You are right. I'll do better."

"Have you talked to Jerry?"

"No. Lets leave him out of this discussion shall we?"

◇　　　◇　　　◇　　　◇

Jerry's mother doesn't go to work this particular morning. She is out at the hospital seeing about Jerry. They have chosen to keep him overnight for observation.

"He was lucky, Mrs. Collins. The only thing he has broken are his teeth. Other than that he will be sore for a while but he'll be alright. I'll prescribe him some pain pills. They too will help him make it."

The next couple of days . . .

Jerry is at home. He has been to the liquor store and bought a fifth of vodka. He drinks it with his medication in an attempt to stay high.

"Mom, I need to borrow sixty dollars."

"What for? You can't even get out of bed."

"I want to go and pay those guys off so I don't have to worry about them coming here."

"They better not come here. I've still got my old shotgun you know!"

"No Mother, I rather do it the right way. I'd hate to be asleep and wake up with the house on fire."

She gives him sixty dollars and an extra ten.

"You take care of that and come right back home."

"I will."

Jerry puts his homemade pipe in his pocket. Checks his lighter which is about empty. He stops by the store and buys another.

Once in the projects he is approached by several dealers and runners. He rolls the window down.

"I didn't know it was you." Nicks says. The rest of them walk off. "I heard about that little incident the other day. I wish I would have been there. I wouldn't have let them whip you like that. What are you trying to do?"

"I need—"

"I know." Nick walks around to the passenger side of the car. Jerry reaches over and unlocks the door.

"How much do you have?"

Jerry show him fifty dollars.

"Let me get a gram and I'll owe you the rest."

"Well, alright. I'll do it for you."

"You really need to be careful man. You could have gotten killed the other day. The best place for you is at home."

Nick gets out of the car.

"Thanks Nick."

Jerry drives off.

Nick places the pill bottle containing his crack on the ground in a paper sack and walks off. He keeps his eye on it. He just doesn't want to have it in his possession if the police decide to show up.

"I see you took care of the problem rather quickly."

"Yes, I think I'm going to get back in the bed. I'm not as ready as I thought I was."

"I'm glad you realize you need the rest."

Jerry goes into the bedroom, closes the door and locks it. Despite his being at home, he starts to smoke and becomes paranoid. He peeps out of the windows. On his hands and knees he strains to look under the door, making sure no one is listening or watching him. After his second hit of the pipe, he feels no pain.

"Please don't take me to jail! I'll go back to the penitentiary if you do!"

"You should have thought about that before you decided to steal those clothes and run from the police! You could be charged with robbery." Charlene begins to cry.

When they reach the police station . . .

Charlene says. "I would like to speak to a detective."

"Any particular one?"

"No."

Detective Smith enters the room.

"Hello Miss Anderson. I understand you requested to see me."

"Yes."

"What can I do for you?"

"I'm going to be charged with a robbery." She begins to cry all over again. "I just got out of the pen. I would like to know if we can make some kind of a deal?"

"That's depends." Smiling to himself. Detective Smith picks up the telephone and calls the booking desk. "Bring me a charge sheet on a Miss Charlene Anderson. Also tell Detective Carmichael of Narcotics to come in here."

While he is going over the charge sheet, Detective Carmichael walks in.

"How are you doing, Smith?"

"Hello Carmichael. I may have something for you. This young lady was arrested for shoplifting and has been to the pen for it already. Undoubtedly she's on crack. You might could use her." Charlene agrees to show the detectives where some of the crack houses are they don't know about. She has also agreed to introduce an undercover cop to the crack dealers, so that they will be able to purchase some crack from them. They take Charlene's picture and go through the necessary paperwork. "Let her go. We will get in touch with her tomorrow sometime."

"Miss Anderson, I want you to remember that if you violate this deal in anyway, you will go back to the joint."

The following day . . .

Charlene rides around with a very inconspicuous fellow. Despite being a detective, he looks like an everyday individual. He is not neatly shaven and his hair is not neatly cropped.

"All you have to do is act normal. I will supply the money. I need to be introduced as a relative from out of town." After they have made their rounds to different places, the detective gives her fifty dollars. "Thanks. If we need you, we'll be in touch. Don't spend all that money at one crack house."

He chuckles as she gets out of the car. Charlene slams the door in anger and disgust.

"Hello, may I speak to Calvin. Hello Calvin, this is Faye Clark."

"Oh, hi. I've been expecting your call. What can I do for you?"

"We need to talk."

"Where are you?"

"At my mother's."

"I'll tell you what, meet me at your house. I'll pay the cab when you get there." Calvin beats Faye to the house. He walks around and looks at the exterior, seeing what improvements he might have to make. The cab arrives and he pays the cab driver. Calvin and Faye go inside the house. "This appears to have been a nice house at one time."

"We don't have to go through all of that. What are you going to offer me?"

"Do you have the deed to the house and property?" Faye pulls out the papers from the back pocket of her jeans. Calvin looked at them. "We'll have to sign them in front of a notary."

"What kind of money are we talking about?"

"I'll give you twelve thousand dollars, part crack and part cash. You will have to give me a couple of days to get it together." They sign a promissory note. He promises to pay her twelve thousand dollars. He gives Faye two thousand dollars worth of crack and ten thousand dollars.

It is ten days before Christmas . . .

"Jerry, I have to go to work. Take this and pay on my lay-a-ways at the mall. Then go pay the water bill. Here's some money for gas."

While at the gas station . . .

Jerry counts the money. There is a total of ninety dollars. Instead of paying on the water bill and the lay-away, he goes to the crack house. While he is smoking, he is thinking that he will pay on the lay-away and the bill before she knows what happened.

"Jerry, did you pay the bills like I asked you to?"

"Sure."

"Give me the receipts."

Jerry checks his pockets and the car.

"I must have lost them. They're around here somewhere. I'll find them"

The news for this evening is no different than any other day in Pine Bluff in the past years. Police again enforcing another sting operation. More than fifty people are arrested. Jerry reads the day-old paper. He sighs with relief. At least they have not come for him. He recognizes several names including Richard Harris, Nick Stevens, and Marilyn Scott.

Jerry sells his car. He intends to take some of the money and pay his mother's bills. Instead he smokes it all up. He dares not return home. Tonight night and several nights including Christmas he sleeps where he can, under the stairways in the projects and in abandon buildings.

A day later . . .

At Faye's mother's house.

Tony screams from the bathroom.

"Grandma!"

"What is it Tony?"

"Mama is in the bathroom. She won't wake up!"

Faye's mother screams at the top of her voice. She rushes the boys out of the bathroom. She calls the paramedics. The ambulance arrives.

Minutes later the coroner gets there.

"I'm afraid it's too late." The practitioner says shaking his head.

The police are also on the scene.

"Mrs. Clark. Did you know your daughter was on crack? The officer states after finding a crack pipe and several pieces of crack on the bathroom floor.

Special thanks to God.
To my family and friends.

This book is in memory of these special people.

Linda Faye Crawford
Tracy Woolfolk
Debra Haney
Rita Faye McNealy
Angela Baxter
Albert Witmore
Joy
Johnny 'Mack' Jones